The Locket and the Flintlock

Visit us at www.boldstrokesbooks.com

By the Author

Truths

Ghosts of Winter

The Locket and the Flintlock

The Locket and the Flintlock

by

Rebecca S. Buck

2012

THE LOCKET AND THE FLINTLOCK

© 2012 By Rebecca S. Buck. All Rights Reserved.

ISBN 10: 1-60282-664-1
ISBN 13: 978-1-60282-664-9

This Trade Paperback Original Is Published By
Bold Strokes Books, Inc.
P.O. Box 249
Valley Falls, NY 12185

First Edition: May 2012

THIS IS A WORK OF FICTION. NAMES, CHARACTERS, PLACES, AND INCIDENTS ARE THE PRODUCT OF THE AUTHOR'S IMAGINATION OR ARE USED FICTITIOUSLY. ANY RESEMBLANCE TO ACTUAL PERSONS, LIVING OR DEAD, BUSINESS ESTABLISHMENTS, EVENTS, OR LOCALES IS ENTIRELY COINCIDENTAL.

THIS BOOK, OR PARTS THEREOF, MAY NOT BE REPRODUCED IN ANY FORM WITHOUT PERMISSION.

Credits
Editor: Ruth Sternglantz
Production Design: Susan Ramundo
Cover Design By Sheri (graphicartist2020@hotmail.com)

Acknowledgments

The Locket and the Flintlock has existed in various drafts for a while and, therefore, many people have influenced me for the good between the time I typed the first word and now. I can't possibly thank everyone, but I hope you all know I am very grateful. Never underestimate the effect a single word or a fleeting conversation can have on a writer's brain.

There are just a few people I must mention by name:

I am eternally thankful to Radclyffe for creating, supporting, and guiding the wonderful Bold Strokes family. I feel very lucky to be part of that family and I thank all the wonderful BSB authors and associates for your support. In particular I have to thank Sheri for another outstanding front cover.

Again, I don't have sufficient words to thank Ruth Sternglantz, my amazing editor, without whom this novel would never have existed in its current form and whose guidance makes me a better writer, sentence by sentence.

This is the first novel I've worked on while surrounded by some wonderful writing and editing friends. Every member of Nottingham's Sapphist Writers group deserves credit for their constant support and friendship.

I must single out Victoria Oldham, for all the conversations about writing and editing, and for being the organisational driving force helping me connect with so many readers this past year.

Thank you to Michelle Ward, Debbie Silberman, Raych Udell, and Cindy Pfannenstiel for reading draft versions of this novel, or parts of it, at one point or another and giving me their feedback and encouragement. It has been very much appreciated.

There are a lot of people who have affected the way I think, the way I feel, my thoughts about writing, history—and life in general—while this novel was taking shape. I want to mention just a few, though there are many more (and you must forgive me if I've not mentioned you): Amanda Tindale, Lindsey Stone, Michelle White, M.L. Rice, Mark Spray, Ulla Högstedt, Clare Stephens, Al Dharmasasmita, John Hayes, Natalie Martin, David Knight, Adam Nightingale, Stephen Dennis, Melissa McGuire, and especially Cindy Pfannenstiel.

Thanks too, and lots of love, to my family.

And to every reader who reads this book, or one of my others. I hope you enjoy it. Thank you for the feedback, I always love to hear from you, and thank you for letting your imagination fall under the sway of my words for a while. It's an honour.

Dedication

The Locket and the Flintlock is dedicated to Ryan.
There could be no better guide through the dark woods.

Chapter One

December, 1812

The sound was indistinct at first. A distant thud combined with the rattling and bumping of the carriage. Then it became clearer. Hoof falls of several horses thundering against the solid ground. A large shadow passed the window. A cry of alarm sounded in the frosty night.

The carriage halted.

Inside the carriage, Miss Isabella Jane Foxe forgot the dignity of her seventeen years and looked at her father, Sir Spencer Foxe, in blind panic.

"What's happening? Father, what is it?" Her words held a childlike fear.

Their maid, Mary, showed even less restraint. "Oh, it's robbers isn't it, sir? I know it is. There's been talk there has, sir, they've been prowling round these parts of late. Oh, sir, what do we do? Will they kill us, sir?"

"Kill us?" Isabella's blue eyes were wide with terror.

Sir Spencer appeared paralysed by the panic of the two young women and blinked dumbly at the servant girl and his youngest daughter. As if looking for reassurance, he turned to the other occupant of the carriage.

Miss Lucia Elizabeth Foxe, four years older than Isabella, drew a deep and unsteady breath. Her heart was thundering with just as much fear as her younger sister exhibited; she wanted to panic just as

Mary had. And yet somehow she knew fear would achieve nothing. Highway robbery very rarely resulted in murder. The surest way to be one of the more unlucky victims was certainly to panic and infuse their assailants with the same unease. Calm was needed.

"Hold your tongue, Mary!" Her command was sharp. The maid's panic was filling the enclosed space of the carriage and infecting her sister.

"Will they kill us, Lucia?" Isabella demanded.

"Don't be so foolish, Isabella. If they are robbers, their intention is surely only to rob. You do not read of murders by the roadside so often, do you?" Lucia wondered where she had found the authority of her tone. It was in marked contrast to the apprehension surging hotly through her body.

Still silent, Sir Spencer reached beneath his seat. Lucia watched in horror as he brought out an antique travelling pistol. Ornate and aged, she doubted it was loaded or there was any chance her father would actually fire it.

"Father, it seems to me any act of aggression on our part will most likely anger the outlaws. Do you not agree?" Sir Spencer considered her objection and appeared about to protest when a shadow fell over the window blind. Moments later the door was flung open, and the chill December air flooded the carriage.

The night was moonlit, but Lucia almost wished it were not, for the pale illumination gave the countenance of the man who confronted them a devilish aspect. He wore a dark greatcoat and a bicorn hat. His face was obscured by the black scarf he wore over his mouth, nose, and chin. In the patch of light created by the carriage lamp, Lucia had an impression of him as broad shouldered and dark haired, but otherwise indistinct.

Sir Spencer lifted the pistol, but all the action accomplished was a demonstration of his trembling hand. The man at the carriage door raised his own pistol and pointed it calmly at Isabella's heaving chest. Isabella whimpered pitifully and Lucia was outraged on behalf of her sister. The anger almost drove away the fear, but not quite.

"Out." The command was gruff and muffled by the scarf, but the peremptory tone could not be disobeyed.

The barrel of the pistol aimed at Isabella's heart could not be disobeyed.

The occupants of the carriage climbed out into the cold night and stood in a shivering group by the roadside. The moonlight glinted on the frozen puddles and showed the harsh, black branches of the barren trees. A strikingly beautiful nightmare landscape, Lucia observed, wondering how on earth she had the wherewithal to even notice. She shuddered and took hold of her sister's gloved hand. Isabella returned the pressure, though her attention was fixed on the pistol still pointed at her chest.

The dark-clothed robber, who was far taller than Sir Spencer, stood between the huddled group and the carriage. Silhouetted against the patch of yellow light created by the carriage lamps, he appeared even more menacing than he had before.

With a slowness apparently designed to increase their terror by the application of suspense, the man moved his aim from Isabella to Sir Spencer. Lucia was ashamed to feel a rush of relief as he did so. "Your money and jewellery, if you please, sir." His tone held an affectation of politeness yet also a determination Lucia did not feel inclined to cross. She hoped her father felt the same way. That he did not was apparent in the next moment.

"Do you know who I am?" Sir Spencer drew himself up to his full height but was still an unimpressive figure before the outlaw.

"Yes, sir, the coat of arms on your carriage would have revealed it to me, even if I did not. You are Sir Spencer Foxe of Foxe Hall, a few miles hence. Now, if you please, Sir Spencer, your money and jewellery." His resolution was harder, colder, more apparent now. He pronounced Sir Spencer's title with a derisory snarl. Lucia felt her pulse throb in her temples. Isabella's fingers squeezed hers painfully.

"We are not rich." Sir Spencer seemed determined to defend them with ineffective words. Lucia was dismayed by her father's foolish protests. Why resist so fruitlessly and risk angering this armed man?

"You are rich enough, sir," the man said. Uncannily, Lucia could picture him smiling beneath his scarf. "Now, please do as I say, before I feel inclined to shoot one of your daughters." He waved the barrel of the pistol in the general direction of Isabella and Lucia. Lucia heard her sister gasp and did her best to prevent her own hand from shaking and revealing her fear. Mary had begun to sob, but the man did not seem to be interested in the maid.

"You won't get away with this," Sir Spencer said. He began to remove his coin purse from his pocket all the same. "I'll see you hang."

"Perhaps, sir," the man spoke with no noticeable trepidation as he reached out for the purse offered to him.

Three men had opened the door of the carriage on the opposite side from where Lucia and her family stood. These men were now rifling through its contents, clearly in hope of further treasures. Lucia knew they would find little, her father spoke the truth. They were comfortable, yes, but only country gentry, hardly the richest of pickings to travel the roads that night.

The robber now turned his gaze, glinting in the moonlight, towards Lucia. He lowered his pistol just enough to make the threat less immediate, yet still pressing, and looked between her and her sister as he spoke. "Ladies, my apologies, but if you would be so kind?" Involuntarily, Lucia reached for the place where his gaze fell upon her throat and felt a wave of sickness sweep through her body. About her neck she wore a locket which contained a miniature of her long-deceased mother and a lock of her hair, her most treasured possession and all she had of her mother. She stared back at the man in dread, challenging him to make the demand of her. He would not have her locket unless it was forced from her.

"Your jewellery, please, ladies." His irritation at being made to ask again was not well concealed.

Lucia's panic at the prospect of losing the locket was enough to make her abandon her former good sense and inspire her with foolhardy confidence to speak. She chose her words carefully and kept her tone polite, as though she spoke to a gentleman rather than a criminal. "Please, sir, this necklace is of great sentimental import to me."

"The gold will be of great import to us too, miss, I assure you." Again Lucia had the unwarranted notion he was smiling.

"I cannot give it to you, sir." She could barely believe her audacity, the steely resolution in her words.

"Lucia!" Sir Spencer exclaimed in warning, clearly stunned by his eldest daughter's rashness. Lucia paid her father little heed. The idea that the man was smiling rather diminished her fear, although a part of her knew it should have made him more threatening still.

The appropriate dizzying level of horror returned to her as the man approached. He stopped barely half a pace from her, his eyes fixed to hers. Lucia found it extraordinary to look into the eyes of a villain but to see only a man. A wicked man to be sure, but a man just the same.

"If you cannot give it, Miss Foxe, I shall take it," he said, the words softly dangerous. The hard barrel of the pistol made contact with Lucia's body, over her heart, as he reached out his gloved hand. Despite her best efforts at control, Lucia trembled as he grasped the locket and pulled it sharply, breaking the chain. She watched him put it in the pocket of his coat, and protests rose in her throat. As if he sensed her resistance, his pistol was still pressed to her as he spoke again. "Do you ladies have any more jewellery to offer me, or shall I be compelled to search your persons for it?"

Lucia was indignant at the notion and suddenly furious with the man more than frightened of him. The anger was made worse by her inability—the pistol being pressed to her breast as it was—to do anything but comply. She removed her pearl earrings as Isabella took her mother-of-pearl comb from her hair below her bonnet and unclipped the gold earrings she was wearing. Her sister handed these to the man with trembling fingers and reached up to release her own necklace, a gold chain with a crucifix made of rubies, a gift from the uncle whose house in the south of the county they were returning from this night. The robber took the items offered to him with a small mocking bow.

"Very grateful, ladies, sir, I'm sure. Now we will impede your journey no further." He backed away, the pistol still aimed in Lucia's general direction. The three men who had searched the carriage retreated towards their horses.

"I will see you hang, sir, all of you," Sir Spencer called out. His voice was small in the night. The men all ignored him. Lucia looked up at the other members of the band of robbers: two men on horseback who had their weapons trained on the driver and footman. The first of these was mostly indistinct, even in the moonlight, but looked to be a stocky man wearing no hat despite the cold. The other rode a fine black steed, a good three or four hands taller than the other horses. He appeared a slender man, this one in an old-fashioned tricorn hat with a kerchief obscuring his face, a long, dark cloak about his shoulders and draped over the rump of his horse. This man was observant, looking around himself continually.

The dismounted men climbed back onto their horses. To Lucia's surprise, it was not to the man who had taken her locket they looked but to the slender man on the black horse, who gave a slight signal with his hand. The riders galloped away. From distinct shapes they became shadows and eventually merged with the night.

As they returned to the carriage to see what had been stolen, Isabella was still trembling, and Mary began once more to sob. Resentment, anger, and humiliation burned strongest of all the emotions in Lucia's heart. The echoing thunder of the hooves on the frozen ground died away as the footman and driver closed the doors and shut out the bitter cold. Sir Spencer had been travelling with another purse of coins beneath his seat, which he discovered was also missing. There had been little else of value in the carriage, but as Lucia climbed in and settled herself, she realised her new book of poetry, a gift from her cousin, had been taken. It gave her a moment's pause. Her book had not been expensively bound. What use did savage thieves have with poetry?

The carriage jolted into life, and they were driven through the suddenly more sinister night towards the refuge of home.

❖

The horse surged, muscular and powerful, between her thighs. Len Hawkins allowed her body to relax and mould to the movements of the beast in his loose gallop. The air around her was filled with the sound of the hooves of the other horses on the hard ground. In the moonlight, the breath of the horses rose in eerie plumes of steam, as the dark hedgerows and looming shadows of trees flew past on either side.

These were the moments she lived for. Years of conducting her unlawful business had not made her stomach hard to it yet, and there were some nights upon which she wished her task over before it had even begun. Tonight had been one of those nights. One of the occasions she yearned to give sway to her gentle heart. Those pretty, genteel women who her loyal Julian had forced from the carriage were a jarring echo of a time she remembered clearly, though she would rather have forgotten. Their gowns pale in the moonlight, almost ghosts. Her past haunted her still. Why could she not harden herself against the memories? Len never liked it when they robbed women. Not because they suffered any more than the menfolk, but because they stirred the empathy she fought not to feel. She battled it every day, yet still the ache, the edge of self-doubt persisted. She knew she was an excellent leader, she was confident, but the sharp contrast between her illicit actions and the pain of compassion threatened to make her heartsick. If she had a choice, she watched her men work from afar, never dismounting her stallion. It gave her authority. It gave her distance.

If the men knew just how deeply she felt, the sensibilities which taunted her daily, she suspected they would mock her. Even worse, disrespect and disobey her. And that could be fatal. To hide your true self was not so hard after all. Len's life had depended upon it for a long time. Why? Beneath the kerchief tied about the lower part of her face, she smiled. She knew why. The air whistled past her ears and stung life into her cheeks. Her heart beat faster with the rhythm of the gallop. This was what it was all for. Freedom. She needed it with every part of her being. Of all the compromises she had made in her life, one she would not make. She would be free, or she would be dead.

The horses barely needed guiding to find their way from the road and through the thick woodland, as they slowed to a trot to negotiate the more uneven ground. The hoof falls were softened to a rustling *crunch-crunch-crunch* by the winter carpet of fallen leaves. The tall trunks of trees loomed in the semi-darkness, not sinister here. These trees were their protection and their shelter.

Ahead, flickering as it was obscured by a tree trunk and then revealed again, shone a dim yellow light. The group of riders, Len ahead of them all, made for that point of warmth in the pale cold of the night. It seemed to burn steadier and brighter as they approached.

The riders emerged from the trees into a small clearing where a ramshackle building stood, which must have once been quaint and welcoming. Len did not know who had lived here or why they lived here no longer. She did not much care. The abandoned house was their refuge. A place to shelter them from the elements and the law. A reminder of her former civilised life she wished to relinquish entirely, yet was still pleased to indulge. The lantern she had left burning on a stake by the door flickered a glowing welcome.

Len dismounted in one fluid movement. The flagstones of the yard at the front of the house were hard beneath the soles of her riding boots. She pulled the kerchief from her face and left it draped about her neck, glad to breathe freely again. Short, stocky William was by her side in an instant—having dismounted his own mare—to take the reins from her hand. He would see that her black stallion was fed and watered. She could have taken care of the horse herself, but William enjoyed showing her the courtesy, and she knew leadership demanded that she sometimes accept these gestures. The men all knew she was perfectly capable of performing every task they undertook on her behalf. She believed it was one of the reasons she had their loyalty and respect.

She took the lantern from its hook and carried it into the house, a halo of light illuminating the small entrance hall and then the comfortable kitchen where the men spent most of their time. Embers still glowed orange in the grate. Before long a fire would be raging, and meat, if there was still any to be had, would be roasting. Len tried to remember how much food they had left. Starving men did not make good outlaws, they were too easily distracted, too slow. The life they made for themselves here was not a plentiful one. But it was still better than where most of the men had come from.

Len set the lantern on the table and used a taper to light one of the tallow candles standing near her. The extra light made the room feel warm and hospitable, not a hideout but a home. The flame guttered in the draught as someone entered behind her.

"Almost not worth the effort." Julian's voice was gruff and disgruntled.

"That bad?" Len turned to him and watched as he removed his own mask, taking off his hat and hanging it on a hook close to the door. Two of the other men—tall, gaunt Isaac and small-framed but strong Peter—entered behind Julian and made their way to the fireplace, where Isaac began to encourage the embers to grow into flames. The other men, William and John, were still outside, seeing to the horses, perhaps bringing in more firewood. Len waited for Julian's response, smiling slightly at his dissatisfied expression.

"Two purses of coins, a few trinkets from the women—"

"And a book of poems," Len concluded for him.

"That might be a treasure to you, Len, but unless you intend to burn it in the grate or give it to me to wipe my arse, I don't much see the point in taking it, myself."

"It's Byron, Julian. All the women are swooning for him these days." Len watched Julian relax and smile.

"I don't see you swooning for him."

"I am not the swooning kind of woman."

"Not for noble poets anyway."

"I don't believe I've had a faint moment in my life." Len was mildly indignant, as she always was at any suggestion of her weakness.

"No. That you haven't since I've known you." Julian reached into his pocket and drew out a handful of gold and jewels which glimmered in the light. He placed them on the table. Len glanced over them and tried not to allow sadness into her heart. She saw rubies and mother-of-pearl, quality gold. About the neck or in the curled hair of a fine woman, the pieces would be exquisite. Here, in the run-down hideout, they seemed to have lost some of their lustre, reduced to their component parts, their material worth, and robbed of their beauty. Such pieces needed pale skin, ringlets of fair hair, a delicate earlobe, the light of hundreds of wax candles in a crystal chandelier, to show them to their best advantage. Not a stained wooden table and the flickering flame of a stinking tallow taper.

Before she could help herself—for she scorned such riches and the unfair society that provided them for some while others starved—Len reached out a hand and touched the ruby of a crucifix, sanguine and glistening disconsolately. The chain of the crucifix was tangled with another gold chain attached to a rather plain gold locket. Len noticed the break in that chain.

"Why is this necklace broken?" She turned questioning eyes on Julian, who looked uncomfortable under her scrutiny.

"Silly little rich girl wouldn't take it off for me."

"So you *snatched* it?" Len did not hide her disapproval.

"We're thieves, Len, not gentlemen, whatever you like to believe." Len saw Isaac and Peter looking in their direction. Julian was the only one of the men who would dare talk to her like this. Her oldest friend, he did not treat her with deference in the way they did and, indeed, thought it was one of his most important duties to remind her of reality when she apparently lost her grip on it.

"So we are. And thieve we do. But not with violence unless it's unavoidable."

"I was not violent. It is a fine chain and broke easily. You point your pistol just as readily as I do, Len. And you would use it if you were disobeyed."

Len was silent. Julian was correct, and she had no idea why she'd even begun this argument. She'd used violence—and the threat of it—to make her way in the world for years now. There was just something about the gold locket with its broken chain that she did not quite like to look at. And why had its owner been so reluctant to relinquish it, even fearing for her life? A brave woman, obviously. What did the locket mean to her? Unable to resist the urge, Len took the locket in her fingers. The metal warmed rapidly under her touch.

She did not apologise to Julian. She didn't even glance up as she heard her other men enter the room. "If you need me, you know where I am," she said to Julian. Her dark cloak flowing behind her, boots loud on the floorboards, she strode from the room to the place she could be quiet and alone, the locket still in her hand.

CHAPTER TWO

Three days later, Isabella Foxe—who had always been of a nervous disposition—was still unsettled by the robbery on the road. She had taken to her bed, much to Sir Spencer's great concern. Though she conceded her sister was excessively pale, Lucia did not feel much worry on Isabella's behalf. Within the week she suspected Isabella would be abroad again, calling upon their neighbourhood friends to tell them, undoubtedly with much embellishment, of their narrow brush with death.

Sir Spencer still bristled with anger, and Lucia understood it was made worse by its impotence. A group of masked riders had taken money and jewellery—and one poetry book—from them and merely galloped away into the night. They were unidentifiable, untraceable, and probably counties away by now. The chances of Sir Spencer ever seeing any one of them on the gallows were slim.

Lucia found herself more contemplative in the following days. She did not believe they had truly flirted with death on the roadside. The peculiar memory of the masked man seeming to smile softened the recollection and added an edge of intrigue. Who was this man into whose eyes she had stared? What had brought him to thievery? His voice had been that of an educated man. She could not help the curiosity. She might have predicted that an encounter with such outlaws, a pistol held to her breast, would terrify her in similar fashion to her sister. That it did not was puzzling.

Lucia's thoughts, as they often did, drifted to her brother, Georgie, somewhere in the battlefields of the Peninsular, a captain in Wellington's army. Did he feel afraid? Her own fear returned when she considered that he most likely faced the barrel of a French musket every day. Death was so horribly final.

Lucia rarely forgot how close the hand of the Reaper could be. She had been troubled by a particular fear of death since her five-year-old mind had first struggled to comprehend the notion her beautiful mother had fallen asleep never to wake, except with God. She had been frightened to sleep herself for much of the year afterwards, for fear she might not wake as her mother had not. Even now, all of these years later, when she was on the point of slumber, at that transient moment when the darkness falls over the vision and consciousness fades, sometimes she would start awake in a hot terror she was dying.

This night she had not yet attempted to fall asleep. She had taken to her chamber at the front of the house after supper. She tried to concentrate on a novel her sister had recommended to her but could not. In the end, she lounged in the window seat and simply gazed across the parkland, watching the palette of the sky change with the set of the sun and the rise of the moon.

Everything outside was silvery and pale. There was no wind, and the picture before her was so still it could almost have been a painting. From her window on the second floor of their modest, half-century-old, red-brick manor house, she could see the driveway. It took a winding path through sculpted shrubbery to the main gateway from the road. The entrance itself was hidden from view by a small, shadowy thicket of elm and birch trees. The whole of the small park was surrounded by a brick wall, six feet in height. From her vantage point, Lucia saw where it stretched out across the front of the land, marking the place where the road ran along the perimeter of the property.

Again, through force of habit, Lucia's fingers went to the bare place on her throat where her locket usually rested. She felt its loss badly, for now it seemed her mother had receded even more distantly into the past. She would have been quite happy to see the man who had snatched it hanging from a gibbet until the flesh rotted from his wicked bones.

At that moment, a movement at the periphery of her gaze drew her attention. She made out a group of riders on the road on the other side of the wall, well illuminated by the light of the moon. She peered keenly at them. Six riders! One could plainly be seen to wear a tricorn and was mounted on a horse considerably taller than the others. Her heart pounded hard in her chest. Lucia knew at once with an unshakeable certainty that the group she saw were their assailants of three nights previously. She stared at them for a little longer, and then almost without a conscious thought of it entering her head, she had decided what to do.

She discounted waking her father or the male servants. The risk of what she intended did not make her falter, although she had never considered herself a brave kind of woman. Bravery was not something regularly of necessity in her life. Possible consequences were of no concern to her. Retrieving her locket was all that mattered.

In an instant, Lucia took up her warm outdoor cloak from the foot of her bed. Slipping out of the house unheeded was really a very simple matter. The servants were, by this hour, either slumbering or below stairs. Isabella had not left her bed all of the day. Her father's chamber was at the opposite end of the passageway from her own, and he slept heavily.

Quite why she felt compelled to such secrecy she did not consider closely. Somewhere in her heart she knew if she roused any of the men in the house, she would be sent back to her chamber and the matter taken out of her hands. It was a matter of principle that she do this alone, confront the man who had humiliated her and taken her most precious treasure from her. Pride drove her forward. Pride, and that dreadful secret need *to know*, that desire to understand more of the world she had glimpsed when she'd looked into the villain's eyes.

The night smelled of damp cold when Lucia opened the front door of the house. She stole across the courtyard to the entrance to the stables. The moonlight pierced the dusty air through the small arched windows and allowed her to make her way easily. She entered the first stall where her own favourite mare, a chestnut named Sally, was standing peacefully.

"Hello, Sally," Lucia whispered. She stroked Sally's nose. Sally snorted softly but was not apparently disturbed by Lucia's sudden appearance at this unaccountable hour. Murmuring platitudes, Lucia removed Sally's bridle from its nearby hook and eased the bit into the horse's mouth, the rest of the bridle over her head. Sally looked at her through only half-interested eyes. Lucia was very glad she had insisted, some years ago, that Jenkins, the old groom, show her how to place a bridle on a horse correctly.

"Now we're going for a short ride." Somehow, being with Sally made Lucia feel safer than she would have done without her. She led her to the mounting block just outside the stable entrance and pulled herself tentatively onto Sally's broad back. She clutched at the reins and a sizeable portion of the mare's mane and clicked her tongue to encourage her forward.

The first wave of anxiety did not engulf her until she turned Sally onto the driveway in the direction of the road. The park was suddenly large and full of shadows, which only deepened as she progressed. The thicket of trees hid the moonlight, and Sally's hoof falls on the frosty fallen leaves sounded very loud. Still, she had to attempt this now she had come this far. To fail now would be a weakness she could not tolerate and would leave her with questions for the rest of her days, she was sure.

Foxe Hall did not have a large enough park to require a gatehouse and keeper, of which Lucia was glad tonight. She urged Sally through the iron gate and let it close behind them, flinching as metal crashed against metal, a harsh sound that echoed in the night.

There was a slight breeze on the road, and the air was bitter. Outside the gate, she was small and alone. But she felt a fierce determination like nothing she had ever felt before. The road appeared to be deserted in both directions, and she wondered if the opportunity had been missed. However, she had come this far. She turned Sally in the direction she had seen the shadowy riders travelling and encouraged her into a trot.

❖

"We are being followed." Len drew her horse to a halt and spoke urgently to Julian at her side. The other men stopped their horses alongside the pair who had been leading them. Her tone was calm, factual, with no trace of panic. She was only mildly alarmed. Melting away into the night was all too easy with the open fields and woodland surrounding them.

"Are you sure?" Julian asked.

"Yes."

"Out here? We're miles from town." This was Isaac, who sounded considerably more anxious.

"It's most like to be a farmer on his way home from the tavern," Peter said in his thick local accent.

"You're right. Still, it does us no good to be seen by more eyes than we have to be." Len considered for a moment. "Will you deal with it, Julian?"

"Yes. William, stay with me." Julian turned to the well-built man on his left side, who nodded his hatless head briefly. "You too, John." John acknowledged the command with a brief gesture of his hand.

"The rest of us will go back to the house." There was some strain in her voice now, for she hated these moments. Her appearance never gave her away, but she dared not risk a situation in which she might be asked to explain herself, for experience had taught her that her voice could arouse suspicion. That she had to allow Julian to deal with such predicaments frustrated her endlessly, however much she trusted him. Sometimes it seemed she should really relinquish leadership of their group to her friend. But though Julian was solid and capable, intelligent and sharp-witted, he was not a leader. His temper was too easily frayed, his patience tried too quickly.

"Yes. We will make out we are merely travellers. No doubt whoever it is will warn us about highwaymen and let us on our way."

Len smiled. "No doubt. For dangerous villains haunt these roads by night. Be safe." Her first words were in jest, her final ones entirely in earnest.

"You too."

Julian, William, and John turned their horses to face the direction they had just come from. Len nudged her horse into a trot, and the remaining men followed her lead. As a precaution, as soon as she could, Len steered them off the road and into the woodland, following a track made by the charcoal burners at first and then threading a path through the trees towards their cottage.

Perhaps she had been foolish to ride along the main road in the first place. Certainly they could have kept to the shadows and not run any risk of being followed. But it had been a quiet night on the roads and so not particularly profitable, and the men were discontented. She had wanted them to reach their home comforts as quickly as possible, had been confident no one was abroad on this cold night to see them. A wave of anxiety swept through her at the reminder of how close to the edge they lived their lives. She quelled it swiftly. Julian and William had her complete trust, John was very capable, and she and the others were now merely shadows in the trees.

Len smiled and wondered what tale Julian would have to tell her later. Would it be a drunkard as Peter had suggested, or maybe a keen-eyed groom, suspicious of such a large group of riders by night? A lone traveller? There were endless possibilities. That it was not the militia she could at least be sure. Everywhere they travelled it was impossible to escape the rattling of their arms—muskets and sabres—with the movement of their mounts. Besides, the militia were cowards, soldiers too afraid to be part of the real war in Portugal and Spain, and they never travelled the roads alone. Len was sure their follower had been a single rider. She would just have to wait awhile to find out if she was right.

Chapter Three

The night air was cold on Lucia's hands. She moved them in closer to Sally's warm neck and wished she had remembered to don a bonnet to keep the chill from her head. She focused on the road ahead, looking for traces of the riders who had passed before her.

The minutes seemed to stretch endlessly as she let Sally trot briskly onward. She had ridden past the boundary of her father's park, and there were now fields and hedgerows at the sides of the road. For an unexpectedly exhilarating moment, alone in the night, she felt as though she was the only being in existence and fancied herself completely safe, untouchable. Then with a jolt of apprehension her thoughts returned her to the present danger and the ludicrous nature of what she was attempting. Suddenly afraid, she almost turned Sally and retreated to the park and the warmth of her chamber.

She heard a sound out of place around the next turn of the road.

Peering in the darkness, her heart hammering incessantly, Lucia slowed Sally to a walk as she rounded the turn. She almost let out a cry when she found the way blocked by three men on horseback. The middle figure of the three had something in his hand. A pistol! Her heart turned to ice as she knew she had been mistaken. There were only three men in the group before her and only one wearing a bicorn. These men could be any group of villains, and she would have no claim on their attention at all. Panic began to seize her and her hands trembled.

"Miss Foxe?" the middle man said, in a surprised tone. Lucia was relieved to recognise his voice in an instant. It was the man who had taken her locket. He did not wear the scarf across his face tonight, and she could see he had a well-trimmed dark beard.

Directly confronted, words escaped her for a moment. Driven by a quest for her lost locket and to satisfy her curiosity, she had not thought to decide what she would say to the men when she caught up with them. In her naïvety she'd assumed, having not hurt her previously, they would treat her in a similar fashion now. She was no threat to them, a young and defenceless woman all alone. She gathered herself again, remembering her intention was merely to ask for her locket, to explain its significance if necessary. In her experience, men were usually kind to young, fair women.

But those rules by which she lived her life seemed suddenly irrelevant here on the moonlit highway.

"Yes, it's Miss Foxe," she called in a nervous voice. She was relieved to see the man lower the pistol. She saw him turn to the companion on his left and caught their soft laughter. It angered her as she recalled all of the resentment and humiliation she had felt on the night of the robbery. She drew courage from those feelings. "I believe you robbed me three nights ago, sir, and I have come to ask that you return to me one item, no more."

"Couldn't have been us, Miss Foxe, we've been out of the county," he said, infuriatingly, as though Lucia was playing a game with him.

"Sir, you took from me a locket which was very precious to me. I want it back."

"What will you give us in return?" called the stoutest man, astride an equally stocky horse. All three of them sniggered.

Lucia thought quickly. "I am willing to offer you money if you will return the locket to me. I promise I will not tell anyone of our transaction." Her attempt to sound as though she was in control of the situation did not succeed out loud in the way it had done in her head.

"Shouldn't young ladies be in bed at this hour?" the man with the pistol said, ignoring her offer completely.

"Young ladies should be in my bed at this hour," the stocky man jested. His crude words jarred in Lucia's mind. These were a kind of people she had no experience dealing with. The fear which had somewhat dissipated when the man lowered his pistol began to creep back.

"I was by my window, sir, and I saw you pass." Lucia addressed the man in the middle, judging that he held authority here and was certainly the more decent to converse with. The man into whose eyes she had stared. Hard to conceive she'd been that close to a criminal. She shivered as her fear intensified.

"You recognised us from your window?" he asked, genuine surprise in his words.

"Yes, sir. I have had many occasions to miss the presence of my locket. Such thoughts have crystallised your image in my mind."

As soon as those words left Lucia's mouth, she knew they had been a mistake.

"You'd recognise us anywhere?" the man asked.

"Yes. But I assure you, sir," she added hastily, "return my locket and I will never reveal to anyone what I can recall of your appearance." She hoped her pledge would put them at their ease again.

"Are you threatening us, Miss Foxe?"

"No, sir, I am merely asking for my locket." She drew in a deep breath and tried not to remember that she was sitting bareback on her horse on the road in the middle of the night, conversing with three highwaymen.

"Do you actually have Miss Foxe's locket?" said the man on the left.

"No, I don't, as a matter of fact," said the man in the middle. Lucia's heart began to pound more heavily. She was losing control of the situation. She knew she had never really had any control. Fear coursed through her veins as she realised the extent to which she had underestimated the danger she was in.

"Did we sell it yet?" asked the stocky man.

"Not yet," the man in the middle answered.

"I think this is one for the boss."

"Yes, I quite agree," the man in the centre said. He looked back to Lucia, who was unsure whether she should attempt to flee or simply hope to be allowed to leave unharmed. "Miss Foxe, we can see about returning your locket, but you will have to come with us now."

Lucia felt quite ill with fear and certain they meant to kill her. "Is this because I recognised you?" she demanded, her voice tremulous. "You have it on my honour that I won't inform anyone."

"Nevertheless, Miss Foxe, you will have to come with us now." Two of the men began to ride towards Lucia, leaving the other to watch.

"No, please. I will just go back to my chamber, without the locket," she said, panic rising in her throat, as the pistol was raised to point at her chest.

"Miss Foxe, do as we say, and I assure you of your safety," the man in the bicorn said. She still had the acuity to think it an odd statement from a man who threatened her with a pistol but did not choose to say as much out loud.

"You will return me to my home unharmed?" She tried to sound braver than she felt. How could she even begin to trust these men?

"I promise, as far as I can," he said. His words sounded so polite and genteel. He smiled, and the notion of him as a gentleman made him even more terrifying. The smile seemed so earnest and trustworthy. "There is one thing, though, Miss Foxe…"

"Oh?" Lucia asked fearfully.

"Yes, we cannot allow you to know the route we will take," he said. The stocky man had brought his horse very close to where Lucia sat on Sally. The pistol remained levelled at her as the man holding it leaned forward to take her reins from her. More alarming still, the man to her side passed a ragged piece of cloth around her eyes. Terror paralysed her, and she did not move nor could she form a word of protest in her mouth as she found herself blindfolded. Sally began to move under her and Lucia clung to her mane. Her heart urged her to scream or protest, even fling herself from Sally's back and run for her life. However, terrified by the pistol, almost entranced, she simply allowed them to lead her.

And a small, traitorous, foolhardy, barely acknowledged part of her was quivering with the thrill of it.

❖

Len leaned back in her chair and stretched out her arms, trying to force herself to relax. Waiting was not something she had much patience with, and though she trusted Julian to handle any situation, she felt helpless not knowing by whom they had been followed.

Standing up, she sighed heavily and walked the length of the small room. This was her private space, the one part of this house she claimed for herself. A few chairs, an old desk, and very little else furnished the room. Items of particular interest to her found their way onto the desk, amidst a pile of papers and books. She acquired the newspapers as often as she could, for it was important to glean clues as to the movements of the militia, the chance of patrols, and the like. She wanted to know too how the war against Napoleon progressed, how well the harvest was expected to do, what other manner of criminals stalked her night-time territory. The newspapers were undoubtedly essential to her. The books were an indulgence but one she would never relinquish.

She perched on the edge of the desk and stared at the spot where her cloak and tricorn hung against the wall. Her gloves and kerchief were beside her on the desk. Those garments defined her to the world and protected her from it all at once. She often smiled at how surprised that world would be to know what lay underneath the kerchief. And yet her amusement was tempered by the necessity of hiding. Freedom was all very well, but she had to acknowledge it had its price. Some nights she longed to reveal herself, let someone other than her men see who the rider of the black stallion really was. But to give any clue was a risk she feared she could never take.

Her eye fell on the gold locket which lay next to her newly acquired book on the desk. It belonged to one of the Miss Foxes, though Julian claimed he'd not been able to tell which was the younger or older of the two fair-haired women. Though she'd kept the locket in her possession since the night Julian had taken it, she had still not opened it to see what secrets it contained. Stealing the gold for its value was one thing. But there was something so personal about this unremarkable piece of jewellery. Len feared opening it, as though doing so would rob her of more of her soul. And yet she knew it was a weakness. This willingness to empathise, to regret her actions and those of her men. This life demanded that she harden her heart. She reached for the locket, determined to look inside.

Just as her fingers made contact with the smooth gold, she heard the hooves of a solitary horse arriving at the front of the house. One horse? What could possibly have gone wrong that only one of her men returned? And who was it? Anxiety gripped her heart as she made her way from her sanctum near the back of the house to the front door. John was just dismounting his mare.

"What has happened, John?" Len asked. She did not bother to hide the urgency of her words.

"Nothing bad, Len," John said. "It was a woman that followed us."

Len frowned, wondering with interest just what kind of woman was on the road alone at night. "A woman?"

"Yeah. Reckoned we took a locket from her the other night and wants it back."

Len felt surprise and consternation in equal measure. "Miss Foxe—one of them anyway—rode out onto the road alone in order to ask for her locket back?" She wondered what on earth could make the locket so important. But this was not the most pressing concern. "How did she know it was us?"

"Saw us from her chamber window. Recognised us at once."

"She did what?" Len's consternation quickly became alarm.

"I know. Silly girl told Julian just that. He's bringing her here. I rode ahead to let you know."

"Here?"

"Yes. With precautionary measures." John smiled as though he had found something amusing in the chain of events. Len did not smile back. Her mind was already working on how on earth she would handle this situation.

"When they get here, bring her to me at once. Alone." She gave the order and retreated into the house. She did not know what to think. Begrudgingly she admired this Miss Foxe's bravery, while at the same time scorning such foolish risk taking. Clearly the girl was far from sensible. But she was also a threat. Len sighed as she reached her private domain and reached for the kerchief to cover her face.

Chapter Four

Lucia did not dare move her hands from where they clutched Sally's mane, for fear of losing her balance. The movement of the horse beneath her was disconcerting without her sight. Nor did she want to brave lifting a hand to adjust the blindfold, since she had no way of knowing if any of the three men was watching. She wasn't even sure there were still three men, since she was almost certain she had heard one of the horses gallop ahead of them. They seemed to travel a very long time, but Lucia could not tell if they remained on the main road or if they had made a turn.

She tried not to dwell on what these men were leading her to. She concentrated instead on understanding they had left her little option. It was surely better to be blindfolded and led to an unknown destination than to already be dead at the roadside.

Eventually she heard the sounds of the hoof falls change, as though the horses were now walking on flagstones. A moment later, they stopped. Lucia waited, rigid and unmoving, wondering what on earth was to happen. She heard the men dismount, one after another. There were only two of them. Where had the other gone? Sally shifted uneasily on her feet, and Lucia had to grip her mane again to retain her balance.

She felt the presence of someone near her. Hands on her arms, pulling her, lifting her down from Sally's back. "Apologies, miss, it's easier this way. Your horse will be watered. You'll be able to remove the blindfold when we are inside." Lucia recognised the voice of the man with the bicorn and pistol as he set her on her feet on the ground. She wavered dizzily and he caught her arm. "Come on, Miss Foxe, with me."

He pulled her after him. She had little choice but to trust his guidance since she could see nothing. She smelled woodsmoke and cooking meat, and heard her guide lean forward to open a door, through which he ushered her. The door closed behind them, and she felt his hands at the back of her head, removing the blindfold. She blinked and looked around the room.

A large table stood in the centre, upon which rested a partially carved ham, a half-eaten loaf of white bread, an earthenware ale flask, and two red apples. A large fire blazed in the hearth on the other side of the room. There was a clutter of boxes, bags, and pouches about the room, on the end of the table, and on the floor. Lucia wondered if they contained further profits of the men's thievery. Despite the fear constricting her throat so it was hard to swallow, the warmth in the room and the glow of the candles were surprisingly reassuring. Lucia had never given much thought to the notion that outlaws must exist when they were not committing their terrible crimes. They must eat and sleep and seek the warmth of the hearth. She found herself in an unremarkable place, cosy and almost welcoming. This was no lair. The realisation was disorientating.

A lean man with greying hair was bent by the fire, apparently cooking something in a pan he held into the flames. A younger man was squatting on the floor, prying at the lock on a small wooden trunk. Both men looked up as Lucia stood bewildered in the doorway.

"Now that's a pretty profit you've made tonight," the older man called, his eyes sweeping Lucia up and down.

"Eyes off," said the man behind her, and she suddenly felt grateful for his protection, despite his having kidnapped her under the threat of his pistol. No feeling was straightforward, and her mind was a morass of contradictory impulses. "Allow me to introduce Miss Lucia Foxe. She's come to claim an item of property she suspects we may have in our possession."

"And how would that be? Did she lose it somewhere?" The older man sniggered.

"Should be more careful, miss," the man squatting on the floor said. Their humour only made Lucia angry. She would have shared her furious disgust with them but calculated she was—distressingly—largely in their power, and it would not be wise.

"You taking her to Len?" the older man asked.

"Yes," the man behind her said. He seemed to have some authority over these men, although he clearly was not their leader. "So don't be getting any ideas."

"Hadn't crossed my mind," the old man muttered, turning back to his pan. Lucia wondered, with a cold shudder, just what notion might have crossed his mind.

"If you'll follow me, Miss Foxe," her kidnapper said, stepping around her. Having little option, she obeyed, passing after him through a door to the right hand side of the hearth into a small and gloomy central hallway. She tried to imagine where they might be, just what deserted house these criminals had taken possession of. The blindfold had done its trick however, and she found herself entirely confused as to how far they had travelled and in which direction.

They stopped outside a closed door. The man rapped firmly on it and entered without waiting for a reply. Filled with trepidation as to the character of the man she would find inside, Lucia followed him through the door.

This chamber was smaller than the first room and not so well lit. A small fire burned in the hearth, sending an orange glow through the darkness, and two lanterns flickered at the farthest end from where Lucia stood. At that end of the room there was a wooden desk. Seated behind this desk was a man Lucia knew at once as the slender figure she had seen on the tall black horse. He still wore his tricorn hat and the kerchief covering the lower part of his face, which struck her as odd until she considered he probably had warning she was approaching and did not want to reveal his identity.

In the scant illumination, he was little more than a shadow. He did not stand up when they entered the room, merely looked up from the desk, upon which she noticed several books, a bottle, and a tankard, as well as several folded newspapers. A civilised and educated outlaw then. Lucia had ceased predicting anything about this encounter. The thick sickly sweet odour of cigar smoke filled the air.

"May I introduce Miss Foxe of Foxe Hall, sir, she's seeking a locket, and for some reason she feels we might be able to help her locate it." Lucia saw the tricorn move slightly as the man behind the desk nodded, almost imperceptibly.

"We found her roaming the roads, bareback on her mare, sir. Miss Foxe recognised us from as far away as her chamber window." Lucia was intelligent enough to understand that her ability to recognise them from afar was the most significant information he had to impart. Why had she not thought to conceal that fact? She could have been safe in her chamber even now. With a peculiar pang of excitement, she realised she did not quite regret the course events had taken.

The man behind the desk raised a gloved hand to his face, in a movement suggesting he was contemplating what to do next. His protracted silence was unnerving, and her fear began to creep back in. She wanted to address him herself, but the authority he emanated silenced her.

After a long pause, he signalled to the man at her side with a dismissive gesture of his hand that his presence was no longer necessary. The man left silently and quickly, and Lucia was surprised to find she missed the semifamiliarity of him standing close to her.

"I have told your men already, sir," Lucia began tentatively. She wanted to explain and, hopefully, save herself from this horrible situation. "Although I did recognise you, my only purpose is to regain my locket, which is of sentimental value to me. I will tell no other what I recall of your appearance."

She expected a reply, but her only answer was another long silence, during which she felt his gaze on her in the most unsettling fashion. Finally, he pushed his chair out and stood up. He was not as tall or as broad as she had expected him to be, but in his dark cloak, his figure had a naturally commanding air about it. Beneath the cloak, she saw he wore cream breeches, shining black riding boots, and a white shirt and waistcoat.

To Lucia's surprise, he removed his tricorn and placed it on the desk. She saw he had very dark hair, worn long and tied at the nape of his neck. The hair was full and thick, suggestive of youth, not the maturity she had expected.

He walked slowly towards her. Her courage drained from her and she wanted to back away, but the door behind her was closed and she had no wish to demonstrate her own cowardice. When he was close to her, he bowed his head slightly and spoke.

"Miss Foxe? Allow me to introduce myself to you." Something unexpected about his voice caught Lucia's attention. In the next moment she saw why, as he pulled away the kerchief masking his face.

❖

The woman Julian had brought to her was undoubtedly very beautiful. Her beauty was refined and aristocratic, delicate. Pale, almost luminous skin clearly kept sheltered from the elements, golden hair with a natural curl, shining warmly in the candlelight. Her eyes were anxious shadows, but Len imagined them to be blue and clear. Intelligent.

She knew at once that this was the elder Miss Foxe, Lucia. The younger, she knew, was no more than a girl. The vision in the middle of her private chamber was no child. Taller than was usual in a woman but of a very slender build, she held herself like a woman with no small measure of pride. And she was not as frightened as Len had supposed she would be. Intriguing.

As soon as Julian brought the unfortunate Miss Foxe into the room, she had known there was no other way forward than to discuss the matter with her herself. If she had been presented with the undoubtedly silly younger sister she might have reconsidered, allowed Julian and the men, and her own shadowy but speechless authority, to frighten the girl into keeping her silence. But this woman, Len knew instinctively, would not be so easily scared.

Len had taken note of Julian's surprised expression when she had asked to be left alone with their hostage. She was sure he was dubious about her plan but thanked him silently for his loyalty and trust. His faith in her was one of her greatest sources of strength. One of the reasons she was sure to use her most considered judgement every day. She could not let Julian down and betray his trust.

When Miss Foxe spoke, it was everything Len could do not to smile. Her tone was so measured and even, though it was not hard to hear the anxiety in the words. And yet she was haughty too, this Miss Foxe. She expected to get her own way. No doubt she usually did, in her life of servants and admirers. Len remembered that life all too well, though she had never been so pampered herself. However, Miss Foxe was no silly, sheltered rich girl. Her words showed intellect and understanding. And a woman who would ride out on the highway in the middle of the night after the thieves who had stolen her locket was certainly worth her interest. Len did not have the pleasure of female company these days. She told herself she did not miss the complications, the unsettling emotions. And yet Miss Lucia Foxe intrigued her unbearably.

She moved towards the woman with deliberate slowness. She wanted to watch her reaction, wanted a moment or two to understand and prepare for what she was about to do. She saw the instant Miss Foxe's courage failed her and made a conscious effort to suppress the kindness and empathy that burned in her heart. She needed this woman to be afraid of her. The safety of her men could depend on it, whatever her own feelings.

And yet, however frightened she was, pretty Miss Foxe did not back away from her. She stood her ground and looked Len in the eye. Breaking her silence was not so hard, even as she saw the question in Miss Foxe's face. But she was surprised how nervous she felt as she reached for the kerchief and pulled the mask from her face.

CHAPTER FIVE

Lucia stared in confusion and tried to grasp hold of a sensible reaction. The face revealed to her was indeed young, without a line of age. The jaw was soft, with no hint of a beard. A striking woman's face.

Briefly, she thought her eyes must be deceiving her in the gloom. But then the woman spoke again, making a slight bow as she did so, and though the voice was deep and smooth, it was also distinctly feminine. "Len Hawkins, pleased to make your acquaintance, Miss Foxe. Miss *Lucia* Foxe, I presume?"

Social etiquette was not the first notion to enter Lucia's mind, and she did not return the politeness. She simply stared, open-mouthed. Dumbly, she looked down at the woman's legs and feet, to be sure this was the same breech-and-boot-wearing figure she had seen approaching from the desk. She looked back into her face and saw pink lips curve into the faintest of smiles. Her eyes were as dark as her hair, and she was regarding Lucia with what seemed to be a combination of amusement and contempt.

"You know my name?" Lucia said at last. It was really the least of the questions she had but the only one she could then form into words.

"Of course. Miss Lucia is the eldest daughter of Sir Spencer. Miss Isabella is the younger. Their brother is off terrorising the French with Wellington." Her voice sounded well-bred and educated, but she spoke with a far from reassuring sneer in her tone. Lucia, though unnerved, was not wholly surprised this woman had such knowledge of her family. What it revealed was that she was familiar with the society of the local area, where the Foxe family were well known enough. "I assume I am more likely to find the eldest daughter abroad in the middle of the night in pursuit of a trinket, and I presume therefore that you are Miss Lucia." The words were spoken with total confidence. Lucia bridled against the arrogance of the assumption but suspected it was grounded in an intellect used to being correct.

"Yes," she confirmed, searching for further words. "I don't understand," she said eventually, unable to do anything but confess her confusion.

"I don't imagine you do," was the smooth reply in a tone Lucia did not appreciate at all, as though she knew nothing of the world.

"He called you sir," she said, trying to express her bewilderment and refusing to acknowledge to herself just how coloured by intrigue her confusion was.

"So he did." Len shrugged. "A term to show his respect. Besides, he did not know I would choose to reveal myself to you."

Lucia understood at once. There was no way she would ever have expected the leader of the robbers to be one of her own sex. If this Len Hawkins had chosen to keep her face covered and had not spoken, Lucia would have left the room with the impression the leader was merely a slender man who rode a black horse. Calling her sir strengthened that disguise. Lucia was forced to wonder why indeed she had chosen to show herself now.

"You are the leader of these men?" she asked. She realised she felt almost more threatened by Len than she had her male companions, the fear infused with incomprehension. It took a great feat of will to summon her courage to ask any questions at all.

"Yes."

"They follow you?" Lucia was incredulous not to be offered an explanation of something so extraordinary.

"Is there any reason why they should not?" Len's tone revealed a resentment Lucia had not expected.

"You are a woman."

"Cleverly observed, Miss Foxe. So are you." The contempt was undisguised now, and it quickened Lucia's own temper.

"I would never expect to lead a group of men," she replied. Of course she would never expect to rob carriages on the highway either, but that seemed beside the point in the moment.

"You are not me, though, Miss Foxe. I would not expect a group of men to follow you." Len's eyes fixed to Lucia's, full of hostility. Lucia decided she must bring this encounter back to its purpose.

"Miss…Miss Hawkins?" she began, unsure of the required form of address.

"You may call me sir."

"I have come for my locket."

"So I understand. Of what import is it to you?"

"I don't believe that is of your concern." Lucia felt her resentment rising.

"I may be inclined to find this locket of yours if you can give me to understand its import. Otherwise, I may be inclined to tell you I have never seen such a locket." Her tone was sardonic and threatening, more unnerving because these were shades Lucia had never heard in a woman's voice before.

"It was my mother's. It contains a portrait of her and a lock of her hair."

"Your mother is dead?" Len asked, with little audible sympathy.

"Yes."

Len did not offer her condolences. "As is my own," she said, and Lucia was surprised by a moment of understanding between them. Len's face, however, remained hard.

"Then you might understand the significance of the locket to me." Lucia matched this strange woman's lack of compassion as well as she could. Perhaps Len was not so strange. Lucia well understood the effect of losing one's mother. Len's hard face struck her as an adopted mask to hide her true emotions. There had to be more than such cold reserve in this woman's heart. Lucia could not help but wonder what secrets Len kept.

"Yes, I might," Len said. Her expression still gave nothing away, and she seemed in a hurry not to dwell on their common understanding. Why? Lucia found questions in her mind she did not dare to ask. "But there is still the matter of your being able to recognise us so adeptly."

"On my honour, if you return my locket to me, I swear I will never breathe a word to a living soul." Lucia did not like to make the promise, but ensuring her own safety and regaining her locket were her first priorities. She fully expected Len to take her at her word.

"Your *honour*?" Len scoffed. "Yes, you have honour aplenty I imagine, Miss Foxe."

"More than I can say for you and your men." Len's derision wounded Lucia, emphasised that Len was not a woman like herself, that it was ludicrous to be drawn to her at all. Her words were spoken before she had time to consider them and their possible consequences. She realised how reckless they were at once but remained quiet and held her head high. This woman would not get the better of her, whatever the threat.

Very slowly, Len reached for the pistol at her waist. Lucia watched her hand, frozen and barely able to breathe. A frightened apology crept into her throat, but pride would not let it pass her lips, even as the barrel was raised to her chest.

"If I had no honour, Lucia, you would be dead by now," she said in a very quiet voice. Lucia looked at the barrel of the pistol held steady inches from her body and, breathing hard, raised her eyes to meet Len's dark gaze, defiantly. Lucia concentrated on hiding her fear, on not being intimidated. Would this woman really consider shooting her? Why was she actually more afraid now than she had been of the man with the pistol that night on the roadside? Were the feelings making her tremble inside coming from her fear? If not fear, then what?

Len's face relaxed perceptibly, and she gave a soft chuckle, lowering her pistol before she finally returned it to its holster at her waist. "You're brave, Miss Foxe, I'll allow you that."

She turned her back to Lucia and strode to the desk. Lucia watched her, relief and inquisitiveness swirling together. To be called brave by such a woman stirred a sort of exhilaration she could not deny. Len picked something up from the desk. Lucia recognised her locket at once and took a step forward, as Len held it up by its broken chain and inspected it as it dangled from her fingers.

"Average craftsmanship really, wouldn't you say?" They both stared at the locket as it twisted slightly, reflecting the yellow candlelight.

"It is not the craftsman's skills I value." Lucia took another step towards Len and reached for her possession. Len allowed Lucia to take it, the chain sliding through her fingers.

"I suggest you guard it closely then, Miss Foxe," she said. "Do not be so careless with something so valuable."

"I did not expect to be robbed." Lucia was irritated by the tone of Len's voice, though buoyed at holding her locket in her fingers once more.

"A hazard the wealthy face daily," Len replied, as though it was no concern of hers.

"We are not so wealthy."

"Wealthy enough to own a carriage, horses, and a gold locket, Miss Foxe."

"That is not so very much."

"Depends what you relate it to, does it not?"

Lucia felt her anger growing, made worse because she also felt somehow ashamed of the small world in which she moved. She had no reply for Len, and mutual resentment infused the air between them with greater tension. Len broke the silence. "There is only the matter now, Miss Foxe, of your being able to recognise us. You understand, I hope, the reason my men brought you to me was nothing to do with returning your locket. It was rather so I might decide the risk you pose to us for myself. In the back of their minds, I believe they thought I might rather see you dead than risk you exposing us. We have never, you understand, been so easily recognised before now. You are uncommonly observant."

"I understand," Lucia replied. She shuddered involuntarily at the mention of how easily she could have been killed, and yet she knew, from some strange instinct, she would not be harmed.

"Good," Len said. "So if I have my men return you to your house, this will be the last time I have cause to concern myself with you? I know you value your life."

The threat was all too real, the menace sharp, even in Len's feminine tones. Lucia stared at her and wondered if she had underestimated her. Why had Len revealed herself? Lucia had been more terrified of her as a silent and mysterious man. Perhaps that was the point. Terror did not breed trust. By revealing her true self, the woman hoped to engender some degree of trust in her. How did she know Lucia would not betray that trust? And yet Lucia felt the effectiveness of Len's strategy, for now she found herself inclined—indeed obliged—to give her word of honour in return.

"You need not be concerned. I have my locket. It is all I wanted. On my honour."

"Then it is time for us to say goodnight, Miss Foxe." Even as she said it, Lucia felt a peculiar reluctance beat through her heart. So many questions swirled suddenly into her mind, but she knew she could not stay to ask them. How had this well-educated woman fallen into a life of crime? And how was it she appeared to relish her illicit power? Lucia longed for time to unravel her own feelings. Why was she so compelled by this woman of whom she knew she should wholeheartedly disapprove? What was it that made her heart beat faster and her breath come harder, that felt keen like fear and yet was not? There was so much she wanted to know, but all she could do was leave, return to the dull safety of her home.

"Goodnight then," she said. Len bowed her head slightly, walked past Lucia to the door, and called to the kitchen. She did not look at Lucia again.

Lucia was taken home in the same fashion as she had arrived, blindfolded atop Sally's broad back, her reins in the hands of the man in the bicorn. He spoke little.

Later in her chamber, unable to sleep, Lucia sat by the casement and watched the early daylight creep across the park, her fingers stroking the smooth gold of her locket.

❖

Len was restless for the rest of the night. Try as she might, she could not stop thinking about her encounter with Lucia Foxe. Eventually she lit one of her remaining supply of cigars—taken from a lone gentleman on the road two weeks previously—and wandered through the kitchen, where John, Julian, and Isaac were still awake and engaged in a game of cards. She acknowledged them with a nod and passed through the door to the courtyard of the house.

The air was bitingly cold. Despite the moonlight, it was dark here, deep among the trees. The darkness held no terrors for her. She was a creature of the night-time now; in many ways she was more comfortable after the sun fell below the horizon. Being so at ease in the hours between dusk and dawn gave her an advantage over her prey. Besides, the shadows allowed her to be more or less whoever she wanted to be.

Why had she abandoned her disguise with so little caution tonight? Just how had Lucia Foxe bewitched her into letting down her guard? Why on earth did she trust such a naïve and sheltered woman? Oh, Lucia had been brave, Len could not deny it. She felt a begrudging admiration for Lucia's courage, even with a pistol to her breast.

She was also painfully aware of disappointment. She did not know what she had expected of Lucia and chided herself for wanting anything more from the eldest daughter of a country gentleman. But somehow, she had hoped this woman who had climbed on a horse in the night and chased after outlaws would be more like herself. Lucia's dignified confusion and refusal to understand how on earth Len could lead a group of men had angered her. She had hoped for acceptance, possibly curiosity. And yet she had seen scorn in Lucia's expression, concealed though it was.

Len leaned against the wall of the house, the stone cold at her back. She reached up to release her long hair from the ribbon which held it at the nape of her neck and massaged her scalp with her fingertips. Part of her had wanted to just talk with Lucia Foxe; she knew it and hated herself for the weakness. She wanted to explain, reveal something more of herself. Instead she had used her power and the threat of violence as another kind of mask, keeping her distance from the other woman.

And she was deeply concerned that her trust in Lucia was misplaced. Lost in the moment, craving to be perceived as more than merely an ignorant criminal, she had let her guard down. She acknowledged that Lucia's fragile, pale beauty—such a marked contrast to her apparently stubborn temper and degree of bravery—had affected her more than she had thought a woman's beauty ever would again.

She drew on her cigar and leaned her head back against the cold stone wall, eyes losing focus on the woodland before her, as she remembered. The life she had known; the woman who had been its turning point in so many ways. Hattie had looked nothing like Lucia Foxe, with her light-brown hair and green eyes, and she'd been a dressmaker not a gentlewoman. And yet there was a quality she saw in Lucia she had also seen in Hattie. The emotion she had perceived just below the surface when Lucia spoke of her mother, the pride she had demonstrated in not allowing her fear of Len's pistol to show. Hattie would have reacted in just the same way.

Len smiled at the memory of Hattie, holding onto it and fighting the sadness which threatened to engulf her. She heard the door to the house open and close. Julian came out into the night, looking around him.

"Over here," she called from her place against the wall of the house.

"Cold night." Julian came to lean against the wall next to her, rubbing his hands together.

"Aye, that it is. A bad winter this one, Julian."

"Worse for some than it is for us, no doubt."

"Yes. I wonder how many Death will claim before spring is here."

"Too many."

They stood together in companionable and reflective silence for a short while. Len looked across at Julian. He reminded her so much of his sister. "I was thinking of Hattie," she said. She had no secrets from Julian, knew they were unnecessary.

"I think of her a lot."

"Do you miss her, Julian?"

"That I do. A man couldn't ask for a better sister."

"No. I still miss her too. However many seasons pass." Len heard the emotion in her own tone but knew Julian would not view it as a weakness.

"She'd be so proud of you."

"Of a thief in the night? Not so. Hattie was a good woman." Len hated the idea that Hattie would have objected to her way of making her living every bit as strongly as Lucia Foxe had shown she did tonight.

"She would have understood. And she would be proud of your strength, Len. How free you are." Julian's voice was gruff. Len knew such talk of emotions made him uncomfortable.

Silence fell between them again. Len wondered what Julian was thinking and waited for him to speak first. "What did you think of the little rich girl then?" he said, after a few minutes.

"Miss Foxe? I'm not sure, to be honest. She was braver than I thought she might be. But stubborn with it." Len did not feel inclined to reveal her deeper reflections in that moment. She sensed Julian's unease with Lucia and with her own method of handling the situation.

"Do you trust her?"

"I trust she will not betray us."

"Are you certain?"

Len considered, drawing on her cigar. She exhaled the smoke before she replied. "It would be foolish to be certain on such a matter. We can never be certain of anything. But I'd be inclined towards having faith in her discretion. She has her locket now after all."

"An odd woman, to chase thieves for a trinket."

"Indeed. How unladylike of her."

Julian looked in her direction quickly. "I did not mean—"

"I am in jest, Julian." Len smiled, although she knew he could not see her face in the darkness. "You would hardly follow me if you were worried about the appropriate behaviour of the fairer sex.

And as for Miss Foxe, I do not know if she is foolish or brave. Whichever, I think we are done with her."

"I hope so." Julian paused. "Can I ask why you let her see you, Len?"

Len wondered how honest to be. "You can ask, Julian. But I am not sure I can answer."

CHAPTER SIX

If the dark shadows beneath her eyes the next morning did not give her away, Lucia was convinced one of the grooms would notice something amiss in Sally's stable, and she would be forced into an explanation of what had occurred in the night. And yet Lucia found she had managed her escapade in complete secrecy; not one question was asked of her.

Of course, she could not wear her locket. The chain was broken, and besides, there was no way she would be able to wear it in the presence of her father or sister again. It made her angry once more. There would be no reasonable explanation as to how she had retrieved it, and therefore they could not know she had it back in her possession. She had slipped it beneath her pillow, so she might at least be close to her mother as she slept.

After breakfast, Lucia took a novel into the garden. Sitting in the arbour where the damp smell of morning foliage surrounded her, she wrapped her shawl tightly around her body, for it was really very cold, the winter sun thin in the sky. She opened the book and pretended to read. In reality, she was lost in thought.

Her adventure of the night haunted her. In the light of day, she was astonished at her nocturnal courage. Surely if she had seen the riders pass the gate now, as she sat in the garden, she would not have been brave enough to rise and follow them. For a fleeting moment, she was proud of her courage. Then she reprimanded herself, recalling the danger she had been in, the risk she had brought upon herself and her family. Sickness swept through her as she remembered the pistol pointed at her breast. She closed her eyes and breathed deep of the frosty air until she felt calm again.

She read a sentence or two of the novel she held in her cold hands. Any attempt to distract her thoughts was useless. The image of the leader of the robbers crept into her mind once more. A woman! Even now, it seemed the fabrication of a dream. Only her picture of the woman—several inches taller than her, with that lithe figure and broad shoulders, the glossy dark hair, and the mocking eyes—was far too clear in her head for her to have dreamed her. Lucia doubted she could ever have dreamed up such a person, someone so beyond her comprehension. So many questions still cried for answers. Why did the men follow her? And why had she chosen to reveal herself to Lucia?

As she contemplated these things, she remembered that odd reluctance to part from the mysterious outlaw woman. Never had she encountered anyone who had so bewildered her. Lucia did not remember her amiably, indeed, she recalled her hostility, her sardonic smile and felt the resentment rise inside her. She had made Lucia feel inferior and naïve. Who was this Len Hawkins to judge her? *Len?* What manner of name was that? She was surely more properly called Helena or the like. Lucia found it all ludicrous and puzzling. And yet still she wished she could have spent a little longer in Len's presence, maybe begun to understand her. Was there a part in her heart which still mourned for her dead mother, as there was in Lucia's? Did Len Hawkins have a man who loved her, or did she shun marriage? Lucia couldn't help but wonder what impression Len had formed of her and hope the scorn Len had shown did not reach very deep. Len had called her brave, after all, and trusted her word of honour in the end. She wondered if Len would think of her, entertained the foolish hope that she would.

In her musings, she almost forgot Len Hawkins was a thief and robber, who had not only stolen from her family but also held a pistol to her breast. It took some effort to keep in her mind that, woman though she was, Len was as dangerous as any man.

❖

As the days passed, Lucia's moments of contemplation grew not less frequent, as she expected, but more so. As that night receded further and further into the past, it became hazier in her recollection, and so she began to doubt herself. Had she really heard such menace in Len Hawkins's voice? Had the woman really contemplated killing her? Did the men really have the respect for their unusual leader she had sensed they did?

Isabella was much recovered from her ordeal by now and was busy planning what she would wear to Lord and Lady Netherfield's ball a few weeks hence. She had good reason to believe a certain Lord Hyde would be in attendance with his sister. Isabella spent a good many hours in her chamber with Anne Drew—her closest confidante—and from the sound of their giggles as Lucia passed by the door, being robbed on the road was a very long way indeed from Isabella's thoughts.

In contrast, Sir Spencer's worried glances now fell upon her own countenance, although she voiced nothing to him and did not think her complexion was yet reflecting the restless nights she was experiencing. True, she spent many hours alone with the novel she was reading, and it was a slim volume she would usually have managed in a day, but she did not think her father likely to be alert to such details. Lucia believed he simply noticed she had less to say for herself than usual. He did not however make enquiries after her health, and so she was excused the need of finding answers for him. This was just as well, since she had very few answers for herself.

Once, she even tried closing her eyes, to see if by doing so she could recall the movements Sally had made beneath her, the turns they had taken to bring them to the robbers' hideout. Of course, this was a completely ineffective exercise. Even if she had been able to recall the way there, what would she have done? Simply saddled Sally and trotted off to call upon a band of thieves, and in so doing show them not only did she recognise them from a distance, she also knew the way to their hideout? Impossible and ludicrous even to entertain the notion.

And so Lucia was left with fading recollections and a queer curiosity she had no way to satisfy. She struggled to recall a time in her life she had felt so restricted, so unable to satiate her thirst to know, to comprehend. As the days passed, the feeling only grew. Never had something seemed so difficult to understand and yet so important that she understand it, as if in the full comprehension of her night-time escapade and encounter with Len Hawkins she would learn something of great value. And never had it seemed so unlikely she would ever find the answers she craved.

Ten days had come and gone since Lucia's nocturnal adventure. There had been a touch of snow, dusting the trees decoratively but already melted from the paths and roads. The sky had been yellow and ominous all day. It was almost entirely dark by the time Lucia took tea with her sister. She retired early to her chamber, where even the fire in the hearth seemed suffocated.

She had intended to sit at her desk and write a letter to her friends in Bath but, after many minutes had passed in which she could think of no way to begin the correspondence, she put aside the paper and undressed, crawling—already half in slumber—beneath her heavy blankets. On this night, even the contemplative mood of the previous days did not prevent sleep from overtaking her quickly.

Lucia thought she was still in the throes of a dream when she awoke, hearing a sound out of place in the darkness. She was used to the groans of the house, to the cries of the foxes in the park, the way the large oak at the side of the house creaked in the breeze. This sound was different, closer.

She turned onto her back and opened her eyes. The darkness of her chamber was disturbed somehow. The shadows before her eyes were not exactly as they should be.

One of the shadows close to her moved.

Before she had chance to comprehend fully she was not dreaming, the shadow loomed even closer, assumed a human shape, and pressed a gloved hand to her mouth. She cried out, but the sound was muffled. Fear filled her, making her heart pound most alarmingly.

"Miss Foxe." She heard the voice in her ear, familiar yet still terrifying. "Your presence is required. There is someone who wishes to speak to you," the man said. He was not wearing his hat, but she recognised him nevertheless. She could hear her heart in her ears, and her thoughts buffeted around inside her skull. What did he want with her now? How did he come to be here in her chamber? Was he more or less of a threat than a stranger would have been? Who was it who wanted to talk to her? Len Hawkins?

His hands pulled at her, forced her to sit up in the bed. She tried to move away from his grip, but he was stronger. Another shadow stirred, and she saw there was another shorter man in the room. The dying embers in the hearth were reflected upon something in his hand. She saw he held a knife with a long blade and felt nauseous with terror.

"We will not hurt you, Miss Foxe, but you have to come with us," the man with his hand over her mouth said. His words were far from reassuring. She reached up to pull at his arm—to give herself a chance to reply—but his response was simply to haul her to her feet. "Apologies, miss." He held her firmly while the other man came closer.

Lucia fought him as he forced her arms behind her back and wound a coarse rope around her wrists, but it was useless. When she felt the cold tip of the knife pressed against the skin of her throat, she did not resist, nor did she dare make a sound as the taller man released her mouth, only to force a piece of fabric between her lips, which he knotted tightly at the back of her head. Her legs were ready to collapse, the blood pulsing with unbearable force throughout her body as, once more, she found herself blindfolded. Still the cold of the blade touched her throat, and she remained motionless, terrified. She could not, strangely, comprehend the idea of her own potentially imminent death, but the threat of very great pain, the harm they could do her, rendered her barely able to breathe, a state not helped by the gag.

And still the questions circled in her head. Why was this happening? Where did they intend to take her? What could she say to save herself from whatever they threatened?

Although she did not faint, terror overtook Lucia, and she felt barely conscious as she was lifted onto the tall man's shoulder—as though she was a sack of grain—and carried from her chamber. Through the haze she wondered if the intruders had broken the lock of the front door and was suddenly aware in the next moment of the cold of the night air through her nightdress. She thought of her father and sister and wondered if she would be returned by morning, as if this was simply a bad dream in the night.

They travelled once more on horseback; she was aware of the steady rhythm, sickening in her disorientation, and the feeling of his strong embrace behind her, keeping her on the mount. But it all felt like the most farfetched of dreams. The fear had abandoned her, but so had the capability of rational thought.

The smell of damp trees and woodsmoke, a recognised scent, brought her somewhat back to her senses. She knew at once they had returned to the same place as they had brought her before. Foolish curiosity fluttered inside her. Surely she would meet with Len Hawkins again. For a fleeting moment she was almost thrilled. Then Lucia recalled how dangerous Len was, how readily she pointed her pistol, and terror crept into her heart once more. Whatever questions she had asked, however she had painted the outlaw in her head, Lucia really knew nothing of Len Hawkins or what her reception would be tonight. The indications were that it would not be favourable. And why would it be? A woman like Len would have no conceivable reason to want to see Lucia again, unless forced.

Lucia needed her abductor's strong grip to steady her as he guided her towards the house. To her relief, as soon as she heard the door open and felt the wooden floorboards of the kitchen beneath her feet—still in her bed slippers—he removed the gag.

She was silent, despite the new freedom to speak. What was there to say? He removed the blindfold and she blinked, looked around to see the kitchen was much the same as before, only neater.

Many of the boxes and chests that had littered it before were missing, and there was no food on the table tonight.

She turned to the tall man at her side, who was by now alarmingly familiar. "What do you want with me?" She was dismayed by how tremulous her voice sounded.

"It's not me, Miss Foxe, who wants anything with you," he said. He put one hand on her bound wrists to push her forward. She went with him, as she had before, into the central hallway of the house, and they proceeded without knocking into the same room they had previously.

As soon as they entered the room her kidnapper turned and left her, closing the door after him. Lucia looked at the shadow behind the desk. The room was as gloomy as it had been on her previous visit, although an extra candle burned on the desk. Len had made no attempt at disguise tonight: there was no hat, no kerchief. Still, if she had been seeing that shadow for the first time, she would not have believed it to be a woman. Len's posture in her chair behind the desk was not like that of a woman. Her shoulders seemed too broad, however slender she was.

Len put down the book she was reading and stood up. She was not wearing her cloak tonight. Instead, as she came closer to the candlelight, Lucia saw she wore simply her cream riding breeches above the black boots, and a loose man's shirt beneath her dark-coloured waistcoat. The shirt was open at the neck and revealed something of a slender throat. Lucia felt Len's power, her authority in the room, even as her eyes lingered on that patch of bare, vulnerable skin. The hair on the back of her own neck stood on end with an impossible tension, a thrill that unaccountably came from being in Len's presence once more, and she shivered in her thin nightdress.

Len's eyes were now fixed to Lucia's face. There was no trace of sympathy or mocking tonight. Her gaze was enough to freeze Lucia's heart. Lucia cleared her throat, her thoughts whirling tumultuously as she tried to make sense of this predicament.

"Why have I been brought here?" she managed to say at last, her confusion all too plain in her voice.

"I can't imagine you are as ignorant as you try to pretend, Miss Foxe. You are lucky to be here. It was suggested to me you be dispatched without being allowed to answer to me first," Len said. There was such a veiled threat in her smooth tones.

"I have no clue as to why you wish to see me." Lucia's resentment failed to give her courage, and she was dismayed by such a cold opening to their conversation. "Nor do I understand why it was necessary to take me from my house in so dramatic a fashion."

"Would you rather I had sent an invitation?" Len said cuttingly. She had moved close to Lucia now, to stand just in front of her. Her proximity made Lucia feel more vulnerable.

"Do you think I'm likely to attack you?" Lucia tried to match some of Len's sarcasm and looked into her eyes with hostility, as she moved her arms in agitation against the rope binding.

"In truth, Lucia, I don't know what you are likely to do. You have betrayed your honour once. I misjudged you. That's not a mistake I care to make twice."

Lucia's mind flew into panic instantly, as parts of the situation began to make sense. "I have betrayed nothing!"

"I don't believe you."

Lucia saw at once, whatever she was accused of, it would be almost impossible to prove anything to Len she did not want to believe. Anxiety seized her heart. "Please tell me how you think you misjudged me," she said. She tried to remain calm, sure her only hope was to convince Len she was honourable after all. She thought she saw a moment of indecision in Len's dark expression.

"You swore you would tell no one what you knew of us," Len said.

Lucia was more frightened, as she understood what Len thought she had done, and also indignant Len believed she would break her word so easily. "I made that promise on my honour. Are you questioning my honour?"

"Yes, Lucia, I am."

"But why? I swear to you I have not breathed a word to anybody."

"Maybe then you will explain to me why, within days of your being able to recognise my men from your chamber window, one of our number was arrested in town, having travelled there safely once a week for three years, never having been recognised before?"

Cold dread crept up Lucia's spine. If Len believed she was responsible for what had happened to her man—what surely would happen to him when the course of justice had been run—she could have no compunction in taking Lucia's life in return. Len appeared to be studying Lucia's reaction closely now, and Lucia hoped her innocence, her genuine surprise, would save her.

"You have to believe me, I have told no one!" Lucia said as firmly as she could, though her voice broke on the last word, giving her fear away. The candle on the desk guttered in the draught.

"Your father promised to see us hang. Then, just days later, you recognise us, run after us seeking your precious locket. The very next week one of us will indeed hang. That's coincidence, you tell me?" Lucia could sense the pain in Len's voice, the anger.

"My father's promise was not mine. I cannot explain the misfortune to have befallen your man, but it was not my doing." In her distress Lucia was chafing her wrists sore against the rope holding them.

"What reason do I have to believe you?" Len's hand travelled to her waist, where it rested menacingly upon her pistol.

Lucia struggled for an answer to convince Len, to save her own life. In the dizzying darkness of her thoughts, suddenly she found a reply.

"You are underestimating me. Do you not think that, if I wanted to see you hang, I would bring the militia here, in the night, to capture you all?"

Lucia saw Len pause to consider this. "You have no idea where you are, therefore you could not do as you say."

"I know we are within five miles of Foxe Hall. We rode no farther. I could bring with me a company of militia and describe to them the house for which they should search. I could describe every one of your men to them." Lucia said the words with a challenge in her voice, fortified with the very last of her courage.

Len did not reply instantly. Instead, she seemed to contemplate for a moment. Her jawline set firm, her lips tightened, and her eyes narrowed. Hope rallied in Lucia's heart as she knew she had cast a shadow of doubt across the other woman's certainty.

Len took another step closer to Lucia, so Lucia had to tilt her head back a little to maintain eye contact with her, for Len was at least three inches taller. She stood her ground, though she wanted to step back. Even through her alarm, she looked at Len with a certain sort of fascination. Eyes so dark, concealing far more than they revealed, faintly lined with experience. Skin still youthfully smooth over a hard jaw, and lips that seemed set in a determined grimace. Lucia could identify with that stubborn streak, that desire to keep herself hidden. It was very strong in her right now, as her heart beat faster and she felt perspiration prickle her skin, despite the chill. The mystery of it all made it hard to breathe. It was as if she needed to reach out and touch Len to fully believe that she existed. Her fingers burned with the urge. How would it feel to touch her, just for a moment? She was almost consumed with the want to do so, only fear held her back. Len was fascinating yet terrifying, for Lucia had no way to predict what she would do next.

Len took a deep breath and her face relaxed. She appeared to examine Lucia's expression with her keen dark eyes, then fixed her with an even stare.

"On your honour, Miss Foxe?"

"Yes. On my honour, I have done nothing to jeopardise your safety, nor that of your men." Lucia's heart began to beat more steadily, though her head was giddy with relief.

Len said nothing. Slowly, she circled around to stand behind Lucia, and Lucia felt Len's fingers begin to loosen the knot of rope that held her wrists fastened. Len's flesh was warm where it brushed against her cool skin. The touch she had wanted so badly just moments before alarmed her now. Len was very real, her fingers very warm. Lucia's chest tightened. When Len spoke again, as she untied Lucia, her words seemed to creep around the back of Lucia's neck, leaving a warm trail where they passed. "I believe you, Lucia. Now, you will stay and take some refreshment with me."

"No, I'm sorry, I will not." Lucia was firm in her reply, before her curious heart could even contemplate the notion. There was more danger here than the pistol Len carried at her waist. Lucia did not understand it, but she knew she could not remain. "You have stolen me away from my chamber in the night. I demand you return me at once."

The rope fell with a soft thud to the floor and her wrists were loose. Suddenly, she felt Len's hand heavy on her shoulder. "My apologies, Lucia, but you *will* take some refreshment with me. It's either that or I will have Julian lock you in the cellar. I can't take the risk of returning you to your home. Not until I'm certain."

Lucia's heart stuttered, but she was not entirely sure it was fear that caused it to do so.

❖

Len kept her hand on Lucia's slender shoulder and did not miss the slight shudder that passed through Lucia's body. But it was only slight. She was a brave woman, undoubtedly. But such bravery could lead to danger. Len wanted to believe what Lucia told her; her intuition told her Lucia's story was true. And yet she dared not take risks with her men. Besides, at this point, it was in Lucia's best interest to remain with her here. She wondered if this foolhardy gentlewoman had any idea of the real danger she diced with. Probably not. She ground her teeth together and kept her silence. Her urge to protect Lucia contrasted sharply with the painful knowledge that she was part of the threat. She had to remind herself that it was not her task in life to educate genteel ladies about the ways of the world. Frustrated at the gulf she felt between herself and Lucia, she was not sure what she should do next. Part of her was tempted to lock Lucia in the cellar, to thoroughly terrify her. That would teach her.

Lucia wriggled out from her grip and turned to face her. Her gaze was level and angry, not as frightened as Len would have expected. She wasn't sure whether she was intrigued or infuriated by Lucia's apparent resistance to any level of fear or intimidation.

Admiration was her first reaction, though she fought the urge. Lucia was her hostage, her possible betrayer. She had to harden her heart. She stared evenly into the bright blue eyes, raised a questioning eyebrow, and waited.

Lucia took a breath, but did not look away. Len saw the traces of apprehension, but Lucia was exceedingly good at appearing angry rather than frightened. "You cannot keep me here!" Lucia said at last. Len imagined what her hostage was thinking. Perhaps of the scandal of the servants finding her missing from her bed in the morning, when they came to dress the pampered eldest daughter. The notion twisted something inside Len, painfully. This girl knew nothing of the world. A world which, for Len, had just got darker, stained by betrayal and new danger.

"I can keep you here." She heard her own words come out as a threatening snarl, watched Lucia recoil slightly, and felt a surge of remorse. She could be as well mannered as any lady. She attempted to modulate her tone to one which, although commanding respect, was also polite. "Though I would rather you simply accept my invitation and choose to stay here. For the time being."

"But why? You believe me, I know you do." Len was less satisfied than she expected to hear the note of trepidation creeping into Lucia's words. She tried not to resent this woman's perceptive abilities. Lucia seemed to know what Len was thinking, and that was unsettling. Len enjoyed being an enigma to her men, none of whom ever knew what to expect from her, even Julian.

"I do believe you." Once she had begun with honesty, Len felt, inexplicably, that she had to explain her reasoning. She owed Lucia nothing, yet she continued. "However, my men will not believe you so easily. If I am right in my suspicions about what has befallen John, he will not be the only one of us, or our like, to be arrested in the next week. If I keep you here with me, they can form no ideas of your betraying us, since you will not be free to do so." There was no safer option, for her or Lucia. She would not have one of her men turn murderer, for all of their sakes.

"But the men listen to you, tell them you believe me!" Lucia said, somewhere between an imperious command and a desperate plea. Len watched her hesitate and consider her next words. "Or do they not follow you as faithfully as you would lead me to believe?"

Len blinked at the sudden and courageous challenge in those last words. The little rich girl wanted to play games, did she? Anger twitched at her face. She willed it back and wondered why she didn't just turn Lucia over to Julian's custody for the night. Knowing the answer to her only question only made the anger deeper. Lucia was beautiful, no doubt, and strong. Len was all too aware of the power of those qualities over her own rational mind. She felt the pull of them now. But women made her weak in ways she did not wish to be, and that road led only to pain and danger. Still, she could not bring herself to treat Lucia with brutality.

"My men would follow me to their deaths," she said simply, her mouth set in a firm line as she fought against the torment in her heart. Anger was not helpful here, and instead she drew on her faith that she knew what she was talking about while Lucia had no idea. It made her feel strong and competent. "However, a good leader understands the men who follow him or her are still only men, and they are not above doubting. Therefore, if I can remove any chance of doubt poisoning their minds against my leadership, I am a more effective leader. Do you understand me?" She felt her passion ignite. Lucia's expression registered her comprehension of how close to dangerous anger she had pushed Len. Len continued to glare, fully prepared to use the advantage. Why was she explaining herself to this woman?

"Why should I help you to be a better leader?" Lucia looked confused, as though she was battling with some emotion other than fear and anger. Len tried not to wonder what that emotion was. She couldn't allow herself to care.

"You have no reason whatsoever to do that." Len maintained her calm exterior, though the question riled her temper further. Had Lucia no fear? Did she not understand who she was dealing with? It was hard to maintain her own strength in the face of Lucia's compelling, though naïve, bravery. Len felt as though she was losing this battle and determined to regain the advantage. "However, I imagine you value your life." She smiled a smile she knew was more threatening than amiable. Lucia needed to understand the world she had blundered into.

"What do you mean?" Lucia asked. She glanced nervously at Len's pistol. Len's hand returned reflexively to her waist and rested lightly on the holster.

"My men are not murderers. If they were, there would be a trail of bodies by the roadside. However, John will hang, there is no doubt." Pain, and the bitterness of being impotent to rescue John, swept through her, and she caught her breath, fighting not to lose control in front of Lucia. "He was like a brother to some of the men here. If they are inclined to believe you brought him to his fate, they will also be inclined to seek an eye for an eye, so to speak." The damned woman was still staring at her with disbelief in her expression. Did she think her wealth and position in society rendered her immune from something as lowly as murderous revenge in the night? "Remember how easily they crept into your chamber, Lucia."

Len's final words seemed to have the effect she was looking for. Lucia stared at her as if frozen, her apparently quick brain fumbling for a way out and not finding it.

"Surely I am in as much danger if I remain here?" Lucia said. Her protest was weak. Len was intrigued by this sudden weakness, for with it seemed to come a spark of something else in Lucia's eyes. Excitement? Clearly the girl was more stupid than she'd thought. But still frightened, of that Len was now in no doubt. Suddenly, contrarily, she wanted to reassure her. Lucia looked so delicate, so easy to break, a figurine of pale porcelain. Len did not want to damage her. She felt that to harm this fragile, frightened woman would be to harm herself too. A fracture in the porcelain would reach into her own heart, already cracked and weakened, and risk destroying it completely. Keeping Lucia safe seemed more important than almost anything.

"You will be under my protection. I'll wager it will be only a matter of days before we have the necessary proof you are not our betrayer, and after that you and your family will be quite safe. I'll even give you my word you will never again be plagued by my men on the roads."

The mention of Lucia's family caused a very visible change in her countenance. Len knew she had struck the right chord. Lucia would not want to endanger her father and sister. Her loyalty was admirable, the look in her eye one of worried affection. For a moment Len envied her and was forced to look away into the shadows at the edges of the room. Family loyalty was something she had never truly known.

"But my father—" Lucia began.

"I have a solution for that." Len did not need to hear the rest of Lucia's words to understand. She took a deep breath and spoke slowly, filling her voice with as much calm and authority as she could muster. "But you must do as I say and trust in my honour as I have put my faith in yours. I will allow you to return to your home once there is no necessity for you to remain here."

Lucia looked hard into Len's eyes. Len kept her gaze steady and open and gave Lucia no reason not to trust in her assurances. She spoke the truth after all.

"I will trust in your honour," Lucia said finally. Len smiled, just slightly. A ripple of pleasure passed through her, and she drew her brows together in a frown, alarmed that she should feel anything of the sort. Gathering her composure, she made Lucia a small bow.

"Then we will take refreshment together, Miss Foxe." She strode over towards her desk, pleased they had finished this useless sparring and a decision had been reached. Before she reached it, she turned on her heel and took in Lucia standing ashen and tense in the middle of the room. Lucia shivered visibly.

"But you are not dressed for company, Lucia, my apologies, I had not considered it before." How thoughtless to leave the poor woman in nothing but her nightdress! Inwardly, Len cursed herself for it. Treating those in her power with respect was one of her maxims. Though she might be a thief, Len could not be cruel. Lucia could not remain in the cold house in her nightdress, prey to the draughts. And the men. For a moment Len was bewildered, and then she recalled she had the answer to the problem somewhere in an upstairs room.

Without waiting to excuse herself, Len left the room and climbed the wooden staircase to the upper floor of the dwelling. She found what she was looking for quickly and returned to Lucia with a bundle of clothing in her arms, a little crumpled from the chest it had been stored in.

When she entered the room again, she found Lucia still rooted to the spot but looking about her in the flickering lantern light with a tentative curiosity. The light cast shadows over the planes of her face, and Len could not make out her expression. Lucia seemed suddenly mysterious and intriguing. Her posture was rigid, but Len could not help but see the soft, curving lines of her form through the thin nightdress. Swiftly, she looked away, back to Lucia's face. Lucia's gaze seemed to be directed at Len's hat and cloak hanging against the oak-panelled wall. Len couldn't help but wonder what was going through Lucia's mind. She had barely moved when Len opened the door.

"I think these will do for you," Len said, feeling bizarrely uncomfortable at having interrupted Lucia's reverie, and she dumped her bundle on the nearest chair. "I will leave you whilst you dress." She acted on her words at once. Outside the room, she paused to breathe the cooler air, unsettled by the stirring of emotions she did not want to feel.

Len returned to the kitchen. Julian was there, drinking—most likely small ale—from a tankard. William was seated at the table, eating a leg of chicken. Peter sat hunched by the fire, staring into the dancing flames. The silence in the room was heavy and she could feel the tension. John had been taken and would undoubtedly be hanged. The idea of riding the turnpike to see their friend's lifeless body in the cruel metal cage of the gibbet—a warning to others who thought of turning highwayman—was something none of them could stomach easily. Not only was John's loss hard to bear, it reminded them far too keenly of the dangers they flirted with every day. She knew the men were frustrated they could not break into the Nottinghamshire County Gaol and free John from his cell. There was no way she could condone any such attempt, but it did not stop her entertaining the notion, the mere fantasy of hope.

Indeed, her refusal to even countenance a discussion of rescuing John told them all there was no true hope. Theirs was not a life of hope, it was a life of darkness and of clinging to existence, of moments of joy and adventure. But not hope. Freedom they had until the day the law caught up with them and took not only their liberty but their living breath. A life free of convention and conformity, and more food on their table than many of their standing. But for friends they had only each other. Love was too great a risk and impossible anyway. The contemplation of a quiet and retiring life, a death safe and warm in a comfortable bed, was something they did not allow themselves.

Many of the men had never dared hope. But for Len, who once had, it was doubly bitter. She understood why the men lurking silently in the kitchen were so on edge. And into their midst had come Lucia, rich and delicate, her life comfortable and cushioned. The suspicion of her betrayal of them was bad enough, but that such betrayal could have come from one with so little understanding of their world, whose motivation could only be a mindless adherence to the law or some sort of revenge despite the fact she had not been harmed, only made the tension worse.

Len looked at each of them, trying to gauge their moods. Though as a group they were all subject to the same tensions and moods, she knew too that her men were individuals. The thoughts of one were not always the thoughts of the others. Julian's loyalty she never doubted. William too she would trust with her life. But she had no such faith in the rest of the band, and now, it seemed, her judgement had been proved terribly correct. But how did she suggest to the rest of them that it was one of their own number had betrayed them? And which was it? For now, she concluded, the answer could wait until there was proof. She would not have them doubt her or think her head had been turned by a pretty gentlewoman.

"Any food spare?" she asked, matter of fact, in a tone that did not encourage questions.

"Some roasted chicken, old bread, and a few apples," William said. He was eying her as though he wanted to ask a question but was not sure how to.

"Does Miss Foxe not get enough to eat at her dining table? I wasn't aware the rich needed our charity." Julian's words were surly. Not a challenge to her directly, but a voicing of some of the tension in the room.

"Miss Foxe is not accustomed to being in the middle of the woods in the night-time. I think it would behove us to show a little kindness." Len picked up some of the remaining chicken, a little bread, and an apple, placing them and a knife onto a wooden platter. She grabbed a bottle of wine from a shelf at the side of the room and left without another word. The men were not questioning her yet. But it would come.

Chapter Seven

Len found Lucia wrapping the worsted shawl she had provided around her slender shoulders. She had the appearance of having dressed very quickly and seemed a little flustered when Len opened the door. Pushing the door closed behind her with her foot, Len ran a brief appraising eye over Lucia's appearance. The pale-yellow muslin gown suited her well, though it was admittedly not the latest fashion. Still, the cut was expensive, and though the garment was clearly designed for a taller woman, the way the fabric gathered below Lucia's bosom accentuated her slender figure perfectly. Len found she rather regretted that the winter air made the considerably ugly worsted shawl necessary for her hostage's comfort. It hid a form of perfect proportions upon which her gaze was inclined to linger. Lucia was pulling the shawl tighter around her body. Len was unsure if Lucia was cold or seeking comfort and protection from the thicker fabric. Her heart ached a little to see Lucia made so vulnerable, to the cold, to the danger of a den of thieves, to Len's own admiring eyes. She fought the compulsion to apologise and glanced down at the rather delicate leather slippers on Lucia's feet. Lucia watched her but seemed uncertain what to say. Len was fairly sure her captive understood she was dressed in fine clothes stolen from the carriage of a travelling lady and found she wished it were not the case. Suddenly Lucia's opinion of her seemed to matter more than it should. She tore her eyes away and deposited the food and drink on her desk before she trusted herself to speak.

"It does well enough," she said gruffly in the end.

"Yes," Lucia said, then hesitated. Her gaze fell on the roast chicken.

"Are you hungry?" Len asked. "I talked my way into some roasted chicken, some day-old bread, and a few slices of apple, though the buggers were reluctant. Sit down and help yourself to the banquet." She gestured ironically at the platter and was disconcerted when Lucia responded with a small smile.

"Thank you," Lucia seated herself in the nearest chair.

"Drink?" Len offered. Lucia's apparent confidence was bewildering, especially since her expression belied her true apprehension. "I brought wine, since I imagine you're not used to ale."

"No."

"To the wine or the ale?" Len smiled before she could help herself.

"The ale."

"I think you need the wine." Len poured a large measure into a tankard that stood on the desk and passed it to Lucia, who was in truth very pale and clearly needed something to fortify her. She did not want the inconvenience or the remorse of a swooning woman to deal with.

"Thank you," Lucia said. She took a sip and appeared steadied by the drink. After a moment of apparent reflection she turned an astonishingly lively gaze on Len's face. "What do I call you? You never told me." Len raised her eyebrows. It was as though sitting down to eat a meal had reminded Lucia of her ingrained etiquette, despite the unusual nature of their situation.

Len found she could not resist. "Sir?" She couldn't help but feel slightly triumphant when Lucia flushed and eyed her in a way that suggested she was not sure whether or not she was in earnest. Finally, Len allowed herself to smile. "If you permit me to call you Lucia, then you must call me Len," she said with a shrug. Such formalities were pointless to her.

"Len?"

"Yes." She saw Lucia's mental speculation as to what her full Christian name was. But she had not been Miss Helena Hawkins for years now and had no wish to lay a claim to a name that reminded her too painfully of her former life.

While Lucia took another sip of her wine, Len perched on the edge of the table, her feet on the other chair, and raised the bottle to her lips, taking a long drink. She could feel Lucia watching her and knew she drank in the way she did, contrary to all good manners and expected feminine behaviour, partly in the face of Lucia's all-too-apparent good breeding. She was suddenly compelled to reassert just how free of those rules she was. Yet when Lucia did not stop staring at her, she grew uneasy under the scrutiny. "Eat," she commanded, an edge of annoyance in her tone.

Lucia reached for a piece of chicken from the platter and began to eat. Len did not watch her, instead she looked away, at the floor, anywhere but at Lucia. Already she was wondering if her decision to keep the gentlewoman here had been a wise one. This felt too complicated, too awkward. Lucia was at once a very real threat and responsibility in Len's present and an echo of a past by which she would rather not be haunted. The feelings stirring were difficult to ignore. But ignore them she must. That path would lead only to danger and distress, and she had the men to think of. She suspected Lucia's presence would only torment her heart more with every moment with the reminder of what she had once known and could never know again. And yet, what choice did she have?

❖

Lucia ate a piece of bread and some more chicken before Len raised her head and glanced at her again. Lucia wondered what was going through this extraordinary woman's mind to make it appear she had almost forgotten her presence in the room. Silent still, Len reached for a slice of apple and bit it in half, chewing slowly, her eyes on Lucia's face. Lucia found her gaze, intense and speculative all at once, unnerving and looked away.

"You have to write a letter as soon as you have eaten," Len said at last.

"For what purpose?" Lucia was taken aback by the sudden instruction.

"You must convince your father that you are safe and prevent him from searching for you."

"I do not know how—" Lucia began, the mention of her father a heavy pain in her heart, though she tried not to let the emotion into her voice.

"I will tell you what to write. It will only be for a few days after, all." Len's tone allowed little disagreement. And yet Lucia felt the need to protest. Did this woman really not understand what it was to have a family who would be concerned for her welfare?

"He will be greatly worried."

"A father's prerogative," Len said, with more bitterness than Lucia expected. Her barely concealed scorn sparked further curiosity in Lucia's racing mind. What was Len's story? Where was *her* father?

"Let me write it now." Reminded of her family and also wondering what Len would have her write, Lucia could not bear to sit eating roasted chicken and drinking claret. The servants at Foxe Hall would be awake in the next hours. This would no longer be an obscure dream she was living. The daylight hours asked questions the dark of night did not.

Len pushed the other half of her apple slice into her mouth and slipped down from the table to go to her desk, from which she took a piece of plain paper. She picked up her pen and inkwell and brought them to Lucia. Moving the candle from the corner of the desk to the table in front of Lucia, she made the shadows dance. Nervously, Lucia took the pen in her hand and lowered it into the ink.

"Write as I say," Len instructed, as Lucia held the nib to the page before her. "Dear Father. Do not be alarmed on receiving this letter and finding me away from my chamber. I assure you of my safety. I will be absent from the house for a few days, and I cannot explain to you where I must be for those days until my return. I appreciate this is a peculiar turn of events, and I know you will be concerned for me. I beg you, do not be, I am quite secure. I am doing nothing to bring worry or disrepute upon our family. Indeed, what

I am doing is, in part, to protect yourself and Isabella. If a reason is sought by our neighbours for my absence, I believe you might tell them I am visiting our cousins in the Lakes—"

Lucia had so far written as instructed without question, considering whether her father would be convinced or reassured by the letter and reaching no firm conclusion, but now she was compelled to interrupt. "How do you know about our cousins in the Lakes?"

"Local society is a source of continual interest to me, Lucia," Len said witheringly. Lucia, more inquisitive than she was offended, had no choice but to return her attention to the letter as Len went on rapidly. "Again I assure you of my safety and apologise for my unusual behaviour and any worry it may cause you. I will explain all in a few days when I will return to you."

Len paused. Lucia glanced at her and wondered if there was any more to come. A few days? What would those days hold?

"Sign it as you usually would," Len ordered. She watched as Lucia did so. "Will he accept it?"

"I don't see he has much option. He will worry, naturally, but what else can he do?" Lucia imagined the concern on her father's face and her heart swelled with compassion. Yet at the same time came a strange feeling, something like excitement, which she had never before experienced. For the first time in all her years, her father would not know where she was, in whose company she was, or what her activities were. Where she should have been afraid or ashamed, she felt oddly light, a sort of liberation she found it hard to understand or accept.

"Julian will take this letter to Foxe Hall, so your father may read it when he wakes."

"Julian?"

"Your abductor."

"He took my locket from me at the roadside. And it was him I followed on the road."

"Yes. You did pay attention to us, Lucia, didn't you." Len's tone was menacing again. Lucia was relieved to see her face relax into a small smile. "Julian is my most faithful friend," Len went on more amiably. It seemed odd to Lucia for any woman to have a man as her close friend, but when Len stood next to her in breeches and riding boots, she could not expect anything to fall within her usual realm of comprehension.

"How many of you are there?"

"There were ten at one time. But our numbers seem to be diminishing."

Lucia had so many questions burning in her brain but no idea how to voice them. Len's voice betrayed some degree of anxiety and sadness, though those emotions were carefully veiled in her expression. Lucia glanced across at Len's desk, searching for words to continue the conversation without prying. She recognised a quarto edition among the few books on the desk surface.

"You have my book!" she exclaimed, pleased rather than indignant and heedless of how inappropriate her pleasure was.

"You mean Lord Byron's?" A smile flickered on Len's lips. "Yes, I do. I must say, it was most fortunate you had it with you. I've wanted to read it for a while now, but I would never have purchased it, not the price they're asking for it."

Len's honesty about her theft and personal circumstances took Lucia aback for a moment. She wondered about Len's life, the conditions of her men's daily lives. There seemed to be food enough and warmth, yet her words suggested something more of a struggle than appearances showed. Lucia forced her thoughts back to the book. "Have you enjoyed it?" she enquired, genuinely interested.

"It has made me think."

"Then I think I must take it back from you and read it for myself."

"I may allow it," Len replied, with a dark smile. Lucia found herself unable to look away from that smile. It had so much of a threat—or a promise—hidden within it. "The book has made the Lord himself very famous, I understand."

"Yes," Lucia said, collecting herself. "My sister's bosom friend is quite in love with him, although she has never so much as seen his carriage. We have not been fortunate to be in his presence. He has been largely away from Newstead, on the Continent I believe, until very recently, and our small circle is not his, anyway."

"My circle is rather different too, of course," Len returned. Lucia felt her cheeks grow warm and she did not reply.

A knock on the door startled Lucia. It opened to admit the man she now knew was named Julian. He looked at Lucia with a combination of inappropriate familiarity, amusement, and an edge of hostility. "I was just wondering if you've decided what we're going to do with her?" he said, addressing himself to Len.

Lucia took a moment to study him more carefully. He was tall and strongly built, his hair and beard dark, his eyes intelligent. He appeared to be of around the same age as Len, who she guessed was thirty or a little older. Lucia was puzzled how a woman only of the age of the men she commanded could maintain any authority at all. And yet, the longer she spent in Len's presence, the easier it was to believe. Len, despite her years, sex, and slender form, had an air of authority and easy control about her. Lucia was oddly drawn to such unexpected power, fascinated by it, and watched intently as Len addressed Julian.

"Miss Foxe will remain with us for the next few days," she informed him. Lucia saw his look of enquiry. He was not so much questioning Len as waiting for her reasons.

"A prisoner?" he asked.

"If you like, at least until I have come to a final decision," she replied. Len was relaxed and casual in her bearing, clearly at home in her authority and certain her decision would be respected. Lucia found she almost envied that easy power. The notion of being a prisoner, however, unsettled her in the same moment. She had not considered that aspect of this arrangement since she had escaped the threat of being locked in the cellar.

"Shall I take her down to the cellars?" Julian enquired, glancing briefly at Lucia and apparently reading her mind.

"No." Len was firm. "Miss Foxe is a gentlewoman and we must treat her as such." A flood of relief and gratitude washed through Lucia. "Besides, I think it is unlikely she will try to flee." Gratitude was replaced by a sort of humiliated anger. Len clearly thought Lucia was incapable of or unwilling to take any sort of action to escape her captivity. Had she forgotten that she was dealing with the woman who had ridden after a band of robbers in the dead of the night? Lucia glared at Len and was prepared to protest but quailed when both Len and Julian turned their eyes on her at the same time. She straightened her back proudly but kept a dignified silence.

"I want you to take this letter to Foxe Hall before daybreak," Len told Julian. She handed him the folded piece of paper. "Leave it somewhere a servant will discover it."

Julian took the letter and glanced down at it. When he looked at Lucia again his brow was furrowed and his expression dubious. "Miss Foxe has written it?" he asked, suspicion in his tone.

"It is her hand but my words. You may tell the others of the situation, and you will warn them Miss Foxe may be a prisoner, but she is also a guest and to be respected. Or I will deal with them personally." Len met Julian's gaze evenly and her words allowed no arguments. Lucia held her breath as she waited for Julian's reaction. He did not look pleased but nor did he seem inclined to cross Len.

"Of course," he said. "Hope you know what you're doing, Len."

"As always, Julian," she said, with a small smile but a hardening of her eyes. "You should go, there are not many hours before dawn," she told him.

"Yes. Until later then." He turned to Lucia and bowed his head slightly, "Miss Foxe." With that, he left the room.

Lucia watched his retreating back with curiosity, wondering just how it was that this articulate and physically strong man had come to respect Len so greatly and bemused by what seemed to be a friendship between Len and Julian. Such a thing was unheard of in her world, and she found herself almost envious.

"He is a handsome man," Len said, with a slight narrowing of her eyes.

Lucia flushed as she realised she had been caught gazing after Julian and that Len had taken her curiosity as something quite improper. "I had not considered such a thing. I was merely wondering how it is he obeys you so faithfully." Candour was remarkably easy with Len despite the tension between them. Perhaps it was the unusual situation, or maybe it was the casual confidence Len herself exuded. Lucia felt able to admit to her curiosity.

"He trusts me." Len shrugged slightly. "That is all a good leader needs."

"But how did it come about in the first place?"

"I can see you have many questions on your tongue, Lucia, and I'm tired. I will show you to your bed now."

"But I—"

"I will give you some of the answers you seek. Take breakfast with me."

"Yes." Lucia acquiesced, as though she had a choice in the matter. Len's manner almost made her feel she did. The notion that she would now try to sleep, and wake a hostage of outlaws still, was one she could barely comprehend. As Len rose, Lucia followed suit and allowed herself to be ushered from the room towards the wooden stairs in the centre of the building.

The chamber Len showed her to on the first floor of the house was small and shadowy, with a narrow bed smelling of damp. However, Lucia was tired, and despite the extraordinary situation she found herself in, she fell asleep remarkably quickly.

❖

Len slept little that night. She waited for Julian to return from Foxe Hall before she even contemplated her rest. His report that all was calm at Lucia's home gave her some peace of mind, though she could well imagine the uproar Lucia's disappearance would cause in a few hours. She knew the note she had dictated to Lucia would do little to relieve Lucia's family's fears, and for that it was difficult not to feel remorse.

She could not take the men's questions and suspicions tonight and scorned even Julian's company to be alone in the night with her thoughts. It was not long before those thoughts drove her from the oppressive silence of her private room and out into the dark woodland. She leaned with her back against the rough bark of an aged oak and allowed herself to feel part of nature, not something abhorrent and strange within it. There was peace in the world, away from the rules and conventions of society, away from the ludicrous constraints she had never had the ability to withstand. How did women such as Lucia manage it and appear to be so happy? And how was it that she had been born to be so different? An outsider. An outlaw. Sometimes she could scarce believe her own choices. To live a life of violence and terror, of crime and villainy, and to know her end was, like as not, to be on the gallows. This had been her choice? What had the alternative been? Could Miss Helena Hawkins have lived the life of Miss Lucia Foxe? Impossible.

And now Lucia saw a glimpse of the alternative in Len. Len saw the spark of excitement in her captive's blue eyes. Dangerous. Too dangerous. Part of Lucia was already drawn towards the freedom she saw here. But she did not yet recognize it. Hadn't there been a time when Len herself had not known just what it was she longed for? And yet still she had craved it. It would be far better for such desires never to be awoken in Lucia. The longing for liberty was an ache like no other. In Len's experience, only one other pain had surpassed it, that of loving as she was not allowed to, desiring someone she could not according to all the laws and conventions she had been taught. To love a woman was surely the most bittersweet of experiences. Was it possible Lucia, still unmarried, had felt something of that yearning? And could Len herself be its object? There was a glimmer in Lucia's gaze, behind the fear and confusion, something underlying that secret excitement. If unrecognised desire was the cause, Len could not encourage it.

Len clenched her fists in frustration. A woman's reputation was so delicate. Lucia had shown remarkable bravery when she had left her bed and ridden out on the turnpike. She did not deserve to be repaid by the shame and possible ruin that always waited around the corner for a respectable woman who deviated from the norm. Len had escaped that fate herself. Instead of disgrace and humiliation she had sacrificed that life forever and now dared the hangman to take her life in the name of justice. Such an escape was not one she could countenance for Lucia. Len was so far removed from Lucia's world now. It was not fair to draw a brave but delicate woman into her own fateful existence.

Yet some part of her wanted Lucia to remain here, to begin to understand. She knew all too well the kind of questions Lucia had for her. An intelligent woman, courageous and beautiful. Life could suffocate such a woman. But she was safe in her constrained existence. Len had to remind herself that it was not her duty to liberate womankind. Lucia could not be made discontented with her own life. She must be glad to return to her cosseted existence, her warm chambers and plentiful meals, the round of social engagements and expectance of a marriage proposal. Len's choices exposed Lucia to dangers she had never even contemplated. However much her heart yearned to free Lucia—and selfishly longed to keep the woman here—she knew she must be guarded in their conversation in the morning. She could not allow the yearning in her own foolish heart to sway her. Lucia was beautiful and looked at Len with something secretive, thrilling, and not quite understood in her gaze. To unravel that was an excruciating temptation. But, outsider though she was, there were rules and responsibilities in this life too. To keep her men safe. To keep her own heart and soul safe. Lucia was her prisoner through necessity. There could be nothing else between them.

❖

Bright sunlight shone outside when Lucia awoke the next morning, although all she could see of it were the rays which crept around the edges of the heavy curtain obscuring the window. Although she was instantly aware she was not in her own bed, she did not realise quite where she was and looked around her with confusion. Recollection returned with a jolt of nervous alarm. Her father would have read the letter by now. Miss Lucia Foxe was the prisoner of a gang of robbers. Only she did not feel quite as she supposed a prisoner should and wondered at her own contrary nature.

Lucia rose from the bed and wrapped the worsted shawl about her shoulders. She had gone to bed fully dressed. Looking down at her crumpled skirts, she reflected that it barely mattered how she appeared here. It was the first morning in memory she had not had to bother herself about how she was dressed for breakfast or to receive morning visitors. She wondered what time it was. There was a cobweb-covered clock on the mantelpiece in the chamber, but it read four o'clock and looked as though it had not kept the correct time for some years.

She went to the window and lifted the curtain, heavy with dust, and peered out at the bright day. If she had hoped to orientate herself as to where this house was located, she was disappointed. All that could be seen beyond the small plot of cleared land in which the house stood were the bare branches of winter trees. There were many patches of woodland within the vicinity of Foxe Hall, and since Lucia had no clue in which direction they had travelled, it was impossible even to guess at where she was.

The snow of the previous day had entirely melted, and today the sky was clear. The pane of glass she looked through, which was cracked clean across, misted with her breath upon it. Lucia gazed at the jagged outlines of the branches against the blue of the sky and thought of her father and sister. They would be torn apart with worry. She missed them suddenly, and a surge of recrimination swept through her. How could she have done this to them? It was only a moment later it occurred to her that she had not had an option in the course events had taken. She was a prisoner, after all. How odd that she had been considering the matter as though she had chosen her fate, as though she had made some decision which had led to her waking here, in a robber's hideout. It was not her fault. Not at all. And yet she was not reassured.

She let the curtain fall, plunging the room back into deep shadow. Through the gloom, Lucia inspected the chamber a little more closely. There was little furniture, and it did not appear to be regularly used. The cobwebs suggested it was unlikely a fire had been laid in the hearth for some time. She shivered and pulled the shawl closer around her shoulders.

Standing in the centre of the room, Lucia wondered if she should wait until she was summoned, or whether she could venture to leave the chamber. She did not like the idea of blundering into the kitchen only to find the men who had robbed and abducted her there. The notion that they harboured suspicions she had betrayed them made her anxious to the extreme.

Her indecision was cured by a firm knock on the door a moment later. Lucia went to the door and opened it, to find Len leaning against the door frame. She was dressed as the night before, only her collar was fastened, she wore a white necktie, and she had donned a gentleman's blue frock coat over her shirt. Lucia could not help but stare. "Good morning," Len said with a slight smile.

"Good morning," Lucia stammered back. She had not seen Len in daylight before. The light from the large, dusty window at the end of the passageway was plenty to illuminate her. It lent an edge of reality to Len's appearance the guttering candlelight could not, and in this she was rather more extraordinary than she had been before. Lucia could see the tones of rich brown in what had seemed to be black hair, the faint rose in the otherwise pale cheeks, the mole on her left temple.

"I trust you slept well?" Len asked, rather formally.

"Yes, thank you." Lucia looked into Len's brown eyes and questioned her own sanity. She was not remotely afraid. At the very least she should have been angry, indignant, *humiliated* by Len's power over her future. She was not so brave as to be careless of the danger she was in. Yet standing facing Len in the doorway, all that filled Lucia's mind were the questions she burned to ask. She felt an emotion she had no name for but which made her senses heighten and a tension form deep inside her. It seemed to make her reckless, hoping Len would not send her away, glad to be in the company of thieves. She would have sworn she saw the same tension in Len, that something between them entwined inextricably. Something that told her Len was not so very different from her, after all.

"Would you like some breakfast?" Len asked. The words were stiff and she looked away from Lucia's eyes and over her shoulder.

"Yes, please." Lucia marvelled at the mundane nature of the conversation and wondered why Len seemed suddenly so uncomfortable. Silently she followed Len across the landing and down the stairs, across the hallway, and into the kitchen.

The kitchen was warm, the fire in the hearth blazing already. Lucia was surprised to see it was empty of men. She wondered where they were and, comprehending suddenly what the nature of their activities might be, felt a lurch of tension in the pit of her stomach.

Lucia sat down tentatively on one of the wooden chairs by the table. Moments later Len placed a plate in front of her, upon which were a slice of bread, a boiled egg, and a thick slice of fatty bacon. She was aware suddenly that she had quite an appetite and began to eat at once. Len took a seat opposite, eating a slice of bread spread with bacon dripping. Lucia watched her eat, pulling the crust from the bread with her fingers, pushing it hungrily into her mouth, before eating the softer part of the bread in large mouthfuls.

Lucia sliced off a small morsel of bacon, which she chewed thoughtfully. All of her upbringing and education told her she should despise Len, for her table etiquette if nothing else, and yet she did not. An intriguing puzzle.

"The bread's fresh," Len said at last. She looked vaguely perturbed by Lucia's contemplation of her.

"Yes."

"I suppose fresh bread isn't uncommon in Foxe Hall, though?" There was an edge of bitterness in her tone, but Lucia did not think it was directed against her personally.

"No. Jones, the cook, bakes bread every other day."

Len snorted disconcertingly and took a drink from the cup of water in front of her. Lucia was offended by her hostility yet, at the same time, felt a strange and previously unknown shame at the privilege she took for granted in her life. However, Len was educated and well spoken. Surely she had not been born into poverty. There were questions which needed to be asked.

"There seems to be food aplenty here too," Lucia said. She did not mean to sound defensive of her own privileges but managed to all the same.

"We don't starve," Len said. "But have you stopped to think about what we must do for that food?" She pushed the last of her bread into her mouth and raised her eyes to Lucia's.

"You steal food too?"

"No, we steal money. The money we steal allows us to buy food." She spoke as though she was explaining the facts to a child or simpleton, and this fired Lucia's temper.

"Forgive me for not understanding the way thieves operate," she snapped. "I understand a world which works for its money to buy food."

"You, of course, work very hard for your food."

Lucia's face flushed. "I am fortunate. But there are many not so fortunate who do not turn to robbery."

"True enough. But there are also many starving to death because the work they cling to no longer feeds them. Do you know how much a quartern loaf costs, Lucia?"

"No." Lucia did not meet Len's searching glare.

"In town, it costs one shilling and eight pence."

"Oh."

"Which means very little to you, doesn't it?" Len's tone grew sharper. "Do you know how much your precious work earns a man?"

"What sort of man?" Lucia's confidence was faltering as her ignorance was exposed.

"Say a skilled man, a stocking weaver, there are plenty of those in these parts."

"No, I do not know."

"A stockinger earns around seven shillings a week."

It did not take Lucia long to calculate how scant such wages were. She did not have a reply. Len's anger infused her words and made her eyes shine. She was frightening and somehow enchanting all at once.

"And he needs more than bread to live. His family need more than bread. And that's a skilled man. Imagine the plight of a labourer. Is it any wonder there are more and more men turning to thievery and violence?"

Lucia swallowed a piece of bread and laid her knife aside. She could not answer to the poverty of the masses. But she was determined to learn more about the woman across the table from her who spoke with such knowledge and conviction. "You talk of men. But you are not a man. I cannot imagine you were ever a labourer."

"And you ask why then I have turned to thievery?"

"Yes." Lucia took a deep breath, calculated that Len was not truly angry with her, and dared to continue. "You are educated, you are no labourer's daughter."

"You are educated, Lucia, and no labourer's daughter. Yet if your father cast you from the house and refused you a penny of aid, how would you make your living?"

"Is that your story?" Curiosity and unexpected compassion competed in Lucia's heart. She wanted so badly to know more of Len, to understand what drove this woman into her unconventional life, what fired her passion, and what sank her into despair. It was partly through wishing to comprehend more of such a woman, and it was partly out of that strange, tight empathy which came upon her again. Even the slightest hint of Len's story told her she had experienced things Lucia had never contemplated. And yet, somehow, she felt that connection between them and needed to know why.

"It does not matter if that is my story or not." Len was clearly not going to expand, and Lucia was disappointed. "The point is, Lucia, a woman has virtually no chance of earning money. Yes, she can sell herself as a slave into the factories and, for the risks she takes with her life, earn less than her male counterparts. She can take in needlework and buy a loaf a week, enough to survive and know the pains of her hunger more acutely. An educated woman can go as a governess, an uneducated woman as a housemaid, but only if there is someone to speak for her character and reputation, and such work is only another form of slavery. All women are dependent on their fathers, husbands, and masters. If her father refuses her admittance to his house, and she has no wish to marry herself off even if she could find a man with money enough to support her, what is she to do? Prostitute herself?"

Lucia stared at Len in silence. There were no words to answer her. Of course Lucia knew there was such a world as she spoke of it, but she had never confronted it before, never had it seemed so immediate. There was such fierce anger, such a hint of desperation in Len's tone, yet her words were eloquent and effective. Lucia felt a spark ignite in her own soul, a fury at the injustice, which combined with a longing for Len to go on, to share more of this raw passion so uncommonly seen in Lucia's world. She held her breath as she waited for Len to continue.

Len seemed to be watching her reaction, and Lucia was dismayed to see her sigh. It was as though she feared dwelling on so emotional a subject in Lucia's presence, and her next words were not infused with the same enthusiasm and became bitter. "You would be surprised, Lucia, how many women turn to thievery. The gaols will soon be full of them. At least the crowd always enjoys seeing a woman hang."

Her last word echoed around them, and Lucia shivered with cold horror. It seemed so desperate. The world appeared a bleaker place than it had ever before. Yet here was Len, well-dressed, with plenty of food.

"But how did you come to be what you are? You're no common cutpurse. The men follow you."

"Yes." Len's face lost some of its bitterness but remained stony. "It is because I refused to take the hand that fate dealt me, Lucia. I could have been as you are now. Not so rich, maybe, but just as blissfully unaware. I could have been dead in a gutter or on the gallows, or sold myself to a wealthy man. But instead I am as you see me."

"But *how*?"

Len hesitated as if pondering exactly what to reveal. She took another sip of water, and Lucia waited with bated breath for what she would say.

Len sighed. Lucia's questions were too tempting, the answers too ready to be told. She'd already revealed more than she'd resolved to. Those innocent yet intelligent blue eyes trained on her face betrayed such a desire for understanding. Lucia was infuriatingly naïve. Could Len destroy that? Risk everything that made Lucia who she was, in the name of curiosity and freedom?

The urge to tell her tale was so great, the urge to share such things with Lucia in particular almost irresistible. Len wanted this woman to know who she really was, a desire she'd not experienced in years now. She'd shared the deepest parts of herself once before, with beautiful Hattie who had listened intently and shared so much of herself in return. That was lost, had faded so far into her past. Lucia was not Hattie, and Len should not want to let her guard slip. Yet the yearning to expose her soul, to allow this woman to see who she really was, was overwhelming.

How could Lucia have bewitched her so quickly, penetrated her defences so effectively? It was disconcerting, and in the life she lived now, it was downright dangerous. And yet she could not scorn Lucia, could not entirely resist the urge to liberate her mind. The look in Lucia's eyes was unmistakeable, and Len felt the thrill of inspiring it. Lucia had no concept of her stirring desire, but Len saw it all too clearly. All the more reason to harden her heart. But she could not. She searched her thoughts for a reply to Lucia's last question. How she came to be as Lucia saw her today was a long story, and she was terrified the sharing of it would push Lucia away. But she wanted to say something. She took a breath.

"I suppose you have to go back to when I was sixteen. My father—" Len broke off as her keen hearing caught a pounding rhythm approaching the house. Horses. Two of them, unless she was very much mistaken. Something was wrong. In an instant Lucia was all but forgotten. She turned her eyes to the window. The door was flung open and Julian entered, breathless, stocky William close behind. As soon as Len saw Julian's face she knew something terrible was had happened. She felt her instant reaction to threat: the surge of heat through her veins, her heart beating faster, the back of her neck prickling. Her senses sharpened as her stomach contracted with tension.

"They've taken Isaac," Julian said. Len heard how the urgency in his tone barely concealed his fear. It was the worst possible news. "And the talk in the taverns is they know where to find us. We have to go, Len, there's no choice."

"Yes," Len said, standing up. She had to be in control. Julian and William were looking to her, Lucia's eyes were wide as she listened. She could not let her fear show. "Gather what you can carry, we'll leave the rest. Leave no papers." Julian nodded. "Does Peter know of this?"

"Yes, we separated in town. Only William and I returned to warn you."

"Good. He'll know where to meet us. Take what you can, quickly, both of you, and go. I will follow, but I'll take another direction." Though she had always known this day would come and planned for it, now that the moment was upon her, Len found herself fighting fear. She always told herself it was healthy to feel fear, it made her alert, always on the edge. It kept her and her men safe. Only now she wished herself braver. She put the thought aside, she had no time to consider why she should feel differently today. She did not wish to look at Lucia.

But Julian glanced at Lucia then, and Len did the same. The woman looked scared but also inappropriately animated. The foolish rich girl clearly had no idea of the danger which threatened all of them. However, the more immediate threat to Lucia was from the suspicion in Julian's expression. "It wasn't her," Len said firmly. "She wouldn't know her way here even if you'd left the blindfold off." Her words were disparaging. She had no time for kindness nor did she wish Lucia to think them friends.

"Leave her here," Julian said.

"What, so they can find her and she can tell them everything she knows of us?" Len knew her reasoning was sound. She also knew this logical objection was not her only motivation. She was worried for Lucia's safety. And she was reluctant to lose sight of Lucia so soon. Her heart objected so fiercely she knew her judgement was already fatally flawed. She simply could not relinquish Lucia's company, the tremulous beginnings of desire, the notion of a woman who wished to know her. It was selfish and unfair to both Lucia and her men, but abandoning Lucia was not an option now.

"She could have done so already, for all we know." Julian's anger was barely concealed. Len railed at the way he dared challenge her authority in front of William and Lucia, her resentment made worse because she suspected Julian knew some of what motivated her. His disapproval troubled her. But now was not the moment for such debates.

"Then it is better that she is with us." Len took a deep breath and looked at him evenly. "If she had informed them, they would have been here already, not in town. No, it is someone else who has talked to them. Miss Foxe stays with us, so we may be sure of her silence."

Lucia was listening to their exchange keenly. Len wondered fleetingly what on earth she could be thinking. Did she want to flee? See hope in Len's disaster, sense her freedom close at hand? Well, she could not have her freedom yet. A stubborn streak in Len asserted itself. She had told Lucia she must stay with them, she had explained her reasons to Julian. Lucia would stay with them because it was what Len ordered. This was a test of her leadership and she would not fail it.

"Very well." Julian's expression was still hostile, but his words brought Len some relief.

"Now, there is no time. Hurry to take what you must and then go!" In her command was also the implicit request that he not question her now. Julian walked quickly through from the kitchen into the hallway of the house. She saw the tension in his shoulders, but he did not argue.

"But what has happened?" Lucia spoke finally. The question was so innocent, it almost irritated Len. Why on earth did she want Lucia here at a time like this? Why not just let her go? She most certainly did not have the time to explain the situation and its implications to the silly child and knew her tone was abrupt and distracted as she replied.

"This morning I sent the men into town to discover what rumours were abroad about us. The taverns are always the best places to learn who has spoken to whom and who has heard what information. It seems someone was expecting them. Isaac has been taken, and it is likely they are coming here. We must leave. You will come with me."

Len fixed Lucia with a determined and authoritative glare and set her jaw firmly. Would Lucia dare to argue? Her mind was already several steps ahead of this moment, working out the best plan for the safety of herself and of her men. She would take no arguments. But Lucia did not argue. A glimmer of something Len recognised ignited in her eyes, and she nodded her acquiescence all too enthusiastically. Len frowned, her heart uneasy, before turning her attention to gathering the possessions she needed. Lucia she would deal with later, when she was sure her day would not end in the cells of the county gaol.

Lucia waited awkwardly in the kitchen as Len gathered the few items she wanted to carry with her. Lucia guessed most of them had once been the possessions of one frightened traveller or another. She found herself listening anxiously for the pound of hooves outside that would bring the judgement of the law upon Len. Though she surprised herself with the realisation, she knew she had not one hope the authorities would arrive before their escape. The idea of Len struggling upon the gallows was horrific, and the urgency filling her heart to the bursting point was that they might escape before Len was discovered. Julian and the stocky man, William, soon galloped away towards the road. Lucia's hands trembled as she waited alone and willed Len to be ready to leave quickly.

At last, Len was striding through the kitchen towards the door. "Come on," she said peremptorily, and Lucia followed her outside. Len had donned her tricorn and her cloak, which, now in the bright light of day, Lucia saw was a deep blue. It billowed behind Len as she went to the black stallion Lucia had seen her riding before, already saddled and tied up just outside of the door. Lucia guessed Julian or William had prepared Len's mount for her, to speed her retreat, and understood just how well the band worked to help each other survive. The beast was one of the finest horses Lucia had ever seen, with glossy hair and bright eyes. As Len led the horse to the mounting block, Lucia took in his magnificent height and toned flanks and could not help but wonder, with a twinge of misgiving, if the stallion had been stolen from an unfortunate traveller.

Len held the reins and gestured impatiently for Lucia to mount the horse. She climbed onto the mounting block and pulled herself up tentatively onto the saddle, which was not a lady's and thus difficult to balance upon, especially on such a tall mount. Moments later, Len mounted the stallion without the need of the block, sliding into the saddle behind Lucia, legs astride, in the same way a man would ride a horse. Lucia felt Len solid behind her and knew her to be a good horsewoman by the firmness of her seat, the ease with which she reached her arms around Lucia's body to grasp the reins lightly. The warmth and steadiness of her proximity put Lucia at ease but produced a oddly uncomfortable sensation which swept through her at the same moment and caused her to grip a little more tightly to the stallion's glossy mane. To feel any person in such close contact was new and unsettling. That Len's form pressed to her back, warm and vital, that Len's arms, strong and reassuring, encircled her sent a thrill through her body which seemed wholly inappropriate to the very real danger they were in. How it was that Len made her feel this way and what these feelings meant she could not answer, but for a moment she was giddy with it and closed her eyes as her breath caught in her throat.

Lucia felt Len's body move as she nudged the stallion into a walk. She leant forward in the saddle, and her breath warmed the back of Lucia's neck, just below her ear. The tickle provoked a shiver in Lucia's body that was not at all unpleasant. Len turned the horse in the direction of the path. As they began to progress, Lucia opened her eyes and looked about her, still unable to glean any clue as to where they were. The woodland was thick despite the bareness of the winter branches. However, Len guided the horse onto a track and at once urged him into a rocking canter. Lucia felt Len's arms a little tighter to her body and was glad of the support, of the contact. She grasped at the black, silky mane and tried to relax into the rhythm of the stride, of Len's body rocking gently behind her.

Soon, Len encouraged the stallion to go faster still, and Lucia felt his pace transform into a smoother gallop. The cool air rushed past her face, chilling her skin and pushing her hair—already unruly after a night spent in its pins and without the maid's usual morning attentions—back from her brow. The worsted shawl did not prevent the chill of the swift air from penetrating her clothing, the cold in marked contrast to the warmth of her back, where Len was pressed against her.

Lucia was used to riding, so the speed of the gallop did not alarm her. However, it was an odd sensation indeed not to be in control of the beast beneath her, instead to be balanced precariously, dependent upon the skills and direction of the extraordinary woman behind her. It was not the same as when Julian had taken her, bound and blindfolded from her home. Then, every sensation had been strange and frightening. He had given her no option. Now, she was not paralysed by terror. She was keenly aware of everything, from the blur of trees, the panting of the horse, the jangling of the bridle, to the strength of Len's arms. And she trusted Len. She felt only the steady warmth of Len at her back and the chill rush of the air over her skin. She watched the trees slide past, the woodland thinning, and finally the brown hedgerows as they emerged onto a wider track between fields. The sun was still shining brightly, and Lucia could not deny the exhilaration of the ride.

After some time, they turned from the track and through a narrow opening in the hedge. Lucia found they were in a wide green pasture, across which the stallion galloped freely. A large oak grew to their right, and somewhere to the left, where trees grew more thickly, she could see a thin skein of white smoke, as though from a cottage chimney. Lucia found the surroundings were entirely unfamiliar, although they still could not have been a very great distance from Foxe Hall. Though she had ridden the local fields upon Sally's broad back, she had always taken a circular route which would lead her home before too long. She had never travelled farther abroad outside the comfort of the carriage. To look about her and see fields and trees unknown only added to her incongruous delight. She breathed deeply of the air as it rushed past her, though the cold stung her nose and throat. She had never breathed, never lived, never seen the countryside, before that moment into which Len had brought her.

Her joy was tempered just a little by shame. Where she should have been anxious through concern for her father and sister, maybe panicking for herself, she simply felt delight. She could not and did not attempt to account for how powerfully the emotion arose in her. It was simply impossible to resist.

Chapter Eight

As they crossed one pasture and a more uneven meadow, Lucia saw they were approaching a shallow rise in the ground, upon which grew a cluster of low trees. Len slowed the stallion to a trot as they climbed up the slight bank. Lucia felt Len looking around, ever observant, although the chances of them having been followed seemed slim. They had, after all, left an unmarked hideout in thick woodland, taken a track which wound its way through the trees confusingly, followed another path surely only known to the local farmers, and crossed two open fields. A pursuer would have needed to follow them directly, and there was no sound of hooves behind them. Still, Len's alertness reassured Lucia.

They reached the place where the higher ground levelled out, and Lucia saw, beyond the thicket of trees, a collection of jagged rocks. Len reined the horse to a gentle walk as they approached. On closer inspection, Lucia saw the grey, mossy stones were actually the remnants of human settlement, though whether they were the forgotten traces of some medieval fortress or merely the ruins of an abandoned cottage from the last century, it was impossible to say. Time marched on, bringing progress and change, power was forgotten as if it had never been.

Yet those stones were a reminder that it was possible to make a lasting mark. Lucia did not know why the stones were here, or who had positioned them, but traces of their story remained, lingering, humanity and nature all mingling together. There was something eternal, constant, tenacious about the stones. To be part of such a story, to be distinct and noticed, to be remembered, seemed glorious and worthy aspirations indeed, though they were new to Lucia's mind. Life had always felt so fleeting, a short period of outrunning Death before finally succumbing. But now she felt something else. Each person who lived and breathed made their mark. What mark would she make on the world? Where would her story take her?

On the back of the fine horse, Len's arms around her, Lucia felt as though she was on the edge of finding out.

Len pulled the horse up and dismounted. Lucia felt unbalanced and cold without her support behind her. The loss of contact, of the embrace of Len's lean arms, left her a little desolate. She was glad of the hand Len offered to help her dismount. The grass was wet and cold through her too-dainty slippers. Len's gloved fingers were firm around her own, and she did not release her grip at once.

"We're the first here," Len said, more to herself than Lucia. "There's a problem." She still held Lucia's hand a little too tightly, as though worried she would lose her balance. After a moment of silence in which Lucia was acutely aware of that contact, Len loosened her grip and took a step back from Lucia. She seemed uncomfortable. Lucia herself wondered why she mourned the loss of Len's hand around her own quite so much. But she could not ignore the tension in Len's last statement.

"What do you mean, a problem?" Lucia was frightened by the anxiety in Len's expression.

"If ever we were forced to abandon the house, our plan was to gather here. There are several ways to arrive and it is a well-hidden spot. Being on raised ground also gives us warning if anyone approaches. But Julian should have been here before us, as he came more directly." Her words were matter-of-fact, but Lucia heard the strain in her voice.

"What are we to do?"

"Wait. There is nothing else. They should arrive before morning."

"Wait here all night?" Lucia's fear was returning all too keenly.

"Yes, Lucia. Do you have any better suggestions for me?" The words were accompanied by a hard stare.

"No." Lucia was downcast by Len's renewed hostility.

"I know it is hardly usual for a gentlewoman—"

"No. But it is necessary." Lucia was not sure if Len was attempting to mock or apologise, but she was eager to show she was not wholly feeble. Len nodded slightly, and Lucia took it as an acknowledgement of her own strength of mind.

"We cannot make a fire. The smoke would give us away," Len said. She looked around her as though she was thinking out loud rather than addressing Lucia.

"Are they really looking for you?" Lucia could hardly believe the truth of it. She looked down from the raised ground to the winter countryside of brown trees and fallow fields and saw no trace of humanity, save the thin white smoke from the cottage nearby.

"That is one thing I cannot know. Not knowing is always the greatest risk. It leads to complacency since the heart wants to believe there is always hope, always a light in the dark. I have to act as though there is no chance. If I believe they are hard on our tail, that all hope is lost, and act accordingly, I can assure myself of my safety."

"That is no way to live, always on the lookout for bad tidings and terrible happenings." To Lucia, Len's world sounded a desolate and frightening place. Her heart filled with compassion and concern for this woman. What had brought her into so dark a place? And would she survive it? The thought that she might not was unbearable.

"Nevertheless, it is how I live, how I must." Len concluded as if there was nothing more to say on the matter. She reached for the stallion's reins and patted his nose then led him towards a low branch, where she could secure the reins. Lucia followed them.

"He's a wonderful horse," she said.

"Yes."

"What's his name?"

"Oberon."

Lucia was surprised. "The fairy king?"

"Yes." Len studied Lucia's expression. "Are you astonished, Lucia, that I have named my horse after the king of the fairies, or that a common criminal such as I am might have read Shakespeare?"

Lucia's cheeks grew hot. She was angry at Len's continual assumption she was making judgements based on values society had educated into her and indignant because Len was correct.

"You have read Byron, why should I be surprised you have also read Shakespeare?"

"But you are, nevertheless." Len took a bag from the side of her saddle and began to stride towards the stone ruins. Her cloak flowed behind her as she trod her way through the long grass, and as Lucia followed her more tentatively in her gown, she was impressed once more by Len's sheer presence. She seemed larger than the lean woman she was.

When they reached the remains of the house, or fort, or whatever building had once stood there, Len sat astride a smooth piece of masonry. Lucia perched opposite her on the remnants of the wall. She shivered, the stone cold through her garments. Len opened the leather bag and took from it a small bottle, which she uncorked and sipped from. She closed her eyes as she swallowed the drink. Then she offered the bottle to Lucia. Lucia eyed it cautiously, reached out and took it. She raised it to her nose and smelled the strong alcohol. "Brandy?" She raised her eyebrows.

"Yes, French brandy too. It will take away the chill," Len said with a challenge in her expression. Lucia put the bottle to her lips. It was still warm from Len's mouth. She tipped it slowly. The brandy flowed into her mouth, scorching across her tongue. She lowered the bottle, swallowing too quickly. The liquid seared down her throat and she spluttered, handing the bottle back to Len hurriedly. Len laughed gently, and as the warmth spread through Lucia's chest, she joined her mirth.

"I have never taken brandy before," Lucia said at last.

"You do surprise me."

For a minute, or maybe longer, they sat in quiet contemplation. Len took another drink from the bottle and placed it back in her bag. Lucia watched her for a moment and then looked away across the countryside. She wondered what type of building had stood here and if the view from this spot was much changed in the time since it had fallen to ruin. She doubted it. She looked back at her odd companion, to find Len regarding her speculatively.

"You are, what, two-and-twenty, Lucia?"

"Yes." Lucia was no longer shocked how well informed Len seemed to be but was surprised she had interest enough to ask. Still, they had to speak of something as they waited, and she did not resent the question.

"And you are not yet married?"

"Clearly."

"Are you promised to a man?"

"No, I am not."

"Why not? Two-and-twenty is growing old not to be married. Or at least engaged."

"It may be, but I do not believe in marrying simply because another year has passed and I will soon be considered too old. If I do not marry, I do not believe I will regret it greatly." Len looked surprised. In truth Lucia had astonished herself with her candour.

"You have never encountered a man you wished to marry?" Len pressed.

"No. I have met handsome men and kind men but not one I can imagine sharing my life with."

"You have had proposals? Surely a woman with such fair skin and golden locks is sought after."

Lucia flushed at the favourable description, secretly pleased Len saw her in such a light. She had not imagined Len would have any time for noticing her looks, so to hear the tone of admiration was surprising but welcome. "I have had but one proposal, when I was seventeen. I was in no humour to accept the man, who was then aged forty and who I do not truly believe can have been serious in his addresses to me. I do not look to attract gentlemen and have received no further advances." Lucia remembered the encounter with a barely repressed shudder. If courtship and marriage meant that sort of sacrifice, she was prepared to remain a spinster. Now she was conscious of Len's increased attention and sensed she had suddenly aroused her interest in a way she had not up until this point. She was pleased to think Len now comprehended she was not simply another gentlewoman intent on a good marriage. It mattered, somehow, what Len thought of her.

"Your father must be disappointed." Len's casual question belied a new level of interest. Lucia ignored the twinge of anxiety at the mention of her father and answered with as much honesty as she could.

"I have no doubt he would be happier if I were to marry. However, he loves me and wants me to be happy. Besides, two-and-twenty is hardly ancient. There is time yet."

"Yes, I suppose that is what he thinks."

"You are not married." Lucia attempted to divert the conversation back towards the questions she wanted answered.

"No." Len's eyes hardened, as though Lucia was about to challenge her.

"And you are older than me, are you not?"

"Yes. I am in my thirty-first year."

"Is it not of concern to you?"

"Does it seem to be of concern to me?"

"No." Lucia hesitated, seeing a new tension in Len's posture. "What about your family?"

"I have no family." Len looked away.

"Oh, I'm sorry," Lucia said, more softly. Had she asked one question too many?

"Don't give me your pity, Lucia. The men are my family."

"What happened?"

"Nothing happened. They still live, except my mother. They are merely not my family any longer."

Lucia was silent. No reply presented itself. Still she burned with curiosity but was impotent as to how to form the right questions. Despite an almost fierce expression, Len's eyes had grown misty, and the demonstration of her emotion was unnerving. Lucia's hand twitched with the urge to reach out and comfort her, but she was not sure how Len would react to such a comfort and tightened her hand into a ball instead.

A chill breeze sent another shiver through Lucia. She wrapped the shawl more closely around her shoulders. A stray tendril of Len's hair which hung down near her ear moved gently in the breeze. Lucia watched, fascinated, wondering briefly how that silken hair would feel in her fingers if she were to reach out and touch it. Her fingertips tingled, and quickly she turned her attention to the grass near her shoes. Eventually, she felt brave enough to look up at Len again. Len appeared to be thinking of something Lucia was not to be privy to. Many minutes passed before her jaw tensed, a certain resolve coming into her countenance, as she turned her eyes to Lucia's.

"I am the daughter of a hosiery manufacturer," Len said hurriedly, as though she might lose the urge to explain at any moment. "I was born into comfortable circumstances and educated so I might make a good wife and find an advantageous marriage, to better our social position. It was very important to my mother." She looked down at the ground and plucked a blade of grass, which she rolled distractedly between her thumb and index finger. Lucia waited expectantly, hoping she would go on but fearing she would not. She sensed Len was trusting her with a story that she did not often tell, one she seemed reluctant to share even now. To be given the honour of hearing Len's story touched her heart and frightened her at the same time. She wanted to know Len but was rather concerned that, in knowing Len, she would learn just how different she was from herself.

Len glanced quickly at Lucia, as though for reassurance, and then looked down once more as she went on. "My father was not a loving man, though he was not unkind exactly, not when I was very young. He merely had very little to do with our upbringing. I have one elder brother, one younger, and two younger sisters. Only my elder brother commanded my father's full attention. The rest of us were merely expected to do as we were bid and give him no trouble. His business was everything to him." She looked into the distance, as though she was remembering. She let the blade of grass drop and pressed her hands together.

"When I was sixteen, I was introduced to a man with a round belly and his hair already greying. He owned the land adjacent to our own and was willing to give my father a good price, so my father could expand his workshop, in return for my hand in marriage. My father was selling me in return for a piece of land."

Lucia saw the anger still fresh in her expression, the remembered pride and hurt, and felt it burning in her own heart too.

"I could not bear the man, although he might have made a good husband. I have no reason to think otherwise of him. It was simply the notion of being handed over to a stranger like a piece of property I could not abide. To have to promise to honour and obey a man I had nothing but hostility towards. It was impossible!"

Lucia remained silent, confused by her empathy. Len's circumstances were not as unusual as her reaction to them. She knew many women who had gone quietly and outwardly content into marriages designed to suit their families. She had always been grateful her father had never had cause to have such expectations of her or Isabella and felt sorry that Len could not have experienced such parental compassion. Yet she shared the anger, had a part in it, felt that her feelings and Len's were not so very different, whatever their circumstances. But Len was still talking and Lucia did not want to miss a word.

"Of course, I refused him. At first my father reassured him I was merely being coy. But when I refused him again, at the fourth time of asking, I was by no means polite, and he finally withdrew his offer. That night my father took his riding whip and he beat me."

Len paused and pressed her lips together. Lucia's stomach churned with the horror of it. She could not imagine such a thing, and she ached that Len had been subject to it. Her mind reached for words of comfort, but she found none. She tried to compose her face, moulding the expression of shock into one of understanding and concern. But could she really understand? Could she really offer anything in the way of comfort to someone like Len, who had been through such things?

Len glanced at Lucia and watched for a reaction. She was concerned her revelation had frightened Lucia, and she was suddenly acutely aware that she did not want fear to drive Lucia away from her. Closing the distance between them was all in her hands, and she had done it quickly, throwing caution to the wind. For what? In hope of some comfort? Out of a longing for Lucia to know her, see her as she really was, not merely as an accomplished thief? Why could she not stop talking? She had vowed never to talk of these things again. Only Julian knew her story, and if it had not been that he was Hattie's brother, she would probably never have told him. She still bore the faint scars of that long ago beating. The outrage and humiliation made her chest tight even now.

She tried her hardest never to dwell on her past life. And now she was compelled to reveal it to a silly young gentlewoman, a perfect stranger who was only in her presence as a hostage. It was ludicrous and risky. Yet she could not resist the urge to go on. It was as though, having taken a lantern into a dark cellar, she wanted to explore every dark nook and corner, despite her trepidation and to hell with the danger. Lucia listened attentively and with a hunger to know, to understand, that Len recognised. There was a powerful lure in being paid such attention. And she had not missed the compassion in Lucia's expression either. Her life presented very few opportunities to see that emotion in another's eyes. Len drew a deep breath, ignored the warnings her logic gave her, and continued.

"I had seen coldness in him before, disinterest, but never such anger. And then he told me the only way I would leave his house again, unless it was in his company, would be as the bride of a husband he chose for me. I was confined to the house and gardens, mostly to my chamber. I was allowed visitors, and sometimes I accompanied him on visits when he wanted to show me off as a piece of his property to be bartered for.

"Of course there were the servants for company. It was in talking to them I realised how poorly off many of the people of this county were, how indeed my father's own business was making them poorer still!" Len made no attempt to hide the outrage in her voice, still as fresh today as it was when her eyes had first been opened. If Lucia was so curious, she would hear the whole story, however uncomfortable. She remembered her own shame at the knowledge her comfortable life was built on the misfortune of others. She would not shield Lucia from the brutality of the world. She looked into the distance for a moment, gathering her thoughts to at least make the story coherent.

"I grew to resent my father to the extent I could no longer exchange a civil word with him. More and more, I fell back onto the companionship of the servants. Even my own siblings refused to sympathise with me, for fear my fate would befall them too. My younger sisters were sent away to school. I think my father blamed my lenient governess for my behaviour and was determined to see they turned out more favourably. My mother had little choice but to take my father's side. She was a weak woman, and though she still showed me moments of kindness, for which I will always be grateful, she supported him.

"And so I befriended the servants. I had many hours alone in the house, when my parents were away—on visits to London or the north, where he had business interests. I saw no reason to keep my distance from the servants, and gradually they lost their deference and came to see me as a friend. They taught me skills usually considered inappropriate for a woman in my position when I asked them to. They were not inclined to be favourable towards my father and I believe demonstrated their dissent towards him by showing kindness to me." Len smiled, remembering the warmth and companionship she had discovered in the bustling servants' quarters of her home. In the end she'd resented that she was excluded from that world when her family were at home. She rubbed her hands together for warmth as she went on, barely even noting Lucia's reaction but intent on concluding her tale now.

"That was how I first met Julian. He was the brother of the dressmaker who visited us often, for of course, the women of the house required clothes in the latest fashions. She was one of the few acquaintances I could send for regularly, on the pretence of needing a hem altered or a bodice stitched.

"She was called Hattie. A small woman, with hair a little lighter than Julian's. Eventually she became my very close friend. I shared everything with her." Len felt her face colour as her heart ached. Hattie was beautiful, like no woman she had seen before or since. But there were some details she would not share with Lucia. Those were hers and hers alone, locked safe in her heart forever. She fought the lump in her throat and moved on quickly from talking of Hattie. "She wanted me to know Julian, since she loved him very greatly. He was the eldest son of the family and had been reasonably educated by doting parents. He was expected to join the militia as a low-ranking officer. However, he'd chosen against that, not being of a truly martial temperament, and came to our house looking for work, as clerk or the like, with my father. Hattie made sure to introduce him to me. Immediately, I recognised something indefinable in him that was reflected in me, and we became friends quickly. I would meet him secretly in the fields—creeping out was not hard with the servants to help me avoid my father's scrutiny. I believe the housemaids and footmen thought themselves to be aiding a secret courtship, which they were not, of course."

"Of course." Lucia responded to Len's closing words but did not truly understand the tale she was hearing. Hattie and Julian seemed to have a key part of play in this story, but Lucia could not fathom just what that role was.

"Do you doubt my sincerity?" Len looked as though she was struggling not to feel angry, a notion that alarmed Lucia greatly. She no longer feared that Len's reactions might lead her to draw her pistol, to turn on her hostage. Now she worried she would offend Len or stop her concluding her story. She was no longer merely curious. She needed to know how Len had fought her way through such things to where she was today.

She needed to know Len.

"No. I think you are in earnest." Lucia tried to sound reassuring. But how to articulate her feelings? "It is just—"

"Irregular? Indecent maybe? I do not doubt you are shocked at the sort of woman I am, Lucia." Len's tone had a challenge in it. Lucia was aware Len not only expected her to be shocked but partly wanted it too. As though, more than mocking, she was trying to educate Lucia about her world, to demonstrate its dangers. But Lucia's stubborn streak would not allow it. Besides, she could not believe Len truly wanted to be seen as an indecent woman. Her demeanour and words so far suggested anything but.

"No, no—I am not shocked." Lucia's protest was genuine. She wanted Len to understand that she already saw more than the unusual woman who robbed travellers. "I am merely interested how this tale brought you to where you sit today."

Len held Lucia's gaze for a long moment. Lucia prayed Len would see her honesty, understand that, whatever world Lucia came from, she was not being judged. It was only that Lucia had no idea how to understand such a story, it being quite unlike anything she had ever contemplated before. But she knew that in understanding the story she could come to understand Len and dearly wanted her to continue. She was relieved when Len seemed satisfied, her demeanour relaxing slightly.

"Well, then listen. I shall tell you." Len sounded as though there was still a lot more to tell. Lucia wanted to hear it all.

"Please go on."

Len paused for a moment. Lucia wondered if she would hear the whole tale or if Len was also deciding what to tell and what to keep for herself. Len seemed to carry so much darkness with her. Lucia wanted to tell her not to be afraid of sharing it all, that she was brave enough to bear it. But she was not, in truth, sure that she could. So she simply waited in silence for Len to speak again.

"To begin with, I watched Julian demonstrate the military skills in which he had been educated, showing me his swordplay and how to fire a pistol. Eventually, I demanded he show me how to hold and wield the weapons myself. He laughed at me at first, but he soon realised I was in earnest and taught me the skills quite happily. I found it all fascinating." Len smiled, her eyes showing the recollection of exhilaration and wonderment. Lucia pondered how it must feel to hold a sharpened blade for the first time, to thrust and jab and parry, how it would be to fire a deadly pistol. Such lessons sounded unconventional, frightening perhaps, and yet just knowing Len had experienced them gave her a small vicarious thrill. How freeing it must be to do something so active, needing such strength. Lucia doubted she could do any of it herself, but in those doubts, her admiration for Len only increased all the more. She was almost envious of a life that had allowed such experiences, despite its pain. But though she wanted to stop Len and ask her questions, she was even keener to hear the conclusion of the story and let Len go on without interrupting.

"And so I was reasonably content in the small society I had created around me, and the years passed. I made myself so unpleasant to potential suitors I received no further proposals. My sisters were married satisfactorily, both before the age of nineteen, and my father grew happier. He no longer beat me when I refused to dress for company, he simply locked the door to my chamber and refused to allow me out until the morning."

Lucia could not hide her astounded expression as Len related these things as though they were commonplace. Len had borne so much in her life. Lucia's heart was aflame with compassion and anger on her behalf. Len, on the other hand, seemed unnervingly calm. Lucia was dreadfully afraid she would realise how different they were from each other after all, how Lucia could not possibly understand this story, and stop before the conclusion. She was glad when Len continued to speak.

"However, I knew he would not bear his daughter remaining in his house eternally. I had become an embarrassment to him, and I started to fear he would marry me to any man, however lacking in advantage the match was, merely to be rid of me. I began to ponder solutions to my problem. Hattie was my close confidante, although I see now we were both very naïve." Len closed her eyes, as if in pain. When she opened them again, Lucia saw there were tears. Again she debated: should she acknowledge the pain she saw in Len, try to comfort her, or simply pretend she had not noticed? Len's shoulders were now very stiff. She did not seem like a woman who would welcome a kindness, so Lucia checked her natural instinct. But curiosity burned. Just why had the mention of Hattie brought this strong woman so close to tears? Lucia sensed they were coming to the most crucial part of Len's story, and anticipatory tension grew inside her.

"One day, my father happened upon Hattie and me…talking of ways I could escape…and he grew very angry. Of course, Hattie was not employed by him, and all he could do was expel her from the house. She left at once. I was frightened by what I saw in my father's face, and I was sure he would beat me again. However, he did not. Rather, he took hold of one of my arms rather roughly and dragged me from my chamber, down the stairs, out of the front door, and to the road. There he pushed me so I fell to my knees in the dirt and told me I was no longer his daughter and could have no claim on his affections or his finances any more. The ground was damp from a recent shower, I remember."

Len gazed into the distance, but Lucia knew, instinctively, she saw nothing of their surroundings. Len was looking into her past, reliving those feelings. Lucia ached to comfort her, as she began to understand. However, one aspect of the story did not quite make sense, and as Len's silence stretched on, she chose a moment to ask, hesitantly.

"He did this simply because you were talking with your friend?" Lucia tried not to sound incredulous, though she suspected Len was keeping something from her. She felt a twinge of pain that Len still did not trust her with every detail, despite such personal revelations. Just what could be so bad, so shocking, that Len would not tell her? Could Len not feel the compassion flowing from her heart? She was braver than Len thought she was. Though not brave enough, she acknowledged, to tell Len so.

Len did not look at Lucia as she lied. "Yes. It was after many years of displeasure with me. I believe that finally sealed it for him." A thin excuse, but no doubt Lucia would be taken in. She would have to be, for Len would not talk of what had passed between her and Hattie in any more depth than she already had. There was too much pain in the recollection, too much danger in exposing Lucia to such ideas.

"But what did you do?" Lucia clearly could not imagine how anyone could survive such a predicament.

Len shrugged. "I could have begged him to take me back, promised to marry. But my pride would not allow it. Whilst he still stood there, I rose from my knees and walked away from him along the road, vowing to myself I would never return to him." Pride elevated her spirits, even this many years distant. "Instinctively, I went to Hattie's house. Thankfully, her parents were away from home, and only Julian and she were there.

"At first I suppose I had hoped I might be able to stay with Hattie. But they were not rich people, and it would not be long before word of the supposed shame I had brought to myself spread throughout the neighbourhood. Besides, I did not want to be in a place my father could find me, should he have a change of heart. I told them I wanted to travel out of the area, and I asked Julian to accompany me. He was out of work and had the time to spare. I had a half-hearted idea I might look for work as a governess in some distant area, where I could forge a character for myself." Such an innocent notion. Len found it hard to believe she had seriously considered that as her path into the future. How differently things had turned out. She could not help a vague smile. Outlaw she might be, but at least she did not have to endure the trials of working as a governess. She suspected Lucia was struggling to imagine her in that role too, from the way her brow furrowed. Was there an expression in the world that did not look well on Lucia's face? Len sighed, determined to finish the story now.

"But Julian and Hattie did not have a carriage, and their parents were away in their pony trap. I would have to travel on horseback, and Julian did not like the notion of travelling with a vulnerable woman on horseback any great distance, especially taking into account the recent rumours of highwaymen in the area." She laughed briefly at the turnaround in her concerns these days. "That was when I suggested that if I were to borrow some of his clothing and wear a kerchief over my face as a mask, I would be less vulnerable on the roads. Julian was reluctant to begin with, but Hattie and I convinced him it was a sensible plan.

"As soon as I put on his breeches and coat, large though they were on me, I felt the freedom of that style of dress, both in terms of my own movement and in how I knew the world would perceive me. I felt stronger, more able to take on the challenges ahead of me. I also armed myself with a pistol, to be sure of my safety."

Len paused and looked at Lucia, challenging her to be astonished by the story so far. In actuality, what she saw was something like envy. Had she made it sound simple and painless? If so, she had failed. Her tale was not one to covet. She watched Lucia as the other woman's mind worked over some contemplation. Perhaps Lucia was wondering what she would have done in such a situation. As she reached some sort of conclusion, Lucia's eyes dropped to the floor, and she seemed intent on a dead leaf fluttering in the grass. Len realised she wanted to know what was behind that downcast expression.

"We set off that night. It was hard to leave Hattie, but we told each other it would not be for very long. Somehow, we would work out a way we could see each other before too much time had passed." There was that pain again. Len went on swiftly.

"We had travelled only a few miles and had not yet made it to the turnpike when we heard horses both in front of and behind us. Just as Julian had feared, a band of robbers had happened upon us. However, they were a small band and we were quicker than them. Julian's teaching stood me in good stead. Shots were fired on both sides, and I felt a pistol ball pluck my sleeve, but before they could reload, with pistol butts and Julian's sword, we had overpowered them. Julian kept his blade to the throat of the nearest man, to remind them not to resume their resistance."

Lucia became aware she was staring open-mouthed. Len told her tale as the most commonplace of happenings, without a hint of sensation.

"It became apparent to us then, from their general demeanour and the poor state of their clothing, that these were not professional thieves, and there was no obvious leader. A bold notion occurred to me, though I know not what prompted it. I whispered questions to Julian for the frightened men, so that my voice might not give me away. They answered reluctantly, but soon I ascertained that they were hungry stockingers, turned to crime rather than starve, and that they had no definite leader.

Lucia did not hide her astonishment now. The story seemed so fantastical, so frightening, it was hard to believe. Yet here Len was, and Lucia knew she was being told the truth, being allowed to see the steps which had brought Len to her side on this cold hilltop today.

"You look quite astounded Lucia. Is it surprise at my unwomanly behaviour?" Len looked keenly at Lucia, who realised that she had not even considered that aspect of Len's tale. That Len did not behave like any woman she had ever expected to encounter had, at some point, become entirely irrelevant. There was an odd excitement to that, she found.

"No, I had not thought of such things. I am merely contemplating the dangers of that encounter. And wondering how it was those men allowed you to become their leader."

"Then I will continue," Len said. Lucia was sure she saw something like relief in her expression. Perhaps Len had never before related this tale, simply carried it with her, and found some release in the telling of it. Lucia hoped that was the case, and waited for the conclusion.

"The most confident of the men seemed to recover himself at this point. With a challenge in his tone, he suggested our curiosity was owed to our wanting to lead them. A flutter of fear and potential passed through me. I had meant to suggest hiding with them, maybe stealing only enough to survive, while I decided on the best course into my future. But now fortune presented a new notion to me. Julian looked to me for guidance, and I nodded. We had reached the same conclusion without exchanging a word. One of the men protested then, but Julian told him if they did not allow us to join their band, we would go directly to the authorities, describe the wounds they had sustained, and see them hang. These were not experienced criminals and were, in truth, very frightened. They allowed us to stay with them, though they resisted the idea that either of us should lead them. We went to their shelter in the woods."

Len glanced at Lucia then turned her dark, expressive eyes to gaze across the countryside. She had apparently concluded her tale, and Lucia was astonished. Her eyes and her mind had been opened to notions she'd never known existed, she'd heard of dangers more fitting to the plot of a novel. But more than that, she understood now something of Len, this remarkable woman. Compassion and admiration sparked inside her, as well as gratitude that Len had trusted her. Len had allowed her to witness pain and despair, but also hope. She saw the root of the darkness she sensed in Len, the courage and passion which surely helped her combat such sadness. It was impossible not to be drawn to that, to yearn to know those details Len had kept from her. Lucia felt she needed to know more of Len, having been given the thrill of hearing her story.

And she had not yet told what, to Lucia, was the most important part in understanding why they were seated together in this hilltop ruin today. Lucia summoned up the courage to press her on it.

"When did they discover your true identity? Did they accept you at once?" Len seemed mildly amused by Lucia's keen interest.

"They discovered it that night. I could not very well remain silent and masked all night. At first, when I removed my mask, took a drink of ale, and said nothing, they simply stared. I think they presumed I was a young boy. Slowly, it dawned on them. But they had seen my actions at the roadside, and they were more than a little frightened of Julian and me together. In the end, it was novel to them and they began to laugh.

"They accepted me as one of their number almost instantly. It took a little longer to be able to lead them. To begin with, Julian was the one they looked to. However, he was not happy to lead them—he did not like the responsibility of making decisions, whereas I discovered I thrived on it. I soon proved myself—with sword and pistol and on horseback—to be more capable than any of them. My knowledge of the workings of society, of the liveries on coaches, of the richest pickings all helped increase their profits and, with that, their confidence in me. And finally they concluded that to have a leader who could go unidentified—for who would ever suspect a woman?—was also to their advantage. Eventually, they came to understand who my father was and why my sympathies were with them. We became friends, in a manner of speaking."

Len made it sound very simple. Lucia guessed, from the determination she saw in her face as she spoke, from the way she said the words very definitely, she had been forced to prove herself many times over before she had been truly accepted by the men. The mere fact she had achieved it, however, could be considered nothing short of impressive, almost beyond belief. Lucia's pulse beat faster simply with the thought of it. She wanted to reach out and touch Len, feel her solid and strong, the survivor of these things. The emotion burned so hot, for a fleeting moment she wondered if it was envy she felt, of a life of freedom and bravery, of having been challenged and having won that battle.

But it was not envy. She did not want to be Len. She wanted to know her, in every way she could possibly know her. Her head was still full of questions which threatened to spill out. Lucia forgot her former caution with Len and dared to ask.

"Were you never afraid of them?"

Len smiled, and Lucia wondered if fear was something too simple, too unnecessary in Len's life to be worth a question, and felt silly for having thought of it. Len was matter-of-fact in her reply. "They're not bad men, only poor and desperate. Besides, they were most certainly afraid of both my own and Julian's skills with a weapon. Before long, they saw the advantages of accepting us, and then there was nothing to be afraid of."

She adjusted her position and brushed the stray strand of hair behind her ear. Lucia watched, imagining once more the feel of that silken hair on her fingertips. She bit her lip and tried to suppress the thought, since Len was still talking.

"That was five years ago now. I have never chosen to move on. It is a different life, and I know its risks every morning I awake. However, I cannot imagine returning to become a governess, or worse. The men have come and gone. We had ten with us at one point. William is the man I wounded in the shoulder, and Isaac was the man Julian took his sword to. The other two left us two years ago but were quickly replaced. There are many dissatisfied men in these parts willing to turn to crime. Ours is an old and established profession, with its glory days behind it. There are not many gentlemen of the road anymore. The turnpikes and militia put paid to that. And yet, in these times, the risks seem to be worth it."

She concluded and looked down at the ground, her expression distant and contemplative. Then she reached for the bottle and took another drink of brandy. It was not a happy tale Lucia had heard, yet she could not help the sentiments it aroused in her heart. She was nothing short of excited. Len was strong, she was free, and she had succeeded where failure had seemed more likely.

And here she was Miss Lucia Foxe, amid grey ruins in the deserted countryside, beside her.

Waiting.

CHAPTER NINE

They sat in silent contemplation for some time after Len concluded her tale. Then Lucia asked, "What about Julian's sister, Hattie?"

Len's face transformed into an unreadable mask in an instant. "Hattie died of a fever, within a year of our leaving. I had visited her several times in the night, but I was not with her when she died. Julian was."

Len rose and walked away from Lucia, climbing up onto a piece of ruined wall and looking out across the fields. Lucia felt the strength of her grief form a barrier between them, where there had been none as she related her story, and regretted at once that she had asked the question. She felt oddly envious of the friendship Len had clearly shared with the dressmaker. Lucia had good friends but none to whom she had ever felt truly close. To know Len in that way must be wonderful. Even today's revelations had not satiated Lucia's curiosity about her. She deliberated whether to go to Len now, try to offer some scant comfort, perhaps an apology, or whether to remain seated where she was.

Lucia heard movement on the opposite side of the hill. Lucia saw Len listening, watching closely. She had an almost animal quality about her, as all of her attention was focused on what—or who—would emerge from behind the thicket of trees and shrubs. Her hand went instinctively to her waist, ready to draw her pistol if necessary. Lucia's heart thudded, and she marvelled how Len could appear so controlled. Was she so settled inside?

A figure on horseback came into view. Lucia breathed a sigh of relief and watched Len's stance relax as she recognised Julian. After him came two men Lucia had not seen before, on foot and breathless. William followed them and dismounted first.

Lucia rose to her feet, unwilling to sit and watch as an idle spectator. She had viewed the expression on Len's countenance change from one of relief to one of suspicion and curiosity when she laid eyes upon the two strangers.

These two men looked about them hesitantly and ended staring at Len open-mouthed. Thin men both, one considerably taller than the other. Both had unkempt brown hair, and their clothes were poor, if not quite ragged. The taller man was the younger, the other's face creased with age. Both looked weary, though natural hostility burned in their eyes and disbelief suffused their expressions.

As Lucia moved towards the little group, they turned to her, took in her fine yellow gown and unruly hair, and directed their gazes back to Len. Lucia pitied them in their bewilderment. Len wore no manner of disguise, and Lucia saw them glance from her woman's face to her boots and breeches and back to her face, much as she herself had done when she had first encountered Len. That confusion seemed so long ago now. Len no longer left Lucia bewildered with her unusual attire and unladylike mannerisms. Those things simply did not matter.

In fact, watching Len now, Lucia realised she had begun to delight in such things, that she felt privileged to know the secrets behind the façade Len presented to the world. That in itself was another sort of confusion. Why did she yearn to know Len in this way? Why was she so compelled to watch Len's every movement? Why did it make her ache inside to do so? Lucia could not fathom it and tried instead to focus her attention on understanding whether there was new danger on their hilltop.

"Who are these men?" Len asked of Julian. Lucia sensed no anger in her tone and understood how much Len trusted Julian. More than she would ever trust Lucia, surely. Lucia resented Julian for that, however unreasonable such sentiments were. But Len was still suspicious of the strangers.

"We found them at the roadside, poised to rob us if you can believe it," Julian said. He dismounted his horse and allowed William to take the reins. William led both horses to the nearest tree and secured them to low branches.

"We stopped, of course, to politely explain the error of their ways." Len looked from Julian to the two men, who could not meet her gaze.

"It appears they are not robbers at all," Julian said. "They tell us they are frame-breakers. We were about to release them when they told me something I think you need to hear."

As soon as he described the men as frame-breakers, Len had looked at them more keenly. Now Lucia saw her interest deepen further. "What is it?" she asked.

"Tell her of your plan for the coming Friday," Julian urged.

Sensing they were in no immediate danger, the men relaxed perceptibly. Their shoulders loosened and they stood less stiffly. The younger, taller one spoke first. "The noble men of General Ludd's army will attack a workshop that is bringing shame upon the trade," he said archly.

"Shut your mouth if you're only going to talk twaddle," the older man reprimanded his companion. His accent was broader and Lucia struggled to understand him perfectly. He turned to Len himself. "There's a lot of us now, madam, been making our point slowly but surely. A frame or two here or there. Sure you've heard of it. Only it's not enough, the bad practices is still going on. So we're going for a whole workshop this time."

Lucia saw the comprehension in Len's face as she glanced quickly at Julian for confirmation. "Which workshop?" she demanded.

"The one belonging to Mr. Nathanial Hawkins, miss."

Lucia was surprised how little reaction she saw in Len's face as she heard her father's name. How much strength did it take to maintain that mask? Lucia felt the pain of that necessity and was filled with compassion, alongside tremendous admiration. "And how has this man offended you?" was all Len said.

"By cutting and with colting," the younger man said, as if he hoped to mystify her.

Len was far from bewildered, and her tone was friendly but authoritative as she replied. "Then I see your grievance. Stay and eat with us. We have food and drink. I wish to hear more of your plans."

"Thank you, madam," the elder man said, "but why should you be so interested?"

"Because I am considering helping you in your enterprise." Len's words were calm, and she spoke as though there was nothing extraordinary in her considering such an idea. Lucia stared in surprise and her heart fluttered in her chest. She was frightened, true, but she was also enthralled by the world she had discovered in which it seemed it was impossible to predict what would occur next.

Len left the two men with Julian and William, who retrieved bread and salt-meat from their saddle bags and shared it with their guests. The news that the men would attack her father's workshop had produced a strange sort of dark exultation in her heart. It was the only justice a man like Nathanial Hawkins would ever face, and she wanted very badly to be there when it was meted out to him. True, these men were hardly the instruments of the people she would like them to be. However, if they were to be believed, they were part of something. She felt the thrill of potential, of the risk too, but mostly the desire for revenge.

She watched the small group squatted on the low wall of the ruins. Criminals all, but in her eyes they were men, betrayed by their masters and their country. She looked from the men to the lonely figure hovering a little awkwardly a short distance away. Lucia was watching the men too. Her countenance was full of wonderment and something like fear. Oddly, Len sensed Lucia was more alarmed by the presence of the frame-breakers than she was to be the hostage of a band of robbers.

Len sighed with the reminder of the world Lucia belonged to. Of course she was more frightened of the frame-breakers. Robbers were a commonplace and constant threat to travellers and had been for centuries. But in this county, frame-breakers, men whose only means of protest was to smash the machines of their masters, had become the representation of evil itself. They were storybook villains to be feared, though rarely encountered.

The papers were full of the disturbing detail of the Luddite raids, as they had come to be called. The frame-breakers, it was claimed, pledged their allegiance to a mysterious General Ludd, who was rumoured to hide out in the thickest part of Sherwood Forest, like some modern-day Robin Hood. Chilling letters and mocking poetry sent to workshop owners added to the atmosphere of fear. If the manufacturers did not cease their offensive practices, General Ludd's foot soldiers would smash their machines in the name of the defence of their historic trade.

It was almost laughable that the people of the county were more afraid of these ragtag gangs of workers than of the organised highwaymen who stalked the roads. And yet the rumours fuelled the terror: The machine-breakers were revolutionaries, sponsored by the French. They were plotting an uprising which would bring the guillotine to England. Tension and suspicion were heavy in the air, and the militia were more interested in frame-breakers than thieves.

Len had discounted most of the rumours. These were hungry men, treated so badly by their employers they were forced into violence. They were no more French revolutionaries than she was. Yet she could not help her own curiosity as to the way the Luddites plotted their raids, who their leaders were, and how such attacks were coordinated. Now she saw a chance to see into the heart of the shadowy rumours and to gain, at last, the revenge over her father he deserved.

Watching Lucia, Len knew what was going through the gentlewoman's mind. These men did not look as though they had been sent by Napoleon. They wore no masks, nor were their faces sinister caricatures, blackened with soot. They were simply ragged, hungry, aged men. Yet Lucia looked as though a nightmare had come to life in front of her. Len couldn't help a wry smile that Lucia was more afraid of these men than she was of a gang of highwaymen.

Then she reminded herself that Lucia's fear could be her only protection. Lucia was unsafe, a stranger in this world too. It was right that she was frightened, even if the cause of her fear was misguided. She worried that in telling Lucia her tale, compulsively and selfishly as she had, she had made such things seem commonplace, when they were in fact extraordinary and should remain terrifying. Lucia looked so very vulnerable here, out in the wild countryside surrounded by thieves, frame-breakers, and hardships she'd never encountered. Len's urge to protect her surged fiercely. She would not have Lucia tarnished.

Slowly, she made her way to where Lucia stood. Lucia appeared startled when Len reached her side but managed a tentative smile in greeting. Len said nothing to begin with, trying to choose her words carefully. She noticed Julian looking in their direction, suspicion in his expression. It did no harm that she showed her confidence in Lucia now. She knew instinctively that Lucia had not betrayed them, nor would she. She turned so that she could not see Julian and he could not catch her eye.

"They intend to attack your father's workshop?" Len was startled out of her contemplation by Lucia's boldness.

"Yes."

"And you are considering helping them?"

"Yes." She knew Lucia wanted an explanation, but having revealed so much of herself already today, she felt vulnerable now and further words deserted her.

"What did they mean by cutting and colting?" Len sensed Lucia needed a longer answer more than she really wanted to know the men's grievances.

"Cutting means making cut-ups. They're stockings that are cut out of a large piece of cloth made on a wider frame and sewn together. They are cheaper but fall apart before long. Colting is their term for employing unskilled apprentices. Making cut-ups means you don't need as many skilled stockingers. Hence the unskilled boys, who are paid less, take the jobs of the men."

Lucia appeared impressed by Len's knowledge. "And your father does this?"

"Of course he does." Bitterness made her tone sharp. "Money is all that matters to him. He began by gathering his workers into shops rather than allowing them to work from their own homes. It is hardly a surprise he has moved on."

"But you cannot support the idea of these men destroying his machinery?"

Len raised her eyebrows at Lucia's naïvety. Did the woman forget she was in the company of outlaws? She could not allow her to forget. "If I can countenance robbing a traveller at gunpoint, do you think I will have a problem seeing my father's workshop destroyed?"

"But these are evil men."

Len couldn't help a surprised snort of derision. "Evil? They are no more evil than I am." For a moment she resented Lucia's simple and sheltered view of the world. Then she met the questioning but frightened blue-eyed gaze and found she could not hold the resentment. She sighed. "They are not French revolutionaries Lucia, whatever you might have heard. Do you know they leave the frames of the men who are good masters untouched? Even when those frames are in a shared workshop alongside the ones they break. Does that sound like revolution to you?"

"No."

"No, not to me either. My father need not have his frames broken. He knows well what the grievances of the men are. Only he is arrogant enough to think he can escape their justice."

"You call it justice?"

"Do not sound so offended, Lucia. The men are starving, and they protest their starvation by causing financial damage to men with money enough to stand it, the very men who cause their starvation. Is that not justice?"

"Not according to the law."

Len swallowed her frustration. Lucia's view of the world was not her fault. "The law wants to hang a man who breaks a frame because he has not enough to eat. Even your good Lord Byron could not countenance that, when he spoke in the Lords. You would defend that law, would you?"

"No." Lucia's concession was not so much reluctant as thoughtful. Len was pleased Lucia did not seem surprised at her knowledge of political events. She knew it should not matter whether Lucia thought her an ignorant wretch, yet it seemed to be of exceeding importance to her. And she wanted Lucia to understand.

"You will comprehend then, Lucia, why I am considering joining them."

"You mean becoming a frame-breaker yourself?"

"Just for the one night." She heard the grim determination in her own words. "Can you blame me for wanting to gain the satisfaction of seeing my father's property destroyed?" Len found some comfort in the knowledge that Lucia knew her story now and would perceive just why she craved such satisfaction.

"No, I cannot."

They watched the two frame-breakers eating their bread and meat hungrily. It seemed odd to Lucia, she could put her confidence in Len and her highwaymen, yet she had been instantly terrified of two frame-breakers. But now they were frail to her, weak, and at the mercy of a system which no longer needed them. She had never contemplated the world in such terms, and it was a revelation which quite startled her. For a moment she experienced Len's own rage at the world that had tried to suppress her and which she now fought against every day. Feeling quite giddy with the unexpected emotion, she was forced to draw a deep breath.

"Where is Peter?" Lucia gathered herself and found more questions ready to be asked.

"I don't know." Lucia saw the concern in Len's face, the strain around her eyes. "He should have been here by now. I fear he has met with the same fate as Isaac and John. Or worse." Her mouth set in a grim line.

"Worse?" Lucia felt infected by Len's tension.

"Yes. For us, not them. I fear it is either Isaac or Peter who is responsible for the attention which has suddenly been cast upon us, through some perverse motivation or conducive promise. If that is the case and we are betrayed, I hope it is Peter. He does not know of this place. Isaac does, and if he is the snitch, we are in danger if we remain here."

Lucia hoped her alarm did not show on her face. Clearly she was not so good at hiding it as she wished, for Len glanced at her and then attempted some manner of reassurance. "I do not imagine you are in danger, Lucia," she said. Her wry smile seemed to mock Lucia. "I do not think they will take you for a robber or frame-breaker."

"I am not concerned merely for myself."

"I know you find Julian handsome," Len said soberly.

Lucia had to glance at her to understand that she was in jest. A slight smile played at the corners of her mouth even as her eyes showed a new intensity. Of course Len understood that Lucia felt the connection between them, that her concern was for Len. At least, Lucia hoped she did and thought she saw the acknowledgement of it in Len's eyes. She wondered if that sense of a bond was at all mutual. Surely Len could not have shared so much of herself with someone with whom she did not feel some kind of unspoken empathy? Lucia looked into Len's eyes and willed her to understand, realising as she did so that she was also seeking answers, imploring Len to help her. Len looked to be about to say something, then she paused. Lucia held her breath, and the pain was almost physical as Len turned away.

"Do not let your sympathies fall too strongly with us, Lucia," Len said, to Lucia's consternation and profound disappointment. "It is dangerous for you." She turned and walked away to consult with Julian. Lucia watched her go reluctantly and clenched her hands against their inclination to tremble.

Later, as night drew in, Lucia sat shivering, pulling the shawl ever tighter. Suddenly she felt a heavy warmth about her shoulders. She glanced up to see Len above her, draping her own cloak around her. It was still heated from Len's body, and instantly Lucia's chilled muscles relaxed into the warmth.

"No, I cannot take it," she protested half-heartedly.

"Nonsense, I have a coat and you have a muslin dress and a thin shawl." Len sat down beside her on the ruined wall. "Besides, I don't suppose you are used to nights in the open."

"No." Lucia pulled Len's cloak closer, knowing some of the warmth seeping into her was from Len's own body. It inspired a little thrill—of excitement and awe, of pleasure that Len would even consider sharing her cloak with Lucia. The evidence that Len cared about her, even in the simplest sense, made her want to smile. There was something protective about that heavy cloak too. Whilst it was wrapped around her, she felt safe. Len made her feel safe. It took a lot, when Len was near her, to remind herself of the danger they were all in. She felt a nervous stirring in the pit of her stomach. She had been managing well enough to avoid the reality of the situation, even as she had sat with only her own thoughts for company, watching Len talk to the men. However, Len seemed determined she should confront it now.

"Do you not worry your father is missing you?" she asked.

"Of course I do. Only, somehow, Foxe Hall and my father and Isabella seem part of quite another world. I can scarce believe they're out there, barely a few miles away."

"They are your world, Lucia, don't lose sight of it." Len sighed.

"I see the limits of that world," Lucia said. It was a surprising confession, even to herself, for she had not thought such a thing before she spoke the words.

"That is dangerous for you, and I am sorry for it," Len said. She took out the bottle of brandy again and tilted it to her mouth.

"Why should you be sorry for it?" Lucia asked, with some hostility. "You should be pleased I begin to understand you."

"And what place does understanding the thoughts of a criminal, be it a robber or a frame-breaker, have in your world, when you return to it? Do you think Isabella will giggle over it with you?"

Lucia was wounded by her tone and wondered what fed this renewed tension. "Isabella and I have not giggled over anything together since we were children."

"But still, you will return home unable to speak anything of your time here. Even if you could speak of it, would they want to listen to you?"

"I wouldn't want to tell them."

"That is even worse, surely? Are you in the habit of wanting to keep secrets from your family?" Len passed the bottle to Lucia, and she took a drink of the fierce brandy without as much as a hesitation. Though it burned her throat, she welcomed the sensation. It complemented the anger stirring in her blood at Len's words, seemed appropriate to mask the other fierce sensations, the ones she could not name, that talking with Len compelled in her. For Len to question her now, to risk the growing bond between them, was heartless. Lucia could not bear many more questions.

"It is not your concern." Lucia's expression was supercilious, her tone proud.

"True enough," Len said, "except you are in your present predicament because of me. And I believe I can now convince William and Julian you have no responsibility for our new danger. Besides, we have other things to think about for the time being. You can return home."

At her words, delivered so matter-of-factly, Lucia felt hollow. She did not understand where it came from. She had no reason to expect to remain with them for any considerable amount of time, and all of her common sense should have led her towards fear, homesickness, and anxiety. However, at that moment, the notion of returning to Foxe Hall, of never seeing Len again or learning what the outcome of her frame-breaking plan would be, was terrible.

"But I do not know the way to Foxe Hall from here."

"Julian will go with you. We are closer than you probably think."

"No," Lucia said, more decisively. She felt angry and did not understand why. "I won't go." She turned, her eyes blazing defiantly into Len's.

Len contemplated briefly before replying. "I could use force to make you ride home. Do you forget you are here because you were kidnapped at the point of a pistol, just last night?" No real threat coloured her tone. She could not bring herself to use fear to persuade Lucia to act. The sheer act of terrifying Lucia seemed to risk a betrayal of her own heart, her own sensibilities. She did not want Lucia to be frightened of her, and knowing she wanted quite the opposite was something she did not know how to respond to. Besides, she could not argue a case she did not favour. She did not want to lose Lucia's company so soon.

"No, I do not forget," Lucia answered.

Watching her reaction, Len knew she was, in fact, rather close to the truth. She was at once alarmed and pleased, the contradictory emotions waging a war in her heart but neither quite triumphant. The terror of Lucia's abduction from her chamber had been eclipsed by her fascination with all she had discovered since. Lucia was caught up in an adventure. Len was profoundly aware of her own role in that adventure and in Lucia's fascination. She could not ignore it, even as she tried to pretend she hadn't noticed.

Lucia's next words confirmed her new determination to continue in this thrilling new world. "Indeed, you *will* have to use force if you want me to return home now."

Len was dismayed and yet oddly relieved to hear the passion of Lucia's resolution. "I am not going to do any such thing, and you know it," she said, looking at the ground. Concern made her feel exhausted. She was worried for Lucia, the dangers she was now exposed to, and for her own pathetic heart which would not listen to reason. On top of that she had the men to consider, almost surely betrayed by one of their number, the shadow of the gallows upon them all. Her wish to damage her father was bitter and heavy, and she knew that smashing his machinery would only give her slight satisfaction. She could not undo the years. She looked up at Lucia again. Why on earth would she want to see Lucia drawn into the life she had been cast into without seeking it? "But you must assure me, Lucia, when you return to them, to your world, you will forget me and all you have seen here."

"Do you still think I would inform the authorities about you?"

Lucia's words sounded somewhat desolate. Len knew then she had offended Lucia with her request. Oh, was the girl really so lacking in understanding? Lucia was far from stupid, that much was clear. What would it take for her to understand?

"No, I don't." She shook her head slightly. "You mistake my meaning. I worry for you and your place in your family."

"Nothing will have changed with them," Lucia replied. A slight waver in her words belied her certainty.

"*You* will have changed, I fear," Len said. Her words apparently had the effect she wished, for Lucia fell silent as she digested them. Len allowed her think on it for a long moment.

"Surely I will know if that is the case?" Lucia said, in the end.

"But will you?" Len let the question hang. "And when exactly do you intend to return to them?"

Lucia hesitated, and Len knew she was right to challenge her in this way, to fight off the selfish urge to keep Lucia with her. It was not fair to allow her to be seduced by freedom and excitement, not when she would return to her cosseted life before long. Len knew she had the power in her hands to change Lucia's perceptions entirely. To change Lucia's world.

She could show her liberty and danger, how not to know her place but to fight against small minds and crushing traditions. She could show her what it was to love because, God knew, she saw the signs that Lucia was halfway there already. Len checked her thoughts before she lost control of them entirely. Such a change could destroy Lucia. Thief she might be, but she would not take Lucia's life from her for the sake of a self-indulgent urge and a notion that Lucia was the same as she was.

"I would like to see the outcome of the attack on the workshop," Lucia said.

"If you return home, I will send a messenger to inform you of it," Len suggested. She knew it was an unacceptable scenario. Would Lucia sit at supper with her father and Isabella as night fell, then take to her chamber, imagining the crimes committed by shadows in the thick night, waiting to receive a message conveying the outcome? It was ludicrous.

"No!" Lucia's firm refusal only confirmed Len's expectations. "That will not do. I must be here." To Len's consternation tears sprang into Lucia's eyes. Lucia wiped them with the back of her slender hand.

"And just what is it enchants you so, Lucia?" Her tone was soft, though she struggled to hide her scepticism. "Do you think, perhaps, you have stumbled into a novel? Are we like the mysterious bandits of the Apennines to you?"

"I do not read those novels," Lucia countered, "and I am not enchanted." Despite the twilight, Len saw the colour rise in Lucia's pale cheeks.

"Do you find crime romantic perhaps?"

"No." Lucia's voice had thickened as though there was a lump in her throat. The cool air between them suddenly seemed filled with a new tension. Len's gaze caught Lucia's and neither looked away.

"Do you look for thrills not present in your day-to-day life?" Drawn by feelings she barely acknowledged, Len leaned closer to Lucia. Her shoulder touched Lucia's.

"Do not mock me." There was real pain in Lucia's plea.

"I don't mock you," Len said gently. "I hope merely to warn you."

"Of what?"

"You propose, Miss Lucia Foxe of Foxe Hall, to remain in the company of outlaws for another week and to have knowledge of a frame-breaking plot. It is probably enough for you to hang alongside the rest of us. At the very least, do you not think that Foxe Hall will seem a little mundane when you finally return to ease your father's worries?"

Lucia's eyes widened. "They wouldn't hang me?" she asked, her stomach in a knot of disbelief. Even in her wakeful night-time hours, the chill of death had never seemed so close. A shiver ran the length of her spine.

"These days, they hang anyone," Len said with a shrug. "Though I'm sure your father would vouch for you not being an outlaw yourself and save you from the rope."

Len's face was still very close to Lucia's, and she spoke in nothing more than a loud whisper. To Lucia she seemed to breathe magic into the air. For every warning, prediction of dire consequences, or reminder of the life from which she had been snatched, she only thrilled to Len more. As the night deepened, in that moment, in the dark ruins, she could believe herself truly enchanted as she kept her eyes on Len's.

"I want to stay with *you*," she said softly, her voice trembling.

"Then you may," Len whispered back, as if she had never protested otherwise. She paused, her eyes locked to Lucia's through the thickening gloom. A mist was beginning to rise from the plains around them and her breath was a cloud of vapour. Everything was obscure except her eyes and the pounding of Lucia's heart. For a brief moment Lucia felt their hearts beat to the same rhythm, that they were not so different after all. Then Len looked away and said, more loudly, "I will insist on certain conditions. You will spin a more convincing story for your father to justify this unexplained absence. And you will learn to fire a pistol."

"A pistol?" Lucia asked, horrified and thrilled in the same moment.

"Yes. I don't expect you to turn robber or frame-breaker, but you are a liability if we have to defend you."

"Oh." Lucia was almost disappointed this was all Len required of her.

Len stood up and, with a brief glance down at Lucia, strode towards where Julian was perched on a higher fragment of wall, a shadow in the descending night. Lucia watched her go and felt her heart ache in a way she had never known it to before.

CHAPTER TEN

Lucia slept little that night wrapped in Len's cloak, hunched into a corner of the ruined building in an effort to keep warm. The fog crept over their low hilltop and froze, encrusting the leaves and the moss-covered stones with a layer of white. She drifted between sleep and wakefulness. In her waking moments she seemed always to hear the screech of an owl or a rustling in the undergrowth nearby. She curled and uncurled her numbed fingers and pulled the heavy material of the cloak closer in around her.

Every time she opened her eyes, she looked for Len. Sometimes she saw her figure shadowy and distant, other times not at all. Once, she looked about her only to see Len sitting very close to her on the wall, brandy bottle in her hand, a thin wisp of cigar smoke rising from her other, and her eyes almost certainly trained on Lucia. To know Len's gaze was on her, to wonder hopelessly what Len might be thinking, warmed Lucia almost enough to banish the chill of the night. To know Len was thinking of her was oddly exciting, having Len watch over her remarkably comforting. Len never slept, not that Lucia saw at least.

When the first signs of dawn crept murkily into the sky and she knew she could abandon the pretence of sleep, Lucia was filled with relief. She rose stiffly to her feet and, stretching her arms, looked in the direction of the sunrise. Her breath steamed from her mouth in the bitter cold air, and the grass and cobwebs were jewelled with frost, but the growing daylight warmed her.

"Breakfast, miss?" Lucia heard a voice beside her. She turned to see Julian offering a piece of bread. He was hatless for once, his dark hair hanging in loose waves to his shoulders. She took the bread, aware how hungry she was, but eyed him warily.

"Thank you."

"Do I worry you, Miss Foxe?" he asked, that vaguely sardonic tone still in his words. Lucia reminded herself he was Len's closest friend and tried not to be quite so alarmed by him.

"The first and last times we properly met, sir, you pointed a pistol at me." Lucia took a bite of the bread.

"I cannot apologise enough," he said, with a slight bow of his head.

Lucia did not believe him and did not reply, merely went on eating the bread.

"Len tells me she trusts you have not—and will not—betray us," he said, more seriously.

"I would not. And have not."

"I trust her judgement."

"I am glad of that." Lucia wondered if this conversation would reach its point soon.

"She also tells me you wish to stay with us for now."

"Yes."

"You see this as a form of country jaunt I suppose. Similar to a fox hunt?"

Lucia resented his insinuation. "I have never hunted," she said, "and you are wrong about me."

"Maybe you will explain it to me, Miss Foxe? We are suddenly a small company, we thieves and frame-breakers. We sleep in the cold and do not have enough to eat. I can see no reasonable cause for you to remain one of our number. We will travel more quickly without you and will not be forced to consider your safety."

"I am to learn to fire a pistol."

"Excellent!" He laughed bitterly. "But why put yourself through such an unusual lesson? Why not return to your dancing and novel reading and pianoforte tuition?"

"Do you ever ask Len why she does not return to her father?" Lucia did not hide her hostility.

"Do not speak of what you do not understand," he returned.

"I understand more than you think." Lucia saw the realisation dawning in his expression, as he comprehended that Len had chosen to confide in her. His expression was somewhere between wounded and surprised. He certainly did not seem pleased.

"Your life at Foxe Hall was happy, I believe, Miss Foxe. Why would you abandon it?"

"It is not abandoned, sir." Lucia was alarmingly aware she doubted her own words as she spoke them. "It is merely that I do not intend to return to it just yet."

"How will you explain it to your family?"

"It is no matter to you."

"No, miss, you are correct. But the safety of the men, of myself, and of Len are of great import to me."

"Len does not need you to protect her."

"Nor does she need you to bring her danger."

"Nor does she need either of you to be discussing what she does or does not need," said a voice behind them. They both turned quickly to see Len, dark circles beneath her eyes which were yet as sharp as ever, regarding them evenly. "Good morning," she said, with a wry smile.

"Morning," Julian said. Lucia remained silent. She was still offended by Julian's words, worried by his hostility. In truth, he had made her consider the reality of what she was taking on in more stark colours than she cared to. Len glanced at Lucia and addressed her words to Julian.

"We are to go to the frame-breakers' hideout in the forest," she said. "It is the safest option, whether I would assist them in their raid or not. We can't spend a week on this hilltop, too exposed to make a fire. They have some food and shelter. We will be outlaws together."

"I'm sure Miss Foxe will be glad of the food and shelter." Julian turned hostile eyes on Lucia.

"I shall be glad of it myself," Len said sharply.

Julian looked angry to be spoken to that way. Lucia felt uncomfortable as the cause of hostility between friends. Julian turned away from her. "Can we speak alone for a moment?" he said to Len.

"Of course." He strode away and Len followed. Lucia could not hear what they said, but she saw his angry gestures, his constant glances in her direction. Equally she saw Len's determination, the way she stood straight, looked him in the eye, and did not lose possession of her temper. It was ludicrous to Lucia to believe Len was defending her and her decision to remain with them, yet it had to be the case. Eventually Julian's shoulders seemed to relax. She saw him slap Len on the back in a friendly fashion and then make his way over to the horses.

Quickly, Lucia turned away, although she could not explain why she did so. Having watched Julian walk away, Len had turned back towards her. Suddenly Lucia felt shy of her in a way she had not in the gathering darkness of the previous night.

"Of course, if I was sensible, I would listen to Julian," Len said, as she reached Lucia's side. Lucia turned quickly to look at her, hoping she had not decided to be sensible in that way. "Don't look at me like that. If *you* were sensible, you would listen to him too. You were not unhappy at home, after all."

"No, I was not. Only I was waiting for something to happen that never seemed as though it was going to."

The sky was beginning to clear, and the early morning sunshine was breaking through in places. Lucia looked up to the scattered cloud rather than into Len's eyes.

"What were you waiting for?"

"That's what I asked myself. I have no idea. I merely thought something else was bound to happen, that life must be more than what it is."

"What if there is no more?"

"But there is," Lucia said, looking back to Len. "I knew it as we galloped across the fields yesterday. I even knew it whilst I shivered in the night. I'm living it now, and even if after I return to my home it feels as a distant dream, I will at least have tasted it for a short time."

Lucia saw Len's comprehension of her emotions. She saw the clouds of doubt in Len's eyes. All Len said was, "This is why I do not choose to be sensible as Julian suggests and send you home."

They stood in silence, the bond of empathy tenuous between them, and watched as the last of the fog melted away and the morning became bright. Len appeared to shake herself out of her reverie. "It is ten miles across country to the edge of the forest. They will not tell us how deep into the forest their hideout is, though since it is hardly the forest it once was, it cannot be more than a mile or so. Will you ride with me?"

A small thrill swept through Lucia's body as she remembered yesterday's ride. "Yes."

"And have you thought how to reassure your father for another week?"

Tension rose in Lucia's stomach at the notion of lying further and bringing additional concern to her family. Yet they seemed distant, and it was remarkably easy to give Len the answer she required. "Yes, I have. If you can give me paper, I will write another letter to him. I will tell him I am on my way home and quite safe, only that I have taken ill with a head cold and want to wait for it to pass before I go on with the journey. I will inform him I have found a kindly lady to stay with. I will neglect however to tell him of the village I am writing from or the route I am taking. He will be concerned, of course, and I will have many questions to answer upon my return, but at least he will be reassured of my safety."

"You could develop the mind of a criminal yet." Len smiled. "I have paper and ink, I'll fetch them for you. I'll send Julian to deliver the letter."

"It would be better if he could send it by the post, do you not think?"

"Yes, you're right," she laughed and made for the horses, where most of her belongings were still loaded on the saddle.

❖

Len did not miss the way Julian eyed Lucia's letter suspiciously when she handed it to him and asked him to see it into the post safely. She did not blame him; it was not a lack of trust on his part, more an urge to defend her and his friends. Peter and Isaac had still not arrived on the hilltop. Len forced herself to harden her heart. One of them was the traitor. Maybe even both of them had betrayed them, who could guess for what reward? Either way, they were lost to her and she could not dwell on it now. There was no time for anger or sentiment. Decisions had to be made.

Did Lucia find it strange? Len found herself pondering what her pretty hostage was thinking. How did Lucia see her now? She seemed to have become accustomed to Len's manner of dress and deportment. But what of her occupation, her ability to lead a gang of outlaws? Did she seem hard to Lucia? Eccentric or indecent? Or did Lucia begin to understand what this way of life necessitated? Had her eyes finally been opened?

Though it had been her intention from the start to make Lucia see that another reality existed but her own sheltered one, she could not quite help a pang of regret, as if she had somehow destroyed Lucia's innocence. And yet innocence was not the helpful virtue the world painted it to be. She sighed and cursed herself.

Why did it matter what Lucia was thinking, and what her opinion was of Len? She knew she was anxious for Lucia to see the woman, not just the outlaw with a mask and flintlock. And she knew why. The thought of Lucia's approval, of something beyond approval, was almost unbearably wonderful. But she could not allow it to influence her actions. Lucia's expression was pensive, as if she was thinking of the family who would be worried for her. But Lucia had been given the choice and refused to return home. She was a prisoner no longer but here at her own volition. Len would not force her will upon the other woman. And thus Lucia must learn, for she was in as much danger as the rest of them now.

Len watched as Lucia stood on a part of the grey ruin and mounted Oberon. As she settled in the saddle, she looked about her with something like regret. Something had changed in Lucia during that long, cold night on this hilltop. She did not yet understand that it was not the hilltop that had caused it, it was not a change she would leave behind. It was in her heart and her mind and would be with her always. Lucia straddled worlds now. There really was no going back.

Len smiled a little sadly and pulled herself up into the saddle behind Lucia. She slid one leg either side of the horse's flanks and eased herself closer to Lucia. She felt the other woman's heat along the whole front of her own body and clenched her jaw hard against her body's impulsive reaction to the sensation. She reached around Lucia to grip the reins. Lucia shivered. Well, it was cold and Lucia was not warmly dressed. And yet the sensation of a woman shivering in her arms was something Len found difficult to ignore. She had never thought to feel it again.

Oberon stirred beneath them and recalled her to her senses. She thought quickly over her plan for the day. Julian had taken the elder of the frame-breakers—whose name was Daniel—with him, since he would need a guide to their hideout. The younger man—called Tom Smith—who was distinctly ill-at-ease without the support of his companion would lead her and William, already mounted on his bay mare, to this mysterious place of safety and plotting.

Len nudged Oberon and he surged into life. She steered him in the wake of the guide. Since Tom Smith was on foot, they would make frustratingly slow progress. Len only hoped Tom had good sense enough to lead them a route that would keep them safe from discovery.

They made their way down the opposite side of the hill to that which they had climbed the day before. Here a kind of faint track wound its way down to the level ground, between tufts of long grass still painted white by the frost. Occasionally Oberon slipped on a patch of mud frozen hard and Len tightened her arms about Lucia's frame as she regained her balance.

At the base of the hill, this path joined with a broader track, but their guide instead cut through a gap in the hedgerow immediately across from them. They followed him as he turned to walk alongside the hedge on the field side. The ground was more uneven here, and the ride was not smooth. Their progress felt painfully slow, and gradually a knot of tension returned to the pit of Len's stomach. She hated the sense of not being in control of this journey across country.

In truth she had spent half the night wondering if her selfish desire to deliver justice to her father was clouding her judgement.

Why trust the frame-breakers? Why lose some of her control over the actions of her band and give it to a pack of disgruntled textile workers? Was she really taking the safest and wisest course? The anxiety had made it impossible to sleep and weighed heavy on her tired shoulders now.

They crossed several ditches dividing the fields. After about half an hour, they found themselves on a small track which skirted a hamlet of five or six cottages. Though Len prided herself on her knowledge of the local countryside and she knew the distance they had travelled, she found the hamlet was unfamiliar to her. A brown-and-white dog, tied by a length of rope to a stake in the yard of one of the cottages, barked furiously at them as they passed. Len held her breath, full of anxiety the barking would draw unwanted attention to them. She felt Lucia tense in her arms until they had passed by the yard and the dog had desisted from its noise.

After this, they began to cross the country again, turning briefly onto what appeared, to Len's consternation, to be the turnpike, before breaking through another hedge to ride at the side of a fallow field. Gradually, Len began to relax once more. It surely would not be too much longer before they reached their destination. Sometimes she had to trust in others.

Suddenly a sound out of place reached her ears. She stiffened in the saddle and removed one of her gloved hands from the reins to signal to William behind them to stop, as she pulled Oberon to a halt. Ahead, Tom Smith noticed and turned questioning, anxious eyes on her. They all listened carefully. Len could feel Lucia's pounding heart, and she was suddenly conscious of her proximity to the other woman. She heard the odd sound again, only this time she recognised it. Abruptly, she threw herself from the saddle, pulling Lucia with her. They landed heavily on the soil, and Lucia cried out slightly as her ankle jarred. Lucia looked askance at Len, but she held her finger to her lips and glared in such a way there was no mistaking her message. Now was not the time for questions.

They remained crouched on the ground as William, who had dismounted with just much urgency, came to squat next to her. He held his mare's reins, as she did Oberon's, and they both pulled the beasts towards the fortunately dense hedgerow, which was just about the same height as Oberon's ears. Thankfully, William's mare was a little shorter. Tom Smith joined them on the ground and Len saw his hands were trembling. She had little pity for him. This new threat was his fault for leading them too close to danger.

"The turnpike runs alongside here?" she demanded of him in a whisper.

"Yes," he confirmed. Len fought her rising anger. It would do no good and Tom Smith was too frightened to pay heed to his error.

"I heard horses," she said. "You know the militia patrol the turnpike, looking for frame-breakers and highwaymen?"

"Yes," Tom Smith's eyes were filled with terror. Len saw Lucia's expression alter as she heard the sound too. Distant yet horribly nearby, a horse whinnied. Listening keenly, Len made out the rhythmic rattle of metal against leather. Then the hoof falls were unmistakeable. This was certainly not a solitary traveller.

Len did not take the time to comfort Lucia, though the woman had turned almost white with fear. The best comfort would be protection. She peered through the branches of the brown winter hedgerow, scarcely breathing, her free hand on the butt of her pistol. She would not be so foolhardy as to take on a militia patrol, but the weapon at her side gave her some reassurance.

Lucia watched Len and prayed she would stay hidden, not expose herself to danger. Suddenly the danger was real and sharp. The heavy anticipation clarified for her the nature of the life this woman and her men led. Her own loss of property at Len's bidding, her abduction, even a night on a frozen hilltop, all seemed a dream compared to this. Her pulse throbbed vehemently in her temples, and her throat was so tight she felt she could not breathe; then she gasped for air too quickly, and her head began to swim. It struck her fully then: these moments decided questions of life and death. By the end of the day, her three companions could all be in dark gaol cells, awaiting the noose. What would become of Lucia herself should such a dreadful fate befall them was not, strangely, uppermost in her thoughts.

William's mare shifted position behind them, and Lucia started, the noise the horse made terribly loud as they crouched in deathly silence at the base of the hedge. William looked up at her anxiously and reached up a thick-fingered hand to pat her shoulder soothingly. Oberon stood calmly, as though he was used to such dramas.

The ground close to the hedge had not yet seen the sunlight and was still frozen white and solid. Though it prevented them sinking into the mud, the cold began to creep through Lucia's thin shoes, numbing her toes. She envied Len her leather boots. Unused to being kept in such a position, her knees were aching, and she was forced to put one hand onto the ground to keep her balance. Len could apparently stay crouched and motionless all day, if it were required of her.

Lucia's attention was snatched back to the other side of the hedge, as she heard a man's voice raised in laughter, alarmingly close. The heavy thud of the hoofs and the rattling of bridles and other clanking, most likely of weaponry, were more distinct now. There was more laughter. Clearly a morning patrol of the turnpike was a light-hearted business. Lucia had a sudden thought of her brother, so far away in Spain, and wondered if he had been forced to hide in hedgerows from patrols of enemy cavalry. A wave of sickness and hot fear swept through her.

Len was still stock-still, watching. Lucia copied her, trying to see through the brown branches to the road beyond. It struck her that since she could see the road rather clearly, they would themselves be equally visible should one of the soldiers choose to peer through the hedge. She prayed silently they would have no cause to do any such thing.

Suddenly a horse's legs came into view. She held her breath. The first horse was a chestnut with white socks. There were another four horses following. Shifting her gaze upwards, she saw the boots and breeches of the riders, clearly military issue. She could even make out the red coats, the green facings, of their uniforms. Lucia had danced with the officers of the militia at balls, talked with them in sitting rooms, and now she sheltered behind a hedge, her feet numb and her legs aching, not daring to breathe in case she should be discovered by them and, in so doing, betray her three companions. Never had she felt so responsible for the welfare of another human being.

At the soldiers' sides she saw the dangerous glint of curved sabres. These were not regular soldiers, and she doubted they would have given Napoleon's columns fighting for Spanish territory any cause for concern, but she knew they would still have been trained well enough in the skills of the cavalry officer for those sabres to be a real danger. She shuddered and, in her mind, urged Len—whose hand was still on her pistol—to remain behind the hedge, in hope of safety.

Thankfully, Len showed no signs of imminently attacking the patrol. Maybe she had never had that intention, or maybe if it had been one or two men she would have taken the risk. Lucia wondered what Len was thinking, how she made the decisions she had to.

Lucia could not watch as the men rode past. All it would take was a sideways glance to notice Oberon's black ears in the hedgerow, or for William's mare to shift again. She heard one of the military horses whinny as if she sensed the presence of two of her kind nearby, but her rider urged her on with a cross word and a jab of his spurs.

None of them moved until the militia were not only out of sight but also until they could no longer hear any trace of their clinking and thudding, of their grating laughter on the slight breeze. Tom Smith broke the silence first, exhaling all of his fear in one breath and then swearing softly, rubbing his face with unsteady hands.

Len rose to her feet and rubbed Oberon's velvety nose. "Good lad," she crooned softly to him.

William also stood and patted his mare. To Lucia's surprise, he offered her his hand, which she accepted, grateful for the help in straightening her stiff legs. Pain seared through her frozen knees and into the ankle she had jarred when Len had forced her rather hurried dismount from Oberon's high back. She gasped but bit the cry of pain away quickly. She looked at William, whose face was unreadable, and wondered what had made him suddenly willing to offer her assistance. She saw Len glance at him in a similar fashion and, as his eyes met hers, he looked away.

Lucia understood. Len's point had been proved, Lucia had shown she could be trusted. It would have been very simple for her to have risen to her feet, cried out to the militia patrol, and seen Len, William, and Tom Smith on their way to the gallows, herself on her way back to her family. The fact she had not done so had clearly convinced William she had no intention of informing the authorities about them and had never done any such thing. Despite her still-thudding heart, she was almost glad of their close encounter with the agents of justice, since the outcome was to her advantage after all.

Another result of their brush with danger was a marked change in Lucia's own feelings. Where she had previously felt as an impostor in their small group, like a creature from another world set apart from their own, all at once she felt as though they were her people after all. The officers of the militia in their scarlet coats were her true social acquaintances, the men who were employed to make her family and their like feel safe and, she suspected, to provide the ladies with gentlemen in uniform to dance with in the assembly rooms. Yet now they seemed to her as enemies, as surely as if they were in fact Napoleon's men come to English soil. Lucia had crossed a boundary somewhere, and she had not even been aware of its happening, only that it had, indeed, been crossed.

William helped her mount Oberon and Len was quick to mount behind her. Lucia felt the solid warmth of her at her back and closed her eyes as Len's arms slid around her body to reach for the reins. Even in the midst of such danger, Lucia could not help a feeling of belonging, of being where she was meant to be. She opened her eyes and wondered how on earth Len's arms could be the place she was meant to be. There didn't seem to be an easy answer. She sighed. Len still had not spoken, but Lucia sensed a trepidation in her she had not noticed before the encounter with the militia. And Len was also angry. Lucia could tell from the rigidity of her body and the urgency with which she kicked the horse forward.

Chapter Eleven

Tom Smith had underestimated the amount of time it would take them to reach the frame-breakers' hideout. Len grew angrier with every passing minute, though she kept her composure. Clearly these frame-breakers thought themselves invincible by daylight. Perhaps they felt safe behind their daytime status as impoverished artisans. Such a cover was not a luxury Len and her men had. By the time they reached the edge of the forest her whole body seemed to be aching with the tension of holding back her resentment. And yet the warm, solid presence of Lucia's body so close to her own brought a comfort she did not like to admit to herself.

They did not approach the forest by one of the roads that cut through it, rather they crossed more fields and edged an estate of parkland, which Len recognised as Rufford Great Park. Finally she had a bearing on where Tom Smith had led them. Instantly she knew she could have navigated a safer course across the country than Tom Smith had provided. It was of no matter now though, as they forded a shallow river and found themselves beneath the trees. The horse's hooves crunched through the thick carpet of yellow and brown fallen leaves, stark black branches overhead. In summer the green canopy would cut off the light from the forest floor, the trees were so thick here. Len allowed herself to breathe deeply again. She was back in her element, surrounded by timeless and strong trees, shadows to protect her, nothing but the rules of nature to plague her. She loved these ancient woodlands, so long the shelter of outlaws.

The very air itself seemed to change once they made their way between the tall trunks, following no apparent path. Tom Smith knew his direction with some certainty now. Len was content to trust him now the group was shielded from common view. The sunlight reached through to the leafy floor, yet somehow lost its strength, as though its warmth was torn to pieces on the bare branches. It was colder here, and they inhaled a damp scent of mould and moisture, with none of the crispness of the winter morning about it. Yet Len found comfort in that.

They rode through the woods for around twenty minutes until they came to a small clearing. Tom Smith stopped and turned to her expectantly. Looking beyond him, Len had her first view of the frame-breaker's hideout. She had not been sure what to expect, but the place presented a very dismal prospect indeed. She found herself, against all good sense, disappointed with what she saw. General Ludd's army trailed no glory at all. They squatted in a cold, damp, overgrown clearing.

The trees leaned inwards into the clearing, making it darker than the woods around it. Clearly the rain penetrated the forest here, for the ground appeared boggy, the leaves stuck into it and rotting quickly. To one side of the clearing was a circular area of stones surrounded by large logs, apparently a place to make a fire. To the other side was a building. Len wondered how such a place ever came to be here in the depths of Sherwood Forest. It was not like the house she and her men had found in the woods close to Foxe Hall. That was an old servant's or gamekeeper's dwelling and had once been quite respectable. This was a virtually ruined cottage, with the appearance of not having been lived in for at least a century. One storey high with low eaves, the thick thatch of the roof was rotten and holey. The windows were glassless, dark openings in the muddy brown of the walls, which might once have been whitewashed. Ivy grew over most of the building, long tendrils reaching out away from the cottage, as if looking for further masonry to conquer but finding none. The whole building sloped alarmingly towards the middle of the clearing. Both the building and the clearing were deserted. In fact, the silence was almost too perfect.

Tom Smith picked up a thick branch from the ground and beat out a short rhythm of taps on a nearby tree. Len shifted in the saddle, irritated. Coded warning signals were entirely unnecessary, and she disliked the self-important pretence of organisation where there was clearly little. An emphasis on such masquerades prevented the men from focusing on what was most important: survival.

However, the coded tapping did its job, for moments later, four men emerged from the trees surrounding the clearing where they had hidden. One of the men looked very much like Tom Smith, tall and thin, only a little younger. Another was shorter even than William, his small stature exaggerated by his stooped back. A light-haired, youthful man stood near him. The fourth man reminded Len a little of Julian, although his hair was fair. It was this man Len deduced to be their leader—if there was such a thing here—since he came nearest to her while the other three hung back.

She met their gaze with hostility and waited for their questions. She would have had plenty herself if their positions were reversed. Would their leader be sensible and ask the most important questions? Or would his hostility obscure practicality? She waited, ready to judge the man as soon as he opened his mouth. First impressions were all important. Could she trust him?

"We expected you back last night, Tom," the fair-haired man said. Len knew she had been correct in assuming him their leader, since he had a certain edge of authority in his tone. His local accent was broad but his words clear. His keen but tired eyes looked with some hostility at the intruders in his clearing.

"I know, Bill, sorry, wasn't a lot I could do about it." Tom Smith mumbled.

The fair-haired man was now staring at Len, and Lucia in front of her in the saddle, with a combination of fascination and anger. His expression was just further fuel to the fire of Len's irritation. "Never seen a damned woman before," she muttered to herself, before dismounting quickly. Lucia was looking at her with a startled expression. Len ignored her. Lucia was the reason behind the man's confusion, and she would not have Lucia become the focal point of her first encounter with the frame-breakers. It would distract from what was important. If the man was going to be bewildered by the presence of any woman, it would be Len herself. She pulled the scarf from her face and glared her challenge at him.

Len saw the surprise on the man's countenance and knew her disguise had fooled him effectively. Now he looked from her to Lucia, who was blushing, and back to her again. He was satisfyingly confused and Len enjoyed wresting back control of the situation.

The man recovered his countenance quickly. He smiled slowly. "Fancy a good night of it, did you Tom?"

"What?" Tom Smith cast a nervous glance at Len. He was afraid of her. Good.

"Why else would you bring me whores?"

Indignation rose in Len's chest. For a moment the anger caught at her breath and gave her pause for thought. She'd been called names of many kinds, and usually they only amused her. But now she was offended. Glancing to her side she saw Lucia's shocked expression and knew the reason she was so insulted by the man's words. Lucia. She sighed. Had she not known this would happen? Lucia's presence was already clouding her judgement. Why had she not forced her to return to Foxe Hall?

Len rested her hand on the pistol at her hip. "You are General Ludd, I assume?" she asked, her voice heavy with sarcasm. She looked ostentatiously around her, a disgusted sneer on her face. "And this is your headquarters, where you muster and train, what is it, thousands of sworn heroes? That's what your letters claim."

"Those letters were not sent from here," the man said calmly. The fact he did not seem afraid of her only made her more annoyed.

"So you are not General Ludd?"

"No, I am not. I am Bill Wilcock."

"Oh, forgive my disappointment, Bill. Tom, here, led me to believe we were journeying into the very heart of General Ludd's glorious army." Len's tone was withering, and she saw the resentment in Bill Wilcock's face as he looked back at her. He was clearly unsure just how he should respond.

"Who are you and what is your business here?" he said at last.

"I wish to aid you when you attack Hawkins's workshop on Friday," Len said. There was no time to dance around the matter.

But nor did she wish to dwell on her reasons or her identity and offered no further explanation.

Bill Wilcock laughed. "And why should I require your help? Two women? Only the one useful man amongst you!"

Len would not rise to his small-minded insults. She knew well enough what was expected of a woman and that the only way to prove otherwise was with action, not words. "There is another man of ours coming with your Daniel. They had to do a small duty for me first."

"Perhaps I will consult with him." Bill Wilcock might have been described as handsome, but now a sneer made him ugly in the extreme.

"You will consult with me or with no one," Len said. "We could have killed your men at the roadside last night, but we chose not to. Instead we are here, offering you assistance."

Bill Wilcock frowned. "You would have killed them, would you?"

"Since they attempted to rob us?" Len was aware of the irony behind her indignation. "Of course I would."

"So, what are you? Travellers?"

"No." Len paused for a second or two. How far to trust him? What to reveal? She was still in the position of power, knowing this man's crimes and his hideout while she was still a stranger to him. But she had to risk some degree of revelation to win his trust. That was only fair. "We are outlaws just as you are. Only we use our pistols to get our bread."

"Highwaymen?"

"If you have spent many weeks in the neighbourhood, you will have heard of us."

"I have heard of a band of highwaymen in these parts. A band of seven men. Their leader rides a black stallion, sure enough, but there are no women."

"How do you know this for sure?"

Bill looked her up and down. Len endured the inspection impatiently. "In the dark *you* might pass as a man," he conceded, "but she would not." He jerked his head in Lucia's direction. Len turned as Lucia steadfastly looked at the ground. Len understood she was embarrassed to have all of their gazes directed at her.

"Does she look like an outlaw to you?" Len said.

"No. That's what I mean. What is she, your sweetheart?" Tom Smith laughed out loud at his leader's joke. Len's lips set tighter, and she felt the colour in her face heighten.

"She is our prisoner, who I want to keep in my sights." Len did not look at Lucia. If the girl was offended to be reminded she was a hostage, she would get over it before long. It was the only explanation Bill Wilcock would trust.

"And your other men?"

"Arrested, I believe." Len did not like to say it.

"What? Four of your men arrested, and you think I would want your help?"

"*Three* of my men arrested. I believe the other to be their betrayer." She kept all emotion from her voice.

"How do you know it wasn't her ladyship there?"

"That is precisely why she is my prisoner, what do you take me for?"

"A woman who thinks she's a man." Bill made it sound as though that was explanation enough for doubting her ability and judgement. She felt the prickle of resentment and refused to allow it to take hold of her.

"So you've lost your men and you're looking for help?" Bill said.

"No. My men were taken but I will find more. We will continue to work, in the meantime, without them. I am here because I want to assist your cause this Friday. After it is done, you need never see us again."

"And what interest do you have in frame-breaking?"

"That is of no concern to you, beyond the knowledge that we need shelter for the week and will assist you if you allow us to stay with you."

"You could be sent to trap us."

"Do you think it likely that the Lord Lieutenant would send me to trap you, when you have as little trust for me as you would if the colonel of the militia himself were to appear in your clearing?"

Bill Wilcock was silent for a moment, conceding her point.

"You will stay with us for the week, assist us in our work of Friday night?"

"Yes."

"I have one condition."

"Name it."

"Your men are better clothed, better fed than we are. You take some rich wages in your work. Provide us with food, or the coins to purchase food, and you may join us."

In answer, Len walked back to Oberon's side. She did not look up at Lucia, still in the saddle, as she reached into one of the bags she had burdened the stallion with and removed a small leather purse held tightly closed by a drawstring. She tossed it to Bill Wilcock, who caught it easily and opened the string with rather more eagerness than she expected of him. These were hungry and desperate men. There had never been any doubt Bill would allow them to hide here, not while he contemplated the prospect of food or money. But the game of convincing him had been necessary for his pride and his legitimacy as a leader. She understood that very well.

"That is a gesture of goodwill," Len said. "Now, where can we tie up the horses?"

❖

Julian arrived in the clearing with Daniel—the older frame-breaker—about an hour after Len and her party. Bill Wilcock was instantly more respectful of Julian than he had been of Len and began to act as though the true leader of the band had finally arrived. Lucia could see how Len was irritated by this but respected the restraint she showed in not protesting and causing unnecessary discord.

Len and William had tied their horses to a rail at the side of the cottage, loosened their girths, and ensured they had water to drink. The men who used this hideout had been collecting rainwater, and there was plenty to fill the trough. Meanwhile, Lucia had stood awkwardly where she dismounted Oberon, uncomfortable under the silent scrutiny of the men, until William, whose kindly attention was still remarkable to her, gestured to a large fallen tree and suggested she take a seat.

"We'll see about some food and drink, and a fire," he said. She smiled her thanks weakly as she sat gingerly on the tree. It was really very cold in the forest, and the damp had penetrated her thin clothing to reach her very skin. The idea of a fire was overwhelmingly appealing.

The kindling was just beginning to catch alight, bright orange and comforting in the clearing of greys and browns, when Julian strode into the scene, leading his mare calmly behind him. Despite his hostility towards Lucia, she found herself pleased when he arrived. Not only did he lend Len more credibility in the eyes of Bill Wilcock, his safe arrival meant surely nothing else terrible could face them today. She also looked forward to the conversation he would have later with William, when the latter revealed he believed she was to be trusted after events on the road today.

Len spoke with Julian, William, and Bill Wilcock before her attention returned to Lucia again. Lucia could not help the feeling of being rather unnecessary and out of place. She thought unavoidably of her father and of Isabella. Her thoughts touched but did not linger on the agonies they would be going through, even after the receipt of her latest epistle. Rather, she imagined they could happen upon her now, in this damp clearing with thieves and frame-breakers. What expression would she read upon their countenances? Surprise and astonishment, no doubt. Yet she suspected there would also be bewilderment, disgust, and maybe even horror. She did not like to picture such things, for they pulled at the place in her heart where she knew what she was doing was terribly, awfully wrong. She brought her attention back to the cold place in the woods. Clutching her shawl to her body, she was gazing at the ever-growing fire gratefully when Len seated herself astride the log next to her.

Lucia smiled faintly at her and tried to think of something useful to say.

"You've been thinking of home?" Len said, to Lucia's astonishment.

"Yes," she confessed, "how did you know?"

"I remember, Lucia." Len paused.

"Are there only these six frame-breakers?" Lucia asked, when Len said no more.

"These are the men who organise the attacks. The other men are workers. There is no short supply of angry, hungry men ready to take up sledgehammers against the machines, they tell me."

"Are their lives really so awful?" Lucia asked the question before she considered her words.

"Did you not believe me before?" Len asked. A shadow clouded her eyes. "There is no food here, other than what we have carried with us and a rabbit Bill caught yesterday. One of the men will take the coins I gave them into town tomorrow, and it will be the first real meal they have eaten this week. That is why Tom and Daniel were contemplating robbing Julian and William."

Lucia had always imagined the frame-breakers to be a well-fed group of men, organised in their hideout, feasting from ill-made gains, planning their next raid. The truth of it was apparent to her now: these men were desperate. Criminals, yes, and—if Bill Wilcock was anything to judge by—thoroughly unpleasant men. But it was their desperation she felt most powerfully.

"You still mean to go through with your plan to help them?" Lucia asked.

"Why would I change my mind?"

"I just thought, with them already having so many men—and with him being so rude—you might think differently."

"It is not that they need my help. It is that I want to assist them, and it does us good to hide in the woods with them these few days." Len's face was grim. "Bill's rudeness is nothing to me and should be nothing to you either."

"How do you grow used to such manners?" Lucia was not, in truth, offended on her own behalf. But for Bill to mock Len, to try to diminish her before the men, was an affront she felt very powerfully.

"It is not hard." Len smiled slightly. "I know you are very used to the import of manners, Miss Lucia Foxe, but really, you must consider, have his words done me any real harm?"

"No, I suppose not."

"Then I choose not to contemplate them further."

"It is a skill I am yet to learn." Manners were everything in Lucia's world. To abandon them so completely seemed impossible.

"Like so many other skills you have had no need for before." Lucia remembered then, Len had once not been so very different from herself.

"You did not tell them the workshop is your father's."

"No." Her face darkened.

"Why not?"

"It was unnecessary," Len said shortly. That seemed to be the end of the conversation. Len stood up, went to her saddle-bags, and then disappeared in the direction of the house. Shortly afterwards she returned with a pot of water which she set over the fire.

"I am quite sure this is the first time fine China tea has ever been made in the heart of Sherwood Forest," she said, with an amused smile.

Lucia was about to question how on earth it was she had fine China tea in her possession. Then she noted the quality of the small silver-and-enamel tea caddy Len had set on the muddy ground at her side and could well imagine it having been among a traveller's precious possessions. For a moment her recollection that Len was a thief caused a pulse of fear through her veins. Then she looked from the caddy to Len's still smiling face, and she could not help but smile in return. Something about the way Len looked at her made her fears dissolve with alarming ease.

Later that evening when, warmed by the fire and with tea, salt meat, and stale bread comforting her hungry stomach, Lucia found herself in her first conversation with Bill Wilcock.

She was still sitting on the fallen tree, having had no cause to move anywhere else. Len was sitting to her side but turned slightly away from her, in conversation with William and Julian. Tom Smith and the man who looked so like him—and proved to be his younger brother—were visible through the flames of the fire, talking with

Daniel. The eldest of the frame-breakers sat alone, gazing at the fire with a fixed expression of sadness. Bill Wilcock and his other men had been inside the house, but now they emerged and crossed into the glow of the fire. To her consternation, Bill came to stand directly behind her. Lucia glanced at Len, but she had not yet noticed. Bill bent forward so that Lucia might hear his quiet words, yet however she tried to turn to face him, she could not quite see him.

"You are treated well for a prisoner, miss?"

"Miss Foxe. And yes, tolerably," she replied. How far did Len expect her to take the pretence she had begun when she had described her so coldly as a prisoner?

"Miss Foxe. You do not have a family to search for you?"

"I assure you sir, I do have a family."

"I am a little alarmed, you see, Miss Foxe, that your family will be calling out the militia to find you and putting me and my men at rather more risk than we would like."

"You need not concern yourself."

"Your family are not searching for you, perhaps?" Lucia's presence clearly confused him, and he was not happy to remain bewildered.

"I imagine not." Lucia tried to remain calm and not actually think of her father and sister.

"Why would that be?"

"It is of no matter to you."

"If you are not what you seem, Miss Foxe, it is of very great matter to me," he replied, in nothing short of a growl.

"I am responsible for Miss Foxe's presence. If it is a problem to you, you address yourself to me." Len had turned and caught his last words and was now looking him square in the face. Lucia turned to him too.

"It is getting late," he said. "We will talk further in the morning." Obviously, he was not as comfortable challenging Len as he was Lucia. Lucia smiled slightly to herself, and he glared at her as he noticed.

"You ladies will, of course, sleep in the house," he said. Lucia was mildly surprised by this concession. Len, however, seemed irritated by it.

"I will not sleep in the house," she said firmly. She got to her feet and faced him squarely. "I will remain here, with my men."

"I do not mean it as an offence to you," he said, "merely a consideration."

"I do not need your considerations."

"I sleep in the house when my men make their beds here by the fire," he said. "I am their leader, and it befits my position that I do. It is not that I require the greater comfort, it is only that they remember I am their leader."

"I am one with my men," she said stubbornly. Despite her words, Lucia recalled Len's private room at their own woodland lair and knew she did not wholly speak the truth.

"And yet you are separate from them because you lead them," Bill said. For the first time Lucia understood there was more to Bill Wilcock than the unpleasant, arrogant criminal she had taken him for.

Len merely glared at him.

Bill went on when neither woman spoke. "I like to preserve such a structure. Like you, I need the men to be loyal. They are loyal more easily to a man—forgive me—to a *leader* who knows how to lead. Yes, be one with them, but do not let the distance between you ebb away. Sleep in the house."

"I will not do anything because you tell me to," Len said.

"No, I imagine not. But think on it. Your men will be here with mine, they will be able to talk, to grow to trust each other. No men, however good, are free to do so when their leader is present. I will not spend the night with them either. Your men are loyal to you, you have nothing to fear from not being with them all night. And besides, I fancy Miss Foxe would like to sleep in the house. I would feel safer if you kept a guard on your prisoner." He looked at Lucia, and she saw he was still dubious of her status.

To Lucia's surprise, Len, after a moment's pause in which she apparently struggled with her pride, let out a deep breath and replied, "I will sleep in the house."

CHAPTER TWELVE

When Lucia entered the ruined cottage, she almost wondered if it would have been better to sleep outside in the warm orange halo of the fire. Len was not with her, having stayed behind to exchange hurried and urgent words with Julian, just outside the circle of firelight.

The ceiling of the first room was low and sloping. In this room were a large fireplace, the grate empty, and a square wooden table with a bench at one side. It was dark, even the faint light of the fire obscured by the ivy which grew over the window and into the room, as though the cottage had stood here so long the forest was claiming it for its own. Someone had left a lighted lantern on the end of the table, but its light was weak, suffocated by the gloom.

The floor was wooden, but the boards were lifting and warped, and moss grew in the corners. The oppressive smell of damp obscured even the scent of the woodland outside. To Lucia's right was a dark doorway which led to the only other room in the building. She picked up the lantern from the table and went towards it.

"Not exactly what you're used to, yet again," came Len's voice from the entrance. Len walked a few steps into the cottage. Even as she'd said her last words, Len wished she had not. It would not do to keep reminding Lucia of the differences between this world and her own. She was also aware that she was in danger of treating Lucia with the same condescension she resented so much from men like Julian.

"No," Lucia agreed and allowed the subject to drop. Len sensed that Lucia was determined to prove she could bear hardship with reasonable stamina. Len could not help but admire this evidence of Lucia's strength.

"I think it was drier outside," she said, to express her own distaste. The lantern light did not allow her to make out Lucia's reaction clearly.

Lucia walked into the next room, holding the lantern before her, and Len followed. This chamber was smaller but felt marginally drier. The smell of burnt wood suggested a fire had been lit in this room within the last few days, and sure enough, when Lucia held the lantern towards the grate, the remnant pieces of blackened wood and ash confirmed it. Lucia swung the lantern around to look at the rest of the room. As she did so, the yellow glow illuminated her face briefly, her eyes shining and her hair golden. Len drew a deep breath as her whole body, even her soul, reacted to that glimpse of Lucia's beauty in the midst of the dark and the damp. She was like a pure, perfect light in the squalid place, and Len wanted her, she could not deny it. With effort, she made herself ignore the burning longing which could never find its release and pay attention to the rest of the room.

To one side, beneath a glassless window—which was also covered by the relentless ivy—was an old bedstead, complete with sagging mattress and blanket. Len supposed this was where Bill Wilcock had made a habit of sleeping. There was a table, smaller than the one in the other room, and two chairs which looked as though they had once had wicker backs but were now merely stools with spindles rising from their back corners. The odour in here was musty rather than damp, with that hint of acrid smoke.

Len moved closer to Lucia. "It's not exactly what I'm used to either," she said. She wanted to create a sense of unity with Lucia. There were lines she could not risk crossing, but there was no reason not to foster a greater companionship with the woman.

"It has to be better than another night on a hilltop."

"Yes. Probably."

"Do you trust the frame-breakers?" Lucia's question was either coincidently well-timed or perceptive. Len felt vulnerable alone in the cottage with Lucia while the men talked outside. Before she'd left them alone for the night, she'd made sure to tell Julian just what could and could not be revealed to them. She trusted him, but she also knew how secrets could slip from careless tongues by the light of a midnight fire.

"No." She answered Lucia's question honestly. "But I do trust Julian and William. And I do not need to separate myself from them to prove myself their leader." True enough. She would not have Lucia think she was sleeping in the cottage because Bill had better leadership skills than she did. Somehow, she found herself explaining her reasons. Even as she did so, she found it remarkable. Len rarely explained herself, not even always to Julian. And yet she wanted to tell Lucia her reasoning. She wanted Lucia to know her. She knew all too well why that was, but she went on anyway. "However, his men are used to such things, and I do not want to disturb them from their patterns. There are, after all, more of them than us, and we are in their territory. I think, perhaps, Bill is also reluctant to have two women to distract his men in the night."

Len suspected the latter reason was the one uppermost in Bill's mind, and it was only some rudimentary politeness which prevented him stating it. Still, it was nothing unusual. Even in Lucia's world, ladies were considered a distraction to men.

Lucia asked, "Do you not wonder what happened with the other men?"

"No." Len could not help but wonder. But she knew such thoughts were unwise and had no intentions of confessing to them. It was a weakness she should not allow. "It does me no good to wonder. I do not care to know if Peter or Isaac betrayed us, or why. I care less to imagine any of them in gaol or on the gallows."

"Could you not save them from their fate?" Lucia sounded cautious. Part of her was apparently still a little afraid of Len. Well, that was probably healthy, though part of Len's heart was saddened by it. She did not want the barrier of fear between them. If Lucia was afraid, she was seeing the highway robber, the authoritative leader. Len was those things. But there was so much more to her she wanted Lucia to understand. Her life might bring freedom, but in that moment she felt imprisoned by it.

"This is no novel, Lucia," she said with a sigh. "There is no action I can take will save them. Even if there was, do you think I would risk my own life or that of Julian or William to do so? All of the men know the risks, as I do. We thieves are essentially selfish creatures."

Her words sounded brutal. To Lucia no doubt they sounded harsher still, and she said nothing in response. "Our life is not perhaps as ideal as you thought it to be," Len said, careful to keep any mockery from her tone.

"I did not think it ideal," Lucia said, and she sounded thoughtful still.

"In truth, Lucia, there is no ideal life," Len said, trying to understand what Lucia was pondering. She fell back on the answers she had found in answer to her own questions. "There are only choices between the kinds of life we wish to lead."

"And you chose this," Lucia concluded for her.

"I chose to be able to choose," she returned.

❖

At Len's insistence, Lucia slept on the creaking bed that night. There was really no alternative; she could hardly suggest Lucia sleep on the floor and did not dare suggest they share the small bed. It seemed entirely dangerously inappropriate to Len, though she doubted Lucia would see anything improper in two women sharing a bed. Len would not use that naïvety only to find, later, Lucia felt her trust had been betrayed. It was not that she did not trust herself. But if Lucia were ever to learn the nature of her desires, and Len suspected she might, she could not bear the thought of her feeling even slightly taken advantage of.

Lucia gave Len the old woollen blanket from the bed and spread her shawl out over her upper body to provide her some warmth. She looked so small and fragile in the lantern light that Len wanted to take the blanket and wrap her slender form in it. However, Lucia was no child, and she clearly wanted to be treated as an equal. She had given Len the blanket, and Len would accept the kindness.

Len laid the blanket on the floor, not far from the side of the bed, and slept beneath her cloak. Listening to Lucia's breathing, she was asleep quickly.

When she awoke in the morning, the thin forest light was filtering through the ivy in the window frame and casting a shadowy green illumination into the room. Lucia was still asleep, and Len wondered how restful her night had been. She picked up the threadbare blanket and laid it over Lucia's legs. Even in the weak, green light, Lucia was beautiful in her repose. Her pale hair awry and her cheeks flushed, her lips slightly parted, breathing softly, she slept on her side with the fingers of one small hand curled close to her face. She looked peaceful, and Len would not wake her and drag her into the world of outlaws and violence she was so drawn to. Let the girl rest in her easy bliss. It was a luxury she herself had not enjoyed for many a year.

Len watched Lucia sleep for a little longer. Such pale and fragile beauty in the murky, damp, derelict cottage. Lucia was out of place here yet somehow not sullied by her surroundings. Len hoped desperately her reputation would not be sullied by the company she had chosen to keep. She did not want to destroy Lucia's beautiful innocence. Yet she feared the destruction was already inevitable. Was it her fault? Or was Lucia searching for a place in the world just as she had been? How could she do anything but allow that?

Sighing, with a heart heavy with responsibility and a longing she fought not to acknowledge to herself, Len turned her back on Lucia and left the cottage, hoping to find Julian and a report on how the night had passed in the company of the frame-breakers.

❖

Lucia emerged from the cottage, blinking in the daylight, to the smell of cooking. Len and Julian were near the fire, along with Tom Smith and Bill Wilcock. She heard a rustling of leaves to her left and saw Tom's brother and Daniel walking into the woods. The other men were not to be seen, but she guessed they would be drawn back to the fire and food before long.

As Lucia approached, it was Bill Wilcock who looked up and saw her first. "Your prisoner has little trouble sleeping then?" he said to Len, who looked in Lucia's direction.

"No," Len said. "Good morning, Miss Foxe."

Slightly taken aback by Len's formality, Lucia tried to mirror her reserve. "Good morning," she said politely.

"Give her something to eat," Len ordered Julian, who glanced at her, curious too it seemed about this pretence she was attempting to maintain. Lucia wondered what his feelings were about the frame-breakers after his night spent with them. Did he trust them more than Len did? Had he confided such sentiments to Len yet?

Julian handed Lucia a piece of bread he had been toasting in the fire. She took it gratefully and turned her eyes back to Len. It was difficult to know how she was supposed to behave towards her. Lucia saw Bill Wilcock looking at her with some amusement in his expression. "Look," he said, "I know Miss Foxe here isn't a prisoner in the usual sense of the word. I really haven't a clue in what sense of the word she is, but seems to me we can trust you."

Len was looking at him with a startled expression on her face, as if she could not believe he had intelligence enough to have worked out anything of their peculiar situation.

"She is our prisoner," she insisted, and Lucia tried not to feel offended.

Bill looked to Julian. Lucia knew Len would be angered by his seeking confirmation from Julian rather than believing her.

"It is true enough," Julian said with a shrug. "Why else would we drag someone like her across the country with us?"

Bill looked at Lucia suspiciously and back at Len. "Do you not think it would be more practical to release her?"

"That is just the point," Len said. "Who is to say, if we release her, who she will tell of our secret places, our appearances, our plans for Friday night?"

Len did not meet her eye, and Lucia wondered if there was any truth in her words. Len said Lucia had her trust, but was she allowing her to stay with them as a precaution? It seemed possible. It was also a perfectly good reason to give to Bill Wilcock, by whom she was still intimidated, and Lucia did not choose that moment to launch a defence of her honour.

"I was under the impression there was a certain amount of trust between you," Bill said. "She hardly seems as terrified as I would expect of a prisoner."

"There is as much trust as necessary," Julian replied for Len. "Miss Foxe knows we will not harm her."

"But how will you ever be able to release her if you fear she will reveal your identities? That will not change after Friday." Bill was clearly enjoying this demonstration of his intellectual abilities.

"I will tell nothing of what I have seen," Lucia put in, compelled to speak for herself. Len glared at her, and she looked away quickly, part chastened and part indignant.

"Then you should be released now," Bill said.

"Miss Foxe remains with us until I decide otherwise," Len reasserted herself. "That is all there is to say on the matter." She sat down on the log by the fire and folded her arms stubbornly.

"Not while your decisions affect my men as well," Bill said, a hint of anger in his words.

"Look," Lucia said firmly, ignoring the warning glance from Len. "I am here because I choose to be. I was their prisoner, it is true. My family was robbed by them upon the turnpike. Shortly afterwards, this man abducted me in the night from my bed." She glanced quickly at Julian, who was watching her with what seemed like enjoyment coloured by no small surprise. "This woman insisted I stay with them until it could be proved it was not I who betrayed them. Of this they are now convinced, I hope. I have given my word I will reveal nothing of them to anyone once I return home. They offered to release me. Only I am reluctant to return to my ordinary life so soon." Lucia levelled her gaze at Bill Wilcock's cloudy blue eyes. She did not dare look at Len. Her heart was racing and she felt a little breathless. She held her head high and straightened her back.

"A small taste of our freedoms and you want more, Miss Foxe?" Bill said.

"I do not choose to enter into a discussion of my reasons with you, sir." Lucia filled her voice with as much pride and determination as she could muster.

"Or maybe you have fallen under the spell of the charms of your abductor?" Bill said with a glance at Julian, who raised his eyebrows and waited for her reaction with interest.

The colour rose in Lucia's cheeks at the improper suggestion. "Hardly likely," she said coldly. Julian laughed. In that moment Lucia warmed to him for his good humour.

"Perhaps you have ambitions yourself to lead a band of robbers. After all, you see now a woman can do such a thing, surprising to us all, I'm sure. Or maybe at home you are betrothed to a man you wish to escape?" Bill was merciless, and Lucia found that instead of her usual inclination to back away from any confrontation, she was compelled to answer for herself once more.

"I would not expect my reasoning to be clear to you, sir, and I ask you to desist from your game." She paused. "Because your breakfast is burning." Bill turned his attention to his food with a muttered oath. Lucia gasped for breath, amazed at her own audacity.

There was silence. Bill, while clearly not defeated, chose not to continue with the conversation. Lucia felt Len's eyes on her, but still she shied away from looking in her direction. Julian handed Lucia a metal mug of strong tea, and she sipped the steaming liquid gratefully. He smiled at Lucia as she did so, and she felt the thrill of his acceptance. It mattered greatly to her, because he was Len's closest confidant. Lucia was oddly proud of herself as she warmed her hands on the tea and steadfastly avoided looking at Len.

Later, after a long time walking alone in the woodland, Len approached Lucia as she sat alone by the fire once more. Lucia pressed her hands together uncomfortably. Len did not like to see Lucia awkward in her presence again. She guessed Lucia feared her disapproval after her outburst of earlier in the day. Len was only undecided as to whether she should reveal her admiration of Lucia's newfound courage, or not. Lucia had shown a self-confident passion and a stubborn temper, and Len was quite enthralled by these unexpected qualities. But they were unexpected because Lucia was well schooled in not allowing them to show. Should such a change be encouraged in a woman who would soon return to a world where such self-expression was generally condemned? Surely that was the path to social condemnation and, worse, a level of frustration Lucia had not known before.

Len could not stop thinking about Lucia. Although she had spent her time alone with the trees trying to weigh up her trust in Bill and his men, her best strategy for the week ahead, she found her thoughts returned inexorably to Lucia and her earlier defence of herself. Lucia was too proud to explain herself to Bill Wilcock. But could she be induced to talk to Len? Was she flattering herself? Lucia clearly had condemnation aplenty for Bill, the frame-breaker. What was to say she had any more regard for Len, the highway robber? And yet somehow she knew she had to take the risk, presume on the growing friendship she dared to hope existed between them. She looked at Lucia now, perched on the large log, and hoped she would not be humiliated by a rebuff equal to that to which Lucia had subjected Bill earlier.

"What are your reasons?" Len asked in greeting. Her tone was soft but her eyes serious.

"I'm sorry?" Lucia looked taken aback.

"Your reasons." Len was determined to know more of Lucia now. "You wouldn't tell Bill, but I want to know. What are your reasons for not returning home?"

"I would not have thought *you* needed to ask that question."

Len suspected Lucia was correct. And yet she did not trust her own instincts enough to make the assumption. "Why not? I see that we are both women, Lucia, but beyond that we are hardly the same."

"No. We cannot compare our families, our upbringings, or even our personalities. Yet I think you understand enough of my reasons. I do not need to explain them."

"*Can* you explain them?" Len asked. She saw comprehension in Lucia's pretty eyes.

"That you ask shows you do not need me to."

"I can explain my own reasons for leaving my family." The challenge was necessary; Len wanted to force an answer from Lucia, for her own good if nothing else.

"No, you cannot." Lucia's eyes flashed a new confidence. Len caught her breath, not used to being so blatantly contradicted. Defiance transformed Lucia's face from sweet to striking. "You can explain the facts, the events. You have never explained why you did not do as so many young women have and simply marry the man your father chose and make the best of it. There are whole hosts of wives and mothers across England who do not and have never loved the men chosen for them, and they are tolerably happy. Why was that not enough for you?"

Len did not answer immediately. Though she had recovered from the surprise of Lucia's newfound self-assurance, the question forced her to reflect. Were there words to explain such things? She drew a deep breath and almost resented that she thought it necessary to explain herself to Lucia. "You are right, of course. I can try to explain it, talk of humiliation and freedom and justice, but nothing truly pins it down." She levelled her gaze into Lucia's eyes, almost daunted by the fascination she saw there. The question came to her again: What did Lucia see? An outlandish curiosity to be marvelled at? Or did she see beneath the surface, to the places Len allowed no one access? It was an unnerving notion at the same time as it was alluring, and she did not dwell on it. She turned the interrogation back to Lucia's reasoning. "But you are not to be forced into a marriage, nor are you unhappy in your life. Those might be my reasons, in their simplest form. They are not yours."

"No. Yet I have never encountered a man I would willingly promise myself to. I have heard younger women whispering that I will never find a husband now I am old as I am. So I learn to be accomplished. I read French, play the pianoforte, dance well enough. My manners in society are impeccable. And now I see it plain before me—though I sensed it before—that is all my life will be. I will essentially be a failure, to my family and our acquaintance, because I have no husband, am not a mother. I will be an accomplished maiden aunt to my sister's children. Then I will die. My only escape from this would be to marry a man I do not love and who, for all the good it will do me, might as well have been selected by my father."

Lucia stopped, as though surprised by her own words. Len remembered that feeling well. The life she described was so familiar, the feeling of suffocation so easy to recall, that Len almost shuddered. The abrupt realisation that there was more to the world, that one's heart has been constrained and imprisoned, that ignorant contentment is not the same as happiness was something so very difficult to put into words. The sensation was one she could not explain herself. But as she looked earnestly at Lucia and waited for a further reaction, she knew with certainty Lucia's heart was not so different from her own.

It was a curious feeling. She had liked to think herself unique and alone. She gleaned a certain strength from being isolated in the world, fighting a struggle all her own. Was that something that could—or should—be shared?

"Come on," she said, standing up and beckoning to Lucia. Time to show the girl a little more of this life she seemed so drawn to.

"Where?" Lucia asked.

Len smiled. "I'm going to teach you to fire a pistol."

When Len removed her pistol from its holster at her hip and handed it to Lucia, its very weight frightened her. They had ventured a little distance from the clearing and were among the taller trees, ankle deep in the fallen leaves. A slight breeze crept around Lucia's face to ruffle her hair, but she was not cold. The wooden stock of the pistol was smooth and cool, the metal of the barrel colder, more brutal. Lucia held it at arm's length and regarded it as if it could kill her without her so much as touching the trigger.

"It's not loaded," Len said, grinning at her anxiety. Lucia was not reassured.

Len took the pistol from Lucia's hand, holding it naturally, comfortably. "Watch me load it," she said, and Lucia did, entranced by the deadly mystery of it.

From a pouch at her side, Len took a small metal ball wrapped in what looked like a patch of cotton, and a horn. Lucia knew enough to recognise the horn contained black powder. She watched as Len poured a little of this into the muzzle of the pistol before dropping the wrapped ball after it into the barrel. She removed a small metal rod from below the barrel and pushed it into the muzzle firmly, twice. Opening the pan of the pistol, she poured a little powder into it, then shut it with a snap. Every action was fluid, second nature. Far from frightened now, as Lucia watched she grew fascinated, even envious of the easy movements of Len's hands, the knowledge her skilled fingers displayed. Though her fingertips were rough, and more than one scar traced faintly over the back of her hands, Len's fingers were dextrous and strong and worked with such fluidity and precision that Lucia couldn't help but feel transfixed. She imagined holding her smaller, paler hand against Len's, feeling the difference, yet the connection.

Len took the pistol in her right hand and showed Lucia how her fingers were positioned around the stock, her index finger resting lightly on the trigger. "Now watch carefully," she said, though Lucia was already doing so.

She raised her arm until it was outstretched, straight at the elbow. With her thumb, she clicked something on the pistol. Turning her head, she looked along her arm. Lucia watched her eyes focus on the distance and then on the pistol in her hand. She stopped breathing, and Lucia did the same. Her finger moved on the trigger, and the loud bang made Lucia jump. She watched Len's arm absorb the kick of the shot, and a small cloud of smoke floated from the pistol to be carried away on the breeze.

Lowering her arm, Len strode away from Lucia through the trees in the direction she had fired. Lucia hurried after her. About fifty feet away, Len stopped to peer at the trunk of a large tree. She smiled triumphantly and placed her hand on Lucia's arm, drawing her in to look at the place where the metal ball was lodged in the tree trunk.

"You'll have to take my word this was the tree I was aiming for, of course," she said.

"Of course." Lucia did not doubt her.

"Now it's your turn," Len said. A nervous thrill quickened Lucia's heart.

Before Len passed her pistol to Lucia, she cleaned the barrel with a piece of cloth attached to another metal rod she removed from the pouch at her side. She handed Lucia the pistol once more, and while it was still baffling to Lucia, it did not bear the same menace, now she saw how easily Len had controlled its lethal force. It was not difficult to pour a little powder from the horn Len handed her into the muzzle or to drop the ball in after it. Ramming it home with the short metal rod required more force than it had appeared and gave Lucia her first moment of doubt. Opening the pan to prime it with the powder was equally more difficult than Len had made it seem, and Lucia's fingers had no strength. Merely loading the pistol seemed like an enormous achievement once it was done, and Lucia felt her face flush with pride.

"It's nothing if you can't fire it," Len said, rather ruining the sentiment that had been swelling Lucia's heart. She drew a deep breath and raised her arm.

"Firstly, where are you planning on firing it?" Len asked.

Lucia's eyes scanned the trees ahead. She chose one of the thickest trunks in her view. "At the oak there."

"Very well. Turn so you face this way," Len said. She gestured that Lucia should turn sideways to her target. "Now, stretch your arm more, make it straighter."

A muscle in Lucia's upper arm trembled as she attempted to do as Len instructed. "No. More than that." Len grasped Lucia's wrist firmly with her warm, strong fingers and pulled her arm until it was straight. "There," she said, as Lucia battled to recover from the sudden shock of Len's touch and to ignore the burning ache beginning in her shoulder, unused to such manoeuvres. "Now, look along your arm and along the barrel. When you are ready, press your finger on the trigger slowly, don't snatch at it."

Lucia squinted along her outstretched arm and over the unfamiliar metal of the barrel in her hand. She saw the thick trunk of the oak ahead of her. She fought the trembling in her aching limb and pulled her finger back on the cold trigger.

The explosion was louder than Lucia expected, and she flinched as the pistol kicked back at her arm like an angry creature with a life of its own. There was a prickling sensation on the skin of her hand, and she looked down at it in consternation.

"It's just the powder," Len said, "it burns a little." Lucia smelled the acrid sulphur of the powder smoke before it drifted away through the trees. She handed the pistol back to Len hurriedly but could not help a wide smile creeping over her face.

Together they went to examine the target, and Lucia was astonished and delighted to see the small metal ball embedded in the thick trunk. "Though you could hardly have missed such a big tree," Len said. "And the question is, could you do it again?"

Her words struck Lucia as a challenge she could not resist. She wanted to prove herself to Len, show her capabilities and her ability to learn. She wanted Len to be impressed and pleased with her, and not for a moment did she question why she should want the approval of an outlaw. Len was that no longer. She was the woman who saw with startling ease into Lucia's heart. She was the woman who had opened Lucia's eyes. She was beautiful.

The realisation struck her suddenly and swiftly. Len was beautiful. It was an odd thing to notice at such a moment. Len narrowed her eyes, and Lucia realised she was staring. Feeling her cheeks grow warm, she quickly turned her attention back to the pistol in her hand.

Lucia fired the pistol several more times that morning, until the procedure of loading the ball and priming the pan were familiar, if not habit. She was elated to find she managed to hit the tree she was aiming at, all but once when her ball disappeared through the forest. By the time Len had mercy and allowed her to return to the clearing, her arm ached in a way she had never before experienced, but she was oddly delighted.

It was not until later Lucia remembered, with a cold shudder of fear, you did not learn to fire a pistol so you could aim at tree trunks.

Chapter Thirteen

"But surely you see that is not a practical suggestion? There are the militia, to begin with, let alone the turnpike wardens and various gamekeepers and lodge porters if we were to take that route." Len glared at Bill Wilcock and hoped he would see sense. Julian and William stood by her side, but they knew she was capable of fighting her own battles. Bill's men lurked a safe distance behind him, and it was not clear if they were supporting him or merely wanted to hear the discussion.

"We managed to plan well enough without you, what makes you think you can come here now and tell us how to manage better?" Bill showed no signs of backing down.

"Because I have been the terror of travellers in these parts for years, and yet I have not been apprehended. You are a ragtag bunch of stockingers who terrify no one and have thus far been merely lucky not to end in a gaol cell." Len crossed her arms and refused to give way. She would not risk the lives of her men—of Lucia—and the successful destruction of her father's workshop because Bill was too proud to recognise when he should bow to someone—even a woman—with better knowledge and experience.

"If we are seen, we can be merely village folk who have been making merry and are on our way to our beds."

"A gang of men on the roads in the night is enough to arouse suspicion in these times we live in, Bill, you know that as well as I. The county must be protected from the invasion of revolutionary ideas from France. The gentry are terrified of the people. Shadows in the night are shot at. Is that how you want this to end?"

Bill did not answer right away. Len knew she'd won this particular argument, though she suspected there would be more flashpoints with Bill over the remaining days until the raid. He resented her leadership abilities, her calculating mind, the unexpected presence of a gentlewoman in his clearing. And yet he would not send her and the men away. He knew the raid stood more chance of success with Len's input, and he valued the food and coins she was able to provide his men. She was running low on such things. It was time to go to work again.

Bill looked at his men as if for support. Finding none, he looked back to Len. She raised an eyebrow. "What you say has some merit. I will think on it."

"That is all I ask." Len nodded. Bill turned from her and stalked away into the woods. His men trailed after him. Len exchanged a glance with Julian and William, thankful for their loyal support.

"We must ride out tonight. Keep Bill satisfied."

"You still think it's worth the risk? Hiding here?" Julian's question contained no challenge.

"For now." Len understood. She asked the questions of herself too. Was this all about revenge on her father? She reassured herself over and over again that it was not. This was the safest place to hide for now, the best place to lie low. It also gave her valuable insight into the other goings on in the shadows in the county. She was not so bad a leader that she would let personal revenge take priority over good sense. Was she?

"Tonight. The north road?" William's mind was clearly more focused on the immediate future.

"No. No risks at all. We take the Mansfield road, east of the Rose and Crown inn. Even if there is only one carriage tonight, it will do for now."

"There are only we three," Julian said.

"I know, Julian. But we three have pistols and the element of surprise. It has been enough before and will be again. No well-guarded carriages. Perhaps we will just look for solitary travellers, even if the rewards are poor. For now we must just survive."

"And survive we will, unless God wills it otherwise." William shrugged.

"Thank you, William. Pray that he's on our side." Julian grinned and patted William on the shoulder good-naturedly.

Len smiled with them. Then movement in the periphery of her vision drew her eye towards the tumbledown cottage. Lucia was emerging from the crooked doorway with a pail of water, which she emptied onto the forest floor. Len had no idea how Lucia had occupied herself while she had been debating strategy with Bill, but clearly it was in doing some task not usually suited to one of her social standing. She smiled. Then her heart plummeted. Tonight Lucia would remember just what manner of woman Len was, just how this life she was so drawn to was funded. Would Lucia be frightened, condemning? Or worse?

The contemplation of how to inform Lucia about this evening's plans, and how to be sure she could be left alone with the frame-breakers safely, preoccupied Len for the rest of the afternoon, though she dismantled and cleaned her pistol and helped to gather wood for the fire. She was still very quiet later that night as they cooked meat on a spit in the fire. Clearly Lucia had been washing their scant utensils and plates earlier, for they were suddenly free from the dried remains of previous meals which had clung to them before. Len wasn't sure whether Lucia would want her to comment on her work or not, or what she was expected to say, so she said nothing.

Just after twilight, Len found Lucia sitting quietly in the doorway of the cottage, keeping her distance from the men. She wanted very badly to sit and talk with her, to explain the reasons why tonight's action was necessary. She checked herself before she began to speak. Never had she felt the need to explain herself to anyone. It almost caused her to resent Lucia. How could it be that she had such a hold over Len? Yes, she was beautiful, but Len Hawkins was surely too wise and weary of the world to be swayed so far off course by a beautiful woman.

The problem was she did not feel as though Lucia was compromising her. She felt strengthened by their conversations, by Lucia's mere presence. It was good to have something pure to protect, rather than simply a meagre living to strive for. Was such thinking misguided? No doubt Julian would say it clouded her judgement. She would heed that. She could not allow her feelings for Lucia, however intoxicating, to influence her actions, her ability to think clearly. Especially not tonight. It was too dangerous.

"Julian, William, and I must leave for a few hours," she said, more abruptly than she intended. She saw the alarm in Lucia's face and added, "Bill assures me you will be quite safe. I have come to trust him, you know. He is not a bad man, though arrogant."

Lucia smiled thinly, and Len sensed she found some irony in Len faulting arrogance in another. From anyone but Lucia that smile and its implications would have provoked resentment in Len. And yet she found herself tempted to laugh at herself, to smile along with Lucia.

"If you trust him, I will trust you," Lucia said. Len felt her whole body react to the notion of Lucia's trust in her, and she swallowed hard. "Where is it you must go?"

Len's heart beat harder. Her mouth felt dry. Inwardly cursing her weakness, she found she could not form the right words. Lucia had shown such trust in her. It made her feel more of a criminal than ever. "I do not choose to tell you. You will understand, of course."

She heard the strain in her own words and knew Lucia was intelligent enough to understand their meaning. Their eyes met in acknowledgement, but all Lucia said was, "I will see you later then."

"Yes." Len strode away from Lucia immediately before she felt weakened further. As she mounted Oberon, her tricorn, scarf, and gloves removing any trace of the woman about her, she felt Lucia's eyes on her through the near darkness. Cursing herself, she put the woman out of her mind and nudged the horse into a canter. Julian and William were alongside her on their mounts. Len felt the wind on her face and cleared her mind, let her instincts take over. She needed her wits about her tonight.

Lucia remained in the cottage while Len, Julian, and William were absent, determined not to think on what they were doing. She longed to warm herself by the fire roaring in the clearing, but the idea of placing herself there among the frame-breakers frightened her. For the first time since Len had untied her hands, she felt her own vulnerability. Len made her brave, but without her, Lucia felt lost and quite frightened. She retreated to the musty bed and sat—her knees pulled up to her chest, the woollen blanket around her hunched shoulders—in the darkness. She waited, trying to stave off the trembling of her fingers. Thankfully, Bill Wilcock did not see fit to torment her, and not one of the men approached the cottage while she was alone.

About three hours later, to her relief, Lucia heard the distant approach of hooves. She knew it to be Len, Julian, and William, since Bill posted some of his men to be lookouts at night, and they would have warned of the approach of anyone who did not have friendly intentions.

An odd anxiety knitting itself in her stomach, she stood up and folded the blanket absent-mindedly. She listened to the sounds without, as the horses were tied up and conversations took place. Excitement coloured the voices and movements she heard. Somehow, she did not want to venture outside. It was a jubilation she found impossible to share. She was still standing in the middle of the room pressing her cold fingers together when Len entered the cottage, bringing the chill air of the night with her.

"Lucia?"

"Yes, I'm here," Lucia said dully. She heard Len lighting the lantern, moving around removing her hat and gloves. Len entered the bedroom, the light swinging around her.

Len passed Lucia a bundle of cloth. "Here," she said. "This should keep you warmer." Lucia unrolled the bundle to find a lady's velvet travelling cloak. Matching gloves fell onto the floor. "And these will be better by far than those slippers," Len added. She placed a pair of leather boots at Lucia's feet.

Lucia looked at the items in astonishment. The velvet was expensive and soft under her fingers. She bent down to pick up the gloves and felt they were lined, to be especially warm. Her stomach lurched. "I do not want them," she said flatly.

"Do not be silly, Lucia." There was anger in Len's tone. Lucia knew Len had already guessed the cause of her protest.

"I don't want them."

"And why is that, may I ask?"

"You know perfectly well."

"No, I don't."

"Where have you been this evening?"

"I think you know."

"These things—this fine cloak, these boots," Lucia said, thrusting a hand towards them, "did you take them from a lady travelling the Mansfield road? Did you hold a pistol in her face and demand she give them to you or you would kill her?" Lucia's confused anger was barely concealed now as she remembered her own fear in the situation she described. How could Len think she would want to benefit from such a terrible deed?

"I did not make her strip them from her body at the roadside," Len said, her own anger all too apparent. "They were in a trunk in a carriage. And no pistol was pointed at any lady tonight."

"Her father then, or her brother? Maybe a servant?"

Len's silence gave Lucia her answer.

"I will not wear them."

"You choose your times to be moral when they suit you, Lucia." The accusation was almost a snarl of contempt.

"What do you mean?" Lucia was growing ever more furious.

Len's concealed anger exploded into a rage Lucia had not suspected, and her tone was somewhere between wounded and venomous as she replied. "You have travelled with us, lived with us for several days now. You did not come to us through choice, I will admit, but you have had the opportunity to return home several times since. You chose not to. You eat our food, drink our tea, accept our shelter and protection all so you can experience a breath of freedom. And then, when you are confronted with the reality behind that liberty, you shy away from it, condemning what you previously accepted and those who you seemed to befriend."

"I never accepted it!" Tears prickled Lucia's eyes.

"Do not fool yourself, Lucia, there was not even really anything implicit about it. You have always known us for what we are, and you took the benefits of our life for yourself. Now you have a fit of morality as if refusing a cloak absolves you of it all."

"I do not need to seek absolution." Lucia felt the truth of Len's accusations and her words were shaky. What pained her more than the exposure of her confused morality was Len's all-too-apparent anger with her. To have incurred Len's displeasure seemed the most awful of consequences, though she could not understand why this woman's opinion mattered so very much to her. Len was relentless, her expression hard and resentful.

"You have been as guilty as any of us, in your own way. Do you not imagine the agonies of worry your father and sister go through are far worse than anything they experienced at our hands on the turnpike? You have been fed from the proceeds of our so-terrible actions. Believe me, Lucia, you would not be here now, on this jaunt you seem to be so enjoying, if we were not what we are."

In Len's words, Lucia was sure she heard Len's own regret, her own distaste for the way she earned her living, but also her grim conclusion she had no option but to do as she did. Regret turned to anger with that knowledge, and she found the confidence to speak her mind. "Do not patronise me. You were once little different from what I am and did not always approve of robbing from travellers, I have no doubt."

"No, I did not. But neither did I accept the hospitality of those who did such things."

"You call this hospitality?" Lucia said. She did not really feel the incredulity that coloured her words.

"Oh, I apologise, Miss Foxe, is the accommodation not to your satisfaction?" Len's words were an angry and resentful growl.

Lucia did not reply instantly. Instead she drew a deep breath. The tension of bitterness and wounded feelings between them seemed to thicken the darkness in the room.

"Wear the cloak," Len said, moving towards Lucia slightly.

"No."

"I should have expected nothing more." Len's words were almost muttered to herself. Lucia baulked at the disappointment Len made no attempt to hide.

"What do you mean by that?" Her words were sharp with humiliation and hostility, her own disappointment. She had thought Len had developed a sort of respect for her, that there was something in common between them. Now it lay in tatters and Lucia's skin prickled with anger.

"I mean what I say. I clearly expected too much of you. You have been sheltered, cosseted your whole life, in a way I never was. I thought there was something the same about us, but I was wrong. You are simply acting out a drama. I will not be a player in your performance any longer."

"What do you mean?"

"You are not what I thought you to be." At her statement, Lucia felt a growing hollowness in the pit of her stomach. Len was not done yet. "And I think you should return to your home tomorrow, where you will not be sullied by keeping company with immoral creatures such as we are."

"I will not." Though her head told her Len was right, Lucia could not persuade her stubborn heart which seemed to ache with every hard beat. "You know nothing of what I am."

Len did not reply quickly. Instead, she moved towards Lucia, threatening. She seemed a much larger presence in the shadowy room than Lucia. As she moved, shortening the distance between them, she seemed also to compress the air between their two bodies, air thick with tension and anger, and force it through Lucia's very skin and into her body until her blood seemed to boil. She began to tremble and her face burned. She heard her pulse throbbing and her breathing grow uneven. Yet Lucia did not recognise what she felt as either fear or anger. This was something else. A new emotion she had never known before.

Len leaned forward until her face was close to Lucia's. "You will do as I say," she said quietly.

"I will not," Lucia said, in a tremulous whisper. "I am not one of your men."

"You wish to keep immoral company after all?" Len's voice was a whisper too, not hostile, yet not friendly. Her eyes reflected the light of the lantern, but it was difficult to make out the exact expression of her features.

Lucia swallowed heavily. "I wish to remain with you." The confession made her almost dizzy.

"With thieves and frame-breakers?"

"With *you*."

Len's tone softened as she went on. "Yet you choose ignorance of what I do in the dark hours of the night?"

"I am not ignorant of it."

"You do not approve of it." Len was so close, Lucia felt her warm breath on her own face.

"It frightens me."

"Life can be a frightening thing. But do you feel the thrill it brings?"

"Yes," Lucia murmured, hot tears of something like shame pricking her eyes. The tension between them mounted further. Lucia knew something was going to happen but did not know what. Then for an instant, Len's lips met Lucia's. In surprise Lucia pulled back at the same moment as Len hastily withdrew herself.

"I am sorry, Lucia." There was heavy strain in Len's tone. But Lucia was deaf to the apology. Strange sensations she could not understand had taken hold of her. She stepped towards Len once more. As if they were both drawn by some invisible force in the shadowy room, Len moved at the same moment. Lucia's nose brushed hers as she again sought her lips. Len's mouth was hot and tasted faintly of brandy. Wrapping her arms about Len's lean body, Lucia clung to her with a need only just awakened, as Len's lips pressed hers and they breathed as one.

Lucia was swept away on emotions she felt had always been in her heart without her being aware of them. All their talk of liberation and choice, and the exhilaration of galloping with Len, were nothing to this. She had no learning to tell her if this was right or wrong, and she did not care. She only hungered for Len with a strength of desire she had never known she could feel.

She was aware of every press of Len's hands as they slid over her back and to her hips. She had never been in such close contact with any person, never craved further contact so greatly. She bunched her hands in the fabric of Len's dark velvet cloak, her fingers burning, yearning for more, but uncertainty holding her back.

Gently, Len eased back from her. Her lips tingling from their kiss, Lucia waited in dread for questions, apologies, or refusals. But Len did not speak. Her warm fingers were slightly rough on Lucia's face as she caressed her cheek softly. Lucia turned to kiss those exploring fingertips without a second's thought or hesitation. She heard Len catch her breath. In the next moment, Len's fingers were at her own throat, unfastening her cloak and discarding it on the bed, pulling at the buttons of her coat and then tearing at the layers of her clothing below. Lucia did not help her undress, she watched, transfixed, not able to see every precise detail in the half-light of the lantern, but still seeing wonders unveiled before her. Before long, Len was gloriously naked from her waist upwards before her. The light flickered golden on her exposed skin, the shadows caressing the curves of her small breasts. Lucia's cheeks burned, but she did not think of turning away in her modesty. She could not have turned away.

Lucia dropped her shawl to the floor. The cold of the night could not reach her. Len moved closer to her again and slid one of her hands around Lucia's waist and to her back, pulling Lucia towards her. She bent her head, and her breath, then her lips, were on Lucia's throat. Lucia shivered with pleasure at those caresses, the heat of Len's mouth over where her pulse beat close to her skin. Len moved her kisses lower over Lucia's throat. As she did so, she reached for the already-low neckline of Lucia's dress and eased it lower. Lucia put her hands on Len's naked shoulders and let her have her way, unable to protest or resist. Considerations of modesty and morality meant nothing to her. She closed her eyes and simply let the sensations fill her, beginning to understand just why she was so very compelled by Len and yet still in wonder at what was unfolding between them. Heat was throbbing in parts of her body previously mysterious to her, and she knew she needed Len's touch to cure the ache. That need was all she knew.

Len pulled her gown lower still, and Lucia felt her breasts exposed to the night air. That sudden cold was replaced moments later with the heat of Len's mouth. Lucia could not help but gasp with the pleasure that swept through her. Her gasp became a moan, and she heard the sound as though it came from the throat of someone else.

Len stood upright, her hands still on Lucia's arms. She was breathing hard. Lucia was trembling with pleasure and wonder, in anticipation of she did not know what.

"Miss Foxe, you are in danger..." Len whispered.

"I feel quite safe."

"You are in the hands of an outlaw." Lucia took Len's hands in her own and squeezed them softly, knowing she granted permission with that pressure. Despite that, Len seemed to hesitate, as if her own words had given her pause for thought, for doubt. They were both motionless for a long moment. Lucia's heart throbbed, and she could not stand the suspense any longer.

"You are a thief. What will you take from me this night?"

"What riches do you offer me?"

"Everything I have."

Len caught her breath at Lucia's words. Lucia herself felt giddy with what she had said without a thought and had no wish to retract, even as she was not entirely sure what she offered. Len's lips sought hers, a soft, questioning kiss. When Lucia responded with her own kiss, Len seemed to ignite with passion. Her hands tightened on Lucia's arms. "Everything?"

"Yes."

Even in the darkness, Lucia saw Len's slow smile, felt the intensity of her gaze. "Then you must stand and deliver, Miss Foxe..." Len gripped Lucia's gown and pulled hard. The thin muslin was around her waist and Len's mouth was on her exposed flesh, hungry and demanding. Lucia felt the fire growing in her loins and wondered if one could explode from such pleasure.

Len was almost frightened by her own need, the craving to consume which threatened to overtake her. Lucia's skin was smooth against Len's lips and tongue. She had thought it impossible to ever feel this way again. But the unlikely, naïve Miss Lucia Foxe had crept beneath her skin. The confident, angry, liberated Lucia she had encountered on her return to the cottage tonight had been too much to resist. No longer did this feel like an immoral act, taking advantage of her prisoner or of Lucia's naïvety, with all the dangers and questions that brought. It felt like a coupling of equals. And Lucia's hunger, though Len knew she did not have the learning or experience to understand it, seemed to match her own. Len wanted to feed that hunger, wanted Lucia to know the pleasures she had been starved of.

Len pulled Lucia closer, until their breasts were crushed together, and kissed her again, deeper this time. Lucia moaned sweetly into her mouth, though Len doubted Lucia knew she had made a sound. She could feel Lucia's temperature increasing in every moment.

She gripped Lucia's shoulders and pushed her backwards towards the old bed. Lucia moved with her willingly. Len could not help herself. The urge to possess Lucia was so strong, to show her what she was capable of experiencing. She pushed harder and Lucia subsided onto the bed, Len above her. Len kissed her again, sliding her hand over the softness of Lucia's breast where her nipple tightened against Len's palm, over the curve of her slender waist, until she encountered the muslin of Lucia's gown. It was an obstacle easily overcome. She reached lower for Lucia's hem, and raised it to Lucia's thighs quickly.

Lucia gasped and lifted herself on her elbows. Len smiled, for she could see enough of Lucia's expression to know she was not alarmed.

"Do I offend your modesty, Lucia?"

"Yes."

"Do you command me to desist?"

"No. I cannot forget I am in your power." There was a hint of musical laughter in Lucia's tone, but there was also a need, a desire which called to Len powerfully.

"That is true." Her hand found the tender inside of Lucia's thigh. She was rewarded with another satisfied yet needy gasp.

"Do you mean to ravish me?"

"Yes." Len's hand moved higher still, easing Lucia's thighs apart. Lucia did not resist for a moment. Her sheer trust moved Len, stirred the heat low in her abdomen. "Do you know what it is to be ravished Lucia?"

"I do not."

Her realisation of Lucia's total innocence caused Len to hesitate for a moment. "I would not hurt you."

"I wish to learn." Lucia's whole body stirred with impatience.

"I can show you." Len heard her own voice trembling.

"Then I beg you, do so without delay," Lucia said. Len could do nothing but obey. She pushed higher, shifting the material of Lucia's skirts out of the way, until her fingers found the heat and moisture she sought. Lucia was satin soft against her fingers, and Len could feel the swollen wetness of her desire.

"Breathe, Lucia," she murmured, aware suddenly that Lucia had stopped doing so. Lucia gasped at the air as Len's fingers moved, and Lucia arched her back, one hand reaching for Len, finding her arm and squeezing hard. That pressure was an encouragement, not a warning.

Len left her hand where it was as she moved to lie on the bed with Lucia, her body still half covering her. She slipped one arm under Lucia's neck to hold her closer, feeling Lucia's skin sticky against her sensitive breasts. She kissed Lucia's forehead as she moved her fingers lower, exploring, hesitating slightly.

"You would give me everything?" she whispered. She could feel Lucia's body pulling her inside.

Lucia nodded frantically. "Yes. Everything."

Len eased her fingers forward gently, feeling Lucia's body resist the invasion, before welcoming it with a flood of silky moisture. Emotion built in Len's chest, and her eyes stung with unshed tears she could not explain to herself as she kissed Lucia's soft lips. Lucia tensed in her arms and moaned again, but Len did not hesitate this time. She slid her fingers deeper. Lucia's hips rose and her kiss became hungry, encouraging Len further. Len was filled with want, to show Lucia the fulfilment of those so-very-apparent desires. Before they slept tonight she would reveal to Lucia the mysteries of her body, and in doing so she knew she would find greater satisfaction for herself than she had on any night for many a year. Lucia sighed and writhed in her arms. Len kissed her harder and drew out another sigh with her fingers. Heat pulsed through her, and she recognised the aggressive, wanton urges. But there was something else too. Her heart was full with more than the simple pleasure of a woman sighing at her touch. It was no use denying it. That she loved Lucia was a truth and a burden she would have to accept. It was a love that could go nowhere. But in these dark hours, it could at least find its full expression and fulfilment.

❖

Lucia awoke with a start as the light seeped through the thick ivy. Len's arm was heavy and warm across her chest. She followed its lines to Len's naked shoulder and felt a thrill creep into her heart. She felt she should be ashamed of such a feeling, but she was not. She realised her own nakedness and pulled the blanket closer. Beneath the rough wool of the blanket, she felt the soft, heavy velvet of the travelling cloak. She allowed her fingers to caress it, as a smile she could not prevent spread onto her face.

Len was breathing lightly and regularly. Her dark hair spread over her shoulders and cascaded over half of her face, which was turned towards Lucia. The light in the room was a greenish gloom but still she seemed flushed. Her eyelashes made perfect dark half-moons on her cheeks. Lucia was unsure whether the world would view Len as a handsome woman, but in those moments she was the most beautiful creature Lucia had ever seen.

Gazing at her, Lucia remembered what had passed in the night. A dream, yet one she could not have dreamed until last night. Len had opened her mind and revealed so much to her. The physical sensations she was capable of astounded and thrilled her. And somehow her heart seemed open too, as though she could see it and understand it finally. For the first time she believed she knew a little of what was meant by real love. But was such a thing possible? It had been so clear in the night. In that glorious and surprising moment of crisis when Lucia had almost thought Len had killed her with pleasure, she had felt such clarity. This was perfection, the pinnacle of all she had ever wanted. In the morning light it seemed rather more confusing. Yet, looking at Len in her slumber, it was hard to dwell on the obstacles.

Lucia pulled a warm hand from beneath the velvet of the cloak and touched Len lightly on her shoulder. Her eyes fluttered into wakefulness quickly. After a moment, she smiled.

"Good morning," Lucia whispered.

"Good morning." Len's smile grew wider. "Where is your morality now, Lucia?"

"You have stolen it from me."

"You risk these things when you make friends of thieves."

"I will not be returning home today," Lucia said.

"I was not going to ask you to." Len rose to a sitting position, the blanket dropping to reveal the slight swell of her breasts. Lucia's cheeks burned as she looked away. She felt Len's fingers firm on her chin, turning her face back.

"You are not ashamed?" Lucia heard uncertainty in Len's question.

"I did not think it was possible," she said hesitantly, "and indeed, it should be shameful." Lucia paused. "But I am not ashamed."

"Many more things are possible, Lucia, than you would dream," Len said, as her fingers stroked the side of Lucia's neck. Lucia grew warm at her touch. She watched Len's expression. Her demeanour suggested no surprise at what had occurred between them.

"But you knew…or you…" she said, wanting to understand but unsure what question to ask.

"I knew nothing, Lucia, I only felt."

"But how did you…how could you possibly…?" Len looked away from her, closed her eyes briefly. A shadow passed over her expression. Lucia had seen that shadow once before when they had talked…talked of Hattie, the dressmaker. Realisation dawned quickly. "The dressmaker! Julian's sister?" It was half a question, half an answer.

"Yes," Len murmured.

"She was more than your friend. You loved her?"

"Yes."

Lucia knew then Len had not merely been talking to Hattie when her father had happened upon them. She felt Len's pain, her loss, her humiliation as a sharp tug at her own heart. Compulsively, she reached out and enclosed Len's hand in her own. Len's fingers tensed for a moment then entwined with hers.

"I understand." Did she? Lucia knew she could only imagine the pain Len had felt, first upon her father's intrusion, her forced separation from Hattie, and then, terribly, on the death of the woman she loved. Could she love again after such tragedy? Lucia imagined Len being torn from her in similar circumstances and felt a cold, creeping terror.

Then the horrible comprehension came upon her: Len was not hers; she had no claim on her. Lucia's life was on such a radically different course to Len's the likelihood of Len being wrenched from her grip was drawing ever closer. It had not occurred to Lucia to consider it for more than a passing moment before, but now everything had changed. She could not bear the thought of losing Len. She looked away from her, fighting the threat of overwhelming sadness.

Len rose from the bed and Lucia watched her dress, pleased of the distraction from her melancholy reflections, marvelling at how the breeches, shirt, and waistcoat transformed the lines of her body—which though it was angular, was yet still feminine—into the less distinct form she was used to. Now she contemplated it, Len did not appear wholly like a man, it was only she did not seem to be a woman. That was the secret of the illusion.

When Lucia emerged from the cottage a short while later, to find Len in deep conversation with Julian not that far from the door, she was wearing a heavy, dark green velvet travelling cloak and soft leather boots, which were only a little too large for her feet.

Chapter Fourteen

Tensions grew in the clearing throughout the next day. Lucia, trying to keep her distance while never letting Len out of her sight, heard Len's voice raised on several occasions as she clashed with Bill Wilcock over some detail or another. She even heard hushed words of disagreement between Len and Julian.

Despite the change in the nature of their relations with each other, Len still did not make Lucia party to the plans or the confrontations. Lucia found herself partly envious of the intimacy Len shared with Julian, mildly offended to be pushed aside so easily, and yet grateful she did not need to hear the terrible details or be involved in the arguments. She was well aware her presence was a complication for Len and Bill, but she knew now Len would not send her away. For that she was thankful. Whatever thoughts of home and the future troubled her, the thought of being parted from Len before it was necessary was one she could not countenance. Late in the morning, as she watched Len from a distance in animated but cheerful conversation with Julian, she knew she finally understood what love was. That she felt that love for a woman, an outlaw at that, did not feel so very remarkable. She could not deny the strength of the feeling. That such a feeling could never be carried with her into her day-to-day life was not something she chose to dwell on.

For now, just watching Len, anticipating the touch of those hands, the feel of their bodies pressed close in the night, was enough. Everything about Len was wonderful. Her stride as she walked through the clearing, the shape of her legs in her breeches and boots, the angle at which she wore her tricorn, the self-assurance in her expression, the initial hostility with which she seemed to meet everyone who addressed her: Lucia was able to see all of these things anew, and she delighted in all of them. Once she had thought herself envious, however unlikely she was to don breeches and turn outlaw herself. Now she knew it was not envy, but love.

❖

Early in the afternoon, William and Daniel, the frame-breaker—between whom a friendship seemed to have developed—had gone to gather wood so the fire might warm the men until the fateful Friday evening. The other men were immovable by the fire, rubbing their hands ferociously. Lucia was glad of the cloak and boots, however ill-gotten, and had even resorted to wearing the gloves. The stitching upon them was very fine, which gave her only a slight qualm when she considered what they would have cost their rightful owner.

Len and Julian were standing aside from the other men, as Lucia noticed they so often did, talking easily. Julian appeared to be teasing Len, whose face was distinctly pink, and with a flash of anxiety Lucia wondered what it was about. Had Julian known the nature of the relationship between his sister and Len? Did he now come to understand what had taken place between Len and Lucia in the night? Tension squeezed her heart as she watched Len laugh at a casual comment he made. Not only would Lucia's modesty be embarrassed for him to have understood what had occurred, she also felt a vicious jealousy. The secret was Len's and it was hers. To tell it to Julian's—or anyone's—ears was to betray it, to sully it. The ferocity of the emotion tightened her throat and made it difficult to breathe.

Determined to gauge how much Julian understood, Lucia was approaching them across the brittle carpet of leaves when she was intercepted by Bill Wilcock in the company of Stephen Dale, one of the younger frame-breakers, who was tall and broad-shouldered, with piercing blue eyes rimmed with red and underlined by dark shadows

"You look ready for a carriage ride, miss," Bill said, looking Lucia up and down. He had not really engaged her in direct conversation since their confrontation near the fire, and she was a little startled when he addressed her.

"I am ready only to guard against the cold." Lucia hoped to continue her steps towards Len and Julian. However, Bill moved to stand in front of her, and a little intimidated, she halted and glared at him. "What is it?"

"No need to be so unkind, miss."

Lucia sighed and remembered Len had confided in her that she trusted Bill, even liked him. She moderated her expression. "Can I help you?"

"Yes, as a matter of fact. I've been wanting to speak with you."

"Yes?"

"You're part of the scenery here it seems, whatever I have to say about it," he began, "and since you don't seem to be causing us any trouble, I'm happy to have you. Nice to have a pretty woman about, if you'll forgive the sentiment." He leered at Lucia alarmingly and she withdrew slightly. Stephen Dale smiled in a way she did not like. "But you see, I'm wondering what exactly you're going to be doing while the rest of us take up arms and go to work. You going to stay here on your own? Because we might not be able to come back here, and I don't like the idea of you being left here. Could you even find your way out of the forest?"

"I am sure I could." In truth Lucia was terrified by the notion she might have to do so.

"And if I know her like I reckon I do," he gestured with his head towards where Len stood, "she ain't going to be letting you stay here alone, just in case. But equally, I don't want you coming with us. Too dangerous."

"I will keep myself safe."

"He don't mean dangerous for you, miss," Stephen Dale put in. Lucia looked at him with some hostility. These were the first words he had spoken to her. She wondered if his concerns had prompted this address from Bill. However, the question he confronted her with was indeed a good one. She knew she had not really considered what she would do while the workshop was raided. She had certainly not contemplated the possibility this hideout would be abandoned. She truly had very little concept of exactly where in the forest they were, and the chances of her making it out safely were not good. She did not want to put the safety of the men—and, more particularly, Len—at risk. As she looked at Bill, bewildered, she was relieved when the rustle of leaves heralded Len and Julian's arrival at their side.

"Bill?" Len said. She tried to keep her tone friendly. Lucia's discomfort could be plainly seen but she had to restrain her anger, her urge to defend, at least until she understood what Bill and Stephen wanted. "And Stephen too? How can Miss Foxe help you?"

"Maybe you can answer for her?" Bill's tone was challenging. Len knew he was unhappy with some aspect of the planned raid. That would not do. They had to work together, to cooperate and trust, if such a plot was to succeed.

"They wish to know what I will do. During the attack," Lucia said.

Her eyes met Len's, and it was all Len could do not to smile with the surge of emotion in her breast. God, but Lucia was beautiful. To know what lay behind that beauty gave her a joy she had not known she was still capable of feeling. But the joy was tainted with a sense of foreboding. Love had only led to sadness for her before. And now the threat to her elation was imminent and very real. For now, she had to appease Bill and Stephen. She made herself focus, looking directly at Bill as she spoke.

"Of course they want to know." She smiled in a way which suggested she had a ready answer for the question. She did not, of course, but she would not have Bill know that. She would not have him accuse her of what even she suspected was the truth: Lucia's presence did cloud her judgement. There was no way to justify Lucia's presence here, which could actually prove a danger to them all.

Now Bill waited and Len sensed Lucia did too, to see what her answer would be. "Miss Foxe will accompany us, since I cannot countenance leaving her here alone. But you have told me there is a thicket near the workshop, where we will take cover. Miss Foxe will stay there, hidden. She will hold the horses."

Bill raised his eyebrows. Len wondered if he thought it strange that she had not wanted to reconnoitre the workshop and its surroundings before the raid and had merely accepted his description of the landscape. Of course, she knew it far better than any of the frame-breakers, though she still had not informed Bill who Hawkins was to her. Bill looked dubious about her plan. Len turned to Lucia who looked pale and frightened, probably imagining herself in the said thicket, witness to a frame-breaking raid. Neither Lucia nor Bill spoke.

"Do you think that is a good idea?" Stephen Dale asked in the end, directing his question at Julian. His demeanour was agitated, as though he could not understand the casual manner his leader—and Len—adopted. Len would not have liked Stephen Dale in her band of men. She did not entirely trust him. Still, she had trusted Peter and Isaac, and that had led them all to this predicament. Was her judgement to blame? Was she about to make an even worse mistake in allowing Lucia to remain with her? But what would become of Lucia if she were to send her home now? What would become of her own heart?

"Miss Foxe is under my protection," she said firmly. "I think, in fact, we will need all of the men to attack the workshop, and it will be useful for her to attend to the horses."

"*We* have no horses to attend to." Bill was clearly not satisfied with her answer.

"We do and, therefore, in case we do not return, it is necessary we take them. They will aid in our escape should there be any trouble." Len made herself sound more certain than she felt.

"They will aid in your escape." Stephen Dale looked angry.

"They will aid us all, since it will be in our interest not to be found together." As Len spoke she realised her words made good sense, and she grew in confidence. "A band of many men on foot will attack that workshop. Two or three well-dressed riders will hardly seem frame-breakers if the militia is called. And if we should meet the militia upon the turnpike, Julian will tell them we saw a large band of shadowy men some miles hence, in the opposite direction."

"But what if the militia should happen to take you for those notorious highwaymen we all hear to be haunting this area?" Bill asked acerbically.

"If there are frame-breakers abroad, they will be the only concern of the militia," Len said. "You bring the threat of revolution from France, we merely inconvenience travellers."

"True enough," Bill replied, laughing good-naturedly.

Stephen still appeared sceptical. "We all know the ringleader of the highwaymen rides a black stallion," he pointed out. "If you are captured you will bring danger to all of us."

"Do you suspect I would give you away, should they drag me to the county gaol in chains?" Len asked him. She did not disguise her disgust at his suggestion she would betray them. She drew a calming breath to enable her to continue with less anger. "You do me little credit. But I tell you again, we will not be captured. You have there another reason why we must take Miss Foxe with us. The militia are hardly likely to take her for a highwayman. A lady with her groom, brother, and a manservant will be trusted and able to direct the militia as we wish." Her expression was triumphant. That Lucia's presence would lend credibility to their disguise had only just occurred to her, but the observation was valid.

"And Miss Foxe can now fire a pistol," Julian put in. "She will not need anyone to defend her." Len grinned and looked to Lucia, who smiled back. She clearly knew Julian's mockery was good-natured. Len was pleased to see the animosity between Julian and Lucia had faded.

Bill laughed and slapped Julian soundly on the back. He shook his head, looking at Len, "Who'd have thought?" he said, as if to himself. "But very well, you have your way, since I see its advantages." Stephen Dale's smile was weak, but he obviously sensed his protests would fall on deaf ears and said nothing.

Len looked at Lucia. Though she smiled, her blue eyes were wide and a little apprehensive. She had, after all, just learned what roles she would play in a frame-breaking raid. And yet Len saw the fear fade as she caught Lucia's eye. Lucia was brave, and what was more, she trusted Len completely. It was a weighty responsibility. But Len was honoured to bear it. She knew then, she would give her life to keep Lucia safe.

❖

As night fell, the men sat in the glow of the fire, uncharacteristically silent. Their thoughts were no doubt beginning to turn to the action before them, which Lucia understood was the largest and most risky raid they had yet undertaken. The anticipation seemed to be affecting Len too. She rose to her feet and made for the cottage early. Lucia waited a few minutes, during which she grew agitated and Julian eyed her curiously, before rising herself and following Len into the dilapidated building.

She found Len perched on the edge of the bed, her hands clasped in her lap, the lantern not yet lighted. Lucia went to sit next to her and the bed groaned beneath them.

"Is something the matter?" Lucia asked, unsure whether she should intrude but compelled to comfort Len if she could.

"Not really." Len's voice was quiet.

"Then what is it?"

"Nothing at all."

"Are you worried about the raid?" Lucia ventured. She had no real idea what emotions Len would be feeling on such an occasion.

"No." Len said shortly, and Lucia wondered whether to press any further. Then Len continued unprompted, "I am not worried by what we will do, or the dangers. But I have not returned to my father's property since he cast me from my previous life."

"And you are worried by this?"

"Not worried. Only it gives me a little more to contemplate than I would like."

"You remember your family?" Lucia longed to comfort Len. Yet Len did not seem to be mourning her former life.

"I think of them. Not with fondness. But my lack of affection in itself is pause for thought, do you not think?"

"They treated you badly."

"No worse than many are treated, as you pointed out, Lucia."

"But you could not settle for that. You wanted to choose for yourself."

"So I did."

"You do not regret that, I know it." Lucia wanted to tell Len just how much she admired her for her lack of regret, for her freedom. How much she loved her.

"I do not Lucia. But when I look at you, the sacrifices you have already made, I am frightened. I see how far I have come from what I was. I would not force you over the same difficult path."

"You do not force me anywhere. I choose my path."

"You are my prisoner. You choose nothing."

"You contradict your own words. I am no prisoner. I could return home now and you would allow it." Lucia was confident in her words, mildly indignant Len would suggest she had no option in her present circumstances.

"Tell me you do not feel bound here."

"I cannot. But I am not in chains."

"Then what keeps you?"

Lucia thought for a moment. Len kept her here. But could she be brave enough to say it? "The feel of the wind in my hair. Of the trees all around me—"

"Liberation, you mean?" Len sounded scornful. "What if that is a myth I have spun and pulled you into with me?"

"It is no myth." Lucia summoned everything she felt for Len. "And besides, you did not allow me to finish."

"My apologies. Please do." Len raised curious eyes to Lucia's.

"I am bound…by you." Lucia felt giddy as she said the words.

"By me?" Len did not look surprised, though the pleasure in her expression was tempered by a sort of weary concern.

"I cannot—will not—leave you now."

"I would not have you leave either."

There was a long pause, heavy with emotions Lucia was sure they both felt but could not express.

"Are you not frightened at all?" Lucia said in the end, when she could not find the words to explain her feelings.

"Maybe a little." Len reached for Lucia's hand. Lucia pulled the velvet glove quickly from her fingers and clasped Len's tightly. "Which is unusual in itself."

"What is?"

"My being a little frightened. I am not, usually, before we go to work."

"This is different."

"Yes."

"I am more than a little frightened," Lucia confided.

"I expect you are," Len said. She turned to face Lucia properly. "What have I led you into, Lucia?"

"I repeat, you have not led me."

"Yes, I have. You cannot deny it. If it were not for me, you would hardly be about to witness a frame-breaking raid. Nor would you be in a forest hideout with outlaws."

"No, I wouldn't."

"Then it is my fault."

"Yes. But it is my choice."

"But did I allow you to choose, truly?" There was a strain in Len's voice.

"Yes, you did." Lucia was positive of the truth in her own heart. "I made my decision to be here."

"Do you regret it?"

Lucia squeezed Len's hand more tightly, certain of her reply. "How could I?"

"But afterwards? What will you do?"

Lucia had no answer for her. The notion of *afterwards*, the inevitable necessity of her return to her family, was distant, still impossible. And now she did not only fear the loss of this freedom she had tasted. Now she feared losing Len too.

Len's hand caressed Lucia's shoulder and her other turned Lucia's face to hers. Her fingers were in Lucia's hair as their lips met. As they sank together onto the bed, Lucia pressed herself to Len's warmth, her strength, and thought, if she had to die, there could be no better time. The cold and dark, the oncoming violence and danger, receded from her mind until there was only Len and the sounds of the forest outside.

Len's kisses deepened, moving over Lucia's chin, her jaw, to her throat. Hot sensations stirred deep inside Lucia as she wrapped her arms around Len's solid form, holding her close. She ran her hands over Len's back and was surprised when Len moaned hungrily into her mouth. To be able to have such an effect, to give such pleasure, to a woman like Len seemed impossible. And yet here was the evidence that it was within her power to do just that.

Len sat up long enough to remove her clothes. Lucia lay breathing hard, missing Len's proximity. The knowledge that Len was naked when she returned to Lucia's side was almost too much for Lucia to bear. There was nothing indecent about this, and she did not even consider the morality. To be this way with Len felt more natural and right than anything in Lucia's previous experience. She was not ashamed. She ached to prove that to Len, to explore her own power over the other woman's feelings.

Gently, she put her hands on Len's shoulders. The warm skin beneath her fingertips was smooth and wonderful. She pushed, urging Len to lie on her back on the bed next to her. Without a question, Len obeyed that pressure, sighing as she relaxed against the mattress. Her stomach knotting with nerves, uncertain that she could give Len what she deserved, Lucia could not help but put her mouth on Len. She kissed her lips, then her throat, mirroring the way Len had kissed her. Len tilted her head back and moaned.

Len's skin against her lips made Lucia's temperature soar. She had never felt so hungry, and she knew only Len could fulfil her appetite. She kissed lower, finding the soft fullness of Len's bosom, that sure evidence that Len was as much a woman as she was. She felt the way Len's body reacted to her, felt her own response as an ache burning low in her abdomen.

Len was breathing hard. Lucia kissed over her rib cage as it rose and fell, tasted her skin, salty on her tongue. Her lips found the softer flesh of Len's stomach, close to her navel. Lucia had never been in such proximity with another person, and kissing Len's stomach felt just as intimate as running her lips over her breasts.

Len shifted beneath Lucia, parting her thighs slightly. Lucia caught her scent and grew even hotter. She was lost in her desire, hardly knowing what she would do next, just needing Len. She moved her kisses lower still.

Len's hands took hold of her hair gently and raised her head. "What are you doing, Lucia?"

Lucia felt embarrassed with the idea she had displeased Len in some way. "I apologise. I…I couldn't help myself—"

Len's finger stroked over her lips and silenced her. "I was not suggesting you stop. I was simply wondering if you have any idea what you are doing."

"I confess, I do not. I simply need you. I am so hungry, it is like nothing I've ever felt before. I like the way you taste…" Her face was hot as she spoke the words she knew she should be ashamed of, but somehow was not.

"Your kisses are like heaven," Len said. She paused, and Lucia wondered what she was considering. Her voice was thick and slightly tentative when she spoke again. Her fingers moved in Lucia's hair. "I would have more of your kisses."

"I would kiss you more."

Len's hands pressed Lucia's head lower. Lucia allowed Len to guide her, given confidence by that gentle touch, knowing she did nothing that was not wanted. Len's slender thighs were warm as her shoulders brushed them, and all of her senses were filled with the moist scent of Len's desire. Lucia's first kiss of that silky, warm skin was tentative, but the sensation was too much to resist. She kissed harder, allowing her tongue to taste, as Len pushed her hips towards her and stroked her head. Massaging with her lips, she drew a deep sigh from Len's lips and marvelled at her own power. Lost in Len's body, in pleasures she had not known could exist, all fears of the future vanished into the night.

It might have been freezing out of doors, but Len and Lucia were warm in their small, creaking bed. Under cloaks and blankets and with limbs entwined, Lucia's head on Len's chest, they eventually slept peacefully.

❖

Time passed slowly, yet all too quickly. Len was anxious for the night of the raid to come. With every hour the tension in the clearing was growing. The plans had been changed and then changed again. She trusted Bill Wilcock, but she did not like relying on him, when she was used to depending only upon herself and her men. Still, her error of judgement in trusting all of her men implicitly had in part led her to this place, and she tried very hard to allow that she was not the only one who clearly saw the correct path ahead.

Though her instinct was to will time to take her quickly to that decisive night, in her heart she would have commanded time to cease ticking away. She knew with a certainty she wanted to diminish, and still could not, that she was going to lose Lucia. Even if the raid on her father's workshop went entirely to plan, that loss was inevitable. And she knew Lucia would take a part of her heart off into her old life, a part she would never be able to retrieve. She could not trespass into that world any more. She was a creature of secrets and shadows, a threat in the night-time. Lucia, with her purity and goodness, belonged in the light. Len would not drag her into the murk. And yet she craved to keep that light in her life in a way she did not even want to acknowledge to herself.

The evening of the Thursday was just beginning the descent into twilight when the sounds of wood striking wood followed by a single pistol shot rang out through the trees. Len started, was bewildered for a moment as the frame-breakers in the clearing rose to their feet as one, their expressions stricken with panic. It took her only a second to realise that the sound they had heard was the warning signal agreed between the frame-breakers to signal the approach of someone who could discover their whereabouts. As the frame-breakers scattered into the woods, Len looked for her own men. William was with one of the frame-breakers on lookout duty. It was probably his pistol they had heard fired. Julian was already striding over to where the horses were tethered, preparing them to be ridden. She started in his direction but stopped when Lucia gripped her arm tightly.

"Is it the warning? Is someone coming?" Lucia asked. Len could see fear and panic in Lucia's expression and felt a pang of remorse. What had she exposed Lucia to now? She turned to look into Lucia's frightened gaze properly. She could not shield Lucia from the truth. "Yes. Which means we are in danger. You will ride with me."

"But what about the raid? What about Julian and William? What of Bill and his men?"

"We have made plans for this eventuality. For now, trust me to keep us safe."

"I do." Len's heart beat just a little faster at the fullness of Lucia's faith in her. But she could not allow herself to dwell on such things now.

"Then come, onto Oberon with me."

Lucia followed her quickly to the horses. Julian was already mounted, holding Oberon's reins ready. Len aided Lucia to mount then took the reins and climbed into the saddle herself. Her senses on edge from the very real danger that threatened, she found a strange comfort and reassurance in Lucia's warm body in front of her, in her arms. That wouldn't do at all, she reprimanded herself. Lucia's presence increased the danger rather than reducing it, and she had to remember that.

"You remember the plans?" she called to Julian. His eyes met hers and she found reassurance there. Julian's trust, his solid faithfulness, gave her courage.

"Of course." Julian nodded. Len saw him glance at Lucia briefly. He knew what was between her and Lucia, though she had not told him in so many words. And she felt his blessing in that glance. He would stand by her. She returned his nod then pulled Oberon's reins and nudged him forward, just as Julian steered his mount in the opposite direction through the trees.

She kicked Oberon into a gallop, taking a route which hurtled them deeper into Sherwood Forest. Soon, the thudding sound of Julian's horse thundering in another direction died away, and there was only the whistle of the wind past their ears and the thunder of Oberon's hooves on the forest floor. Len held Lucia tight in her arms and allowed Oberon his head. He was better at guiding them through the trees quickly than she was.

Len's sense of direction was good, but she was not entirely sure which part of the forest she rode into. She could only hope she had chosen the correct direction to keep them safe. It would be necessary to emerge from the cover of the trees at some point, to find landmarks and make their way to the place where they would be reunited with the men. But for now, while the daylight remained, Len was content to be deep in the woodland, away from the clearing and all evidence of criminal activity.

When the trees began to thin, Len slowed Oberon to a trot, looking about her cautiously, trying to get a grasp on her bearings.

"What is it?" Lucia asked.

"Hush," Len said in a whisper, close to Lucia's ear. "I'm uncertain where we are, and that is a danger." She removed one hand from the reins and wrapped it around Lucia's slender body before she'd even thought about the action. She knew it was not only to reassure Lucia. The feel of Lucia's body, of her real, living warmth, steadied Len. It reminded her what she had to protect.

Len peered ahead through the trees. She could clearly see that they had come upon one of the tracks that led through the forest. They were seldom used since the bigger road through the woods had been cleared, used so little, in fact, that Len and her men gained no profit in stalking these tracks. However, it was possible the track would lead them out of the woods safely, to a place Len knew. Cautiously, she walked Oberon forward and onto the track. It was no wider than three yards and very rutted, overgrown at the edges. It was almost hard to tell it was intended as a route to anywhere. Len looked to her left and then to her right. She saw trees and shadowy undergrowth. Evening was fast becoming night. The sky to the left was vivid orange, to the right it was blue, cold and forbidding. She was not sure where they were exactly, but at least she knew which way was west now.

"We need to find our way to a crossroads beyond Kirkby by nightfall tomorrow," she told Lucia. Lucia reached up with her hand and gripped Len's fingers. "I believe Kirkby is to the east of here, which means we must turn right. However, if I am correct, east is also the direction from which our pursuers approached. Therefore you must help me, Lucia. Keep your senses keen and tell me at once if you hear or see anything which could be a threat."

"Of course." Lucia's voice was timid and frightened.

"I will keep you safe."

"I know."

Len turned Oberon to the left and urged him into a trot. For now she would follow the track. Being lost in the depths of Sherwood by night was something she did not relish. She had found the way out of the woods and she would not abandon it unless danger threatened.

They rode in the deepening darkness for what felt like a long time. Len did not speak, and she sensed Lucia's eyes on the track ahead of them, watching for the slightest hint of danger.

Suddenly, Lucia tensed in front of her. "What is it?" Len demanded, peering into the distance.

"I thought I saw something glint. Ahead. A slight glimmer, like metal."

Len pulled Oberon to a halt. Lucia was barely breathing, but Len could feel her heartbeat. Her own pounded in a similar rhythm. Her eyes searched the track and the trees up ahead. For a moment she thought Lucia's frightened mind had envisioned a threat where there was none. And then she discerned the slightest hint of movement. A bright spot in the dark where the last of the setting sun reflected on metal. The metal of a sabre blade.

"Militia." Len said it softly.

"Militia?" Lucia had begun to tremble.

"Yes. But I'll be damned if they're getting their bloodstained hands anywhere near us." Len's words were almost a growl. She yanked Oberon's reins and steered him into the woods to their right. As soon as they were among the trees, she made him trot at a diagonal to the track, taking them closer to the militia who barred her from the direction she knew she needed to travel, but farther away from the track on which the militia lay in wait. The soldiers in their shiny uniforms would not search the woods. No doubt they all believed in the spectres which were said to haunt the trees. The outlaws of days gone by would be on her side tonight.

She nudged Oberon into a gallop as they drew parallel to the place on the road where the militia loitered. Oberon's hooves were loud on fallen leaves and broken twigs. But they were past the patrol now, deeper into the trees.

A shout sounded in the night behind them. Len did not pause for a moment, she pushed Oberon harder. Even if the soldiers did follow, she had faith that she and Lucia had enough of a head start to be safe. Still, she could not breathe freely just yet. There were stirrings behind them, a rattle of metal and another shout. Another set of hooves, distant but menacing, echoed Oberon's. Len did not think about it. It did not matter. She was attuned only to Oberon, to his flight through the trees, to her arms gripping Lucia firmly. No rider and horse could catch them. Oberon was swifter than any horse she had ever known, and Lucia's added weight was only slight.

After another minute, she could not hear their pursuers. She hoped they had given up the chase, though she was all too aware they had maybe only abandoned the hunt through the forest in order to wait for them elsewhere. They had to find somewhere to go to ground for the night. She did not want it to be in the depths of the forest. And she wanted to find a landmark before she took cover.

The trees thinned again, and up ahead was a far wider road. The turnpike, where it passed through the forest. The most dangerous of all roads, but enough to give Len a sense of where they were. She took a deep breath and galloped Oberon into the open, turning him wildly in the opposite direction from where the militia would be. They were exposed, but it would not be for long. Len looked about her to a familiar rise, spied a small cottage, and knew where they were at once.

"Hold on," she told Lucia. "Close your eyes if you must." She turned Oberon towards a low part of the hedge, kicked him forward, and prayed he did not let her down. They approached the hedge. Below them, Oberon reared onto his hind legs. She felt the powerful muscular surge as he pushed into the air and soared easily over the hedge. He landed well, but heavily, and Lucia was thrown against his neck with a little cry she barely managed to suppress. Len pulled Lucia back close to her own body and did not slow Oberon as he galloped on, across the pasture they had leapt into. She kept the cottage she recognised to her right and knew what she would find on the far side of these two pastures.

As they rode through a gap in the hedge into the second pasture, she slowed the horse into a trot. His flanks heaved beneath them as he recovered his breath, and she could smell the bitter odour of his sweat. He'd never let her down. Len listened carefully and heard no evidence they were being followed.

Lucia seemed to sense her relax. "Are we away from them?"

"I think so."

"Do you know where we are?"

"Yes." Len was confident now and glad to be able to reassure Lucia with an affirmative answer.

"Where?"

Len did not reply at once. Instead, she waited until they had travelled over a rise in the land, and a small village appeared in front of them. Several houses, an inn, and a small church with a pointed steeple. "Here. Underwood."

"Oh!"

Len realised Lucia'd had no sense of which part of the countryside they were in. Maybe she was even surprised to be so close to her own home, which was not so very far across the fields.

"But won't the militia search here?"

"Perhaps. But we are not going to take a bed at the inn, after all."

"Why do we not hide in the trees?"

"They are searching for outlaws who hide in the woods. I feel safer out of the forest. Besides, to get back to the woods, we will have to cross open land again. I would sooner not."

They rode to the outskirts of the village, to where the pasture met the hedge of the churchyard. Just as they neared the hedge, Len heard the sound of hoof falls along the road through the village. "We will go no further into the village," she said. Though she did not suppose the single horse she heard was evidence of a militia patrol, it would not do for them to be seen by any passers-by. "Do the spirits of the dead alarm you, Lucia?"

"No. Why?"

"Because we're going to spend the night with them."

Len dismounted and aided Lucia to the ground. Walking quietly and listening keenly, she led the way to the entrance to the churchyard. In the corner behind the church, a large, old oak spread its dark branches wide and low. In the late evening light it was a looming, dark shadow. Len walked between the headstones in the direction of the tree.

"We're going to spend the night here?" Lucia sounded as though she did not want to question Len's decision but could not quite reconcile herself to it at once.

"Yes. Unless you have a better suggestion."

"Would it not be warmer inside the church?"

"There is Oberon to think of. Besides, there is only one entrance and exit to the church. If we should be discovered, we would be trapped. In the churchyard, we can be through the hedge and into the fields if we must."

"You think of every possibility."

"I have no choice but to."

They reached the oak. Len led Oberon close to the trunk, into the deepest shadow. Beneath the tree, the ground was firm, and dry enough. She sat down with her back against the tree trunk. "Join me, Lucia," she said softly.

Lucia was seated beside her in moments, her shoulder pressed against Len's. Len wrapped her arm around Lucia's shoulders and pulled her closer. "We'll be safe here, my love," she said.

Lucia looked up at her, though it was too dark for Len to make out her expression. "You speak of love?"

Len had barely noticed that she had done until Lucia asked her question. Now her heart acknowledged the emotion with a rush of warmth through her body. "Yes."

"I had thought never to know what love is," Lucia said. Len waited for more, but there was none.

"And do you?" she asked. The importance of knowing the answer was suddenly greater than she would have dared to acknowledge.

"I believe so." Lucia sighed happily and leaned closer to Len. Len held her tightly and smiled in the darkness. Elation and fear waged a war inside her. To be delighted to have the love of a woman like Lucia, or to be terrified of the inevitable loss to come, the burden of knowing she had made Lucia love her and thus exposed them both to greater pain than they need ever have felt?

They were silent for a long time. Len listened to Lucia's breathing as it settled into relaxation. An owl hooted in a tree not so very far away. She looked out across the churchyard. The tall spire was an outline against the deep dark blue of the sky. The moon had risen enough to give a pale illumination to the scene in front of them. Her gaze settled on the headstones between their hiding place and the church itself.

"Do you ever think about death, Lucia?" she asked.

"Yes. Since my mother died I have been quite afraid of it." Lucia said. Len was touched by her immediate and unquestioning honesty. "I had nightmares, even. But now…" Her words trailed off as if she was not sure how to articulate what she wanted to say.

"Now?"

"Now I find I am less afraid. I think I was not so much afraid of dying, as of feeling that I had not lived before my time was over."

"And what has changed?"

"In the last days I have known what it is to really live."

"You think an outlaw life is the one you craved?"

"I think a life with you in it was the one I longed for, without knowing it."

Hot tears threatened Len's composure and she did not reply, not wishing Lucia to see her weakness. Eventually, she said, "But what if there are no more nights after this?"

"Then I will have known this night and the ones immediately before it."

"Would that be enough?"

"No." Lucia's reply hung in the air. It would never be enough, whatever they said now. That awareness was a tension between them. Len was almost nauseous with it. Oh, for the power to keep time from moving forward. She struggled to keep her composure and not rail out loud at the injustice of a world that would snatch Lucia from her.

Len remembered that Lucia was by her side *now*. To be cherished and treasured. She would not waste this night on anger and resentment. Too many of her nights had been wasted that way. She turned to kiss the top of Lucia's head and felt calmer.

They were silent awhile longer. "Do you ever wish for a different life?" Lucia said at last.

"You mean one within the law?"

"Yes. I know you would not go back to your old life or the restrictions it imposed. But to be constantly in fear for your life—to be a shadow, always. Does it make you happy?"

"Death can catch us at any moment, whether by the hangman's noose, a riding accident, or a fever. I am probably less likely to die today than a woman in childbirth," Len said. "And there are times I wish I could be seen, and known. But it is the price of my freedom."

"You make it sound rather noble and romantic. To be a thief."

"Let it be known that I am no common thief, Lucia." Len laughed.

"You are the Robin Hood of modern times I suppose?" Lucia said lightly.

Len grew more serious again, as she contemplated the comparison. "I am not. Though it is true, I do not take anything from those who cannot afford it, and my men and I would be poor if we did not take what we do. But my motivations are mostly selfish, after all." Len toyed with her hat in her hand as she spoke.

"You're very old fashioned, you realise?" Lucia said.

"Do you mean my hat or my thievery?"

"Tricorns are dying out."

"I am aware of that. And so are highway robbers. The turnpikes and the militia patrols are seeing to that."

"Is that not progress?"

"It is the march of time, ever onwards. I do not know if it is progress."

"But if fewer people are turning to crime?"

"I did not say there were fewer criminals, Lucia. Merely fewer highwaymen. Less robbing from the rich at the roadside. But while times are hard and freedom must be fought for, there will still be criminals. I don't mean those intrinsically evil creatures, without a heart or any sense of morality. I mean men and women who are not bad at heart but forced to turn outlaw, through their circumstances, or through their yearning for more than their life is. Only the future will bring indiscriminate thieves. They will steal from those who have no more than they do."

"You think it is better to have highway robbers roaming the roads?"

"I do not know, Lucia. I only point out that the old ways are passing away. There will be no highwaymen by the middle of this century, if you ask me. The world is changing beyond recognition. The speed of it frightens me a little. Because I do not know what the future will bring."

"But the change could bring freedom. The ability to choose you have craved so desperately."

"It could. But those who hold the reins of power—the silly, fat Prince Regent and his insane father, the rich men in Parliament, and the fathers and husbands in every house in this country—will not allow us freedom without a struggle. Perhaps it will be unnecessary for a woman in my place to turn outlaw. Perhaps. But there will be a fight, Lucia. I am sure of it. The old world and the old ways will not simply die away quietly. Look at the streams of blood in Paris and our current war with France, which began because simple people wanted a better life. A world without highwaymen would be no bad thing, I grant you. But what threats will that new world bring in our place?" Len felt her chest constricting as she spoke, with a very real fear of the future she very rarely expressed. It was soothed somewhat by the simple pleasure, the new freedom, of being able to discuss these things with an interested and receptive listener, a woman she loved.

"You make it sound very bleak." Lucia said. She sounded thoughtful.

"Perhaps I am merely realistic."

"Perhaps." They lapsed once more into contemplative silence. Eventually it was Lucia who spoke again. "But there will always be love. I believe in that now. You have made me believe in that."

Len smiled. She could not help it. "If there is only tonight, Lucia…"

"Then there is nowhere I would rather be." Lucia turned her face to Len's. Their lips met in a tender kiss, so full of love that Len was not sure her heart, awash with joy and sadness all at once, could take it. She kissed Lucia more deeply, felt her soft hair beneath her fingers, and knew Lucia was right. Just then, the future did not matter. Lucia mattered, and Len loved her.

Lucia broke off the kiss. "You might be the last of the highwaymen of Nottinghamshire, Len Hawkins."

"Aye, that I might." Heat stirred in Len's loins at Lucia's tone.

"Then you must live up to your future legend."

"My legend?"

"Yes, the shadowy rider of the black stallion, handsome face obscured by a mask. Fearless and devious thief, and the ruination of weak-willed women who fall under your spell."

"Are you under that spell, Miss Lucia Foxe?"

"I am." Lucia took Len's hand and kissed every fingertip. She held Len's hand to her bosom, then pushed it lower, until Len felt the heat at the meeting of her thighs. "And I ask you to fulfil the legend. Ruin me. Again."

Len groaned and leaned in to kiss Lucia again. She pulled Lucia's skirts higher quickly, with urgency, as Lucia breathed hard into her mouth. She caressed Lucia's soft, welcoming sex, felt just how much Lucia wanted her touch. And she held back.

"You would be the mistress of an outlaw?"

"Yes."

Len caressed with a firmer touch and Lucia writhed against her.

"But the lover of Helena Hawkins?"

"I want that more than anything." Len did not doubt Lucia's honesty. She eased her fingers into Lucia's hot body, exulting in Lucia's cry of ecstasy before muffling it with more kisses. The owl screeched again, but apart from that the night was still. In the shadow of the oak, Len made love to Lucia as if the future was as bleak as she predicted, and this was the only night in which love could shine and find its fulfilment.

Because she knew it was true. There was only this night.

Chapter Fifteen

When Lucia awoke from the sleep she had fallen into in the early hours of the morning, Len was already awake. Her hand was still twined with Lucia's beneath the velvet cloaks they were wrapped in, but she looked out across the churchyard pensively. Dawn had barely broken, and the world was blue and violet, the horizon beyond the church a vivid gold. Though she looked towards the sunrise, Len's dark eyes were blacker than ever. A mask had come over her face, displaying all of her desolate emotion at the same time as it displayed none at all. Watching her, Lucia saw her strength and weakness combined, and her heart thudded more quickly in her chest. She was gripped with a terrible fear for Len's safety and, still further, the anxiety that, even if Len was safe, they would be parted. After the love she had felt in the night, it seemed impossible. Yet here she was, in the shadow of a great oak, hidden in a churchyard from the militia. Len would raid a workshop tonight. Terrible things could happen. All the wishing in the world would not prevent it. She squeezed Len's hand.

Len turned to look at Lucia. Lucia caught her breath at the intensity in her eyes. She waited for her to say something to reveal its cause, but Len merely held her gaze for a long moment, then looked away again. Lucia wondered what Len was thinking. Was she still reflecting on life and death and the passing of time? Was she dwelling on the idea of last night being their last? It had been so easy in the night to grasp hold of that notion, to allow the sense of urgency to intensify every feeling. But now, in the aftermath, it was impossible to accept. It was impossible not to want more. There would be more. Lucia refused to accept that this could end. Now that she finally believed in love, she would not let it slip away in the night.

"We must meet the others at the crossroads beyond Kirkby by four o'clock at the latest. I propose we take the road. You will ride Oberon, I will walk."

"Why?" Lucia had expected a return to the forest, to travel between the trees.

"Because you will be a respectable lady on her horse, accompanied by a manservant. We could probably ride through the middle of a militia patrol in the daylight, and they would question nothing. Skulking in the trees would raise suspicions, however."

"You are right, of course." Lucia still did not like the idea of being exposed on the roads.

"Trust me." Len smiled, finally.

"I do. Oh, I do trust you." Lucia felt the passionate truth of her words as she spoke them.

Oberon was nibbling the short grass beneath the tree contentedly. Len stood up and patted his flank. She looked back to Lucia, who watched her every move, determined not to miss a moment of her time with Len. "We should leave the churchyard now. We will travel a short distance, then rest awhile. It is not so far to Kirkby." She paused a moment, considering. "And I suspect you are hungry?"

"A little."

"I am too. I did not have chance to bring any food. But I have an answer for that. If you are ready, we will set off in five minutes."

Lucia rose stiffly to her feet and shook some warmth into her chilled limbs, wondering just how Len intended to find food for them, and nervous about what the day would bring. But for Len, she smiled.

❖

They travelled out of the village unnoticed by all but a man with a handcart who passed them on the road and simply smiled a greeting. Lucia did not like being alone on Oberon's high back and missed Len's body behind her. Len had left off her mask so as not to attract suspicion, but with her tricorn pulled low there really was nothing to suggest to a passer-by that she was the beautiful woman Lucia knew her to be. Quite how they would manage if Len was required to speak, Lucia did not like to think.

After awhile on the road, which was really little more than a track, they reached a crossroads. Lucia was surprised when Len led them to the left. "Is Kirkby not to the right?" she said.

Len twisted to look up at Lucia. "It is. But I promised we would eat breakfast."

Len grinned, then turned back to the road ahead. After about half a mile, Lucia saw a building up ahead with a sign which suggested it was an inn. It seemed an isolated place, probably frequented by farmhands after a day on the land and travellers who had lost their way.

"Welcome to the Red Lion," Len said.

"But it can't be safe." Lucia wondered if Len was growing reckless with the approach of danger.

"This is one of the few places we are safe, Lucia."

"How can that be?"

"Because the landlady of the Red Lion is Annie Birch." Lucia simply looked at Len, bewildered.

They arrived at the front of the inn. It was a very small building, not more than a cottage, with whitewashed outside walls and a crooked roof. There was a small stable block to the side, and a yard was visible to the back. A wooden sign was painted with the symbol of a red lion, though the paint was old and faded.

Len aided Lucia to dismount, then led Oberon to the back of the building. Lucia followed and watched Len secure the horse to a rail next to a trough of water, of which he drank contentedly. Then Len took Lucia's arm and walked with her to the door of the inn. "Now, don't you mind Annie or anyone else. They're friends," she said. Then she pushed open the door confidently and went inside.

The room was low ceilinged, with dark beams only just above their heads. There were a few chairs and tables, and a door at the back of the room. The air smelled of brandy and lingering pipe smoke. A fire was blazing in the large stone hearth at one end of the room, and Lucia felt the heat gratefully.

The door swung open, and a woman emerged. She looked to be in her fifties, her dark hair threaded with white. She was dressed in a simple, old grey dress, covered by a cream apron. Stocky and strong looking, Lucia knew at once this must be the landlady Len had mentioned.

"Well I never, Len Hawkins!" Annie's accent was broad, her voice loud and confident.

"Annie. Good to see you."

"We read about you in the papers, Len. Almost keeled over with fright, I did, when we read that a highwayman had been took. But I said, I did, it couldn't be Len."

"It wasn't me. But we are fewer than we were." Len said it quietly, as though she did not want to think about it. Annie's hazel eyes scanned Len and then looked behind her. She saw Lucia and frowned. Lucia was not encouraged.

"Not Julian?" Annie asked, fear in her words.

"No. Not William either, before you worry."

Annie looked relieved. Her eyes jolted back to Lucia sharply. "Well, since I can breathe easy on that score, you better tell me from what carriage you stole this pretty treasure."

Len smiled slightly. Lucia did not, unsure how to react to being described in such a way. She had never encountered a woman like Annie before. All the etiquette of a formal introduction was useless here. But then Len took her hand and pulled her forward, closer to Annie, who was inspecting her appearance.

"Annie, allow me to introduce Miss Lucia Foxe, of Foxe Hall. Lucia, this is Annie Birch. My friend."

"Her bloody mother, more like. I worry for her like a mother." Annie winked at Lucia, who blushed and looked awkward. "Good to meet you anyway, darling. Foxe Hall? You mean *the* Foxe Hall, that fancy place a few miles hence?"

"A pleasure to meet you. And yes. *The* Foxe Hall." Lucia's nerves were audible in her voice. It seemed as though she was admitting to some fault in revealing that she was from Foxe Hall, and she almost wished Len had left out that particular detail.

"How on earth does Miss Foxe of Foxe Hall come to be with this good-for-nothing wretch in the Red Lion?"

"I am good for some things, Annie, really I—" Len protested.

"I am a prisoner." Lucia said. It was the simple explanation, though hardly one which still applied.

"Hush your tongue, Len, you know I love you." Annie winked again. "And a prisoner?"

"Lucia ran after me for the sake of her mother's locket. And has not yet returned home." Lucia found herself blushing, wondering if Annie would understand the reasons she was still with Len.

"She is hardly bound to the back of your horse."

"No." Len smiled. Lucia was alarmed by the image.

"A willing prisoner then?"

"Are you a willing prisoner, Lucia?" Len directed the question towards her. Hesitant for a moment, she forced herself to breathe, to relax. She had spent a week with robbers and Luddites. Surely the landlady of an inn should be no problem?

"I am a willing prisoner, yes."

"Good for you, my girl." Annie smiled warmly, and Lucia couldn't help but smile in return.

"Thank you."

"Bet you couldn't believe your eyes when a pretty thing like this came running after you, eh, Len?"

Now even Len was blushing slightly. "I don't believe Lucia's looks were the first thing on my mind when she followed us in the night." Len looked at Lucia contemplatively. Lucia wondered what she was thinking. Lucia herself couldn't help but reflect on how short a time it really had been since that fateful night on which she'd followed Len in a quest for her locket. How much had changed since then.

"A brave one too. She would have to be, to be with you, Len."

Len turned even pinker and let the subject drop. "Any chance of some breakfast, Annie?"

Annie grinned. "You know there is, darling. Just give me a minute or two to rustle something up." She winked again and went through the door through which she had appeared when they'd entered the inn.

"Shall we sit?" Len asked Lucia.

"Yes." They sat on a wooden bench in the corner of the room, close to where the fire crackled in the hearth. The only other patron in the inn was an elderly man seated across the room from them. He had not looked up from the tankard in front of him since they had entered, and showed them no interest now. Lucia watched him for a few moments and decided he was no threat. She began to relax.

"How do you know Annie?" she asked.

"Julian knew her before I did. She's well known in…well… certain circles. Annie will always help you out. For a fee, of course."

Lucia felt she should be condemning, or at least morally concerned. But instead she found herself smiling. It was impossible not to feel warmly towards someone as kindly as Annie, who had clearly helped Len, who seemed to love Len. Who apparently understood something of what was between her and Len and who thought nothing remarkable of it, rather seemed to be happy for them.

Annie brought them breakfast then. There was bread, cured ham, devilled eggs, and creamy butter Len said Annie made herself. She also brought them a flagon of ale, which Lucia eyed cautiously, drawing another smile from Len. They were both ready for food and ate hungrily. Lucia thought she had never enjoyed a meal so much.

With the warmth of the blaze in the hearth, a good meal in her belly, Annie's best ale and good cheer, and Lucia by her side, Len was close to contented. It was impossible to entirely dispel the sense of anticipation and fear of the night to come, but the darkness and the raid seemed like a long way away from this warm moment. She began to feel drowsy.

Suddenly the door opened quickly, with a rush of cold air into the room. Len was alert in an instant. Her heart began to pound when she saw a man in the uniform of the militia stride into the room. His red coat with green facings and brass buttons seemed unnecessarily vibrant and formal in the sleepy, cosy inn.

Beneath the table, Len gripped Lucia's hand. She could see that Lucia was staring at the militia man with wide-eyed fright. She looked back to the door and was relieved to see that the man, a mere corporal, appeared to be alone. He came a few feet inside and looked about him awkwardly, just as Annie bustled into the room.

"Hello there, young sir. A corporal in His Majesty's militia no less. We are honoured. What can we do for you, sir?"

Len took advantage of the man's attention being diverted to Annie to whisper hurriedly to Lucia. "He cannot talk to me, Lucia. He might not know who I am, but I cannot draw suspicion onto us. It is dark in this corner, and warm. I will pretend to sleep with my hat obscuring my face. If he approaches, you must talk to him—"

"But I can't do—" Lucia began.

"You must." She hated to make Lucia do anything of the kind and fiercely regretted the illegality of her life that forced her to drag Lucia into the murky realm of disguises and lies. But there was nothing for it now but to depend on Lucia. Len knew she was brave enough and trusted in the rest. There was no time for more discussion. The man was done talking to Annie and was glancing around the room. She tilted her tricorn over her face and closed her eyes, slumping in her chair and pretending to sleep. Her hand still gripped Lucia's beneath the table. Lucia's hand was sticky with perspiration and Len could feel the pounding of her heartbeat, even in her fingertips. She could no longer see what was happening in the room, but the tightening of Lucia's grip told her all she needed to know, even before she heard the heavy footsteps approaching across the oak floor. She squeezed back with all the reassurance she could.

"Good day, madam." A clear man's voice, more youthful than his appearance had suggested. Len was relieved. The young were generally easier to deceive.

"Good day, sir," Lucia said. Len could hear the strain in her voice, but Lucia concealed it well.

"Corporal Harding of the Nottinghamshire Militia, madam." Len imagined him giving Lucia a polite bow.

"Miss—er—Mrs. Western. I hope your presence here isn't an indicator of anything I should be alarmed over, Corporal?" Len prayed the solider wouldn't notice Lucia's slight hesitation. Her tone was the perfect mixture of earnest enquiry and supercilious disregard.

"Oh no, madam, nothing to worry too much about." Highwaymen and frame-breakers were clearly not too much of a concern. "Nothing you need concern yourself about, with the militia on patrol. We are merely seeking the whereabouts of some notorious outlaws."

"Outlaws?" Lucia managed to sound sufficiently alarmed. Len was proud of her, though her stomach still twisted in knots of apprehension and regret.

"Yes, madam, but do not be alarmed. You are accompanied by your husband, I see?" Len tensed, knowing the corporal's gaze had settled upon her and hearing the suspicion in his question.

"Yes, sir. I apologise for my husband's despicable lack of manners. I fear Mr. Western spent his night drinking rather too much ale. He has only been awake for a full thirty minutes so far today."

"And he expects you to pass your day in such a place as this, madam?" Feelings of anger stirred in Len's belly. She resented the implication that Lucia would be uncomfortable or suffering some way by being here in Annie's inn. After all, she had brought Lucia here, exposed her not only to this humble place but also to the interrogation she was subject to now. And the implication in the soldier's tone, that he would have been a far more protective and considerate husband, was hard to miss.

"It is not so bad, sir. I am warm and fed. It is a suitable place to break our journey."

"Where, may I ask, are you travelling to?" He was tenacious, Len would give him that credit.

"You may, sir. We travel from Northampton to visit acquaintances in Yorkshire."

"A long journey, madam."

"That is why I am glad to rest here awhile."

"Of course." There was a long pause. Len wondered if the man was going to suggest waking her, in order to corroborate the story. Then she realised she was thinking too much about it. No one would possibly suspect Lucia was anything other than she presented herself as being.

"Will there be anything else, sir?" Lucia asked the question dismissively. An excellent tactic, Len thought. Exactly how a gentlewoman with no concerns over her own guilt would behave.

"No, madam, I will leave you to your rest. Only beware if you are travelling the north road after dark. There are reports of highwaymen in these parts. And the Luddites are abroad in the small hours too."

"Luddites?"

"The machine breakers." There was extreme distaste in the soldier's words.

"Since I am not a machine, I believe I will not worry myself too much about those men. And I will heed the warning about highwaymen and ask my husband that we travel only by day. Thank you, sir."

"You're welcome, madam. I bid you good day."

"Good day, sir. Happy hunting."

Len did not dare breathe until, after a long moment of silence, she heard the man's footsteps retreating. Even then, she did not move from her pose of slumber until she had heard the door open and the man leave. "Is he gone?" she murmured to Lucia.

"Yes." Lucia's voice sounded weak. Len pushed her hat back and opened her eyes. When she looked at Lucia she saw her face was pale, but there was an alarming glimmer in her eyes.

"I am very sorry, Lucia." The regret was fierce and bitter inside her. She could not bear any harm to come to Lucia, and she did not like the way Lucia's eyes glistened now.

"Do not be. I am quite all right." Lucia said.

"You did well."

"Does that surprise you?"

"Not at all. Only I might have expected you to be more afraid." Len was honest.

"You remember that I am the woman who followed you in the night, for a locket."

"I do, very clearly. But then you were prepared to put some faith in outlaws who had not harmed you once before. That man could have happily seen us both on the gallows."

"I know." Lucia was more sombre. Then she smiled. "But somehow, the life and death of it adds to the thrill, doesn't it?"

"I would not have you think like that, Lucia." The way Lucia's face flushed and her eyes sparkled was terribly alluring, and Len understood very well the feelings she referred to. But still she was alarmed by this development.

"And why not?" Lucia was mildly indignant. "You feel the thrill yourself, I know you do."

"I do, Lucia, I will not lie. But I would not have you talk of life and death so lightly. You should not take life for granted or think the Reaper merely a phantom."

"My mother died."

"When you were a child and did not understand, and of an illness at that. Not at the will of the law, at the order of another person. That sort of death is different and just as ready to strike. Do not forget."

"You forget it yourself."

"I do not. It is why I am still safe."

"And afraid of tonight's raid." Lucia was clearly well at ease with Len by now, and despite herself Len almost smiled at the accusation.

"I am not afraid, Lucia. I am anxious. I know the risks the night brings."

"Yes. I know. And I promise I am aware of it. I am not so naïve, you know…"

Lucia looked away from her, and Len knew she was offended. That had not been her intention. "I am sorry, Lucia. I did not mean you are naïve." Lucia looked back into her eyes. Len smiled. "And you did do very well with the good corporal."

Lucia finally smiled once more, though that dangerous glimmer was gone from her eyes, and Len was glad. "You truly think so?"

"I do. We will make an outlaw of you yet, Miss Foxe."

Lucia looked pleased. Len was not so. In contemplating the idea of indoctrinating Lucia into her own way of life, outside of the law, she saw that life for what it was. And she did not like what she saw.

❖

Len decreed it was not safe to remain in the inn for the rest of the day if the militia were patrolling the area. They were too visible. It was far safer to take shelter in the nearest patch of woodland. Len said her thanks and goodbyes to Annie. Lucia noticed she gave her no information about their plans for the remainder of the day or the raid that night. Then they made their way along the hedgerows, leading Oberon rather than riding him until they reached the treeline.

Neither of them was inclined to venture far into the woods. They lingered instead at the very edge, with a view over the countryside before them, and allowed the weak winter sun to fall delicately onto their skin. It was the time for light and hope, not darkness and secrets.

They were silent a lot that day. Tension grew as the day wore on, the hours of waiting beginning to seem interminable. Lucia knew that in any other circumstances she would be delighted to spend this time alone with Len. But Len had withdrawn more and more into her own thoughts, and Lucia could think of no suitable ways to break the silence. Everything she thought of to say sounded trivial and inconsequential compared to the thoughts she imagined to be tormenting Len's mind. But she kept her hand in Len's or on her thigh, never wanting to lose contact with her.

Their morning encounter with the corporal of the militia had truly brought the frightening reality of Len's life home to her. She had seen the eager expression in his eyes, his sheer contempt for anyone outside the law. He was the sort of man who would take delight in watching a frame-breaker or highway robber in their death throes on the gallows. By not letting go of Len now, Lucia felt she could keep her in the world, protect her from such men. Len was warm, living, breathing, moving. No one would dare take that away from her, surely?

The sun was setting and the approach of night bringing an ominous chill to the air when they mounted Oberon and rode in the direction of the planned rendezvous with the other frame-breakers, Julian, and William. Lucia wished they did not have to. And yet she was swept along with the momentum and did not voice her wish. There was a workshop to be righteously raided, a daughter's revenge on her father to be enacted, and she would have a part in it.

She allowed that feeling to sustain her, until she saw Julian and William waiting at the crossroads with Bill Wilcock and his men. Seeing their faces again reminded her of the harsh truths of this life, the realities of this night. She leaned back in the saddle against Len and hoped the wave of sheer terror would pass.

Chapter Sixteen

They rode slowly, Bill and his men walking alongside them, mostly through the woodland parallel to the road. Though they had spent the last week surrounded by winter trees, these unfamiliar ones seemed to crowd around them, dark and menacing, as the sun set and the sky above darkened further. Len shuddered with the recollection of their escape from the militia just last evening. Eventually they reached a place where the trees suddenly parted ahead of them and allowed them to see much more of the sky. The ground changed under Oberon's hooves, and Len knew they had reached the turnpike.

A stone way-marker was visible in the gloom. She peered at it and managed to decipher that, as she had expected, they were close to the village of Giltbrook, though she could not read the number of miles given below. Without the cover of the trees, she felt horribly exposed and vulnerable. She cursed herself for the level of anxiety that gripped her heart. Was it because tonight she finally gained the revenge she had longed for over her father? Or was it because Lucia was warm in front of her on Oberon's sturdy back?

It was not long before they were off the road again, in fields. Bill did not give his directions in words, he merely gestured which direction they should ride. Len was content to trust him as their guide. The knot of tension in the pit of her stomach was tightening. She leaned forward against Lucia. She was rewarded when Lucia loosened her grip on Oberon's mane and reached backwards to touch her leg gently.

There was no moon, the sky was too heavy, and the countryside was entirely black, without shadow or definition. As they skirted a field of winter crops, Len felt the cold tickle of a snowflake against her face. The snow was falling only lightly, but it clung to the velvet of her cloak, and its wetness against her exposed face only added to the sensation of her blood becoming gradually frozen.

She willed her body to feel the thrill of what she was about to do. Usually her senses were alert and keen, her heart beating fast, her temperature climbing. The approach of danger, the anticipation of the need to fight or run, usually made her feel more alive. And tonight she felt as though she was dying. The raid, her father: they were almost forgotten. Her focus was the woman who was now so solid and warm in her arms, but later tonight could be lost to her, a phantom memory, a reminder of what she could never have. Death had snatched Hattie from her. Life would tear Lucia from her arms. After tonight Lucia could not stay with her, however much she desired it. It was impossible. And yet her hopeful mind insisted on trying to think of ways in which it could be. Did Lucia ponder the same things? Or would she truly be glad to return to the safety of her home and allow comfort and familiarity to take the place of love?

Len lost all bearing as to how many minutes had passed or which direction they travelled. But she sensed her former home, her father's workshop, ahead of them in the night.

Abruptly, Bill led them to the right, into a copse of woodland. Suddenly dark shapes were moving in front of them, and a lantern flickered quickly, was obscured, and then shone once more, before being extinguished. This was the expected signal.

"How many of you?" Bill addressed the closest of these shadowy figures.

"Eleven," the man replied. These were the workers, the men who sat at their frames labouring by day and broke the frames of their masters by night. Bill and his men were their leaders, the ones who plotted the raids, but it was these men who lent the real element of terror to the spate of frame-breaking across the county. These were ordinary men, not outlaws. If ordinary, ignorant workers could turn to such measures, no property and no person was safe. Or so went the terrified whispers. Len was sure Lucia was well acquainted with those myths.

Lucia's eyes strained in the darkness to see the faces of these mysterious labourers, but it was difficult to make out more than vague shapes. She shuddered involuntarily at the stuff of nightmares made flesh before her. Len touched her shoulder briefly then dismounted, giving Lucia her hand so she might do the same. Lucia did not let go of Len's hand at once. She longed to ask how Len was feeling, to demand to know what would happen after the raid. She did not want to leave Len, to go home. And yet tonight was the night their time together was due to end. She must return to her father and sister. If she refused, would Len allow her to stay? And how would she tell her father? It was a terrible predicament she could not resolve. But she could not bring herself to ask Len either. Not now, with so much tension and danger in the air, with the raid on her father's workshop imminent. Lucia squeezed her hand tightly, hoped to convey her love and reassurance with that touch. Len squeezed back, and Lucia's heart beat just a little faster.

Lucia was glad of the leather boots as she stood on the leaf-littered floor. The ride had made her cold to the bone, and she shivered. Julian and William had dismounted beside them, and now they crept through the trees, shadows with rustling footfalls to either side of them, to where the narrow thicket thinned once more.

She heard Len draw in her breath deeply as they peered through the trees. Ahead of them, down a slight slope, was a red-brick, dark-roofed, rectangular building, two storeys tall. Long, white-framed windows stretched the entire length of the building. This must be the workshop operated by Len's father. Beyond the workshop, across a small open space, the shadow of a large house could be seen to loom, its illuminated windows eerily bright in the dark.

Lucia looked at Len. "Yes," Len whispered, "that was my home." Her tone was matter-of-fact. There was clearly no time for sentiment now.

Lucia was handed the reins of the three horses. "Stay here until we return," Julian instructed. He thrust a pistol into her hand

and she looked at it in renewed horror. "It is already loaded," he said. "Fire it if you are in danger or to warn us if you see anyone approaching."

"Of course." He nodded his head briefly, an acknowledgement, she thought, of his trust in her.

"You must come back," she said to Len in a softer whisper. Every moment mattered. Even if they were to part tonight, it would not be now, in these circumstances.

"I will," Len said. Her gloved hand pressed Lucia's quickly before she went to stand close to Bill. He handed her an axe. Lucia looked at the blade and trembled. Bill himself was holding a heavy-looking hammer. She had previously wondered at their lack of weapons or instruments to damage the machines. Clearly the labouring men had brought such implements with them. Perhaps they had been hidden in the copse for days. She knew relatively little of the plans leading to this point, yet they swept her along as much as they did any of the men here. All around Lucia lurked men with axes and hammers in their hands. She looked at Len with her axe and wanted to cry out, to beg her to return to her, not to do this. She bit her lip and choked back the ache in her throat.

Lucia did not even see the signal Bill Wilcock gave, but suddenly, as one, the men began to move stealthily out of the trees. In just seconds they were but shadows, Len indistinct among them. Lucia watched the dark shapes moving quickly down the hill, approaching the building. Her heart was pounding, and with every part of her soul she willed them forward, since the quicker their work was done, the more quickly they would return.

She lost sight of them as they reached the workshop building, for the entrance was on the side she could not see from her vantage point. Oberon shuffled beside her, his nose pushing at her shoulder. Absent-mindedly, she reached up to stroke his soft, warm muzzle. William's mare was restless and pulled a little at her reins.

Lucia thought she heard a muffled sound from the direction of the workshop. The dark windows told nothing of what occurred inside, but it came again, a faint crash. In alarm, she looked to the house with the lighted windows, Len's father's house, the place she had grown up in, been imprisoned in, and finally been cast out of. There was no sign of anything amiss.

Silence fell over the scene before her. She felt she was looking at a painting. Everything was still; it was impossible to imagine what occurred behind the windows of the workshop. Her eyes returned to the lit windows of the house. She could well imagine the scene within, after all, it was not so very different to the one she lived every day of her life. Lucia saw the limits of that life then, so very clearly. That small patch of light was contained within the walls and windows, while outside the darkness and countryside stretched so far. There was a world beyond those walls, just as there was a life beyond those constraints. Len had known and she had seized it. Lucia knew now this was what she had always waited to know. Only she doubted she could ever cling to this larger life with such tenacity as Len had.

❖

Though it was dark in the workshop, it was not difficult for Len to make out the shapes of the square stocking frames positioned evenly around the room. Besides, Len had been here before, many times. The smell was the same as she remembered: the oil of the machines, the slight damp from the floor. She was even sure she could smell the perspiration of the men who worked away their days in this space.

Usually, the workshop was loud with the clattering, clanking, and creaking of the machinery. A rhythmic, repetitive, regular sound, which seemed to get inside your head and rattle inside your skull until you could think of nothing else. Tonight, though, this was replaced by the tramp of men's boots on the wooden floor. Once they were all inside, there was a long moment of silence. And then the first crash, as one of the frame-breakers brought his hammer down on one of her father's frames.

Then all hell broke loose. As one, the men began to pound the machines with their hammers and axes. Len hesitated, briefly awed and even a little afraid of the fury unleashed around her. And then she remembered. She allowed the anger into her own heart out of the locked place where she'd kept it these past years. This was why she was here. To confront the anger she'd never been able to, to wreak her own revenge on the man who'd thought he had power over her life. The man who had beat her. The man who had made her what she was, an outlaw, forced to risk her life daily. Now, although he would not know her hand in it, she would strike at what mattered most to her father. His business.

She gripped the axe in her hands more fiercely and moved closer to the nearest frame. She raised the axe, loving the power of its weight in her hands. It was above her head and she swung it downwards. It struck the frame with a splintering of wood and the clash of metal against metal. The impact jolted along the wooden handle of the axe and jarred her shoulders, seemed to bruise her hands. But she tugged the heavy blade free of the machinery and raised it again. As she slammed it down against the frame again, she realised she was crying out in her fury and tears were streaming over her cheeks. She could never achieve a real revenge against her father, but at least, here and now, she could claw back some satisfaction and self-respect.

For so long she'd repeated to herself that she'd made her own choices, chosen to choose. She'd tried to explain it that way to Lucia. But deep down, part of her doubted that. If her father had been different, kinder, would she have sought out the same freedoms? Would she have chosen thievery and a life in the shadows? Or contented herself with the small freedoms the life of a wealthy woman allowed?

As she crashed the axe into the frame again, feeling the muscles in her arms beginning to burn, she also tried to let go of those doubts. She destroyed her father and the image of him. She destroyed the darkness in her heart, the festering place full of blame—for her humiliation, for her separation from Hattie, for Hattie's death, for her physical pain, and for the necessity of her life of crime. From this moment on she would cease to blame her father and take ownership of that life. She would make her own choices, be responsible for her mistakes, and win the true freedom she was still searching for. And she would present that to Lucia and offer her the chance to choose, in a way she had never been able to.

She raised the axe and brought it down one more time. The machine groaned, and some part of it fell onto the floor with a thud. Suddenly her arms were very tired. Just thinking of Lucia seemed to soothe the fierce rage in her heart, and breaking the frame seemed less imperative. It was already done. Why waste anything more on it? It was time to think of what waited for her outside. Of beautiful Lucia.

Len knew Lucia expected to return home to Foxe Hall tonight or the day after. And return she would have to, since she had a family who truly cared. Yet Len had begun to imagine ways in which they could still see each other. She had started to believe the impossible was possible after all, with a little creativity. She was in no doubt that she loved Lucia. Did Lucia truly love her back? She wanted to believe it. She knew the course of the night and of the next day would answer her questions.

She started to make her way towards the door to the workshop. She wanted to be out of this place of toil and machinery, out from under her father's roof, and in the night-time she shared with Lucia. The other frame-breakers apparently took her retreat as some sort of signal, for the rest of them began to move with her. It was done. Len did not even glance behind her as she left the workshop.

❖

Lucia looked back to the workshop. At first everything was still. Then she saw a dark figure appear around the corner of the building and begin to make for her position. Another followed and the weight began to lift from her heart. It was done. She looked for Len but could not tell one man from another as they came closer.

A noise and a movement caught the corner of her vision. She turned back towards the house. Her heart froze. She was in time to see two men running hurriedly towards the workshop. One of them shouted, whether in alarm or warning she did not know. There was something in his hand. Lucia peered through the darkness, trying to make sense of what she saw. She cried out loud as she realised he held a musket, which he brought to his shoulder. Fear coursing through her, she seized the pistol Julian had pressed into her hand and fired it into the night.

The noise echoed from the trees. Lucia cast the pistol onto the floor among the leaves. The men closest to her, now aware of the danger, were running more quickly towards the woodland. Still Lucia looked for Len; still she did not see her. She knew her to be one of the indistinct shapes struggling towards her, and clenching her fists, Lucia willed them to move more quickly.

Another shot rang out in the night, this time from the direction of the workshop. Lucia saw a man fall, the shadow at his side turning to assist him. A cry caught in Lucia's throat. She longed to run out from the trees, find Len, touch her, know she was safe. She twisted the reins of the now-agitated horses in her hands and forced herself to stay hidden in the woodland.

Lucia saw the flash as the second man fired and the next shot pierced the night. Already some of the men had made it into the woods. As another, breathing hard, rustled past, she turned to look, hoping always to see Len, or Julian, or even William.

She focused her attention back towards the men still scrambling away from the workshop. There was a dark shape slumped on the ground halfway between the workshop and the treeline, and her eyes fixed to it. A man lying motionless in the grass. All feeling left her limbs. Was it a man? Or maybe a woman in breeches, boots, and cloak?

Another shot rang out.

One man, a straggler, had been apprehended near the workshop and struggled in the arms of the man who had fired the most recent shot. "Not Len." Lucia murmured it defiantly. She could not imagine Len being captured, nor struggling in that man's arms. Her gaze returned to the motionless hump in the grass and her head swam.

"Miss Foxe!" An urgent shout from close by. Julian appeared next to her and she looked to him eagerly. She heard her own cry of horror as she saw Len, half-fainting in his arms. Even in the black night Lucia could see her pallor and the place where her shirt and waistcoat were hideously dark with wet blood.

"Julian! What can I do?" Lucia demanded, as Len groaned with pain. She was barely conscious and must have been in very great agonies to have shown any evidence of weakness.

"Nothing," he said firmly. "I will care for her. You must go, now. It will not be long before the militia are combing this place. You must return to your home and speak nothing of what you have seen here. You know where you are. Ride directly over the field behind the copse, keep the wall to your left, and you will reach the turnpike. Turn left until you meet the first junction. Then turn right, off the turnpike. You will most likely be surprised how short a distance you must ride before you are home. Take Oberon and ride fast."

"I cannot!" Lucia cried in desperate protest, her eyes fixed to Len's white face.

"You must, for your sake and ours. Just go!" When she reached for Len's hand, he pushed her roughly. "I will contact you when it is safe. Go to your family and tell them what story you will for the time being."

"But you cannot understand!" Lucia resisted him still, her voice high-pitched with passion and despair.

"I know what she is to you," he said. For a moment the world seemed to stop, and Lucia stared at him through the gloom. "I give you my word, I will contact you."

Desperately, Lucia reached out and held Len's hand in her own for a few seconds. Somehow, she managed to mount Oberon without the aid of a block. With a last look at Julian—whose eyes were now diverted back towards the workshop, looking for further threats—and a lingering glance at Len, as she lay heavily in his arms, Lucia nudged the stallion into life.

❖

Lucia remembered Julian's directions well enough and reached the turnpike quickly, her heart pounding for fear she would be discovered and bring danger to Len and the men. But once she reached the turnpike and turned towards home, urging Oberon into a steady canter—smooth enough to allow her to maintain her balance despite the man's saddle—the full impact of what had taken place overwhelmed her. Tears flooded her eyes and she prayed, as she never had before, that Len would be spared.

Before long, the road ran through a village. Lucia glanced around through blurred eyes, and found Julian was right. She recognised the church, the inn, the row of new-built houses on the outskirts. In less than half an hour she reached the gates of Foxe Hall. She dismounted and eased through the wrought iron barriers.

The relief at having reached safety undiscovered slipped away from Lucia inexorably as she stood at the end of the driveway and gazed at the familiar edifice of her home. It was so different to her yet, unequivocally, the same as it always had been.

No lights were visible from the windows. She had no idea whether it was before or after midnight. Mechanically, she led Oberon to the stable, where Sally, her old friend, snorted a welcome. She loosened Oberon's girth and fastened his reins to a hook in the wall. She saw that he had food and water but barely thought about what she was doing. Her heart was with Len, left in a shadowy woodland.

Lucia passed the remaining hours of that cold night in the gardens. She perched on her old favourite bench in the arbour and waited for the daylight. Somehow she could not face the warmth and shelter of the house. Strange though it was in such a short time, she had grown used to the cold and the air around her. Moreover, she was seized with an overwhelming, superstitious fear Len would die if she lay in her soft bed before daylight. As she waited for dawn, Lucia was alert always for the sounds of militia patrols along the turnpike but heard nothing.

The sun was rising on a far clearer and crisper day than the fateful one preceding it when Lucia finally approached the front entrance of Foxe Hall.

CHAPTER SEVENTEEN

Mary, the maid, was the first person to witness Lucia's arrival home. The young servant was passing through the hallway carrying kindling for the drawing room fire as Lucia came slowly through the door. Mary glanced briefly in Lucia's direction, and then turned, open-mouthed, flinging her basket of sticks to the floor.

"Miss Foxe! Oh, miss, you're home!" She gazed at Lucia, clearly astonished. Then she examined more of the detail of Lucia's appearance. "But look at you, miss, you look half-dead."

There was a mirror mounted on the wall in the hallway, and Lucia turned to it to see if she really appeared as Mary described. She saw a white-faced figure with darkened eyes, her hair awry, loose in its pins. A leaf clung somehow to her hair near her left ear. The green velvet travelling cloak seemed especially dark and harsh, swamping her frame.

Meanwhile, Mary shook herself out of her motionless surprise and approached Lucia, taking her arm as though worried she would faint. Never having been prone to doing any such thing, Lucia put her hand aside gently.

"Please tell my father I am returned home." It seemed such a final request and brought Lucia back to the reality of her life. Mary reached around her to close the door she had left ajar, and she felt suddenly sealed into the house, as though Mary had locked the bars of a gaol cell behind her.

"Miss, you must lie down," Mary said. Concern and duty mingled in her words. Lucia knew the maid was inquisitive, but it was not her place to ask questions and Lucia was glad.

"I am going to. Please do as I ask and inform my father. And please bring me some hot water, to my chamber."

"Of course, miss. I will tell Mr. Foxe, and then I will come and make the fire up for you. I'll fetch the hot water after that." Mary's eyes were kind and Lucia felt close to tears. She looked at Mary and pondered: Would she ever understand, even if Lucia were to explain in precise detail where she had been for the last week? Would anyone ever understand? There was only Len.

Biting her lip to prevent the sobs rising in her throat, Lucia turned away from Mary and crossed the hallway to the foot of the mahogany staircase. She did not look back as she climbed the stairs slowly, her legs heavy with grief and exhaustion. She held the smooth banister to steady herself, to appear stronger than she really was.

Lucia's chamber, her former refuge and place of comfort, felt chilled and gloomy when she entered it. The drapes were closed and the grate bare. For a moment it was difficult to recall when she had last been there. Then she remembered Julian's shadow over her in the night, the terror reaching right into her heart. So much had changed in so small a number of days. She seemed to have been away for months.

Every part of Lucia's body felt leaden, and it was an effort to move to the bed. The sheets and blankets were turned back, just as they were every evening, expectant. She unfastened the cloak and laid it on the foot of the bed. Sitting down, she began to unfasten her boots. They were sullied with mud and pieces of dried leaves. Lucia stared at them, sure it had been someone else who had crouched in that copse of trees in the dark hours of the night. A thought interrupted her reverie: Her locket! Had it been disturbed? The importance of it seemed overwhelming, and she reached quickly beneath her pillow. Relief flooded through her as she felt the metal chain against the sheets.

She heard quick footsteps in the passageway outside her chamber and withdrew her hand in haste. First her father, dressed but dishevelled, as though he had been halfway through the process when Mary had informed him of his daughter's return, and then Isabella, still in her white nightgown, her hair in long braids, burst through the door without knocking, their expressions suggesting they doubted Mary's sincerity.

"Lucia!" they exclaimed as one. Isabella flung herself at Lucia on the bed and wrapped her arms about her sister's body. Her father was more restrained, but she saw the sheer relief upon his countenance. For the first time since she had taken the decision to stay with Len and her men, Lucia understood the full consequences of her choice and her heart filled with regret. Mingled with this was a bitter grief, for she knew she was one with them no longer. She would lie to them now and the lie would continue for the rest of her life. Len had said there was no such thing as an ideal life, and now she was sure of the truth of that wisdom. She held Isabella tightly and looked over her shoulder at their father.

"But where have you been?" he asked. He was looking at Lucia as though she was an apparition.

Lucia recognised how extraordinary her true story was. They would never have guessed such a thing could have occurred. If she told them the truth, they would not believe her, she was certain. Yet she made the lie as close to the truth as possible. "I was taken by the same men who robbed us on the road." She saw the anger and horror form on her father's face. "I think they thought I would be able to identify them. They would not release me until they were sure I had not betrayed them."

"There was talk in town," her father said, nodding faintly, "of highwaymen being captured."

"Yes, I think they thought I had informed the authorities about them."

"They forced you to write the letters, in order that I would not search," her father concluded. "But why you? And how did they know where you live?"

"We are known enough in these parts. And who can know how the minds of thieves work?" Lucia closed her eyes for a moment, shutting off the part of her thinking of Len, hating to speak of thieves in these terms. Her father clearly took it for a sign of her experience weighing heavily upon her.

"Did they hurt you?" he asked, eyes full of concern and underlying fury.

"No, not at all," she said hurriedly. "I am only weary."

"We were terrified," Isabella said. She stood up so she might look at Lucia. "When we found you gone and the door broken into, I thought you were dead!" She began to cry, and guilt tore at Lucia's conscience. How could she have put them through such an ordeal? It had all come to nothing in the end, only caused them very great pain.

"But you see me now, Isabella, I am not dead." Lucia smiled weakly.

"Were you not scared?"

"Of course I was. But they treated me well, for outlaws."

"Could you recognise them again?" her father asked.

"They wore masks whenever they were with me." Lucia found the lie gave her no difficulty to tell.

"Where did they take you?"

"I do not know." That was honest at least. "They covered my eyes. It was not so far away, I do not think, but as to which direction it was I could not say."

Mary arrived in the doorway, bearing a pitcher of hot water. "Excuse me, sir," she said, "I've brought the water for Miss Foxe. And Jenkins, from the stable, asked me to tell you a strange horse has appeared. A fine stallion, he says."

Lucia thought of Oberon in the stable, and her mind raced for an explanation. She had been too distressed to consider it before.

"A horse?" her father demanded of Mary, as the maid set the pitcher down on Lucia's toilet stand.

"Yes, sir, in the stables."

"I rode the horse here this morning." Lucia waited for their reaction.

"They gave you a horse?" Isabella looked incredulous.

"All was in uproar," Lucia said, thinking quickly as she spoke and finding the lies came more naturally than she expected. "I think they wanted me to be gone as soon as possible, before the militia found them. It would look worse for them if I was found to be their hostage. They put me on the horse and told me to ride home."

"Then surely you know where you rode from," her father said.

"They covered my eyes and led me to the turnpike," Lucia replied hastily.

"But will they want their horse back? Will they come here again?"

"I do not know," Lucia said. She could take no more questions, no more lies. Exhaustion swept through her, and she took the easy path away from their enquiries. "I am so very tired, Father." She closed her eyes and passed a hand over her forehead to emphasise her words. "I would like to sleep now."

"Of course," he said. "Come, Isabella, you may talk to her later. Attend to her, Mary."

"Yes, sir." Mary looked as though no duty could have given her more satisfaction. Isabella pressed Lucia's hand briefly and withdrew as instructed. Mary made up a fire in the hearth and supervised as Lucia washed her hands and face in the warm water. She was shocked at the murky brown of the water in the bowl as she rinsed her skin. She allowed Mary to help her into her clean nightgown and then crawled into her bed. It felt soft, almost too soft. She pulled the blankets over her body and found the warmth soothing.

"Can I bring you anything to eat or drink, miss?" Mary asked.

"No, thank you. Maybe later." It was that easy. Lucia thought of the starving stockingers, forced to frame-breaking. She could not even remember how much Len had informed her was the cost of a loaf of bread. How quickly she had forgotten.

Lucia's mind travelled to Len, wherever she was. She could not die. It was quite impossible to contemplate it. Lucia needed to know she was out there, even if she could not go to her. She wondered where Len was, how many of the men had escaped. She thought of the clearing in the forest where she had spent most of the last week, remembered the patches of sky visible through the bare branches. It was too dark in her chamber. "Could you please open the drapes?"

she asked Mary. The daylight flooded in. Lucia could see the sky, pale blue and clear. Len was somewhere beneath that sky.

"I think I'll sleep now," Lucia said. Mary left the room quietly. Lucia lay alone in her bed and stared at that blue sky, tears burning her tired eyes.

❖

Pain, in all of her body, especially sharp in her side, worse with every breath. Weakness, as she opened her eyes cautiously. She was lying somewhere, and it was damp, but the smell was unfamiliar. Pain again, nothing else, darkness.

Footsteps? But whose? Unsure if she was lost in a nightmare or horribly awake, opening her eyes again, Len tried to look around. But it was all a blur. A human shape above her, a sudden strong scent of brandy.

"Julian?" her mouth was dry and her lips cracked. She was unsure if she'd formed the word properly. He held the brandy to her lips, and she took a small, grateful sip. It burned her tongue, which felt swollen.

His cool grip on her warm fingers. She was hot. Why was she so hot? "Yes, it's me."

"Where…what?"

"The workshop, Len, do you remember?"

The sound of a gunshot in the night. Her father. The satisfying crunch of machinery breaking. But something else. Something missing…

"Lucia!" There was panic in her voice. Where was Lucia? Was she injured, or worse?

"I sent her home. She is quite well, Len." Julian held her hand tighter.

"Home?" Nausea swept through her. Whether it was a result of her injury or the realisation of her separation from Lucia, Len was in no condition to ponder. This was it then. Lucia was well, and for that she was relieved, but Lucia was gone. Back into her world of light and good manners. Gone from the shadows, from her grasp.

And Len could not blame her. She half closed her eyes and was glad of the distraction of the pain in her side.

"She did not want to leave you, Len. I had to order her to go." Len's eyes opened wide again and the pain lessened suddenly. She held Julian's hand tighter.

"She would have stayed with me?"

She thought she heard a slight smile in Julian's tone. "Aye, she would. So don't worry yourself about that. The girl's in love with you, all right. But that won't do you any good if you're not here to enjoy it."

Len felt the pleasure of his words wash through her, a soothing balm to body and spirit. Only gradually did she focus on his last statement. "I am not so badly injured, Julian," she said. More a question than a statement of fact.

"You were shot, Len."

"I know…" A wave of nausea. Why was her vision fading? Julian's outline blurred.

"The wound is festering. We are doing all we can, Len."

Len heard but did not listen. She did not want to hear. "Lucia loves me?" She was dizzy now with the effort of thought and speech. Whatever it was she was lying on seemed to be moving.

"Yes."

"Then I cannot die." She said it with as much conviction as she could muster. But she wasn't even sure Julian made sense of her words. He merely held something cold and wet to her forehead. His outline grew hazier, and she closed her eyes. She could feel the sweat making her back and armpits soaking wet, and her stomach was churning. Her heart seemed to be beating too fast. The pain in her side was worse with every breath. But in her mind she saw Lucia. Lucia in the sunshine, with her golden hair and blue eyes, her sweet smile but fire in her gaze. And Lucia in the dark of night, hot with passion, sighing at Len's touch. Len could not die, not if Lucia loved her.

The thought was the last she had before consciousness left her.

❖

Lucia did sleep, fitfully, through that day. Her father and Isabella visited only briefly and did not press her for answers. She ate little, only the porridge Mary brought her at lunchtime, and a slice of bread and butter later in the afternoon. Towards the evening, she slipped her hand beneath her pillow and touched her mother's locket. She remembered it in Len's fingers, and she clasped it tightly as she attempted to sleep again.

When the next morning dawned bright with sunshine and Mary slipped into the room to pull back the drapes and check the fire she had tended in the hearth all night, Lucia knew she could not bear to rise from her bed. She told Mary she had a headache, which she did not have, and that her whole body ached, which it really did not. The maid's eyes were full of worry as she went to inform Lucia's father.

A doctor was called and would visit later in the day. Lucia knew he would conclude she was healthy, only tired with the strain. As she lay beneath the blankets, contemplating her supposed illness, the notion of rising from the bed, dressing, going down to the sitting room felt entirely impossible. She convinced herself of her ill health. She needed the bed rest to recover herself, she was sick. She could lie here in relative comfort because it was necessary. Downstairs, she would see the fine mahogany furniture, the silk upholstery of the sofas, the food laid on the table every mealtime, and everything would be a jarring contrast with the other world she had discovered.

This decision, to remain in bed, was entirely hers to make and it was not questioned. Len had taught her about the freedom of being able to choose. So to stay in bed was her only choice. Fully dressed and perfectly healthy, she could do nothing more than sit and sew or read. It seemed preferable to imprison herself in her chamber than to risk the full comprehension of what her life was. Lucia drifted in and out of sleep, and between slumbers, her thoughts could be with Len. She had no conversation to make, no appearance to keep up. She began to think she would never be able to face rising from bed again.

Several days passed in this manner. Lucia kept resolutely to her bed, claiming a headache. She took the food Mary brought her and ate enough to convince her father and Isabella she would recover her strength eventually. The doctor, who was called back, was mystified, and attributed Lucia's symptoms entirely to her ordeal, which had been confided to him. He agreed there was little to be concerned over since she had no fever.

Yet all of the time in silence, alone, when Lucia should have been sleeping but was not actually in need of the slumber, did not help her state of mind. All she could think of was Len. Julian had promised to contact her. How would he do so? True enough, he had stolen into her chamber once before, but she could not imagine him taking such a risk merely to put her mind at ease.

Was Len alive or dead? For all Lucia knew, she was buried in the cold earth, in an unmarked grave somewhere in the forest. Lucia could see her pale-faced, blue-lipped, and lifeless all too clearly in her mind. But surely Len would fight to hold on to her life? How would Lucia ever know?

The thought came that she would never see Len again. If Len lived, she would slip away into the dark shadows, her own safety her priority, and Lucia would be left in the jarring illumination of her privileged existence. How could she ever see Len? She was an outlaw. Before that night on the roadside she had never encountered a criminal in her life. It was unlikely Len and she would be thrown together by fate. Such a thing would have to be engineered. She had no idea how to even consider it. And would Len even be inclined to contemplate it? Just how did Len feel towards her?

The memory of those kisses and caresses in the night haunted Lucia. In those moments, reality itself had been exposed, clear to her, more vivid than ever. Now, as days slipped by, she wondered if it had been a glowing dream. Could such a thing really exist? But love pulled at her heart, mingled with the grief. Lucia knew it, though it was a sentiment she had once thought she would never understand. But love for a woman, albeit one who conducted herself as a man? Was it possible? It had to be, because it filled her heart to aching. She felt it as sharp and hot as she had that night beneath the oak. Her whole being was filled with longing to see Len again, and yet there was a numb certainty within her she would not. Lucia prayed she was not dead.

Lucia kept to her bed for over a week. Gradually, as her appetite increased, her father and sister shed the looks of deep concern with which they regarded her. She loved their visits just as she hated them. Every time she saw them she was reminded of her lies and, more than that, her sheer otherness from them. Still, it was hard to resist Isabella's warm smile, her father's earnest eyes, and as time wore on, she grew more used to being with them once more.

A week and a day after Lucia's return, Isabella—obviously judging her strength was sufficient now for neighbourhood gossip—perched on the end of her bed to inform her of all she had missed. "Susan Beale danced twice with a Mr. Wood, who is from the north." The most recent dance had been at the assembly rooms, and Isabella had attended despite her anxiety for Lucia. Lucia was neither surprised nor offended, and smiled at her sister's enthusiasm. "But Kitty Thorne was most displeased with Mr. Epworth, if her expression was anything to go by, though he is most handsome, it has to be said."

"And what of Lord Hyde?" Lucia asked. She watched Isabella's face colour.

"We have not seen him, but he is to be at Lord and Lady Netherfield's ball, which is a week hence. And then there's Mr. Shelton's Christmas ball. Oh, I haven't told you of it yet, have I? He is inviting everyone he can think of. He is looking for a new wife of course, and I think Anne Drew has her sights set on him, even if he is nearly forty."

When the important news had been related to Lucia in exclamations and giggles, Isabella rose, since she was anxious to re-trim a bonnet with the lace she had purchased in the week. "Oh, and those awful Luddites have been at it again," she said, as she turned to go.

"They have?" Lucia was unable to entirely hide the waver in her voice. It betrayed the flurry of sentiment stirring inside her.

"Yes, over near Kirkby somewhere, they broke all the frames belonging to a Mr. Hawkins. I've never heard of him though, have you?"

"No." Lucia's throat was tight.

"Well, they caught three of them, apparently, and took them to the county gaol. They are to be tried at the assizes next week, but they will hang of course. Shots were fired, according to Anne's mother—who heard it from Mrs. Steele in town—and she thinks at least one of them was killed."

Lucia marvelled at the ease with which Isabella could relate matters of life and death. She stared at her sister, a lump in her throat preventing any words. She fought against the tears threatening to give her away. Looking anxious at her distressed countenance, Isabella came to rest a hand on her shoulder. Lucia almost jumped at her touch. "Sorry, darling," her sister said. "I should not have told you such a horrible story when you are not well. You're tired. Shall I ask Mary to bring up a glass of hot milk?"

"No, thank you. I think I will just rest," Lucia told her, unable to face the notion of anyone else in the room to intrude on her turbulent emotions.

"See you later, then," Isabella said, and breezed out of the door. Lucia turned her face into the pillow, her fingers clasping the cold of the locket beneath—the cause of all this—which Len had held in her fingers, and she sobbed with longing for her.

The very next day Lucia was awoken early by a commotion downstairs. Isabella came through her door within a few minutes of her opening her eyes, clearly keen to relate what had happened.

"Oh, good, you're awake," she said. "You'll never guess!"

"No, I will not," Lucia said, irritated and sleepy.

"Well, I'll tell you." Isabella was unperturbed. "That horse, the one you rode back on, it's gone."

Lucia sat upright in bed instantly, her heart pounding. "Gone? What do you mean?"

"Just gone. In the night. He was there last night, and then when Jenkins went into the stables this morning, he was gone."

Lucia's mind raced for an explanation. Only one presented itself. "Was there a note of any kind?" She tried to sound largely disinterested.

"A note? Why would there be a note?" Isabella looked puzzled for a moment. When Lucia didn't reply, she continued without waiting. "Well, everyone's in uproar of course. It means the highwaymen have been back here, doesn't it?"

"Yes," Lucia replied weakly. Isabella caught her expression.

"Oh, I'm sorry, I forgot it might frighten you. Can you believe it? But they didn't break into the house, so they cannot want any more from you, surely?"

"No, apparently not." Lucia was sure Isabella took her new distress for a renewal of the terror she had felt when she had been taken from the house. If only her sister knew how, in the secret depths of her heart, she was wondering why they had not come into the house, why they had left no message.

Isabella left Lucia's chamber shortly afterwards. Lucia thought of Oberon being taken in the night. Who had it been? Julian? A weak ray of hope shone though: Oberon was Len's horse. If she needed him, she had to be alive. The flickering optimism was extinguished immediately as she remembered these were thieves and mercenaries. Oberon was too valuable a possession to lose, whether his rider was alive or dead. Above all came the numbing thought: *they have been here, to my home, and they have not contacted me*. Lucia could not have felt her total separation from Len any more strongly.

CHAPTER EIGHTEEN

The very next day, Lucia rose from her bed and dressed before Mary came to wake her. Something about the total despair which had now taken over her spirit galvanised her body into action. She could bear no more hours of silent contemplation.

When she went down to breakfast, Lucia saw the delight on her father's countenance. "You are well, Lucia?" he asked, hopefully.

"Yes, Father, I think I am quite recovered," she said. She would never recover from losing Len, but what else could she answer?

"I am very glad." He smiled. Her father was a man of few words, but his warmth and caring had characterised her upbringing and she smiled back, grateful he was a gentle man.

She ate well of the eggs, ham, and bread they were provided for breakfast, to prove to them she was indeed as healthy as she claimed. As the plates were being cleared, her father told her something to weigh her soul down further. "I have decided," he said, "bearing in mind the ease with which both our house and stables have been invaded, to ask one of the men to be on guard every night, armed with a musket."

"But, Father," Lucia protested, struggling to maintain a calm exterior, "surely now that they have released me and taken back their horse, they will have no cause to visit again." She still hoped Julian would come to her, tell her the news she was aching to hear. The idea that, in doing so, he would encounter an armed guard was quite horrific. She still remembered, all too clearly, the echoes of shots in the night.

"I am taking no more chances," her father said resolutely. "I should never have kept that horse here, I don't know what I was thinking. I will sleep sounder if I know my house and family are safe. What with highwaymen and tales of masked frame-breakers abroad, there is much to guard against."

"We do not have any frames to break, Father."

"No, but if outlaws are prowling the county, I will make my family safe."

"We are safe, I am sure." Lucia knew she could not protest too vehemently.

"I would have thought you, of all people, would welcome the notion of better certainty of that safety." Her father narrowed his eyes, puzzled.

"Yes, I do." Lucia was unable to say anything else.

Lucia need not have worried for the safety of any highwayman coming to Foxe Hall to deliver a message of hope to her. No one came. She did not attend the series of balls and dances preceding the celebration of Christmas. Never very keen on these public gatherings, she now found the notion of attending one—with the false niceties, the structured dances, the heaps of rich food—quite abhorrent. She helped Isabella to dress in her finery and listened with feigned eagerness to her reports of what had occurred on each occasion but claimed always she felt too weak or out of spirits to attend the celebrations herself. Her father watched with anxious eyes, but since Lucia ate well, ventured to walk in the park, and laughed with Isabella, his fears were soothed.

In early January, Isabella was engaged to Lord Hyde. Of course, he had been entertained in Foxe Hall on more than one occasion by that time, and Lucia liked him. He was a tolerably handsome young man with reddish-brown hair and an easy smile. His aspect was one of kindness and good breeding. That Isabella loved him, Lucia had no doubt, and watching his blue eyes brighten as he gazed on her sister, she was convinced the sentiment was mutual.

Her father was overjoyed by the match. Not only did he foresee a future of happiness for his youngest daughter, it was an exceedingly good marriage. Lord Hyde was a rich man of high social standing, with both a country estate and a house in London. As Lady Hyde, Isabella would rise higher than their little world of country gentry, and her fortune was guaranteed. They would be married quickly, before the end of March.

Isabella was positively alight with excitement and love. Lucia was struck by a devastating and bitter envy, which she was—of course—compelled to conceal within her heart. She was happy for her sister, it would have been hard not to be. Yet to see her so fulfilled, so in love, only reminded Lucia of her own loss, her bleak future. She would never make her father happy by a good marriage. And she feared, having tasted love so briefly, she was wounded immutably, never to love again. How could she ever love any man? It was impossible. Yet she knew nothing of whether the object of her longing still breathed, or rotted somewhere beneath the cold earth. As she went through the motions of daily life, Lucia was empty.

Even emptiness, especially when it is hidden, cannot prevent the moving on of time, the expectation of healing. Soon Lucia found Isabella wanted her to travel with her in the carriage into town, to visit the dressmaker or to help her choose a new bonnet or ribbon her fiancé would approve of. Lucia could hardly refuse, since outwardly there was nothing really wrong with her. Despite the heartache the journey caused—seeing the roads and trees she had not set eyes upon since that dreamlike week and which were alive with the ghosts of memories—from the middle of January, they visited town regularly, every Wednesday morning. They would call at the shops Isabella wanted to, perhaps attend upon one of their acquaintances who lived in the town, take luncheon at the inn, and then rattle back along the turnpike in the carriage, to be home by late afternoon.

Lucia came to dread those Wednesdays and wondered at Isabella's relentlessly regular wish to travel to town. She supposed that, anticipating her new London home, Isabella craved the bustle, the opportunities to part with her money.

It was the fifth consecutive Wednesday they had visited the town. Isabella had been fitted for a new riding habit, despite the fact she rarely rode, and they were walking through the square to attend upon Charlotte Willoughby—a second cousin on their mother's side of the family—in her smart town house. Charlotte, who was a year Lucia's senior, had lived in town only since her marriage eight months previously and was still keen to be visited by her country acquaintances whenever there was opportunity for it.

The air was bitingly cold, the sky clear and bright in contrast to the preceding days, which had been gloomy and threatened snow which had never fallen. The brighter day had drawn all manner of people into the open, and it was busy in the square. Several times they had to alter their path to avoid collisions with other people meandering haphazardly. Lucia's attention was drawn to a smartly-dressed couple walking straight towards her and Isabella.

Lucia glanced at the man's face and almost stopped dead. Dark hair, stern eyes, a well-trimmed beard framing a smile. She would have known Julian's countenance anywhere. His eyes were fixed on her face as recognition dawned in her. Lucia glanced from him to the person at his side.

If the woman had been alone, Lucia would almost certainly have walked past her and never recognised her. She wore a long crimson velvet coat in the latest fashion, over a cream muslin gown, with matching crimson velvet gloves, a bonnet trimmed with local lace, and crimson ribbons. It was so different from breeches and a man's coat. But the woman whose dark eyes locked with Lucia's was Len, sure enough. Lucia bit her lip and swallowed to prevent the sound of joyful astonishment escaping her throat.

Lucia wanted so desperately to run to Len and take her in her arms. She was alive! The grief melted from Lucia's overwrought heart. Len lived, she was here in town, she was walking towards her. It was with an effort Lucia kept her pace steady.

"Excuse me." Len addressed Lucia and Isabella with an even expression. At the sound of Len's voice, which had haunted Lucia's dreams through the whole winter, Lucia wanted to cry with relief. Instead, she maintained her composure with some effort and came to a halt just in front of her.

"Yes?" Isabella asked curiously of the strangers. Lucia's heart pounded in her head as she wondered what would happen next.

"Could you tell us the direction to the Bell Inn?" Julian said. "I'm afraid we are new to the town."

"Oh yes, of course," Isabella replied.

Len willed Lucia to speak, though she looked too astonished for words. Len wanted to hear her voice very badly. She wanted to meet Lucia's gaze. She longed to look deeply into those blue eyes, into the countenance she had seen in her dreams all winter long. She was desperate to tell Lucia how important her belief in their enduring love had been to her recovery. She wanted to apologise for leaving Lucia in ignorance of her safety for so long. But she could say nothing, not with Isabella here. Anyway, she would not take the risk in the centre of town. The relief of seeing Lucia looking healthy and happy, and standing here so close to her, made her giddy with a joy it was hard not to express in some way. Making brief eye contact with Lucia, she saw enough to give her hope.

Lucia was intelligent enough, Len was sure, to know it was not coincidence they had encountered her and Julian here. But this was about far more than reassurance. Len wanted Lucia to know she lived. She wanted to see Lucia with her own eyes. But she needed more than a stolen moment of comfort. That would only be a worse torment in the days and months to come. But would Lucia still be prepared to take risks? Would she have written off her time in the woods with outlaws as a queer nightmare she was glad to have mostly forgotten? Seeing Lucia prim and well turned out, walking in town with her pretty sister, was almost enough to deter Len from today's mission. Then Julian pointed out to her that in her outward appearance, her genteel disguise, she looked very little different to Lucia herself. What you saw on the outside did not always reveal what was beneath. She would not know how she stood with Lucia unless she ventured a little more.

"Thank you," Julian said. Len looked at him, confused, and realised Isabella had finished giving him her directions. Why could he have not asked for the route to somewhere more difficult to find? She did not want to move away from Lucia yet. There was so much she wanted to say, so much she needed Lucia to know. So many questions.

"Yes, thank you." Len smiled. There was nothing else she could do. Lucia was looking at her now, and Len saw pain in her eyes. She ached to think of herself as the cause of that pain, and yet somehow, she hoped she was.

"You're welcome," Lucia said. Her tone suggested she did not want to be left out of this conversation of so few words. At the sound of her voice, Len's heart quickened and her stomach lurched. To think of living without Lucia was impossible. And yet today was the day upon which that future would be decided. This could be the last time she ever set eyes on Miss Lucia Foxe. Len felt sick and put the notion out of her head. She had faith in Lucia. She thought she knew her heart.

The note was in her hand, the words on which everything depended, upon which her life seemed to balance. She passed very close to Lucia and pressed the small folded piece of paper into her gloved hand. She glanced very quickly at Lucia's sister, who was apparently oblivious. A very quick moment of eye contact with Lucia, which she wanted so badly to sustain for longer, and she was walking away across the town square, her arm in Julian's.

This was a horrible masquerade. Here she was in her fine gown and velvet coat, on the arm of a handsome man, walking briskly through the town. At any moment in the recent years she would have felt out of place, uncomfortable. Today was worse. Today she had adopted this disguise not to hide in that world but to flirt with it. Today she had to infiltrate that world to get to Lucia. And what if Lucia preferred that world in the end? Len knew, without a doubt, she could not remain in Lucia's world. It felt false, worse than a pretence. But it was not a lie to Lucia. It was her life. Did she have enough to offer to draw Lucia away from that? Lucia had, after all, had the entire winter to consider it. Tonight, Len would get her answer.

❖

Sitting in the window seat of her chamber, as the sky burned with the oranges and yellows of the setting sun, Lucia held the still-folded piece of paper. She had hidden it in the sleeve of her coat for the rest of her time in town with Isabella. Even while Isabella had been busy with her milliner, Lucia had paced the floor and had not dared to look at the note Len had given her. Were the words ones of hope, or ones of farewell? If they were ones of hope, then what did the future hold? At the notion of a future with Len in it, she felt her heart beat just a little faster. Yet it still seemed so impossible. And how could she have a claim on a woman like Len? Lucia would not compromise the freedom of spirit that defined the woman she loved. And love her she still did. Maybe it was better that Len said her farewells now, leaving Lucia to love her from a distance.

She ran her fingers over the smooth paper. For an instant the future was of less importance. What mattered was that Len was alive, and in case Lucia thought she had imagined it in her grief, she held the piece of paper as proof. Joy filled her heart with the knowledge that Len was not cold in the ground after all. Surely, if there was still life, there were still choices, still ways of living that life. Len had taught her that much.

Lucia looked out across the parkland to the countryside beyond. Somewhere Len lurked among the trees, a shadow among shadows. Or maybe she mingled, disguised as she had earlier been, among unsuspecting company. Did she ride out on the roads tonight, her pistol at her side, to terrorise another family? Perversely, Lucia almost envied her prospective victims.

Impulsively, Lucia went to her bed and removed her mother's locket from beneath the pillow, then returned, clutching it, to the window seat. Would her mother have understood this love any better than Isabella or her father? Lucia doubted it. Yet she wanted her mother with her when she read Len's words. The locket had taken on a far greater significance. It was her mother's, holding her portrait and her hair, and somehow, at the same time, it held Lucia's recollections of nights in the dark woods, the sting of the black powder on her skin, and of Len, warm beside her.

Lucia let the locket rest in her lap and unfolded the paper slowly. Len's hand was neat and sloping, the hand of an educated woman.

Dearest Lucia,

You will be surprised, no doubt, over the manner of delivery of this little note. Only be glad your visits to town have been regular enough for Julian to have observed you every Wednesday for the last three weeks. If you are reading this now, it means I have been successful, and today I was able to lay my eyes upon you once more.

Poor Lucia, you must have suffered agonies when Julian sent you away. I am sorry, though you must know I would have done the same. That you are safe is my only wish.

You will also forgive, I hope, Julian's rescue of Oberon from your stable. Once I recovered from my injuries, I needed my horse. Perhaps you thought he would have some message for you and were disappointed to discover nothing of the sort. That was my instruction. I did not want to risk anything of what occurred between us being discovered, for your sake as much as my own.

However, I had to see you once more, Lucia. I do not know what your life has been since your return home. I cannot know if you wish to forget me. If so, I apologise. You may burn this letter and think of me no more. However, if your feelings are not so hostile, I would see you again.

I cannot come to your house. Perhaps, having seen my disguise of today, you will think I could call on you quite respectably. However, I will take no such risks. Besides, I have once before felt the consequences of such relations being carried on in the half gaze of a family. I will not put you through that, nor your family either.

If we are to meet, it must be in secret. Perhaps this is too much to ask of you. If you wish such a thing, tonight, the night you took this note from my hand, be by your chamber window at nine o'clock. Take a candle and place it in the window. As the clock strikes, cover the flame, so from outside it is obscured. Then let it shine again. Repeat this action three times. If you do so, I will see your signal and I will know we can meet again. Tomorrow afternoon, after one o'clock, ride out into your park. Ask to be allowed to go alone. I will wait for you.

You know I live my life in secrets and shadows, beloved Lucia. Now I ask you to do the same. If you cannot, I will understand.

Yours, in hope,
Len

As Lucia read the letter, hot tears streamed over her cheeks. The sheer pleasure of reading words from Len's hand, the evidence she lived, was enough to transport her into realms of delight she had not known since she had shared the darkness with their author.

Lucia ached as Len wrote of her own doubts. How could Len think Lucia would not want to meet her? Lucia forgave her everything she asked and, touching the place on the paper where she had signed her name, longed to be close to her again. The time until nine o'clock, when she could give Len her reply, seemed to stretch endlessly.

❖

Len crouched, motionless, in the undergrowth near the perimeter wall of Foxe Hall. She did not want to risk drawing the attention of the armed guard by attempting to enter the grounds of the house itself. Besides which, she did not need to. She simply needed to see Lucia's window.

Would Lucia disappoint her now? Would Len finally know her own judgement to be faulty, know there was no chance of love for her, after all? Because she thought she saw love in Lucia's eyes. She felt she understood Lucia's heart, her very soul. What if she was wrong? How would she bear the disappointment when she hoped for so much? She'd put her faith in the silly little rich girl. It was ludicrous. And yet here she was.

Julian had offered to accompany her tonight. She had put him off, telling him that she would be safer alone, arouse less suspicion. In truth, she did not want him here to witness her possible humiliation. To see how much she wanted this, and how devastated she would be if her trust in Lucia proved to be misguided.

She wondered what the time was. She carried a silver pocket watch these days, taken from a particularly unpleasant army colonel travelling back to his Yorkshire estate early in January. It was partly because of Lucia that she carried the watch. When she questioned her own morals, questioned the goodness Lucia saw in her, she remembered that colonel, who'd she heard had sent many men to bloody deaths in the wars, and beat a cowardly retreat to his luxurious country estate with his young wife when questions had been asked of his suitability for command. That colonel was still accepted in society, a respected man. He could have proposed marriage to Lucia or her sister. How Len made her living was no worse.

Now she longed to look at the watch, see how close to the hour the time was. But it would be pointless to try to peer at it in the darkness. All she could do was keep her eyes on the house in front of her, and on Lucia's window in particular. She watched, and she waited, barely daring to breathe.

After what seemed like more than the few minutes it must have been, the window was illuminated by the light of a single candle. Len's heart beat quickly, and she felt dizzy. Now was the moment. She tried to peer beyond the light. To imagine Lucia in her room, looking out into the night. What was she feeling?

Len watched the light. She didn't dare blink, in case she missed the signal. The light flickered. And then disappeared. Len stopped breathing. The light shone once more. Len bit her lip and watched. Her chest was tight. The light disappeared again. Still, she would not believe it, even as she saw the light again. *One more time, my love.* She repeated it in her head. One more time. The light was obscured. A moment later it shone into the night again. Len heard her own cry of relief and was glad Julian was not present to see the tears that filled her eyes.

Lucia wanted her and there was still a chance for love. Len wanted to dance with the joy of it. She gazed at the house, kissed her fingers and blew the kiss in the direction of Lucia's window. She swept her tricorn from her head and made Lucia an exaggerated bow. "Until tomorrow, my sweet love," she said to the night.

Moments later she had melted into the shadows once more.

CHAPTER NINETEEN

If Lucia had thought the hours of the previous day drifted by slowly, it was nothing compared to the excruciating time it took every minute of the following morning to pass. Her father had ridden to town, and Isabella was visiting Anne Drew in the next village. Lucia was fortunate she did not, therefore, have to notify anyone of her intention to ride out in the park. She ate luncheon alone and asked Mary to tell Jenkins in the stable to ready Sally for her. Mary was pleased she wished for exercise and fresh air and Lucia assumed her father would feel similarly, should he return to the house before she did.

When she went out to the stables at five minutes after one o'clock, dressed warmly in her riding cloak and gloves, bonnet secure upon her head, she found Sally waiting by the mounting block. Jenkins was making a final adjustment to her girth and nodded his greeting to her as she approached.

"She's ready for it, Miss Foxe. Give her a good gallop," he said. He stroked the mare's neck affectionately.

"Of course." Lucia climbed onto the block. As she balanced upon the saddle, she recalled Len's habit of riding astride the horse, as a man would, and thought how cumbersome and difficult a lady's saddle really was. She recollected the first time she had been mounted upon Oberon, Len close behind her, and felt the thrill of anticipation alive in her heart once more.

"Thank you," she said to Jenkins. He nodded and patted Sally's rump, urging her into motion. Lucia walked her across the yard, for it was a while since she had ridden and she needed a moment to reacquaint herself with the sensations, the balance. As she rounded the corner of the house, where the path led directly into the parkland behind the house, she nudged the horse into a trot, which soon became a swift canter, up the slight bank which rose from the house to the rolling grass of the wilder park beyond. Foxe Hall was surrounded by fields and coppices, and gave the impression of being much larger than it was.

Once Lucia was out of view of all but the highest attic windows of the house, she slowed Sally to a walk and looked around. How would Len know where she was? She was filled with anxiety once more, frightened the plan would be unsuccessful and she would be forced to turn for home without seeing Len. That would be unbearable.

She turned Sally in a small circle, glancing keenly at her surroundings, and set off again at a brisk trot, determined to cover the entire park, to be sure of seeing Len if she could.

She had ridden close to the edge of the park when she heard hoof falls almost exactly in time with Sally's, only heavier, approaching from behind. She drew a deep breath, not daring to look back.

The rhythm of the dull thuds behind her changed into a canter and began to gain on her. She continued the trot, her lips pressed together, gripping the reins until her fingers hurt.

One moment Lucia was alone in anticipation, listening hard, the next Len was there beside her. Lucia saw the shine of Oberon's glossy black flank, the flash of Len's white breeches, the dark blue of Len's cloak, all a blur to her side, as Len cantered up to her. Turning her head, upon which she wore her usual tricorn, towards Lucia, Len smiled, a playful smile Lucia had not seen before. She pushed Oberon further, into a gallop. Lucia dug gently at Sally's side and, as though the mare was herself infused by her rider's excitement, Sally sprang into a gallop nearly as swift as the stallion's.

Len galloped across the open meadow at the upper end of the park. Her cloak billowed behind her, and the tail of long hair at her back flew as she rode. Sally kept pace just behind her, and Lucia felt her own cloak swept backwards. The wind toyed with her bonnet, was cold and pure on her face. The horses' hooves made an exuberant thunder on the earth and she felt she would overflow with the sheer joy of it.

Eventually, nearing the Gothic archways of the old folly which stood at this part of the park, more ruined and overgrown now than it was ever supposed to be when it was built in the previous century, Len slowed Oberon and eventually drew him to a halt. Lucia pulled Sally up beside them.

Len dismounted quickly and turned to Lucia as she sat in her saddle, smiling. She offered Lucia her hand. "Miss Foxe," she said, full of mock formality, as she helped her dismount.

"Sir?" Lucia said, teasing, and was rewarded with Len's laughter. Once Lucia was steady on her feet, they faced each other. Lucia tore off her glove and held trembling fingers to Len's face, stroked her warm cheek. "You are really alive," she breathed.

"Yes." Len's gaze burned into Lucia's.

"You are not a ghost and I'm not dreaming?" Lucia was still scarce able to believe Len stood in front of her, with such warmth in her expression.

"No," she said. "Did you dream of me, Lucia?"

"Yes." Lucia felt shy for a moment.

"I was afraid you would not come."

"I thought I would never see you again."

"And yet here we are." Len smiled that wonderful hint of a smile.

"Yes." The next moment their lips were pressed together, and Lucia felt Len's arms strong around her once more. The velvet kiss soothed away all the pain of the months since she had last set eyes upon her. Love flourished in Lucia's heart and grew stronger to have its subject so close.

Len kissed Lucia deeper, harder, wanted her to know just how desperately she wanted her. She did not need to ask if Lucia forgave her, or had missed her, or wanted her. She could read it in Lucia's clear blue eyes, feel it in her embrace, in her kiss. All the moments when her life had hung in the balance, all the close calls with death, all the moments of joy, and fear, and exhilaration, were nothing compared to how it felt to have Lucia in her arms again.

The grass behind the wall of the folly was damp, though it did not penetrate the double thickness of their cloaks laid on top of one another. The late-February air was chill on their exposed skin, but Len covered Lucia with her body and they were warm once more. As Len made love to Lucia, she glimpsed a clump of snowdrops close to Lucia's golden curls. She kissed Lucia tenderly and reached over to pluck one of the tender white flowers. Lucia, who had closed her eyes, opened them again to see what Len was doing. Len ran the delicate flower over Lucia's cheek, over her pink parted lips, and over her throat. Lucia breathed deeply and smiled.

Len smiled down into Lucia's face. "How long do you think snowdrops have bloomed here?" she asked, softly.

"I couldn't say." Lucia looked at Len with curiosity in her eyes.

Len held the flower to her own lips, felt it tickle slightly and kissed the little bloom. "I can imagine they've been here for centuries," she said. "Nature's way of reassuring us that spring will come again." It was inexorable, the return of colour and warmth and life, even after the harshest of winters. Len felt it so strongly. Her heart had been barren and cold. But Lucia had brought it back, reminded her that spring could come. Now, on this cold day, they drew heat from each other.

"That's a beautiful thought," Lucia said, a dreamy look in her eyes.

Len placed the snowdrop on Lucia's smooth chest, in the shallow valley between her breasts, and bent to kiss the swell next to it. "Not as beautiful as you, Lucia. My love."

"How I have wanted you, Helena Hawkins. How I have loved you…" Lucia's words were a sigh. Len moved her lips over Lucia's skin and drew more sighs of pleasure from her.

"You saved my life, Lucia. In my darkest moments, when I thought I was slipping out of the world, I came back for you."

There were tears in Lucia's eyes. "Thank you. I didn't know how to go on without you…"

Len moved her kisses back to Lucia's soft lips, as her hands rediscovered every beloved inch of Lucia's body. In the remnants of a false ruin, in the farthest reaches of the park, they knew again what love was, and the cold of late winter was banished.

❖

"When will I see you again?" Lucia demanded of Len as they lingered over the necessary parting, dressed in their cloaks and gloves once more. Dusk was approaching, and Lucia's father would worry if it grew dark before her return.

"Soon," Len replied.

"But how I will know?"

Len eased her hand into Lucia's, gripping firmly, wanting very badly to reassure her. "You will know. I always have a way." She would. Whatever it took.

"What am I going to do?" Lucia said.

"What do you mean?" Len's heart stuttered with worry. Was it possible that Lucia would doubt her?

"I do not feel at home in the house any longer. I love my father and Isabella, of course. But I feel separate from them somehow."

Len looked at Lucia earnestly, her heart aching for her with a pain she remembered so very well herself. Her stomach twisted with nerves. Lucia's love she did not doubt. Lucia's ability to let go of the life she was so used to she was not so certain of. "I was afraid for you," she said, "when I first began to see that your heart yearned for more, in the same way as mine. You must remember I told you this could happen."

"Yes, I do." Lucia hesitated, and Len watched her keenly. "And I don't mind it really. Only I cannot see how I can live this way forever. Especially when Isabella is married next month." At Lucia's words, Len felt a stirring of relief.

"You do not long to marry yourself?" she asked. She felt she had to ask the question of Lucia, but there was a hint of irony in her tone, for she really knew the reply she would receive.

"No," Lucia said. "Do I seem as though I am looking for a husband?" She smiled a smile that was nothing short of wicked.

"No, you most certainly do not." Len laughed gently, her heart easier.

"But can this go on forever?"

"Nothing can go on forever," Len replied. She believed that maxim with all her heart. "But change cannot always be commanded. You never know what might happen. That is how I live."

"Is it enough?"

"Not, perhaps, forever. But for today, yes." They were silent in mutual contemplation. "I will see you again before long, I promise," Len said, lifting Lucia's hand to her mouth and kissing her fingers through the velvet gloves.

"I will depend upon it." Lucia squeezed Len's fingers. Len turned reluctantly to mount Oberon.

She took up the reins and turned the horse. She glanced at Lucia and put her hand to her hat, tilting it briefly. "Until later then, Miss Foxe," she said. She made sure to fill her smile with reassurance. She would find a way to make their love possible. Because parting from Lucia felt like tearing out her own heart. Urging Oberon into his graceful canter, she thundered away across the park, to the place where it met the countryside beyond, a gap in the wall allowing access.

Lucia watched until Len vanished. She led Sally to a place where she could stand on the wall of the folly to mount her, and climbed into the saddle. The sun was low and burning orange in the pale sky as she arrived back at the stables, windswept and flushed, her heart alive with the ecstasy of love.

Lucia did not see Len again before Isabella was married. She watched the ceremony with an odd, hollow feeling inside her, knowing she would never stand before the altar with her husband to be, glowing as Isabella now did. She understood all too well that her pleasures and passions would be forever of a more clandestine nature. The small church was filled with family, neighbours, and, as a result of the status of the groom, a fine collection of lords and ladies. Lucia would never celebrate her love in front of such a host of people, all wishing her well. Life held something so different for her. For a fleeting moment, she almost wished herself in Isabella's place.

However, at the feast which followed—during which Lucia had to endure many enquiries after her own lack of suitor and of her late absence from society—she knew she did not, in fact, crave the life Isabella did. That life did not have Len in it. And its rules were fast becoming suffocating.

As Lucia kissed the new Lady Hyde goodbye and Isabella climbed into her splendidly liveried carriage—her husband smiling broadly at her side—Lucia saw the simple pleasure in her eyes and was almost angry with her. Why did she not expect more? Surely there was something she yearned for, something not fulfilled by this marriage? How could she go through with it so cheerfully? Lucia forced her fond farewells and stepped away from the carriage. Isabella was driven into her future by grooms and footmen and four matching bays. Lucia prayed it would be all her sister wanted it to be.

The weeks after Isabella's departure were hard. The house was oddly silent without her, though Sir Spencer and Lucia kept up their usual routines. They read the dispatches in the newspapers for news of the war on the frontier of Spain, and Lucia imagined her brother George in that sun-baked, barren landscape. She had gained a new understanding of the threat he faced, of the powder and smoke, and death, of a soldier's life. She almost smiled when she wondered what her brother would think if he knew his sister had learned to fire a pistol.

In the dense letters covering the pages of the newspapers Lucia also found accounts of frame-breaking in the county and read of its spread farther north, into the woollen factories of Yorkshire. She thought of Bill Wilcock and the others. As her father expressed his disgust at the men turned against their masters in such a way, she thought of the strain she had seen in their eyes. It struck her she would never see them again, never know their fates. They had slipped back into the unknown, mysterious again. Only not so frightening. Lucia was beginning to see that sometimes what lies in the shadows is not a threat, it is only the unknown. She had seen into those marginal places, and she was no longer afraid of the dark.

She read accounts too of criminals found guilty at the assizes and executed upon the steps of the Shire Hall in town. Frame-breakers, thieves, murderers, all were treated in the same manner. Lucia attempted to close her ears as her father read sections of the reports aloud. All too well did she understand that some of Len's men and at least two of the frame-breakers—who knew which?—were among those to have met their deaths by the cruel rope. If Len were captured, no mercy would be shown. Lucia could not bear to think on it.

Lucia spent her time pondering how different the world appeared now. Her notions of justice, of evil, of freedom, her very foundations of right and wrong had shifted fundamentally. She longed to discuss such things with her father, but there was no way she could even begin such a conversation.

She was becoming quite desperate to see Len again, when Len obliged. Mary came to Lucia in the middle of the morning on a sunny day in late March to tell her a servant had called from a Miss Catherine Maltby in town, with a message for Lucia. Miss Maltby was visiting the nearby village and asked Lucia to call on her that afternoon. Mary saw nothing amiss. However, Lucia knew no one of that name and saw Len's hand behind the plan immediately.

Shortly after lunch, Lucia dressed smartly and walked briskly down the driveway, declaring to Mary her intention to walk to the village that she might breathe the spring air, asking her to inform her father of the same when he emerged from his study where he had been ensconced with Mr. Royston, his lawyer and good friend, all morning.

Len waited for Lucia on the road between Foxe Hall and the village. She had left Oberon with Julian at their new hideout in the woods not so far from The Red Lion Inn and walked the few miles to Foxe Hall. It was a fine day, and she enjoyed the solitude. She smiled as she waited, thinking back to her conversation with Julian of earlier that morning. She had just finished washing her face in a bowl of cold water, and the edges of her hair were still dripping when he'd come to stand near her, at the back of the derelict barn they were using as a temporary shelter, and offered her a small Spanish cigar.

"From the cigar box of a certain Mr. Giles, who travelled the Mansfield road but three days ago and met with an unfortunate event."

"My heart goes out to the man. All his pomposity did not save him from losing his purse. Or his cigars." Len drew on the sweet smoke and enjoyed the sensation that crept through her body. "His excellent cigars, at that."

"You'll miss all of this, you know," Julian said then. He looked off into the distance nonchalantly.

Len glanced at him sharply. "What do you mean by that?" she asked. She knew perfectly well what he meant.

"You will miss all of this. Living in a barn, riding the roads by night, the spoils of our work."

"Why would I miss it, Julian? I'm going nowhere." Len didn't even believe her own words.

"Oh, don't pretend you've not thought about it, Len. I know you. Miss Foxe is more than just a pretty distraction. And you don't expect her to live in a barn or a woodland hideout."

"No, Julian. You are right." She coloured slightly. "On both counts."

"I wasn't asking, Len. You're in love. I've seen it before."

"You don't mind it?"

"If you mean on my sister's behalf, not at all. If Hattie had lived, you would have been faithful to her always, I have no doubt. But she isn't here now. And, queer though it is, Miss Foxe makes you happy. I see it in your face every day."

"But on your own behalf?"

"You don't need my blessing." Julian's voice was gruff.

"I should like it, though." Len reached out and touched his arm gently.

"If you want her Len, grasp hold of your chance. God knows, life is too brief to refuse happiness when it presents itself, in whatever form."

"But?"

"But I worry for your heart. A gentlewoman like that, who spent a week in the woods and became a different girl entirely? And what will she expect of you, Len? You are not easily tamed."

Len laughed. "You make me sound like a wild animal, Julian. I do not require taming. And Lucia did not change so much as emerge from her cage. I know that feeling. As for expectations, well, I am not foolish enough to believe love conquers all, but I do think it helps. I am prepared to make sacrifices. I believe Lucia is too. It doesn't feel like a sacrifice."

"You will not move into Foxe Hall, though, Len. She will not live in a barn."

"I know. Do not ask me how it will be done, but I will find a way. I always do, don't I?"

Julian grinned and nodded. "Aye, Len Hawkins, that you do. And Miss Lucia is a very lucky woman."

"Thank you. I consider myself the fortunate one."

"That's why she's lucky." Julian squeezed her shoulder. "Go and get her, Len. With my blessing."

Now, waiting for Lucia at the roadside, Len thought of that conversation with Julian. His blessing had finally released her from the recurring feeling she was somehow betraying Hattie's memory by loving Lucia. Julian had known Hattie better than anyone. And his faith in the truth of her feelings, of the power of her love for Lucia, only strengthened those feelings in her heart.

Her eyes found Lucia the moment she turned the corner of the road leading from Foxe Hall. In her matching mauve cloak and bonnet, she was the image of a proper gentlewoman. But Len knew the truth behind the picture. And she knew she had to find a way to allow their love to flourish. She had to.

Len knew Lucia had caught sight of her, lurking in the shade of a large oak tree, when she quickened her pace. Len felt her own heartbeat respond. When Lucia was close enough that Len could search those blue eyes for traces of doubt, and convince herself once more there were none, Lucia reached out and squeezed Len's fingers in her own. Len smiled and knew she would do whatever it took.

It was not difficult to creep into the fields together, to sit with their backs to a stone wall hands clasped, and to talk, only a flock of sheep to witness it. Lucia's kisses were as eager as they had been in the park, almost a month ago.

"I wish I could see you more often," Lucia said sadly.

"As do I," Len said. "Maybe I can take the air in your park again this week. If we decide upon a time now?"

"Friday, in the afternoon." Lucia's tone was certain, as though she would make the time, even if she found her father had other plans.

"Then it is confirmed." Len smiled.

"I worry for you," Lucia said abruptly. "We read such accounts in the papers."

"Do they write of me?"

"The frame-breakers appear to be more important than you."

"That is not good for my pride." Len was pleased. The attention of the militia was turned elsewhere these days. She had sympathy with the frame-breakers but knew her safety—and Lucia's—to be greater as a result.

"Have you seen them again?" Lucia asked.

"No, not after that night. It is better that way." Len's expression was clouded as recollection drew her gaze into the distance.

"Do you think of it often?"

"No." Len was truthful in her reply. "My father is ordering new machines, of course. I have seen them being delivered. I knew it would be only a minor setback to him. Still, I would not have missed plunging my axe into the heart of his property. If only he knew he had shot his own daughter." Len laughed slightly. The knowledge was too painful to dwell on, and she chose not to. She had not known she would tell Lucia until she was speaking the words.

"It was your father?" Lucia sounded surprised.

"Of course, who else would it have been? I never thought he'd try to kill me." Her voice wavered slightly and she felt herself blush. Only with Lucia would she dare reveal any of her weakness and pain.

"But he did not manage it," Lucia said. She sounded relieved, and Len's anguish was washed away by gratitude, to hear once more that Lucia cared for her, loved her. It recalled her to her own strength, caused a surge of pride in her heart.

"No, he did not. I am, most certainly, alive. He has tried to marry me off, to break me with beatings, to force me to humble myself before him or starve, has even shot me, and yet here I sit, alive and unbroken." Len was resilient again. It was the quality that allowed her to live the life she did. Could she be so now, without Lucia? Or was it Lucia who threatened that resilience? Len did not care. Lucia was fundamental to her now.

"Let it stay that way. I need you to be alive," Lucia said quietly.

"I am careful, Lucia, you know." Len wanted nothing more than to reassure Lucia, though she knew nothing was for certain.

"I know." Lucia replied. She too, was unconvinced. This could not go on. Len knew Lucia needed more certainty. She leant in to kiss her, her mind searching for answers, knowing she would make any sacrifice Lucia needed her to.

❖

And thus the gloriously unbearable pattern of the next six months was established. Len would find some mysterious way to make herself known to Lucia, and Lucia would go to her, her own heart brimming with exultation. Lucia lived partly in terror she would read of Len's arrest in the newspapers and partly under the strain of anticipation, longing for their next encounter. Yet there were moments of joy so pure, she would not have changed those months.

Partly as a result of her preoccupation with Len, Lucia did not notice how ill her father had become. True enough, he had grown quieter and had taken to his study alone more than he was used to but Lucia did not think anything amiss.

Isabella visited with her husband, about four months after her marriage. Her belly was visibly swollen with child, and her excitement at the prospect of motherhood was tangible. Their father shone with pride while Lucia regarded the change in Isabella with some dismay. Her smile was serene and her eyes sparkled still, yet she did not giggle as she used to. Her husband reached for her hand several times as they sat beside each other on the sofa, and Lucia hoped it was a touch of affection, of love, and that Isabella was happy. She had to remind herself that it was possible to find contentment within the conventions of their polite world, that not every woman craved the freedom she did. It made her miss Len, the understanding they shared, all the more.

In late August, on a swelteringly hot day, Lucia's father fell truly ill. He rose from the breakfast table, having eaten little, and immediately slumped to the floor. Lucia summoned Mary and the two women managed to support him, in his half swoon, to the sofa in the sitting room. The doctor attended upon him in the afternoon and recommended bleeding. Sir Spencer was moved to his bed, and Lucia left him alone with the doctor.

The bleeding had no effect. He lingered into the next day, and Lucia soothed his hot forehead with a cool, damp cloth. His eyes wandered gratefully over her face, but he did not utter a word. Whether he had lost his power of speech, Lucia did not know. Later that afternoon, just as the doctor was due to call again, his hand tightened on Lucia's as he drew his last breath. She watched the life pass from him, half fascinated, half horrified by the change in his countenance as his heart beat no more. He did not appear to be sleeping, as she had heard so often said of the deceased. He appeared to be dead. The change was so slight yet so profound, she almost forgot to weep for him. Only as she wished him quick passage into God's keeping, praying he would be finally reunited with her mother, did the grief come.

The next morning, Lucia felt the full consequence of her father's death. She was alone, mistress of Foxe Hall. The building towered around her, so large she could barely contemplate it. She did not want to be its mistress. The feeling so overpowered her she was compelled to run down the stairs—still in her nightdress—across the hallway, and out of the front door, where she gulped at the fresh air. The task in front of her seemed insurmountable.

As it was, however, once Mr. Royston—the lawyer—arrived at Foxe Hall, just before luncheon, Lucia understood she really had very little responsibility in the matter. George would, of course, inherit the house and park from their father. It was a given she would reside there until such a time as she married. George inherited the majority of the financial worth of her father's estate, but Isabella and Lucia were granted an allowance once they were married. Isabella's would go to her and her husband immediately. Lucia wondered if she would ever receive hers. It seemed doubtful.

The next week was a blur of minor details, of arrangements and of visitors all to be politely received. In her black mourning dress, Lucia waited patiently in the drawing room, knowing more callers would arrive before long. Condolences were accepted with thanks. She had not been much in company all winter, and the strain of it all meant she fell exhausted into bed every night. She felt the grief of losing her father but did not truly mourn him. There was not opportunity.

Isabella travelled north for the funeral, her black silk gown decently loose over the growing child in her belly. Lord Hyde did not attend, important business keeping him in London. Instead, Isabella was accompanied by her sister-in-law and that lady's husband. She seemed so at ease with them it was hard for Lucia to imagine Isabella was actually her blood relation and not theirs.

George, the new master of Foxe Hall, was unable to return from the Peninsular. The lawyers gave Lucia their word he had been reached and informed of his father's passing, but it was a difficult moment and George's duty was to remain in Spain with his regiment, preparing for an upcoming battle. There was slim chance he could have travelled home in time for the funeral, they told her. Lucia suspected, despite her faith in her brother, had he been able to travel home in time, he would not have done so. He had thrown himself into the wars as he always had any undertaking. She could not help but be proud of his achievements and vaguely envious of his ability to shrug off his family duties.

Isabella stayed at Foxe Hall with Lucia for a week and then returned to her husband. At first, Lucia thought she was glad to see her sister leave. Isabella was so changed, it unnerved her. However, alone in the house, she grew frightened. What did her life hold now? She did not want to become caught up in managing the estate, especially on behalf of her brother. She knew she would begin to grow old, lonely, lost among the rooms and their memories.

Nor did she have a greater degree of freedom than before. True enough, she could leave the house when she wished, but a large house, even a lesser one such as Foxe Hall, had many pairs of eyes and ears. Mealtimes had to be planned, grooms told if she wanted to ride out. Mary saw her into bed at night and woke her in the morning. Indeed, she was more watchful than ever, in her concern that Sir Spencer's death and Lucia's sudden solitude would throw her back into poor health. There was also village gossip to take into account, and it was noticed if Miss Foxe was away from home when she was called upon, or if she did not return a visit when it was expected she would. While it was maybe a little easier to see Len, still they met cloaked in secrets and shadows. The realisation that even such a huge change as the death of her father had not given them greater opportunity to be together only hastened the urgency with which Lucia contemplated her path into the future.

Eventually, as Len and she sat close together in the September sunshine, once more at the old folly in the park, a way forward—a product of both their minds—took shape.

Chapter Twenty

Len held Oberon steady at the front of the carriage they'd stopped in the road. Her pistol was trained on the driver of the carriage, perched on his box. He did not look particularly terrified, but he was at least doing as he was told. Julian was involved in some sort of quiet exchange with the wealthy gentleman they had encouraged to step out of his carriage and the young woman at his side, who did not appear to be his wife or his daughter. William was searching the carriage for further goods of use to them. Len trusted them to take what they had to, with as much speed as they could. It was better to remain mounted and masked, rather than risk speaking and ruin her disguise.

Her pistol arm was steady, although she knew she would not have to fire. A flintlock was threat enough to keep most men motionless. She knew, as she sat there, she was completely in control. There was no panic or concern in her heart or mind. Her pulse beat slow and steady, her mind even began to wander.

Where was the thrill? True, she might capture it while they rode away into the night or, perhaps, when they examined the spoils later. But the edge was gone. The part of her that could justify this way of life was fading. A smile or a glance from Lucia was more exciting than even the most successful robbery.

Had she grown weak? Now that the need for revenge against her father was eradicated, in the aftermath of her injury, with her heart full of love, had her strength somehow become diminished? Or was there a greater strength in being able to turn away from a life she had thought would always be her lot, in order to pursue a better one, in the name of a love she had absolute faith in? If all of her life was shaped around being able to choose her path for herself, surely she could not turn away from that now?

She was not born to be a highway robber after all. She had fallen to thievery because she had been able to think of no better option. True, she was good at it. There were moments of pure, all-consuming excitement. She was even able to convince herself of the quasi morality of it all, since she stole from the rich and overfed in order to feed herself and her band of hungry men. She was no killer, nor did she pillage indiscriminately. The men followed her, and she relished their trust, the responsibilities of being their leader. But when, as a girl, she had dreamed of the future, it had not been one of running from the gallows and pointing a pistol at unfortunate carriage drivers. She had dreamed of love.

Now she had love. She just had to make the decisions which would allow her to embrace it. It would be the first real choice of her life, and thinking of Lucia, she knew she had the courage to make that choice.

Julian and William were mounting their horses again. Lucia lowered her flintlock and returned it to the holster at her waist. She gave the driver a polite nod, touching her fingers to the brim of her tricorn, and gestured to Julian and William that now was the time to depart. She nudged Oberon into his lurching canter, and soon she was galloping alongside Julian and William, away from the plundered carriage, towards their makeshift hideout.

It was a gallop through the night like so many others. But Len knew, in her heart, everything was different. And it was all for the love of a fair gentlewoman, a love she had never thought possible. If that love *was* possible, anything was. Their plan would work, and the sacrifices would seem as nothing.

❖

Lucia met with Mr. Royston as soon as he would spare her the time. He was an affable man, yet with an air of being in a continual hurry about him. Lucia asked him if he thought it was possible Foxe Hall could be closed, while she spent the winter in Bath with friends.

When he had agreed there was no obvious problem with such a proposition, Lucia ventured a little further. "And I wonder, Mr. Royston," she said, with an uneasy smile, "if there is any way I can receive my father's allowance before I marry? I am, you know, very nearly in my three-and-twentieth year. There is a chance I may not marry. If I am to reside in Bath, I will need some money."

Mr. Royston looked dubious to begin with. The ever-present furrows of his brow deepened further. But he was a kind and sensible man, who understood Lucia's predicament quickly. "We would have to ask permission of your brother." From the honesty and willingness in his intelligent hazel eyes, Lucia had confidence in him to do his best by her. "George controls the estate now. However, I am sure he will consent for an allowance to be paid to you."

"Yes." Lucia's smile was warmer now. "I am sure he will."

It took longer than Lucia had hoped for her brother's permission to be sought. He was somewhere uncertain, his regiment continually on the move. However, eventually the letter came, and Mr. Royston and Lucia were together in her father's study once more. George had no objections either to the closing of Foxe Hall over the winter or to Lucia's being granted an allowance. Technically, her allowance came from her brother, the money reserved by her father for when she married being forfeit by the new arrangement. That settled, she began to write letters.

First, she wrote to Isabella to tell her she would be spending the winter in Bath, with friends she named but with whom she knew Isabella was only vaguely familiar, being acquaintances Lucia had gained on a previous trip she had made alone to Bath. Isabella was now well into her confinement and would be travelling nowhere for several months. Nor, Lucia supposed, with the distractions of her new family and the coming child, would she take much interest in her sister's winter plans. Since their brother had already been informed of her plan, Lucia did not worry there would be any discrepancy, should he and Isabella communicate.

She also informed her local acquaintances she would be wintering with friends in Bath. Some of them voiced their own plans to spend winter at the spa, and Lucia promised to look out for them at the Pump House and Assembly Rooms, while not disclosing the address at which she would be residing. Since they had seen little of Lucia in society for the last year, she knew they would not be especially disappointed when they did not meet with her at the spa.

The next letter Lucia composed was to her friends in Bath, Mrs. Jane Croft and her daughter Annabelle. She begged their forgiveness, told them she had intended to visit them this winter, as they had invited her to do on several occasions, but at the last minute, her aunt from the Lakes had asked her to stay, and she felt she could not refuse. She told them she had already let it be known to some acquaintances where she would be staying, and though she would try to remember to inform them of the change, mistakes could be made. Therefore, there was a chance they might receive letters addressed to Lucia. She asked them to forward any such letters to Foxe Hall, where the servants would send them on to her in the Lakes. This was really a precaution. There was little chance Isabella or George would write to her in Bath, and she had given the address to no one else.

The last part of the scheme was the one Lucia was most fearful over, for it depended upon more than her own resources and ability to mislead, at which she realised she had clearly become adept. One afternoon in October she approached Mary. "I have to discuss something with you," she said.

The maid's face was surprised and yet solemn as she blinked at her mistress. "Yes, miss?"

"Yes. I am to go away for a while," Lucia said.

"Yes, miss, to Bath, I heard you telling Mrs. Drew when she called for tea."

"Yes." Lucia paused. "I mean, no." She stumbled over the words in the face of Mary's easy acceptance of her lie. "I did tell her that," she clarified, "but you see, I am not going to Bath after all." It was the first time Lucia had spoken something of the truth out loud, and she felt she had reached a point from which she could not retreat. She was partly terrified and partly overjoyed. She tried to hide both emotions, as Mary looked at her, clearly bewildered.

"You're not, miss?"

"No, Mary, I'm not." Lucia looked into her eyes and prepared to tell her what was largely the truth. "I have taken a quiet cottage, not far from here. I am looking for some peace, away from people. I have not entirely recovered, you know, from my ordeal of last winter, and my father's death has been very difficult for me."

"I'm sure, miss, but would not a visit to Bath, where you would be amongst friends and could take the waters, be a better cure than solitude?"

"No, Mary," Lucia said firmly. "Bath is a place of society and gossip, even out of season. I do not want to be there. Only it suits me that people think I have gone there. Do you understand?"

"Not quite, miss."

"If they know I am still nearby, they will wonder why I am not here, keeping house in my brother's absence. If they know I have retreated to a hideaway they will think me eccentric. I cannot have that, my reputation is already damaged enough of late, since I have not been much in company. Please do not concern yourself beyond that. What I ask is this: Whilst I am absent, you remain at Foxe Hall and keep it in good order, so it does not have to be closed entirely, should our family wish to visit. I also ask that you keep any letters that should arrive for me. I will call to collect them from time to time. I will pay you a shilling extra a week if you tell no one of my plans."

"Yes, miss," Mary said. She continued to regard Lucia with bewilderment in her expression. However—and how Lucia hated herself for exploiting it—it was not a maid's position to press any further questions upon her mistress. Mary had been told her duty, and Lucia knew her loyalty was exemplary. The extra shilling was not a bribe. It was a reward, a token of Lucia's gratitude towards her, which was truly heartfelt.

And so the web was spun. Lucia hated every lie that had to be told. Yet they were so necessary to her happiness. She understood now how Len could compromise her own moral code and turn outlaw in order to win that so tenuously held right to choose. She had not become a robber herself, but in her society she knew the crimes of dishonesty she had committed, and their eventual end, would be just as soundly condemned.

❖

As October drew to a close, Lucia asked for the carriage to be made ready, and it carried her and her small travelling bag into town. She told the men to return to Foxe Hall, since she would visit an acquaintance then meet with her Bath friends, who were in the area and would take her onwards in their own carriage.

As soon as the carriage was out of sight, Lucia began to walk out of town, along the main Derby road. She was alone in the world, with no one to miss her or question her, and such independence sent a thrill through her that forced a quite idiotic smile to her lips. She had chosen to be able to choose, just as Len had once done.

Before long two riders brought their horses to walk alongside Lucia. They were leading another horse, a pretty grey mare. She looked up at the riders. Julian smiled easily down on her, raising his eyebrows slightly, as though he still could not believe she was the woman he had robbed on the road almost a year previously. Len rode Oberon side-saddle, her dark blue skirts flowing over her legs. Her cloak was her usual blue velvet, but it did not matter it was more suited to a man. Her flower-decorated bonnet met the eye first, and the illusion was thus created. There was nothing to suggest this couple on horseback were anything to do with the highwaymen who terrorised travellers. Len's eyes met Lucia's as they stopped, a little group of well-dressed acquaintances by the roadside, and the intensity of her gaze set something alight inside Lucia, a feeling which had never stopped smouldering since that first horseback ride.

"Hello again, Miss Foxe," Julian said, as he dismounted to aid Lucia in mounting the grey mare.

"Hello, once more," Lucia replied. "No pistol today?" She was no longer intimidated by him as she had once been.

"I thought it unnecessary today, Miss Foxe." He smiled. "Though I can tie your hands if it would seem more appropriate." His eyes danced and Lucia laughed.

Len said nothing, but her silent gaze said more than a thousand words that did not need to be uttered. Lucia rode with them out of town and into the countryside. The golden- and russet-hued trees showered them with their drifting leaves, and the damp air smelled of wood smoke. Lucia wanted to sing with joy at the beauty of it all, which she seemed to see with fresh eyes.

They rode for over an hour, eventually reaching a place where the enclosed land ended. Beyond, the vegetation was untamed and unruly. Here, along a track, and obscured by a large yew, they came to a cottage.

"So, here it is. What do you think of it?" Len asked, as they halted outside. Lucia contemplated the small building. Its roof was of slate and sound, though it sagged a little in the middle. The casement windows were clean, the wood, though old, not at all rotten. The walls had recently been whitewashed. There was a well in the front garden and a patch cleared to the side where vegetables could flourish. A large apple tree, unruly with lack of tending, stretched for the sky to the left.

"It's beautiful," Lucia said, sincerely. No building had ever been as gorgeous to her as the cottage.

"I'm glad you think so." Len looked pleased.

"It is rented in the name of Miss Josephine Grey, who looks suspiciously like a certain Miss Helena Hawkins," Julian said. "But being as Miss Helena no longer exists, it would be difficult to trace the lady who really took out the lease on the cottage. There will certainly be no link to Miss Lucia Foxe of Foxe Hall or to the mysterious rider of a black stallion who haunts the roads by night."

"It is perfect then," Lucia said.

"Providing the rent is met."

"That is no problem."

❖

And so it was Lucia, who had grown up in Foxe Hall and become used to the workings of genteel society, came to be in a small cottage on the edge of humanity's reach into the countryside. The house was far enough from any village to arouse no curiosity and obscured enough from the road not to be often noticed. It was warm and snug in the cottage, even on cold nights, and the darkness no longer held any terrors for her.

Lucia intended to visit Isabella as Christmas drew close. She knew she would tell her sister nothing of the life she had chosen. Still, she entertained idle notions of Len accompanying her on the journey, wearing her fine blue dress, passing for a new acquaintance she had made. She found the idea amusing and rather thrilling in the same moment. To sit beside Len in company—in full gaze of her family and acquaintance—and to look into Len's eyes and see her own secrets and hopes safe, how wonderful that would be.

She was, for the moment, essentially alone in the world. It was at once the price of her new liberty and the facilitator of such freedom. Perhaps, when the war ended and George returned, she would have to look for more excuses, create more secrets. There would be time yet to ponder just how she could continue the illusion she had begun for many years to come. For now, however, she found her liberty had come to her more easily than she could have anticipated.

Lucia remembered how Len once told her they could not command the changes in their lives; they simply had to wait to see what life brought. She loved Len's trust in the path the stars had set out for them, in the hand of destiny. Lucia had never suspected she would understand Len so well before the year was out.

Len had been absent from the cottage for several nights. It was not often she was away for so many days at a time, since Lucia's allowance removed the absolute necessity of her prowling the roads at night. However, she knew Len did not like to depend entirely upon her and her inherited wealth. She was certain it sat uneasily with her principles and her pride. Lucia believed also, more significantly, the unfettered freedom of Len's life on the road called her still. Julian, of course—who now led his own band of men, with William at his side—would welcome Len whenever she sought him out. She told

Lucia she only watched him at work, but somehow Lucia doubted it. The papers reported the notorious band of highwaymen, their leader atop a fine black stallion, was still an occasional but ever-present threat to travellers in those parts. Lucia would wait for Len's return with bated breath, agonies of anxiety for her twisting her insides. But she always returned, dusty and tired, her eyes alight. Lucia trusted Len's skill, her instincts, and her ability to move in the shadows to preserve her.

She knew Len also returned to the copse of trees above her father's workshop. Whether she did so to remember the joy she'd felt in the destruction of his property, to remind herself of how close she came to death, or out of an unbreakable fascination with the life she once had and chose to escape from, Lucia was not sure. One day, when the time was right, she would ask and Len would, she was sure, tell her. Their life was one discovery after another, some small steps, some large, but always together.

As she approached the cottage, Len pulled Oberon back into a gentle walk. Though the temptation was—always—to hasten back and into Lucia's welcoming arms, she always slowed at this point. Just as she turned the corner in the road, passed the last hedgerow marking the bounds of civilisation, and the cottage came into view. Home. Home, she knew now, was a feeling far more than it was a place. It was a feeling Lucia created.

She removed her tricorn and released her hair from its ribbon, enjoying the way the evening breeze played in her locks. The sun was setting behind the little cottage with its crooked roof, bathing everything in a restful golden glow. Len was glad to be back.

True, Julian had been right. She did sometimes miss her old life, galloping through woodlands, breathing in the night air, gambling with the Reaper, cheating the gallows. She even missed robbing pompous aristocrats of their wealth. She missed Julian and William. That was why she visited them often, rode with them by night. But she did not miss holding a pistol to the chest of a frightened young man, nor watching Julian terrify a lady into parting with her necklace.

She knew Lucia did not believe her assurances, but Len did not thieve any longer. Julian told her love had made her soft, but he respected her decision. And knowing she had the strength to give up her outlaw life, a life her father had forced upon her, and to still be able to hold onto her liberty, was all she needed. It was a revelation. She did not have to live beyond the law to be free. Freedom was not about the rules she adhered to or the source of her daily bread. The freedom she had sought for so long was essentially for her heart, her spirit. For that she had only needed love a woman like Lucia.

And the Lord knew, Lucia had made sacrifices enough herself in order to embrace this life. Len knew very well how difficult it was to go from servants and wealth to a life with neither. From being known among one's acquaintance to being invisible. For the first weeks they had spent in the cottage she had barely dared leave Lucia alone, terrified Lucia would one day declare she could not manage this life after all and would sooner go back to the rules and constraints of her safer, more comfortable life. And yet Lucia had seemed to grow ever happier as she embraced this new present, allowing her past to slip away. Len was nervous what would happen when Lucia had to see her brother or Isabella again—as undoubtedly and rightly she would want to—but she had faith that every bridge could be crossed. If she ever thought anything was impossible, she would hold Lucia in her arms and know that anything they wanted could be achieved.

Now, the urge to see Lucia's smile, feel the warmth of her body, was too much to resist any longer. She trotted Oberon along the lane leading to the cottage. She wasted no time in seeing he was stripped of saddle and bridle, provided with oats and water, and secure in his small stable, before heading towards the back door of the cottage and letting herself in.

When she opened the door, Lucia was seated at the table in the central room of the cottage. It was already quite dark inside, and she had lit a lantern, which illuminated her in a golden halo. She had clearly been writing, a sheet of paper covered in her neat hand on the table in front of her, but as Len entered, she put down her pen and rose to her feet.

"You look like an angel," Len said, reaching for Lucia's hands. It was an unfair comparison. In her eyes no angel could ever compete with Lucia for beauty or goodness.

"Thank you. You look like…like…a highwayman," Lucia said. She smiled, her eyes dancing.

"Interesting."

"It is a good thing I have a weakness for highwaymen." Lucia laughed lightly and pulled Len closer.

"Not all highwaymen, I hope." Len said. She leaned in for a kiss. Lucia's lips were soft and warm, tender against her own. "I missed you, my love."

"And I you."

Len kissed her again, then opened her eyes and looked over Lucia's shoulder, her gaze falling on the table. Curiosity drew her attention away from the perfect kisses for a moment. "What were you writing?"

"Oh, nothing of great significance…" Lucia said. She flushed slightly.

"Do not be coy with me, my love. I will drag the information from you somehow."

"It is tempting to hold you to that threat." Lucia's smile was mischievous. "However, I find I want to tell you. I am writing a journal."

Len was puzzled but intrigued. "A journal? Of day-to-day events?"

"Yes. Well, of some days. I am writing the story of how we first met."

Len glanced at the papers. Lucia had been busy. "Is that wise, do you think?"

"I appreciate that our lives hang in the balance still, my love." Lucia looked slightly indignant. Len found it endlessly appealing when Lucia had that spark in her eye. She half smiled and waited for Lucia to continue. "And I promise, I will keep the account as close to my heart as you are. If it is ever under threat of discovery, I will burn it in an instant."

She sounded so passionate, Len could not help but kiss her again. This time it was a lingering kiss which set fire to her blood and only increased the hunger for Lucia which had built over the days she had been away. To feel Lucia, warm and solid in her arms, to see the real love in her eyes, was everything.

Lucia kissed Len back and allowed her hands to roam under Len's dusty clothes. Len shrugged her way out of her cloak and coat, and Lucia's hands caressed her through the thin cotton of her shirt. To feel Len close to her, her living breath on her skin, filled Lucia with a heady mixture of satisfaction and a biting need for more. From the moment Len had opened the door and strode into the cottage, her presence had filled every dark space, erased every slight fear. Lucia pressed closer to her and kissed her harder.

Eventually, Len drew back a little, another question in her expression. "Tell me, why do you want to write an account of how we met?"

Lucia knew the answer instinctively. When she had attended Isabella's marriage in the crowded church, she had lamented that she was forced to keep her feelings locked inside her chest. She could not cry with the grief or sing with the joy of knowing Len, losing Len, loving Len. Even now, the only ones to whom she could make her sentiments known were Len, who knew them well already; Julian, occasionally and modestly; and the birds who danced every morning in the apple tree outside the cottage. Len and she still existed in secrets and shadows, even when Len was not prowling the roads. She had her answer to Len's question very clear in her mind.

"I am writing in solid black letters of ink, marking our story onto that creamy, smooth paper. I am letting it be known. Not that our story has a reader, and nor, I hope, will it find one while we two live. But these letters are testament to everything we have done. It is an extraordinary story, and yet here we are. It is our tale." She paused and examined Len's expression. Len's eyes were soft and her cheeks pink. Lucia knew she understood.

"The letters will always exist. They are inscribed on that paper forever. Even if I do have to burn it one day, the ashes will tell the tale to the wind." She smiled at the thought, and Len smiled back.

Lucia knew that the writing released them both from the secrets. Her own heart felt freed from the burden of keeping everything hidden inside. It was at liberty to expand with the revelation of a love she had not known possible.

"It is a beautiful thought Lucia. Perhaps one day, we will not be a secret any longer." Len's voice was deep with emotion. "Where does your tale begin?"

"On a dark December night. With a highway robber on a black stallion, a flintlock at her waist, and a gentlewoman in a carriage, with a very great attachment to her mother's locket."

"It sounds like a tale I would like to read." Len's hands encircled Lucia's waist and Lucia caught her breath, her temperature beginning to soar. "Although I fear there will be passages which could quite shock me."

"Oh yes," Lucia said breathlessly, hands finding their way beneath Len's shirt to feel her soft, warm skin. To touch Len was a comfort and a provocation to her sharp desire all at once.

"But most importantly, can you tell me, does the tale have a happy ending?"

Lucia smiled, knowing her gaze told Len more than her words would. "Yes," she whispered. "The happiest. But it has not ended yet."

Historical Note

The Locket and the Flintlock is entirely a work of fiction, and none of my characters are based on real people. Similarly, although the places borrow their names from real Nottinghamshire villages and towns, the geography is far from accurate.

There was no Len Hawkins prowling the roads by night. But highway robbers were real. The legends of Dick Turpin, Sixteen String Jack, and John "Swift Nick" Nevison—among others—are all based in fact. Travellers crossing the vast unpopulated areas of Britain, especially taking the main roads from London to the north, were always at risk. The phrase "stand and deliver" has supposedly been around from the seventeenth century.

And a female "highwayman" is not a far-fetched creation. The infamous Moll Cutpurse (born Mary Frith) spent some of her extraordinary criminal career dressed as a man and robbing coaches. A rebellious beauty by the name of Joan Phillips adopted a masculine disguise and robbed travellers at the point of a flintlock. Phillips was captured in Nottinghamshire and executed for her crimes in 1685.

By the time of Len and Lucia's story in 1812, highwaymen were dying out. The advent of the turnpike roads, more enclosed land, and urban sprawl all contributed to this change, along with better policing. It is said that the last horseback highway robbery was in 1831. Highway robbers—via poetry, story, art, and song—became the stuff of romantic legend.

Equally legendary, but less understood, are the Luddites. The frame-breakers were certainly real. The first Luddite attack took place just north of Nottingham, in 1811. The first Luddites did not oppose new technology. Luddism arose in a time of great hardship, when the skilled stocking makers in the outlying villages found their once highly respected trade no longer brought them a living wage, mostly due to a range of new practices on the part of the masters. In protest, they broke the machines, in night-time raids. The government, terrified they were seeing the beginnings of revolution, deployed the militia in huge numbers, and frame-breaking was made a capital offence. Lord Byron really did speak against the bill that made it so, in the House of Lords in 1812. Historians will argue forever whether or not the Luddites were organised revolutionaries or desperate starving men—or maybe both. Letters were certainly sent from a mysterious General Ludd, but there is no evidence he existed. The actions of my band of frame-breakers are based on my interpretation of the known facts.

Could Luddites and highway robbers have worked together in Nottinghamshire in 1812? Both were lurking in the shadows as they moved around the county on the wrong side of the law. Both were relics of a bygone age, their way of life dying out. Both were likely driven to crime by the difficulty of eking out a living within the law. It is not such a very great leap to imagine they could have come together. And there were gentlewomen aplenty in the county. History would not record the story of a foolhardy woman who chased after the thief of her locket in the night-time. But such a tale is not, to me at least, entirely improbable.

About the Author

Rebecca S. Buck was born and bred in Nottingham, England, and has a degree in English Studies from The University of Nottingham. For a few years in her twenties she spent most of her time in Slovenia, in the former Yugoslavia, working as a private tutor and trying to renovate two houses.

Though Slovenia was beautiful, she wasn't made to live in the countryside and was very happy to return to her hometown, around the same time as her first published novel, *Truths*, was released. Rebecca had always dreamed of being a writer, experimenting with words from an early age, and the realization of that dream was incredibly exciting.

After a brief spell in retail, Rebecca found her perfect day job, working as a costumed guide and education facilitator at The Galleries of Justice museum in the old Shire Hall and County Gaol of Nottingham, where she can indulge her creativity and love of history.

Outside of writing, Rebecca loves music and reading in all genres. She's fond of academic books and always ready to learn. She has travelled a lot and especially enjoys the cities of Europe. Her favourite way to spend time is sharing coffee and cake with friends.

To find out more about Rebecca and her publications, visit www.rebeccasbuck.com

About the Author

Books Available from Bold Strokes Books

Dark Wings Descending by Lesley Davis. What if the demons you face in life are real? Chicago detective Rafe Douglas is about to find out. (978-1-60282-660-1)

sunfall by Nell Stark and Trinity Tam. The final installment of the everafter series. Valentine Darrow and Alexa Newland work to rebuild their relationship even as they find themselves at the heart of the struggle that will determine a new world order for vampires and wereshifters. (978-1-60282-661-8)

Mission of Desire by Terri Richards. Nicole Kennedy finds herself in Africa at the center of an international conspiracy and being rescued by beautiful but arrogant government agent Kira Anthony, but is Kira someone Nicole can trust or is she blinded by desire? (978-1-60282-662-5)

Boys of Summer edited by Steve Berman. Stories of young love and adventure, when the sky's ceiling is a bright blue marvel, when another boy's laughter at the beach can distract from dull summer jobs. (978-1-60282-663-2)

The Locket and the Flintlock by Rebecca S. Buck. When Regency gentlewoman Lucia Foxe is robbed on the highway, will the masked outlaw who stole Lucia's precious locket also claim her heart? (978-1-60282-664-9)

Calendar Boys by Zachary Logan. A man a month will keep you excited year round. (978-1-60282-665-6)

Burgundy Betrayal by Sheri Lewis Wohl. Park Ranger Kara Lynch has no idea she's a witch until dead bodies begin to pile up in her park, forcing her to turn to beautiful and sexy shape-shifter Camille Black Wolf for help in stopping a rogue werewolf. (978-1-60282-654-0)

LoveLife by Rachel Spangler. When Joey Lang unintentionally becomes a client of life coach Elaine Raitt, the relationship becomes complicated as they develop feelings that make them question their purpose in love and life. (978-1-60282-655-7)

The Fling by Rebekah Weatherspoon. When the ultimate fantasy of a one-night stand with her trainer, Oksana Gorinkov, suddenly turns into more, reality show producer Annie Collins opens her life to a new type of love she's never imagined. (978-1-60282-656-4)

Ill Will by J.M. Redmann. New Orleans PI Micky Knight must untangle a twisted web of healthcare fraud that leads to murder—and puts those closest to her most at risk. (978-1-60282-657-1)

Buccaneer Island by J.P. Beausejour. In the rough world of Caribbean piracy, a man is what he makes of himself—or what a stronger man makes of him. (978-1-60282-658-8)

Twelve O'Clock Tales by Felice Picano. The fourth collection of short fiction by legendary novelist and memoirist Felice Picano. Thirteen dark tales that will thrill and disturb, discomfort and titillate, enthrall and leave you wondering. (978-1-60282-659-5)

Words to Die By by William Holden. Sixteen answers to the question: What causes a mind to curdle? (978-1-60282-653-3)

Tyger, Tyger, Burning Bright by Justine Saracen. Love does not conquer all, but when all of Europe is on fire, it's better than going to hell alone. (978-1-60282-652-6)

Night Hunt by L.L. Raand. When dormant powers ignite, the wolf Were pack is thrown into violent upheaval, and Sylvan's pregnant mate is at the center of the turmoil. A Midnight Hunters novel. (978-1-60282-647-2)

Demons are Forever by Kim Baldwin and Xenia Alexiou. Elite Operative Landis "Chase" Coolidge enlists the help of high-class call girl Heather Snyder to track down a kidnapped colleague embroiled in a global black market organ-harvesting ring. (978-1-60282-648-9)

Runaway by Anne Laughlin. When Jan Roberts is hired to find a teenager who has run away to live with a group of antigovernment survivalists, she's forced to return to the life she escaped when she was a teenager herself. (978-1-60282-649-6)

Street Dreams by Tama Wise. Tyson Rua has more than his fair share of problems growing up in New Zealand—he's gay, he's falling in love, and he's run afoul of the local hip-hop crew leader just as he's trying to make it as a graffiti artist. (978-1-60282-650-2)

Women of the Dark Streets: Lesbian Paranormal by Radclyffe and Stacia Seaman, eds. Erotic tales of the supernatural—a world of vampires, werewolves, witches, ghosts, and demons—by the authors of Bold Strokes Books. (978-1-60282-651-9)

http://www.boldstrokesbooks.com

Bold Strokes
BOOKS

victory EDITIONS
Drama
LIBERTY EDITION

AEROS e BOOKS
e-Books
Mystery
CRIME
Sci-fi
SPECFIC

erotica
Erotica
BSB SOLILOQUY
Young Adult
MATINEE BOOKS
Romance
BOLD STROKES BOOKS

WEBSTORE
PRINT AND EBOOKS